PERION SYNTHETICS

PERION SYNTHETICS

DANIEL VERASTIQUI

CHANNEL 8 PRESS
Austin, Texas

"The moment they built one who would not die

was the moment they stopped calling themselves human."

- *From The Reflections of Noetica, Volume VI*

PART ONE
CAMERON GRAY

ONE

It's the softest of whispers that demand the most attention.

Frank Gattis had been standing at the back of the break room on thirty-seven stirring his coffee when he first noticed the feed slowing down. The tiny whisperer in his left ear usually let out a steady monologue, telling him in short, stilted sentences the latest happenings in the city, what the clowns in Washington were up to, and how his stock portfolio expected to fare over the coming day. When current events grew stale, the feed turned more social, bringing him updates from personal and professional networks in the form of status messages and location pings. All day, without pause or variance of tempo, the whisperer spoke to Frank, keeping him perpetually linked to the world.

Only the biggest news stories could slow down the feed.

As a senior aggregator for Banks Media Productions, Frank was responsible for seeking out and delivering such stories. Although he spent every moment of every day gathering content to send up the pipe, he was always on the lookout for the big one, the undiscovered stone that could shatter the calm water of the feed and make the other media houses sit up and take note. The ripples would make The White Line out of Atlantic City throttle its political news and tales of corruption in East Coast gaming. Lincoln Continental out of Umbra would ease its incessant technobabble just long enough to turn an ear to Banks Media.

Even the lesser feeds operating in small towns or on college campuses would fall silent, their engineers' fingers at the ready to copy, paste, and rebrand whatever news they might hear from one of the big three media houses.

This time, though, it was Banks Media who was slowing down, stalling stories of corporate influence and Hollywood gossip in anticipation of a ripple from some far-off stone. Whatever was happening out there in the ether, it was big enough for Donato Banks to bring the entire BMP feed to a relative standstill.

It was enough to distract Frank from the task he had been sent to do.

The other aggregators in the break room sensed the ebb before the surge too. There were a dozen of them sitting around with their coffees and donuts, discussing the plentiful but ultimately unusable content they had gathered over the weekend. The group was largely middle-ladder types, those who had been at the company a few years but who hadn't broken a story large enough to get them invited up to the fiftieth floor as Frank had. They traded leads and talked of sports until one by one, they all quieted.

Their mouths held on aborted words as their heads cocked to the left in unison.

Frank watched it play out, watched two-dozen eyeballs scan back and forth as if they were reading the news instead of hearing it in their heads. The resulting silence allowed him to zero in on his own whisperer, to pick out that soft rustle endlessly reverberating in his ear. A soundbite of President Hadden speaking at an anti-MX rally cut out abruptly.

Breaking, White Line Media: 2015.11.09.0605. James Perion. Dying. Cancer.

The ocean had receded, but with those words, it returned as a giant wall of water ready to wash the beach clean.

The message repeated twice and then the feed dove headfirst into the Perion Synthetics hashtag, dredging up recent news stories about the company and reaction from industry pundits.

Panic may have spread through other break rooms throughout the country, but not on the thirty-seventh floor of the Banks Media Productions Tower. These were professional aggregators, men and women whose job it was to stay calm in the face of an earth-shattering calamity. Instead of fleeing before the tsunami, they took the time to calmly but quickly gather their beach towels and umbrellas and head back to their cars.

The crowd stood as one.

Frank stepped forward and put a hand on the shoulder of the man in front of him. When Cameron Gray looked up, Frank winked at him.

Cell phones appeared from pockets; furtive calls went out to stockbrokers as the feed slipped into the financial hashes, turning its focus to pre-market trading. Those without personal investment in Perion Synthetics began narrating into their slivers, the small tabs of metal embedded in their wrists that acted as a PDA, and for aggregators, as their primary recording device. Others pulled leather covers from their palettes to view the BMP feed in graphical format; photos and videos scrolled in an endless loop down the vibrant screens.

Once the last aggregator had filed out, Frank removed his hand.

"That's okay," said Cameron. "It's only the biggest news story of the year, but I'm sure whatever you have to say is more important."

Frank smiled.

The cocky little shit with the throwback skater haircut and unnecessarily tight button-up had no idea what was about to fall into his lap. And yet, Donato Banks had taken a personal interest in him, had decided it was worth his time and effort to mold the mid-grade aggregator with more forced bravado than brains into something better.

"You don't deserve what's about to happen to you, kid," said Frank, shaking his head. "But orders are orders, so I'm gonna take you upstairs anyway. Leave your orange juice; Banks will shit if you spill it on his leather."

Frank dropped his coffee in a trashcan on the way out of the break room. Despite the many conversations spilling from the offices around him, he heard Cameron's footsteps keeping pace. They stepped into the elevator at the end of the hall.

"Fifty," said Frank. "No stops."

Cameron brought his wrist to his mouth as the elevator began to rise. "Hashtag: Vinestead," he said, instructing his whisperer to focus on stories related to the ubiquitous and maligned conglomerate.

"Checking up on the competition?" asked Frank.

"Just trying to beat everyone to the endgame," said Cameron. "If this story turns out to be true and James Perion really is dying of cancer, then you know at some point it's all going to lead back to Vinestead. And I'm going to be there. Waiting."

The kid was sharp. Vinestead was where Frank would have gone had Banks not tasked him with bringing Cameron to his office. Pretty much any story worth feeding about Perion Synthetics would have a footnote related to their biggest competitor, Vinestead International. Their rivalry was more than a political ploy by James Perion to distance himself from Vinestead CEO Arthur Sedivy and his no-morals, all-profit business practices; it was personal as well.

Frank flashed on the memory of Perion and Sedivy appearing on a national news show to speak out against the threat of Chinese cyber-attacks. Both had been united against a common enemy, but somehow their prepared remarks had turned into a debate about corporate responsibility and whether companies served the people or the shareholders. Perion had just raised his fist over his shoulder when the feed went to black.

The elevator doors opened to Donato Banks' office and Frank spied the big boss standing at the floor-to-ceiling windows watching the sun rise between the skyscrapers of downtown Los Angeles.

Frank led Cameron to an arrangement of leather couches and plush chairs, but neither sat. No one sat in Donato Banks' office without being asked.

"I brought him," said Frank.

"And what do you have for me so far?" asked Banks.

Donato Banks was never much for greetings. It was the feed mentality that kept the owner and overseer of Banks Media Productions from acknowledging that conversations usually had discreet beginnings and endings. To him, social interaction was nothing more than a point-to-point feed, an exchange of ideas both ongoing and uninterruptable. Talking to Banks often meant joining a conversation already in progress.

"Excuse me?" asked Frank.

"Not you," said Banks, turning around. "Cam, what do you have on this Perion story?"

Frank expected Cameron to stammer some excuse, but instead, he stepped forward and spoke to Banks as if they were equals.

"Rich people don't die from cancer," he replied. "So either Benny is full of shit, or he's not telling us the whole story."

Bennett "Benny" Coker ran The White Line media house out of Atlantic City, currently ranked third in subscribers. If he had tagged his own name in the story's metadata, it meant he was betting it all on the story being true.

Banks motioned to the couches and sat down in a chair at the head of the coffee table.

"Assume the story is true," he said.

There was an intensity with which he stared at Cameron, an expectant look radiating from brown eyes that were sharp and powerful despite the lines surrounding them.

"Well, assuming Perion has a better health plan than us, for him to die from cancer would mean he's refusing treatment. But why would he do that?"

Banks crossed one leg over the other. "Frank?"

"Follow the trail, kid. Perion goes to his doctor, the doctor goes to the local distributor, to the national warehouses, and small pharmacology centers. A man with his pull would end up at Feather Medical or Cell Scientifics, and those both roll up the chain to one entity. I'll give—"

"Vinestead Pharma," said Cam, his eyes widening. He pulled out his phone and began typing out some notes. "They own the patents on the treatments, don't they?"

"Yes," said Banks. "And given Perion's contentious relationship with Vinestead, you can see why that would be a problem."

Cameron shook his head. "Yeah, but would Vinestead really refuse to help him? That's cold, even for Arthur Sedivy."

"They're more than willing to help out. All Perion would have to do is submit to a Guardian Angel biochip."

The mild excitement that had been growing on Cameron's face fell away. His dim eyes grew distant, perhaps imagining the back of James Perion's neck and the surgeon's scalpel just a few centimeters away. On a nearby tray, a fresh Guardian Angel biochip still in its protective case would be waiting for insertion, its grow-wire coiled up in a small loop beside it. Once installed in Perion's neck, the chip would monitor the CEO's vital systems, and with the right patented code, help his body fight back against any uncontrolled cell growth. And though Perion would live on, it would be with Vinestead technology directly connected to his brain.

Observing. Listening.

Possibly relaying.

Cameron sighed as he came to the realization that Perion would never allow that to happen. He would sooner face death than give Arthur Sedivy, or anyone for that matter, the opportunity to spy on his inner thoughts.

"It's true, isn't it?" asked Cameron. "Perion really is dying."

Banks nodded. "He called me last night and told me personally. I think maybe he knew the story was going to leak."

"Why you?"

Frank noticed the red LED on Cameron's wrist. His questions had activated the recorder in his sliver, just in case. It was a safety feature for impromptu interviews, but also handy when an aggregator needed to be discreet.

"James Perion and I have history," said Banks, turning his attention to the vidscreen on the far wall. Flashy graphics scrolled right to left, detailing the ongoing freefall of Perion Synthetics stock. "Our relationship is one of mutual respect. He produces the most advanced synthetic humans ever known to man, and I run the biggest media house in the world. We're cut from the same cloth."

Frank knew the claim wouldn't pass Quality Assurance, not so long as Lincoln Continental kept crushing Banks' subscriber numbers. And as for Perion Synthetics, all that had come out of their secluded beta test in the wastes of the California desert had been technology only slightly related to synthetic humans.

Pieces of the puzzle, but never a complete product.

"And," continued Banks, "he trusts me enough to not put something this personal and damaging on the feed." He gestured to the vidscreen. "This is all on Benny Coker's head. The panic, the freefall… everything."

"I'm guessing you're not dumping your Perion stock like everyone else?"

Banks scoffed. "Too many people know about my connection to Perion. They would assume I have inside information. And I do." He paused, brushed some lint from his slacks. "Perion doesn't have much time left. Weeks, a month at the most."

Frank watched several seconds tick by on his sliver.

"But even without knowing the truth, I still wouldn't sell. Those people are unloading everything, not because James Kirkland Perion is dying, but because they're unsure who will be replacing him. Will that person, once chosen, be able to fill Perion's shoes? Will they hold to his vision of humans and synthetics living side by side?"

Cameron nodded as if Banks' revelation were old news.

"You already know who the replacement will be, don't you?" he asked.

"I do," said Banks. "His son. Joseph. My godson."

The name made Frank sneer.

At twenty-seven, the son of a bitch was even younger than Cameron and in line to inherit one of the biggest companies in the world.

"Perion's a mess about it," continued Banks. "It's hard enough to have mortality breathing down your neck, but now he has to worry about the future of his company once he's gone."

"But wouldn't his son have help?" asked Cameron. "I'm sure there's an entire team of sycophants just waiting to guide him on the day-to-day."

"It's not that. Perion doesn't doubt the company will continue to do what it's doing. His concern is about what it *doesn't* do. Currently."

Cameron's eyebrow bounced, but no recognition took hold.

"You don't get it," said Banks, "but that's okay. I don't need you to get it right now."

"So what *do* you need from me?"

"How about you show some appreciation?" asked Frank. "There are a lot of aggregators who would kill to be sitting where you're sitting right now."

"What do you know about Perion City?" asked Banks.

Cameron rattled off the clichés. "Darkened streets of endless slag. Neon residents perpetually jacked into the great collective. Skeletons of black metal gleaming in the LED twilight. At least, that's what I've heard."

Frank rolled his eyes.

"It's a niche city," continued Cameron. "Closed beta, employees only. All we have are rumors."

"Which is exactly why I'm sending you there," said Banks. "Perion and I have arranged everything. His employees will be told you're there to do a story about the company's fiftieth anniversary, but what you'll really be doing is checking every crate and closet for any skeletons that might blindside Joseph. And if you happen to find those skeletons in Joseph's closet, so be it. Perion wants to be sure about his company and his son before he goes."

"So it's an exposé *and* a biography," said Cameron. "I can do that." He tapped a few more notes into his phone and then pocketed it. After adjusting his pants, he gestured to Frank with his thumb. "But so can he."

Banks smiled and dipped his head. "And I'd send him if I could, but I'm afraid there's a little too much VTech in our friend Frank here."

Frank thought of the various body augments he had acquired over the years. Though he had never opted for a full-on Guardian Angel chip, many of the mechanical enhancements he had made did run proprietary Vinestead code. His augmented eyes alone were enough VTech to worry a Perion Synthetics employee. Paranoia was the name of the game in Perion City, and Vinestead International was the poster child.

Banks' answer seemed to satisfy Cameron. He sat back on the couch and relaxed for the first time.

"Well?" asked Banks. "What are you waiting for? Diana will meet you down in the lobby. She has some hardcopy and a car ready for you. Now go get me some of that human interest crap you're always trying to pass off as content."

Cameron stood and extended a hand. "Thank you, Mr. Banks. This is a great opportunity, and I won't let you down."

Banks waved the hand away. "I know you'll do great."

Turning to Frank, Cam said, "Sorry. This *was* more important."

"Don't mention it, kid." Frank tapped several beats on the floor with his foot.

Banks stared across the table, his eyes vacant.

From the elevator, Cameron asked, "Who's my contact in Perion City?"

Banks didn't look away. "Sava Kessler," he said. "Perion's head of public relations."

"Watch yourself with her," added Frank. "Word is she's a true believer."

He listened to the doors open and close. The hum of the descending car filled the office and then receded.

Frank tried to tune into his whisperer and keep up the staring contest with Banks, but with the stock market set to open any minute, the frenzy in his ear was getting hard to follow.

When it came down to it, money drove everything. Never mind that one of the greatest innovators of the century was dying from an easily treatable disease.

Banks reached for a small box on the coffee table and removed a Red Velvet whisperer. He pressed it into his ear with his index finger.

Lifting his wrist, he said, "Hashtag Internal: Cameron Gray."

Frank smirked. "You think he has any idea what's coming?"

"No one does," said Banks, "but when it finally gets here, they're going to hear about it on my feed first."

TWO

It took three hours on I-10 to get from Los Angeles to Perion City. Cam passed the time by poring over the dossiers Diana had been sending him all morning, files too detailed to have been the result of VNet searches. He scrolled through write-ups on all C-level players with strong names like Shaw and Phelps, from where they went to school to which political party they backed. Grid dumps showed the relationships between each employee, the under-the-table deals and mutual back-scratching that had birthed Perion's executive team. He studied the many faces and tried to ignore the mild revulsion he felt, a mixture of envy and contempt for men of power.

The car pulled off the highway at the exit for Old Pinto Basin Road, a two-lane blacktop that ran north another ten miles before dead-ending at Perion Terminus. The transit station was a sprawling collection of scaffolding and aluminum siding on an endless slab of gray evercrete. Cam counted twenty-four loading bays set to receive the cargo haulers lined up along the mile-long glide path running parallel to the road. There, grizzled and bored drivers sat baking in the California sun as their massive engines rumbled idly. Left of the main warehouse, the bland siding gave way to Perion's signature silver. The abrupt change in material made the terminal appear tacked on, an afterthought that perhaps people, too, would want to travel to Perion City.

A woman with her face buried in her phone sat on a bench just outside the terminal. A few paces away, a man in a chauffeur's cap stood smoking a cigarette.

Cam pulled the woman's face from the dozens he had seen in the dossiers and identified her as Savannah "Sava" Kessler, fellow Berkeley graduate and Perion's head of public relations. Looking from his phone to the window, he noticed the images in her file were out of date. Sava's previously blonde hair was now a light auburn; it disappeared behind the shoulders of her black blazer instead of curling inward just below her chin. A scarlet blouse led into a black skirt that ended just above her knees.

The chauffeur tossed his cigarette away as Cam's car pulled into a parking spot next to a lone Nissan. He was at Cam's door in seconds, opening it and allowing in the warm desert air. Cam stepped out into the daylight and waited for his eyes to adjust. He squinted as Sava approached.

"Mr. Gray?" she asked.

Cam saw himself reflected in the silver lenses of her sunglasses. The way they filtered the light turned the world to grayscale.

"Ms. Kessler," said Cam, extending his hand.

Sava made a feeble attempt at a handshake and then motioned to her driver.

Cam watched the man approach the trunk of Banks' car. "No," he told him. "I don't have any luggage." Then to Sava, "I didn't have time to pack. I only found out I was coming here this morning."

"Interesting," said Sava, over her shoulder. She waited for the chauffeur to open the rear door of the Nissan for her.

"How's that?" Cam asked, familiar with people who responded with the word *interesting* when they really meant *I could give a shit.*

Sava didn't answer until Cam walked around the car and got.

"Because, this has been on my calendar for a week," she replied. "But I suppose you Banks Media people are used to shooting from the hip."

So that's how it was going to be. Cam took a breath and summoned a professional veneer.

"I take it you're not a loyal subscriber of our feed?"

The car's engine growled an answer for her.

Cam nodded and sat back. The seatbelt resisted his efforts to buckle it.

"Was that question directed at me as a Perion employee or a private citizen?"

"Private citizen," said Cam, finally finding the latch. He tugged on the belt to make sure it would stick.

"It's not for me. Banks Media appears to be in the business of self promotion rather than any actual news reporting. The few times I've listened in, you were running smear jobs on Benny Coker and the other media houses."

"Do you feed at all?"

Sava shook her head. "Maybe if I had a nine-to-five and some time to kill on a commute, but when you work for Perion Synthetics, there really is no downtime. You're either working, asleep, or you're dead. And even then you have to put in a request two weeks in advance."

Outside, the empty California desert sizzled. A sea of shriveled Joshua trees stretched to the horizon.

"You have some time to kill now," said Cam.

"This is an anomaly. I hardly ever get out of the PC—there's really no need to. The city was designed to be a closed ecosystem with every amenity provided. It keeps people where the action is instead of traipsing through the cacti."

Cam pulled out his phone and typed *traipsing through the cacti* at the top of a new file.

"Do you mind if I record our conversation?" His sliver had started recording the second he stepped out of Banks' car, but it was always polite to ask.

"Sure," said Sava, "but our legal team will have to approve anything that goes out. So unless I'm saying something on the record, in an official capacity, it's probably not worth writing down."

"Ah, but it's your unofficial perspective that I'm after," replied Cam. "That's all we really have, right? The world is observed through human eyes, so my job doesn't end at reporting just the facts. I have to show how those facts affect real people."

Sava removed her sunglasses. For the first time, Cam made the connection between the woman sitting in front of him and the photos from her dossier. It was in her eyes, their *aliveness*. Cam shook his head, tried to think of a better word.

"You sound like one of those touchy-feely reporters who do sappy human-interest stories on the evening news. You know, the ones about some kid with a terrible disease whose parents can't afford the treatment?"

"I'm familiar," said Cam. "I actually feed a lot of those."

"Ah, so you *are* one of those people."

"Proudly."

Cam's eyes drifted to the front of the car. He noticed the chauffeur was talking to an invisible partner, maybe through a headset in his ear. His voice was muted by the thin pane of plexiglass bisecting the car.

"And who is that?" asked Cam, pointing to the driver.

"He's the chauffeur. Do you really need to know his name?"

"I guess not."

Sava put her sunglasses back on. "You guess? I was told Mr. Banks was sending over his best aggregator. Don't you have any kind of agenda at all?"

Cam took another calming breath. He did have some preliminary questions written down on his phone, basic conversation starters that might lead to more interesting stories. Sava, however, would probably answer as curtly as possible, giving only the necessary information to satisfy the question. How she became the star flack of Perion Synthetics with such a shitty attitude was a mystery, but one Cam nonetheless wanted to solve.

"Tell me about the Perion Expressway."

Sava answered with a prepared statement.

"The PE is a thirty-three-mile channel following the old Pinto Basin Pass. It begins as a two-lane highway at Perion Terminus and grows to six lanes as you get closer to the Spire. It is the only publicly known road to and from the PC, along with three emergency routes through the mountains. The landscape surrounding the highway is kept purposefully barren to discourage foot traffic. Anti-personnel measures for a mile on each side of Outpost Alpha target anything over two feet tall."

She smirked.

"The speed limit is 85 miles per hour, dropping to 65 at night."

Sava gave Cam a look as if to ask why he wasn't writing any of this down. When he motioned to the sliver in his wrist, she continued.

"In three minutes, we'll be approaching the PNR and an armed outpost consisting of a small squad of Scorpio-class synthetics we call Automated Guards. AGs for short."

"Can I call them AutoGuards?"

Sava exaggerated a sigh.

"And what is a PNR?"

"The Point of No Return, sometimes known as the Deadline, indicates the radial operating limit of a synthetic. The mountains provide a measure of security against anyone trying to take a synthetic out of the PC, but the PNR assures no technology leaves without Perion's authorization."

"Has a synthetic ever left the…" Cam paused; there were so many initialisms. "The PC?" He laughed. "The Perion City?"

Sava shook her head. "Not that I'm aware of. All modern synthetics—we call them synnies—have proximity protocols to keep them close to home. My sister likes to joke that when they rise up and kill us all, at least they'll only be able to wipe out a small radius of the state's population."

"Sounds like a smart woman."

"Yeah, but once you spend some time with the synthetics, you'll understand they're not a threat to us. The threat has always been and will always be human, people who want to take the technology out of the PC and use it for…"

Cam's attention had drifted to the window again, but Sava's pause made him look back. "Use it for what?" he asked.

"For something unbefitting its intended purpose," she replied.

The car began to slow, and Cam leaned forward to get a better look. Ahead of them, the road narrowed as thick, evercrete walls grew up beside it. The blacktop led to a brick of a building sitting astride the road, its wide tunnel reminding Cam of a gaping mouth.

"You were expecting a little shack with one of those traffic bars?" asked Sava.

Ominous warnings dotted the sides of the road like long-forgotten campaign signs littering the landscape after an election. They told stories of private property and reminded travelers of the sovereignty laws giving Perion Synthetics the right to shoot trespassers on sight.

The car pulled over about a hundred yards away from the outpost. On the second floor, shadows moved behind the windows. The driver shifted into park as six black-clad men stepped out from behind support columns in the tunnel. Against their chests, their silver machine guns glinted.

On the other side of the plexiglass, the driver made a silent phone call and waved through the windshield.

Cam noticed Sava tapping her foot. "Is there a problem?" he asked.

"Not yet."

"Note," said Cam. "Armed response appears to be disciplined and formidable. One wonders if this is not perhaps an overly dramatic response to the threat of corporate espionage."

"You're really going to feed that?"

Cam shrugged. "The only bad content is no content."

The driver rapped on the divider and gave a thumbs-up sign.

"Come with me," said Sava. "I want to show you something."

Outside, the mountains came right up to the road, stopping the comforting breeze that had made the heat bearable. Cam followed Sava towards the outpost; she stopped at a thick red line on the blacktop and gestured to an evercrete barrier extending away from the road. Beyond it, metal stakes grew like a row of crops from the cracked earth.

"Proximity beacons. They let the synthetics and their handlers know when they're getting too close. If you walked this line, you'd see they circle the PC completely."

Cam followed the line into the distance, picking out the beacons with some intense squinting.

"Those are the primary measures," said Sava. She kicked at a patch of dirt beyond the edge of the road and revealed a dark gray band extending from one beacon to the next. "Magnetic repulsers give the synnies a sixth sense about the border. They'll feel as if they're being pushed back."

"Are they?"

"Not by much, and it wouldn't stop them if they really wanted to leave."

"Do they want to?" asked Cam.

Sava smiled, but didn't answer. She led Cam back to the car and then waved to the outpost. One of the armed men approached at a leisurely pace.

"Oh, you *shoot* them if they try to escape."

"Of course not," said Sava. "These are multi-million-dollar synthetics we're talking about, Mr. Gray. You don't shoot your product just because it wants to go off the reservation. Haven't you ever read *Your Life, Our Rules?*"

Cam vaguely remembered the self-help book being in the bestsellers list a few years ago, but at the time, Dahlstrom Academics had pulled their advertising from Banks Media and taken their two-million-dollar account to Benny Coker, leaving Banks reluctant to feed any coverage of what he called *new age garbage*.

"No," replied Cam. "I think I have it on my phone, though."

"One of the primary tenets of social engineering is to create within the target a genuine desire to do what *you* want them to do, and at the same time, make them believe it was *their* idea."

The man stopped several feet away from the red line in the road. He touched the tip of his black cap with his fingers, but didn't remove it. The bill cast a shadow over silver sunglasses. For a moment, it appeared as if he were sneering, perhaps put out by having to step out into the sun.

"How can I assist you, Ms. Kessler?" he asked.

"Please come forward," said Sava.

The man took a step; faint LEDs began to flash on the beacons for fifty yards in both directions. On his second step, he faltered and stumbled.

"Please," prompted Sava. "Come closer."

After another step, the man crumbled, as if his knees had given out. Once on the ground, he began to push himself back towards the outpost. He hadn't made it anywhere near the red line.

"As you can see, any synthetic that approaches the PNR will suffer exponential power loss. If he got a running start and threw himself over the line, he'd lose power completely and wouldn't be able to drag himself back to safety."

Cam felt his mouth hanging open. There had been nothing in the man's voice or behavior to suggest he was a synthetic, and yet there he was, unable to stand, betrayed by the fail-safes in his mechanical body.

"You look surprised, Mr. Gray."

The last image Cam had seen of a synthetic replayed in his mind. It was years ago, part of some documentary about replacing humans in dangerous environments. James Perion had garnered an entire third of the broadcast with his ideas about synthetic firemen and astronauts. He talked over video clips from his factories, dramatic sweeps down never ending assembly lines. There were robots hunched over conveyer belts, ready to build the next generation of themselves. There were men in lab coats encircling a completely exposed skeleton, adding and removing synthetic tendons to see which ones worked best.

And while the synthetics they showed were impressive, they were nothing compared to the machine slowly getting to its feet in front of Cam. It was the equivalent of the technological chasm between a Ford Model T and the electric Nissan that had brought them from Perion Terminus—they were simply worlds apart.

"You guys have been keeping some secrets," said Cam.

"Absolutely," said Sava, nodding. Her eyes drifted to the right as if listening to a voice in her ear.

Cam wondered if she had a whisperer installed after all.

Finally, she smiled and said, "We're further along than anyone can possibly imagine."

THREE

Outpost Alpha was bigger than it looked from the outside, a disparity Cam only fully understood after following Sava down two flights of stairs to get to the processing room where they now stood. Two of the outpost's Automated Guards had escorted them down while two others brought up the rear. Cam couldn't stop looking at their faces; Sava's earlier demonstration had left him questioning who was real and who was synthetic.

"Mr. Cameron Gray?"

A technician in jeans and a white Perion Synthetics polo had entered the room while Cam was busy counting the number of blinks performed by each guard. Cam turned at the sound of his name.

"I'm Mr. Ferko," said the tech. "I'll be performing your scan today."

Cam turned to Sava. "My scan?"

"As I understand it, part of the agreement between Mr. Banks and Mr. Perion was that an aggregator would be allowed into the city provided that individual has no ties to Vinestead International or any of their subsidiaries or partners." Sava pointed to Cam's sliver. "That includes endotech."

So Banks hadn't been lying when he said Frank Gattis couldn't go.

Cam held up his wrist. "Katsumi Maximo sliver, second generation. Backside, I've got a BSC iMerse jackport. It's VNet compatible, but it uses third-party transcoding, so no Vinestead IP." Cam tapped his earlobe. "I feed with a top-of-the-line Banks Media Red Velvet whisperer with full-duplex broadcast abilities."

Sava nodded, unmoved. "What do you think, Mr. Ferko? Should we just take his word for it?"

Ferko laughed the question away. "Don't take it personally, Mr. Gray. We scan everyone who comes through here. Even Ms. Kessler will have her turn now that she's been past the PNR."

Sava shrugged and sat down on a couch against the far wall. She pulled her phone from her pocket to check for messages. "Now you see why I don't leave the city too often? Waste of time." Her thumb moved in quick, upward swipes. "The White Line has been feeding this cancer nonsense all morning. I guess Benny Coker's finally found a leg to hump. It still amazes me how ruthless you feeders can be."

Nonsense? So she didn't know…

Cam made a note to keep what he'd learned from Banks to himself.

"Please remove your shoes," said Ferko.

Cam stepped out of his stiff Mark Davids and shook his head at Sava. "Don't lump Banks Media in with Coker and his Atlantic City crew. We're nothing like those Shore Dogs."

"Ah, yes," said Sava, still not looking up from her phone. "Banks Media, the big BM, just the feed that comes to mind when I think of honesty and integrity."

Ferko guided Cam to the scanning chamber and helped him inside.

"Someone hurt you, didn't they?" asked Cam, over Ferko's shoulder.

Sava looked up, pursed her lips together, and returned to her phone.

"Are you sure she's not a synthetic?"

Ferko shrugged. "She's been beyond the PNR, so she can't be."

There was something in the tech's voice. He wasn't exactly lying, but it was almost as if he didn't believe what he was saying.

"Now," said Ferko, "all this machine does is scan your endotech and query for any Vinestead technology. It should be able to read the serial numbers and manufacturing codes from your endo without any kind of discomfort. If you do start feeling woozy, there are handles on either side of the chamber."

Ferko took a step back as the glass partition slid down from the ceiling.

"Are *you* a synthetic?" asked Cam.

"Thanks, but no thanks," replied Ferko, tapping on the monitor next to the chamber. "I like being able to take a walk without worrying about my guts turning to goo."

"I don't follow," said Cam, looking to Sava.

She stowed her phone in her pocket. "Secondary proximity protocol. I was waiting for you to ask the question, but I guess it didn't occur to you that someone could transport a synthetic out of here in some kind of vehicle."

Cam imagined an armored car crashing through the gates of the outpost, a synthetic's lifeless arm hanging out of the back.

"Twenty yards beyond the PNR, a synthetic will self-destruct."

Laughter filled the scanning chamber as Cam grabbed a nearby handle for support.

"There's nothing really funny about it," said Ferko. He was nodding at the data scrolling on the vidscreen. "I've seen it happen once. You'd think because it's a synthetic it wouldn't hit you so hard, but it does. It's like watching a small animal die, except it's sort of human. Imagine if Ms. Kessler's insides liquefied into an acidic green sludge in under thirty seconds."

"So the line of beacons out there is more like a pre-PNR?" asked Cam.

"The beacons are the company line," said Sava. "It's what goes into the handbook for new employees. It's what we teach the synnies when they come off the assembly line. The existence and specifics of the secondary protocol is knowledge limited to a subset of Perion employees who should know better than to run their mouths about it in front of members of the media."

Ferko's head shrunk into his shoulders.

"It's alright," Cam told the tech. "I won't use your name."

"It's Kris, if you do."

"I've noticed you guys don't use your first names much."

"Part of our corporate culture," said Sava. "Mr. Perion addresses everyone by honorific and last name and expects us to do the same."

"So the old man is a stickler for formality?"

"The *old man* is a stickler for respect, which you demonstrate a complete lack of by referring to him like that."

The glass partition rose abruptly; Cam took a step back.

"All done," said Ferko.

"Does he check out?" asked Sava, stepping out of her shoes. She pushed them under the couch with her foot.

"He's clean. Mr. Gray was telling the truth for the most part."

"What's that supposed to mean?" asked Cam.

Ferko pulled a palette from its dock and handed it to Sava. "Nothing serious, just that he's got a first-generation Katsumi sliver, not a second as our file denotes."

Cam felt himself blush; he'd been telling people he had a second gen Katsumi for years.

"Where'd you pull that data from?" he asked.

"You have your sources," replied Sava, "we have ours. Or so I thought."

Cam nodded and took a seat on the couch. He petted the imitation leather with his hand as he wiggled into a comfortable position.

Something felt off about the room.

"Narration," he announced. "The welcome ceremony at *The* Perion City is an understated affair, with no luxuries to speak of save air-conditioned transport, culminating in an unsettling invasion of privacy. The entire process takes place in a small room in the dank bowels of an outpost, far from sunlight or any amenity that would make one feel at ease. One wonders why anyone would want to visit Perion City if this is the reception they are afforded."

Cam swiped a finger over his sliver and paused the recording.

"What you said earlier about all people having to come through here, that's not entirely true, is it?"

Sava stepped into the scanning chamber and slipped her fingers around one of the handles.

"Only those who have high-level clearance can bypass the scanning," explained Ferko. "There's no telling what Vinestead would be able to do with a

man or woman roaming our streets. If that person got behind locked doors…
well, you can understand why we have to be careful."

"Is that the company line, Ms. Kessler?" Cam swiped his wrist again. "Is it
James Perion's position that Vinestead is actively engaged in corporate espionage
and/or sabotage?"

"Perion Synthetics acknowledges that our proprietary technology is the most
sought-after advancement of this millennium. Any inference of misbehavior by
Vinestead International is solely the observer's prerogative."

"And off the record?"

"Off the record, Vinestead can burn in hell for all eternity."

Cam nodded. He had heard the vitriol before, scrawled across the virtual walls
of VNet and on the very real walls of the techno-paradise of Umbra, CA. He made
a mental note to find out which side Sava fell on: fading hipster searching for a
cause or die-hard freedom fighter itching for a scuffle.

"Has a synthetic ever been smuggled out of the city, by Vinestead or a Chinese
syndicate?"

Sava hesitated as the glass partition slid into place. "Once," she said, her voice
muffled. "Before my time, a van was discovered on the Perion Expressway six
miles from I-10. By the time they reached it, the thermite in the synny had
dissolved most of the floor and the drivetrain. There wasn't enough physical
evidence to tie her abduction to a person or persons."

"That's just begging for a dramatic reenactment," said Cam, pulling out his
phone. He opened a notepad application to capture some private thoughts. "Now,
does everyone refer to synthetics by gender? Not by *it*?"

"How would you feel if someone called *you* an it?" asked Sava.

"That's different. I'm human."

"According to this report," said Ferko, "you're only *mostly* human."

"Besides, gender isn't exclusive to us." Sava blinked away a sudden dizzy spell.
"Animals, vehicles, weapons…"

"Yeah, but animals have the equipment that makes them a boy or a girl."

"So do our latest generations of synthetics," said Sava, smiling. The glass
partition retracted, and she stepped out, her bare feet silent on the carpeted floor.

Cam made a note to check out some of this *equipment*. He laughed at the
idea of sending Banks a photo of a synthetic wang.

"I assume I check out?" asked Sava.

Ferko nodded. "You're mostly human too, but no Vinestead tech in either of
you, so I'll sign off."

One of the AGs stepped forward with a palette and had Ferko press his thumb
to it.

Sava slipped her shoes on. "If you don't have any more questions for Mr.
Ferko, we can proceed." She gestured to the door.

They didn't go back the way they had come. Instead, the guards led them out of the room and left down a hallway until it ended at an elevator. As they rode up, Cam tried to discern the sound of synthetic breathing above the hum of the cables.

The doors opened on an expansive hangar that led out to the Perion Expressway. A fleet of company vehicles lined the perimeter of the space. In the middle, twenty or so camo-clad AGs engaged in light sparring, their weapons and helmets set on benches to the right and left. They paused only briefly to acknowledge the new arrivals.

An older man with stripes on his shoulder stepped forward, nodded at Sava.

"Mr. Gray, this is Captain Javier Espinoza. He leads the security team here at Outpost Alpha."

"Pleasure to meet you," said Cam, shaking the captain's hand. He nodded to the AGs. "Fine group you have here. Are they all synthetic?"

Espinoza smirked and glanced over his shoulder at his men.

"What do you think, Mr. Gray?" he asked.

They were all so uniform, yet purposefully unique in their own ways. Some stood tall, breathing heavy. Others were slumped over, sweat beading on their foreheads.

"I can't tell one from the other," Cam admitted.

"That's the point," said Sava. "The ultimate goal is for synthetics to be indistinguishable from humans in every way. Adding routines to make them sweat or appear fatigued serves no real purpose other than to make them more *real.*"

"Seems a little reckless."

"How so?" asked Espinoza.

Cam stepped forward and locked eyes with an AG who was staring a little too intently. "That one there, giving me the stink eye. What if I went over there to kick his ass only to find out he's a synthetic and can't feel pain?"

"Who says they can't feel pain?" asked the captain. "There's a reason we call them Automated Guards and not Killing Machines, Mr. Gray. A certain amount of illusion is required for protection of the city; we learned that early on. Humans respond to aggression and danger, not passive authority. So he'll keep acting tough, staring you down until you move on, but unless you pose a real threat to the PC or its inhabitants, he doesn't have authorization to engage you. He's harmless."

"Right," said Cam, staring at the blank faces, "but how do I know that *before* picking the fight?"

"You don't, Mr. Gray, so maybe you shouldn't. Thank you for your time, Captain Espinoza, but we need to get going. We've got a lunch meeting in the city that I don't want to be late for."

Espinoza bowed slightly to Cam. "Enjoy the city," he said, turning to rejoin his team. Over his shoulder, he muttered, "Try to stay out of trouble."

Trouble? Cam was investigating the state of synthetics in the city of Perion; trouble was inevitable.

He walked closer to the Automated Guards and put up a friendly hand.

"Gentlemen," he said, flashing his press badge, "Could I have a moment of your time?"

There was no response.

"Captain?" asked Cam.

"Alpha Company, attention!"

The AGs assembled in front of Cam and stared straight ahead.

"Alright, if you would, please raise your hand if you're a synthetic."

Twenty-four hands rose into the air.

"Okay," he said. "Any humans in here?"

No one moved; all twenty-four hands remained raised.

Espinoza chuckled. "They don't see a difference, Mr. Gray."

"That's some hard-hitting reporting," said Sava. "Why don't you ask them what their favorite color is?"

FOUR

The PC grew up gradually around the Perion Expressway.

It started with warehouses, giant manufacturing buildings dotting the horizon like teeth, their metal roofs creating blinding glares that brought Cam's hand to his eyes. Sava referred to this part of the city as The Fringe, so called because it employed the healthy minority of Perion City residents who didn't hold multiple degrees and whose only contribution was manual labor. They lived in barracks-like apartments set far back from the road, creating a second city of rough edges and rougher people. Here, Perion turned a blind eye to the lack of polish, allowing businesses to cater to the immediate clientele, provided they kept it close to home.

Cam squinted through the window, spied a giant pink gorilla sitting atop a gentlemen's club.

"Bleeding edge of the technological frontier, the brightest and best of their generation, and there's still a market for depravity," said Sava. "They like to pretend it's just for the laborers, but every once in a while you see someone from the city sneaking out here, looking for some decadence. Human nature, I suppose."

"Well, it's not just that," said Cam. "Evidently you have women in the city who are willing to take off their clothes for money. Unless you've got synthetics showing off their jackports."

Sava rolled her eyes.

"That's not a no, Ms. Kessler."

"We don't have any synthetics in the sex industry, not as strippers or prostitutes or otherwise. Mr. Perion wouldn't allow it."

"And yet you make them anatomically correct?"

"You should ask Chuck about that. We're meeting him for lunch downtown." Sava checked the time on her phone and sighed. "We may be late."

"Chuck?" asked Cam, skimming through the dossiers in his mind.

"Chuck Huber is one of the chief architects of the synthetics program. I've arranged a meeting so he can prepare you for the things you'll be seeing."

"You make it sound like I'm going to lose my mind or something."

"As I said, we're years ahead of where everyone thinks we are. You've already dropped your jaw once today, and that was just a Scorpio, one of the simplest classes we have."

"What would you say is your most impressive application?"

"That depends. Our synthetics are capable of great things, thanks to Chuck's work. He was the one who solved the four fundamental problems of synthetics. If you remember…"

"Oh I do," said Cam, putting up a hand. A buzzing grew in his ear; something was coming down the line.

"Is that so?" Sava raised her eyebrows. "Do tell."

Cam repeated the information streaming from his whisperer.

"Charles Adam Huber, born September 6, 1971. Graduated from Christa McAuliffe High School in Sarasota, Florida at the age of fifteen. Holds multiple degrees from MIT and Cal Tech, and served on the advisory committee of the National Science Foundation prior to coming to Perion City. He is known in scientific circles as the man who wrote the vade mecum on synthetic construction, including progressive modeling of muscle and tendon mimicry."

"You have a thorough research team," said Sava, "but Chuck didn't really hit his stride until he came to work for Mr. Perion. His best work has been here, which is why we've progressed while Vinestead Synthetics is stuck in the mud."

Cam glanced at his sliver. "You know I'll be recording whatever Chuck tells me, right?"

"Whatever ends up on the feed will benefit Perion Synthetics. I can assure you of that. No, we're more concerned with a Vinestead extraction team cutting off your head and reconstituting our corporate secrets from your gray matter."

"Okay," said Cam, rubbing his neck, "now I'm going to have *that* image in my head all day."

"Be thankful you still have one," said Sava. She pulled a pack of gum from her purse and popped a piece into her mouth. "Gum, Mr. Gray?"

"Do synthetics chew gum?" he asked, accepting the offer.

"They can, though I doubt one has ever had the impulse to do so on their own."

Cam tapped his chin with his finger as he chewed. "That means something, but I don't know what it is."

Sava grinned.

Turning to the window again, Cam watched the warehouses give way to cookie cutter neighborhoods that stretched away from the Perion Expressway in logarithmic spirals. Even the city planners were eccentric brainiacs.

"How many Perion scientists does it take to change a flat tire?"

"Seriously?" asked Sava.

"Trick question," said Cam. "They never get past trying to reinvent the wheel."

Sava smacked her gum.

"Speaking of which, doesn't anyone drive around here?"

Since turning off I-10, they hadn't passed a single car, coming or going, and the supply trucks lining up at Perion Terminus were nowhere to be found.

"As I said, there's no unemployment. Most people are at work right now, though we should be hitting the lunch rush when we make downtown. The PC was designed from the Spire out, and mass transit was a large component of that design, which keeps traffic at a minimum. That and bikes."

Cam huffed. "Really? The world's greatest engineers and scientists ride bikes?"

Sava fell into her flack voice again. "Physical fitness is strongly encouraged. Perion Synthetics is one of the few companies that rewards staying healthy."

"Sounds like a great place to live and work. I take it you're happy here."

Something flashed across her eyes, drawing them away. Cam had seen people do that before—feeders distracted by the constant whispers in their ears.

Sava touched the line of jewelry ascending her earlobe, drawing Cam's eyes to the intricate designs and diamond insets.

"Looks like it pays the bills," said Cam.

"Same as your job does," said Sava. "Even a first gen Katsumi isn't easy to come by. And a branded whisperer must be worth more than most Angelinos make in a year."

"Perk of the job," admitted Cam. "If it were mine to sell, I'd replace it with a KLH Tweeter and live off the proceeds."

"And the iMerse?"

Cam shrugged. "What can I say? Virtual reality is where it's at these days."

"VNet is a plague on the scene. No self-respecting technophile goes anywhere near it."

"So you're a darknet kind of woman then?"

"No," she replied, looking up through the roof of the car. "VNet and all the other immersion nets are blocked here. They've been talking about getting some kind of local network going for residents, but nothing's ever come of it. Anyway, you try jacking into VNet from here and you'll find yourself in some cozy null space."

Cam nodded his head and smiled.

"Something I said amuse you, Mr. Gray?"

"No, no, I like it, this whole flack persona you've got going on. Underneath it all, you're just a big ol' dork, aren't you?"

"We all are, but if you want to get anywhere with these people, you probably shouldn't refer to them as such. No dork, geek, dweeb, or otherwise."

"Are we talking about Chuck specifically?"

"Chuck is a good man; he doesn't deserve to be called names. Brilliant in a lot of ways, and dedicated, like Mr. Perion. They're good friends, you know."

Of course he knew. The dossier on Charles Huber was ten pages long, detailing every acquaintance he had ever made, both professionally and personally. None of the names meant anything to Cam yet, but it was interesting that the timeline and Chuck's professional accomplishments seemed to end simultaneously when he joined up with Perion Synthetics. How could a man so prolific in his twenties and early thirties resign himself to R&D at a corporate giant?

"So, Perion put the team together himself?"

"We've always cultivated the best minds, real time travelers," said Sava.

The term made instant sense to Cam, who upon seeing the synthetic guard crumble at his feet had wondered if the whole trip were some kind of dream, an interactive movie being pumped into his brain in the back room of some sim parlor. No amount of promotional footage could have prepared him for seeing the tech in person, seeing that perfect blend of machinery imitating life. Even with his years of experience, Cam had found it hard to disguise his astonishment.

"We need people who can keep up, who won't succumb to complacency just because they met their Q3 quotas."

"The best of the best, right?"

"Is that envy, Mr. Gray?"

"It just raises questions."

"Such as?"

"Well, the big one," said Cam, sitting up in his seat, "is that as far as I can tell, Perion City is one big beta test for your synthetics program, right?"

"In a way. Mr. Perion's first tenet of business is that we're customer zero. If we don't use the product, how can we ever hope to make it better?"

"Ah yes, the Perion Tenets of Business. Number thirty-eight: make sure each product has functioning genitalia."

Sava folded her arms. "I never said they were completely functional."

"Okay," continued Cam, "so ballpark, how many synthetics with partially functional junk do you have running around this place?"

"The PC is home to four hundred and sixty thousand residents, give or take. Almost a third of those are synthetics."

"In what capacity?"

"It varies," said Sava. "You'll see."

The Perion Expressway began to veer easterly, away from the colossal Spire rising up from the center of the city. The car exited and turned onto a side street, giving Cam a proper look at the monument to Perion success. Someone had turned the sharpness filter all the way up, adding details he had never noticed before in marketing collateral.

"It really came out of nowhere, didn't it?" he asked.

"It looks better at night. By day, the mirrors make it practically invisible."

The car pulled over as the Spire loomed, now visible through the tinted glass of the moon roof. They had stopped in front of an open-air cafeteria set behind an expansive patio. Only two of the outdoor tables were occupied; they had umbrellas to shield them from the glare of the Spire.

Sava made no effort to move.

"Do we go?" asked Cam.

"In a minute," she replied, consulting her phone again. "There's something I want to show you first."

"Another demonstration?"

Sava ignored the question. "Across the way there is a child development center."

Cam followed Sava's gaze and took in the squat, two-story building. A large mural adorned the left side of the school, mirroring the orange monkey bars and green swing sets of the attached playground.

"At eleven-thirty, classes will break for lunch, and the instructors will take the children across the street to the cafeteria. You see the policeman waiting by the sidewalk? He'll stop traffic in both directions until everyone has crossed."

"You have your own police force as well? Paid for by the state?"

Sava scoffed. "State money means state involvement, and we can't have that here. Our police force is a blend of Scorpios and humans, mostly prior service military. They were put in place to acclimate synthetics to the idea of civil authority."

A bell rang out across the street and moments later the front doors of the school opened by themselves. A group of children appeared—Cam counted twenty before giving up—chaperoned by four adult women.

"How many synthetics do you see?" asked Sava.

Cam studied the women carefully as they herded the children to the edge of the sidewalk.

"I'm going to guess three."

"Why just the three?"

"Well," said Cam, "to put it indelicately, the fourth one is… rotund."

Sava chuckled. "There you go, proving Dr. Bhenderu correct. The *rotund* woman you pointed out is one of his experiments, a synthetic by the name of Mrs. Albright. Dr. Bhenderu believes a line of synnies with perfect bodies would have a detrimental effect on the body image of their human owners. And while there are some applications that call for a slim chassis, others do allow some leeway."

"Fat robots," said Cam. "Who would have thought?"

"She's not fat," said Sava, peppering her monotone with a hint of anger. "She's slightly above the average weight of an American woman her age."

"Not that I can blame her, right? She's exactly how you designed her. I just wonder what Mr. Albright thinks of his wife's weight problem."

"Don't be simple," said Sava.

"Well, you said *Mrs.* Albright."

"It doesn't mean she's married; it's just part of her imprinted identity. She didn't really get her master's in child development from Vassar either."

"Do the children know their teachers are synthetics?"

"Not at this age. We don't broach the subject until they're much older."

"They don't figure it out themselves?"

"*You* can barely pick out the synnies, Mr. Gray."

"Sure," said Cam. "I'm just a city boy with no reckoning of your new-fangled walking machines. But these are the children of the best of the best of the best. If they aren't smart enough to sniff out the robots, surely the synthetic children can recognize one of their own."

"How did you know?" asked Sava.

Cam smirked. "Yeah, that was the whole point of your little guessing game, right? Look, making that guard eat pavement was pretty incredible, no doubt, and I'm blown away by the attention to detail in those teachers." He sat forward on the seat and looked out the window again. "But look at those synthetic children, look at their faces and those of the human kids next to them, look at how they observe the world. Not even your engineers can reproduce the look of wonder on a child's face. Given how smart you claim your people to be, I'm surprised you even tried."

Sava crossed her arms and narrowed her eyes at Cam.

"This whole aggregator thing you've got going on," said Sava, moving her hand in a circle, "it's just an act, isn't it?"

Cam shrugged and watched the children disappear into the cafeteria. "You people are pushing the limits of human decency here."

Sava pursed her lips but said nothing.

FIVE

"The kitchen is a marvel of efficiency," said Cam.

His sliver glowed red at the sound of his voice.

"There are five stations, each with its own cutting area and sink. Utensils hang above on steel racks, a knife block in each corner. Five synthetics man the stations—if *man* is even the right word—and each one has its own program. They mash their ingredients into a component, drop it on the conveyor, and repeat. At the serving counter, three synthetics dish out the main course, a small selection of sides, and desserts, mostly cookies or Jell-O.

"Two things of interest here. The fundamental difference between synthetics and humans is that the robots don't tire. None of them are stopping to stretch their backs or crack their knuckles. Repetitive movements do not faze them."

Cam swiped his sliver while he considered the phrasing of his second thought. Beyond the serving line, he caught sight of an agitated Sava standing outside with one hand pressed to her ear and the other gesticulating wildly. Chuck Huber, renowned for his contributions to advanced robotics, was evidently a bit of a dawdler—a dilatory scatterbrain when it came to social interaction, as Sava had so eloquently put it. When she excused herself to make a phone call, Cam used the opportunity to slip into the cafeteria kitchen to see if synthetics were being used in the food service industry. With the exception of the mustachioed man in a chef's hat watching a vidscreen at the back of the kitchen, it appeared they were being used exclusively.

"They don't tire," Cam continued. "They don't seem to lose focus at all. Even when I came in, they barely noticed me. Strangely enough, I feel they all know I'm here."

The synthetics were all wearing the same uniform: black slacks, white, button-tab tunics, and aprons as pristine as the floor on which their polished shoes walked. The one closest to Cam had black hair cut close to his head and a light beard on square features. The nametag on his tunic read *Gerard*.

"Excuse me," said Cam, approaching the prep station. He held out his press badge, but the cook didn't look up from his cutting board. "I'm Cameron Gray with Banks Media out of Los Angeles. Would you mind if I asked you a few questions about your work here?"

Gerard remained mute, focused.

Pull a head of lettuce from the pile. Run it under the faucet for fifteen seconds. Make four cuts equidistant from each other. Chop into four piles. Combine in bowl.

"Everything is scripted and precise," said Cam, dictating again. "Dishes are set just far enough away so they don't interfere with the process. The same goes for utensils. Some are balanced—carelessly, I might add—on the edge of the counter, with their blades pointing outward. Where is OSHA when you need them?" He tapped his chin. "An experiment is needed."

When Gerard reached for a new head of lettuce, Cam pushed one of the knives off of the counter. It fell halfway to the floor before the synthetic caught it by the blade and replaced it. His hands moved faster for several seconds to make up for the lost time and then settled into his normal tempo.

"Please don't do that."

Cam narrowed his eyes; Gerard's lips hadn't moved at all. It wasn't until the voice spoke again that Cam realized it was coming from the man in the chef's hat. He had come off his perch to deal with the intruder, and it appeared he was none too happy with the interruption.

"You the aggregator?" he asked.

"I is. Cameron Gray, Banks Media, Los Angeles. And you are?"

"Customers aren't supposed to be back here. Health code and whatnot."

"I'm not here as a customer. Tell me, are all of your employees synthetic?"

"Last time I checked," said the chef. His nametag was conspicuously absent.

"And how long have you exclusively employed non-humans?"

"What is that? Non-human?"

"Sorry," said Cam, consulting his notes. "What do you call them here?"

"This one here I call Gerard. See? That's his name right there on his nametag. That one over there is Wolfgang. And Pikel, Miller, and Cooke."

"The cook's name is Cooke?"

The chef grunted. "Am I going to have to say everything twice?"

Cordial, thought Cam. He looked around to see if any of the synthetics were interested in the conversation, but they seemed unaffected by their boss' hostility.

"You knew I was an aggregator," said Cam. "So you were expecting me?"

A curt nod.

"Which I'm guessing means a memo of some sort was passed around. And it would be a waste of said memo if its only purpose was to inform you of my impending arrival. Therefore, I can only conclude that not only were you told to expect me, you were also instructed to be receptive to my questioning, under the directive of Perion the Almighty." A beat went by. "You get me? Or do I have to say it twice?"

The chef considered Cam for a moment. "Cosimo Castelluccio," he said, forcing a smile. "How can I help you?"

"How long have you worked here, Mr. Castelluccio?"

"Four years."

"And before that?"

"Sous-chef at Mandola's San Francisco."

Cam looked around the modern but unimpressive kitchen. "You gave that up to come here?"

"My little girl goes to the school across the street. I work lunches here to make sure she gets a good meal," Cosimo explained. "In the evenings, I'm executive chef at Chez Cosimo."

"French restaurant, Italian cook. Makes sense."

Cosimo shrugged and nodded to the men and women mixed in with the children at the serving counter. "Like any of these eggheads can tell the difference. The only man in this city with a palate is Mr. Perion, and I'll give you two shakes of my monkey tree as to who brought me in."

"Ah," said Cam. "Tell me about that."

"It's nothing much," said the chef, patting his large stomach. "One night, five years ago, I'm working the line at Mandola's and it's a busy Friday. I have to call in an extra roundsman because my saucier got a little third degree up and down his arm. Everything's going to hell and it's getting late, and like some kind of goddamn celebrity, in walks Mr. Perion. He's got an entire entourage in tow, and Governor Howard, *and* some MX nationals I ain't never heard of before. Mr. Perion sits down, doesn't even look at the menu, and orders pasta fazool for the entire table. I'm thinking, *is this guy crazy or what?* Of all the dishes I can prepare, this guy wants the meal my mother throws together when she's on her period."

Cam shuddered.

"Anyway, I go to town on this fazool, cut all the ingredients myself, and serve it to the suits in our best bowls. Mr. Perion takes one bite and shits his pants— pardon my language. Best fucking meal he's ever tasted, he says to me. Offers me a job on the spot, says he'll give me my own restaurant. Only catch is I have to move from San Fran to this place."

"Most people I talk to can't wait to get out of there."

"You're not from an Italian family, Mr. Gray. You don't just up and leave 'em because some moneybag wants to make you his personal cook."

"And yet you're here."

"You noticed that, huh? Just because I stay here doesn't mean the money does. At least I know Ma is taken care of."

"Does she know about *them?*"

"No," said Cosimo. "I'm not supposed to talk about that kind of stuff with outsiders." He stepped in closer, perhaps afraid of who might hear him. "I've tried to drop hints, ya know, but Ma don't understand so well anymore."

"And you? What do you think about Gerard here?"

Cosimo slapped the synthetic on the shoulder; it barely moved.

"They creep me the fuck out sometimes, but they take orders well. No creativity though. They make the same thing over and over again; it's never different. It doesn't matter much here, but at my restaurant, I'll only trust 'em to prepare the bread."

"You ever get nervous with them handling knives?"

"Ha! I've heard stories about the first synnies, about how they were uncoordinated, not blessed with the fine touch it takes to prepare food. Now the eggheads come and swap out my staff every four or five months, so they keep getting better. Gerard here has been working for me for two and hasn't cut himself once. Neither have the others. It's like they're *learning*."

He let the word hang in the air.

Cam made a few notes in his phone and extended his hand.

"Thank you for your time, Mr. Castelluccio. And you too, Gerard."

"Gerard, directive. Say goodbye to our aggregator friend."

The synthetic came to a sudden stop and cocked his head. "Goodbye, Mr. Gray."

Cam raised an eyebrow.

"Oh yeah," said Cosimo. "Sneaky bastards, huh? You think they're not listening to every word you're saying? Bullshit. And if they're listening, then someone back in the Spire is listening too, bet on it."

"Someone always is," said Cam, reading a message on his phone.

"Ask him if he knows Vinnie the Mouth," Banks had texted. Evidently, the big boss was tuned into Cam's raw feed. It wasn't unheard of for engineers or QA to listen in when aggregators were out on the job, but usually they had the decency to give prior notice.

Cam nodded politely and exited the kitchen through the swinging doors. The crowd in the cafeteria had swelled since he arrived; the tables to his left were full of children, but on the right, a mix of humans and synthetics sat eating lunch. At least, the humans were eating. It was the only tell Cam could identify, seeing how synthetics behaved more or less like humans, nodding their heads to the conversation, smiling when appropriate, and even responding with what, their opinions?

Before he could join one of the tables to listen in, Cam felt a hand on his arm.

"Where were you?" asked Sava.

"In the kitchen, interviewing the automated cooking robots. I'm going to call them AutoCookBots, ACBs for short."

Sava glanced over the serving line. "Well, I hope you got something of value. Chuck's not going to be able to make it to lunch. He's working on some project he can't tear himself away from, so we'll have to meet him at the office later. You hungry?"

Cam nodded and followed Sava to the plastic trays.

"So how long have you two been dating?" asked Cam.

Sava's blush came on fast. "What? What makes you think…?"

Cam pushed his tray along the metal bars. "I'm an aggregator. I pick up on things."

"So it was in my file, wasn't it? His too, maybe?"

"Nope. Two parents, one sister, a dog, but no mention of a boyfriend."

"Then how did you know?"

The smile on Cam's face grew. "It's in the way your voice drips with affection when you say his name. Chuck. Not Mr. Huber, but *Ch-uuuuuck*."

"Goddamn outland feeders," grumbled Sava. She nodded to the synthetic behind the counter and asked for a salad.

"Banks Media presents *Love in the Desert*, the story of a PR flack and an engineer who defied all odds. He discovered universal truths, she made hers up, and yet in each other's arms, they found happiness."

"Sounds like the kind of bullshit Banks Media is known for," said Sava. "Though if you feed any shopped pictures of me and Chuck holding hands in some lab, I'll send an army of synnies after you. Don't think I won't."

"You mean, if they could get past the PNR without dissolving from the inside out, right?"

Sava's blue eyes stared back. "Yeah," she said. "Right."

Cam nodded. "That's what I thought."

"What can I get for you today, sir?" asked the synthetic.

"Pasta fazool," said Cam.

SIX

"The world as we understand it is fundamentally flawed."

Chuck Huber's hands moved like those of a conductor in front of an orchestra, but instead of emphasizing the first beat of the measure, they came down hard at the end of his sentences, as if to drive home the point that what he had just said was the most important statement the world has ever known.

Cam tried to keep his eyes on Chuck's face, on the wireframe glasses resting on a hooked nose, on the deep black eyebrows that stood in contrast to the salt and pepper hair on his head, but there was too much activity taking place in the air between them.

"In that, I mean it is an incomplete system, one without finite rules to govern its occupants. You may think we humans have progressed to a point where we understand how everything works, but you'd be quite mistaken. Science is about expectation. I set two identical tops spinning, and nine times out of ten, I expect them to fall down simultaneously. We have expectations about all facets of life, even those we cannot personally observe."

No kidding, thought Cam, looking from Chuck to Sava and back again. Sava was a good six inches taller than her loquacious boyfriend.

"The average human has a radial consciousness of barely twenty meters. Beyond that, we are guessing what is happening by projecting our expectations onto the world based on previously observed outcomes. The reason we do this is simple: to counteract a crippling uncertainty about the reality we live in. As we grow older, we learn to discount or ignore this uncertainty."

The only uncertainty was where the conversation was going.

Cam looked down at his phone to ask one of his prepared questions, but he was too slow to speak.

"A synthetic mind, on the other hand, cannot process uncertainty, which we represent with a null value. We briefly tried ternary computation with a variant of our Epsilon line—this was prior to our current astrological designations—but it would have required a complete shift in synaptic architecture to implement fully. Null values don't agree with our modern, binary synthetics, the same way dairy doesn't agree with me. If a synthetic's directive is to exist in this world and respond to stimuli, then they must have a complete understanding of the world in order to make the most accurate decision. This was not planned, of course. We didn't know that by asking our synthetics to consider the possibility of a null value, we'd be opening Pandora's Jar of Indeterminate States. That's what we call them in synth parlance, those bits that are neither one nor zero, but something in between."

"I've heard infinity exists between one and zero," mumbled Cam.

Chuck flinched at the interruption. "Yes," he stammered, "I mean no. Nonsense, absolute nonsense. Indeterminate states are a purely human concept. There's no room in the code for them. To have a synthetic understand null values, you'd need to invent a truly artificial intelligence. Simulating ternary computation is not enough."

Chuck trailed off, his mind processing some internal piece of data.

Cam typed a few adjectives into his phone, catching Sava's eyes as he did so.

"He's really quite brilliant," she insisted. "People with the brainpower to keep up find him fascinating."

Cam raised his eyebrows to challenge her.

"I usually can't, but then he doesn't talk much about work outside of the lab. That's why I wanted to meet at lunch, so you could speak to person Chuck, not engineer Chuck. Once he's here in the Spire, he becomes very focused on the prize."

"And what is the prize?" asked Cam.

"Assumed intelligence," said Chuck, approaching a whiteboard. He cleared away some space with the sleeve of his lab coat. "Artificial intelligence is a rush fantasy, a dream birthed by *men* who think themselves *gods*. We don't understand the miracle of consciousness, so how can we ever hope to bestow it upon something we've created? All we can do is program a crude mimicry to make a synthetic *seem* human. And we've done that, to a certain extent, done it better with each revision of software."

"Are you saying your synthetics are capable of carrying on an in-depth conversation? The few I've encountered didn't have much to say."

Chuck looked to Sava, who explained about the cooks at the cafeteria.

"Did you get a look at their wrists?

"No," said Cam. "Should I have?"

"We tag each synthetic," explained Chuck. "Knowing their astrological sign would have told you which revision they were. I'm guessing the cooks you encountered were specialized. Their job functions probably didn't require advanced speech synthesis. Did you try saying their name followed by *directive* and then a command?"

Cam shook his head. "No, but I saw it done. I thought that was a little weird. It reminds me of voice-actuated elevators like the ones we have at the BMP Tower in Los Angeles."

"Ugh," said Chuck, "such a horrible comparison. Those cooks were built for a specific purpose: to make and serve food. They take orders from a human overseer, I imagine?"

"Cosimo," replied Cam. "Funny guy."

"I'm sure," said Chuck, writing the chef's name on the board. He stared at it for a moment, as if wondering why he had written it down, and then promptly erased it. "Are you sure *he* wasn't a synthetic as well?"

"Well now I'm not." He shot a questioning look at Sava. "You would have pointed that out, right?"

"Savannah is a beautiful and talented woman, but she is not infallible in the judgment of synthetic versus human."

Sava shrugged in agreement. "The technology advances so quickly. Every day, there's a better model coming off the assembly line and integrating into the population. Checking their wrists is usually the only way to tell, since not all of us get the memo when a new revision is introduced."

"But you do, Mr. Huber?"

"I *write* the memos," said Chuck. "Well, I mean to say, my assistant writes them, but that's semantics for you. Michelle doesn't have the subject matter expertise to describe our latest advancements, so I simply feed her the information. If we called her in here right now, she could easily recite the specifications and capabilities of our latest model. And if you heard her speak without knowing I had briefed her prior, would you not think she knew what she was talking about?"

"I would… not?"

"That, Mr. Gray, is assumed intelligence. It is all a function of interface versus implementation. Your phone there, for example, has a calculator application, I assume? And when you ask it what two plus two equals, it gives you the correct answer, as if it knew. But without using your calculator, let me ask you this question: what is four plus four?"

"Eight!" said Cam. He made a show of counting on his fingers to confirm.

"See what you did there? The answer is indeed eight, but how did you arrive at it? You spoke before you counted on your fingers, so obviously you knew the answer even without your digital calculation."

"I just knew. Or actually, I remembered."

"Yes, you remembered." Chuck wrote the simple equation on the board. "You've answered the question so many times that you simply pulled the data from memory. But if I asked you to calculate the square root of seventy-six thousand, four hundred and twenty-nine, you wouldn't have a similar table of figures to refer to, would you?"

"You don't know that for sure," said Cam.

"I'm almost certain of it. When faced with a more difficult problem, you have to fall back to calculation. However you decide to come up with the answer—

whether a calculator or pencil and paper—is what we call the *implementation*. When you ask a synthetic what two plus two is, for example, it actually does the calculation every time by representing the numbers in binary and performing a basic add operation on them. But that's simple mathematics, a finite system of rules. So I'll ask you a different question. How are you feeling today?"

"Fine," replied Cam. Truthfully, the pasta fazool wasn't sitting right with him; he made a note to give Cosimo a piece of his mind if he saw him again.

"How do you know?" asked Chuck. "How do you know you're feeling fine? And what does that even mean, *fine*?"

Cam smiled. "I see your point."

"Do you? Do you really?" There was no sarcasm in his voice; he seemed genuinely interested in the answer.

"Well, I think I do."

"Yes, you accept the possibility I have a point, and you are willing to concede its veracity without fully understanding it. So that's how I know you're not a human, er, not a synthetic. Pardon me."

"So… was Cosimo human or not?"

"It doesn't really matter, does it?" asked Sava. "You *thought* he was human."

"The point I'm trying to make, Mr. Gray, is that our synthetics are not intelligent—no matter what our marketing department says. Their cognitive system is based on the idea that humans will accept an interface so long as the implementation is hidden from them. When you ask a synthetic what time it is, it may check its wrist before telling you the answer. Does it really matter that looking for a nonexistent watch or sliver was just for show, that it actually consulted the USNO master clock and adjusted for your time zone?"

"It doesn't matter," said Cam. "I would expect nothing less."

"And thus you define your own reality. But an accurate answer isn't always the most human answer, is it?" He turned to Sava. "Honey, what time is it?"

She glanced at the digital clock on the wall. "Almost two."

"There you go," said Chuck. "Not 1:57, but *almost two*. A slight change to the interface, a fudging of the answer, and you've got yourself a bona fide human response."

Cam was suddenly overcome by a suspicion that Chuck Huber wasn't entirely human himself.

"Chuck, Mr. Gray here will be conducting interviews with employees and synthetics today. Perhaps you could speak to him about that thing you mentioned to me."

"Ah yes," said Chuck, capping his dry-erase marker. "Mr. Gray, I would like to enlist your help as a beta tester. As an outlander, you bring a unique perspective to our field trials. Perion employees have become inured to the presence of synthetics. Advancements are no longer blowing their skirts up like they used to, nor do they appreciate that the robopocalypse remains unrealized."

Cam resisted the urge to check his notes. Hadn't Sava casually mentioned something about the machines running amok?

"I would like you to put our synthetics through their paces. Ask them paradoxical questions, challenge them to go beyond their programming. Create and constantly redefine your own Turing test; present it to every humanoid you meet. Some may fail instantly, but those who pass are of great interest to me. In exchange for your time and effort, I will make myself available to you around the clock to answer any questions you may have."

"Would you mind if I asked you a few questions now?" asked Cam. "I'd like to get an idea of your personal and professional history since you joined Perion Synthetics."

"Unfortunately, I have some pressing matters to attend to. My better half is well-versed in my backstory, and she's a much more visually appealing interface to get the information from, don't you agree? Please speak to her first, and if you still need more for your story, I'll be happy to arrange a follow-up meeting. Until then, it has been a pleasure talking with you, Mr. Gray."

Talking *at* me, thought Cam. He pocketed his phone and shook Chuck's hand. "Any suggestion where I should start my investigation?" he asked.

"Dr. Bhenderu has arranged a demonstration for you at Southpoint Synthetics. He wouldn't give me the details, but I assume it will be worth your time. They have some new and exciting products on display there, and it may be interesting to see how our boys on the front line handle an outlander."

"Dinner tonight?" asked Sava.

Chuck was already walking away; he answered over his shoulder. "I will do my best to be there. Big things are happening upstairs." The silver door swung closed behind him.

Sava turned to Cam. "What's that look for?"

"Your boyfriend, he's... a charming fellow."

"You could learn a thing or two," she replied, putting her hands on her hips.

Cam consulted his phone and exclaimed, "Four plus four equals eight!"

SEVEN

Southpoint Synthetics was a two-story building sitting on an acre of evercrete between an arts and crafts store and the W. G. Walter Spiritual Center. The scaffolding of a rooftop helipad hung out over the edge of what could have passed for a car dealership anywhere else.

Sava explained that Southpoint was the brainchild of Katherine Shaw, Perion's vice president of business development and former rising star at Nixle Chronos. She had been personally responsible for the successful launch of NC's self-contained augmented reality exotech and had been plucked from the company by James Perion himself.

According to her dossier, she was wife to Nicholas "Nico" Shaw, personal assistant to Perion's son Joseph. The list of her accomplishments was a mile long, which was probably why Perion had agreed to let her establish a dealership in the middle of the city and stock it with products and employees, neither of which were actually expected to sell.

"It's the simulation that's important," said Sava, as the car pulled into the parking lot beneath the mammoth Southpoint sign. "Mrs. Shaw wants to get the procedures in place years ahead of the product launch. A few months ago, she sent out a memo telling everyone it was their professional responsibility to visit Southpoint at least once and pretend to be a customer looking to buy. It gives the salespeople something to do."

Cam detected a lack of enthusiasm. "I'm guessing you don't agree with the wasting of resources?"

"It's not just that," said Sava.

The car came to a stop and the chauffeur opened the door for her. Over the roof, she continued.

"It just makes them seem even more inhuman than they already are. Buying and selling *products* that look like humans? And no one bats an eye at this?"

"I guess so long as the synthetics aren't wearing loincloths and bound with shackles, we should be okay, right?"

Sava rolled her eyes and headed for the front door. She was met inside by a man in a blue suit and an outrageously pink tie. He was a salesman head to toe; the only thing more artificial than his smile was his jet-black hair color.

"Ms. Kessler, what a nice surprise. What brings you in today?"

"My friend here needs a new synthetic," she explained, her acting skills strained to their breaking point. "His previous model suffered a water intrusion short after he told it to put liquid dish soap in the dishwashing machine."

The salesman nodded and switched his focus to Cam.

"A shame," he said.

"And ironic, right?" asked Cam. "A machine tasked with washing the dishes using *another* machine to accomplish it. They're crafty, you know?"

The salesman nodded as if it were his default reaction to another human speaking. "All the best ones are," he replied. "We can definitely dial that quality back if that's not what you're looking for."

"We'll see," said Cam.

"The name's Tank Maddox," said the salesman, extending his hand.

"Of course it is. I'm Elliot Graystone of Graystone Prosthetic Extensions. If you've got an itch, we can scratch it. Trademark."

A laugh escaped Sava's lips, but she turned away before Cam could get her to acknowledge it. While she wandered over to a wall of interactive vidscreens, Maddox tried his best to remain in character.

"So, you're looking for a new domestic partner?"

Sava's snort echoed in the showroom. She blushed and tried to find a way to put even more distance between herself and Cam.

"Well, it's the wife really," said Cam. "She's had some augmentation work done on her hips that's really affected her mobility. And with three little monkeys running around the house, that doesn't leave a lot of time for chores."

"I understand," said Maddox. "Let's start with our domestic synthetics and work our way up. I just unpacked an assisted-living model named Amanda. She's versed in physical therapy, and it shouldn't be any trouble to cross-imprint some domestic abilities. How does a full body massage every night sound to you?"

Cam put up his hands. "So long as I'm not the one giving it, it's fine by me. If I have to rub that woman's feet one more time, I may have my own water intrusion short."

"Do you have any blondes?" asked Sava. She was standing by a grouping of inert floor models, examining their clothes. "He's partial to blondes. All I see are brunettes."

Maddox cleared his throat. "Brunette is the new blonde. They're outselling everything else three to one this quarter."

"Shame. He'd buy one on the spot if you had a cute little golden-haired minx to sell him."

"I'll check our inventory. If we don't have one here, I'm sure I can get it for you, maybe order it direct from the factory. In the meantime, please have a look around. Ms. Kessler, all of the private screening rooms are open if you'd like to take Mr. Graystone back."

"We'll wait for you there, Mr. Maddox."

The salesman nodded and walked briskly to the desk on the other side of the showroom.

"He plays the part well," said Sava, as Cam joined her at the display models. "What's he going to do, make a trade with another dealership?"

"So I'm into blondes, huh?"

"According to your last three romantic interests, I'd say yes."

"Well, your intel is wrong. Felicia wasn't a real blonde, so ha."

Cam touched a synthetic on the arm; its skin felt warm under his fingers. For all the time he had spent in Perion City, he hadn't yet held the product in his hands.

"Body heat is a nice touch," he said.

"Chuck's contribution to the design process after a synthetic nurse tried to take his blood pressure with what he called *icy cold hands of death*." Her voice pitched lower. "Absolute zero exists! And it's in this woman's fingers!"

"Would you say your boyfriend is a comedian first, engineer second?"

Sava groaned. "Dr. Bhenderu pointed out that having a completely cold synthetic would break the suspension of disbelief. He and Chuck argued for days about just how much body heat the nurse should have."

Cam caught himself running his fingernails over the synthetic's skin. He pulled his hand away as his cheeks warmed.

"Come on," said Sava. "Let's go check out the screening rooms." Then, raising her voice, "We're heading back now, Mr. Maddox."

"Sure," said the salesman, covering the phone in his hand. "I'll be with you shortly."

"Take your time."

Sava led Cam through a winding hallway with glass walls showcasing well-appointed but empty offices. Each had a thick, L-shaped desk that pushed into the center of the room, a comfy leather chair for the salesman, and two smaller chairs for prospective buyers. VoIP phones sat beside computer monitors on the desks, their screens blank. They passed six such offices, culminating in a larger seventh at the end of the hallway.

"The screening rooms are just through here," said Sava.

"Kind of a walk, don't you think?"

"All part of the sales process. They want you to pass by the offices on your way in so you can see other buyers happily signing their fortunes away. Then, when you're done getting to know your synny, you have to pass by them again." She imitated Maddox' insincere voice. "Now, I know you said you wanted to think about it, but before you go, I'd like to show you some finance options that might make this purchase easier. No pressure; you can still walk out if you want to."

They passed through a set of double doors with rectangular windows and into the screening area, which also had a meandering hallway that broke off at seemingly random intervals into vastly different rooms. There were no windows, but Cam could see into the staged settings through the open doors. They passed a bedroom, a kitchen, and a dental office before Sava led him into what looked like the living room of an expensive condo.

"This about right for you?" asked Sava. "Someone with your salary probably lives in one of those downtown high-rises, right?"

Cam thought about the living room of his three-bedroom house in Burbank. His microfiber couches looked nothing like the ultra-modern appointments filling the fake condo. Staring at the dull, gray stripes of a rug sitting atop the hardwood floor, he wondered why Sava would assume he lived in such a style, especially if his file contained his home address.

He shook his head, trying to sort the important questions from the meaningless.

"Dr. Bhenderu thought you might like to interact with a freshly imprinted synthetic, ask it some questions."

"Are they different on first boot?"

"A little," said Sava. "They have to ramp into their imprint, as well as learn what their owners like and dislike. It's like a training period." She touched a palette on the wall by the door and brought up the Southpoint Synthetics inventory system. She sighed.

"Something wrong?"

"No, it's just that they're overstocked with Leo models. Chuck worked on those for a while, said they weren't exactly a step forward in the revision process. If I recall, we sent most of them to The Fringe for warehouse duty."

"What was the problem?"

"Nothing we could really put our finger on. Chuck thinks it was a tweak they made to the imprinting process, where the synnies get their personalities and technical knowledge. But who knows. Those are the breaks with assumed intelligence. You give them a new way of thinking and they either sink or swim."

"Is it common to have a synthetic come out of the oven half-baked? Also, can synthetics swim?"

"Yes to the second question," said Sava, pausing on the image of a blonde Leo in green scrubs. "The first question is a little tougher. Each model has its own strengths and weaknesses, so it's not a total loss if we can fill a need in the city. But, if they're really bad, or dangerous, they won't even make it out of the Spire."

Cam watched the models scroll by. Each profile was stamped with an astrological symbol, a crouched Lion being the most prevalent.

"Anything blowing your skirt up?" asked Sava.

"That one's missing its symbol," said Cam, pointing to the palette.

On the screen, a three-dimensional model of a woman rotated slowly. The label underneath contained her vitals: five feet three inches tall, one hundred and fifteen pounds. She had eyes the same color as her hair, a deep russet brown that sparkled at the edges of her irises. Cam found himself lost in the shape of her eyebrows, which rose and fell as they extended away from the center of her face, tapering to a fine point. The detail was far superior to anything else in the catalogue.

"Weird," said Sava, swiping the palette to bring up the model's technical data. "I guess they forgot to log her tag when they put her in the system."

"Can I meet her?"

Sava grinned. "You're a salesman's dream, aren't you? Her file says she's imprinted for clerical work. Not exactly exciting stuff."

"I'll make it exciting," said Cam, pulling out his phone. He opened the camera app. "For the story."

"Fine, I'll bring her in. We can check her tag in person."

Sava tapped the button marked *Select* in the bottom right corner of the screen. The palette dimmed and presented a message assuring them their selection would be with them shortly.

Cam took a seat on the couch. The rough base and oddly curved backing made finding a comfortable position nearly impossible. From the door, Sava gave him a quizzical look.

"It's the couch," he explained. "I'm not nervous."

"Sure," said Sava, trying to hide her amusement. She wandered into the hallway for a moment. "Ah," she said, stepping back into the room. "Mr. Gray, meet your new domestic partner."

Cam stood but was unable to take a step forward.

Someone was playing a joke on him. There was no way the woman standing in the doorway could have been a synthetic. They had hired the most attractive woman in the city just to see if Cam would fall for it.

So that was their game.

He put out a hand. "Nice to meet you."

She smiled in return and held out a dainty hand. "Likewise, mister…?"

"Gray," he replied. "Cameron Gray. Friends call me Cam."

"Nice to meet you, Mr. Gray. I'm Roberta." She dipped her head in deference.

"Roberta?" asked Sava. Something made her nose twitch. "Let me see your tag." When the synthetic stared blankly, she added, "Your wrist, let me see it."

"Of course," said Roberta, lifting her hand.

"*Other* wrist," said Sava, reaching out before Roberta could lift her right arm.

Sava scratched a small square of skin on Roberta's wrist; it pulsed white.

"Well?" asked Cam.

"Not a logging error." Sava checked Roberta's other wrist just to be sure. "She's not tagged, which means they've started a new line or she's a prototype." There was a hint of worry in her voice.

"Is that a problem?"

Sava took a step back and considered Roberta. "I can't believe they'd pull a stunt like this. Excuse me, I need to make a phone call."

Roberta watched with detachment as Sava left the room. When she was gone, the synthetic turned her brown eyes to Cam and blinked.

"Your girlfriend?" she asked.

Cam's laughter brought a smile to Roberta's face.

"Absolutely not," he replied. "She's more into your creator."

"My creator?"

"Yeah, you know, the one who designed you."

Roberta cocked her head to the side.

"Interesting," she said.

EIGHT

Cam discovered a manicured garden neatly tucked behind the W. G. Walter Spiritual Center next door to Southpoint. He spotted it as he was escorting Roberta out of a back door while Sava was busy in the showroom arguing in hushed tones with Maddox and whoever was unlucky enough to be on the other end of her phone.

Outside, the air smelled fresher than the artificially scented environment of the screening room. Cam took a deep breath as he sat down on a bench next to a rose bush. Roberta took the seat beside him.

She was no less stunning in natural light, prompting Cam to take another picture to send over to Banks.

His response read *keep it in your pants*.

Easier said than done. This thing sitting in front of him was more than an amalgamation of circuitry and code. And yet, he was having a hard time trying to define just exactly what she was.

"I've got the situation in hand," wrote Cam.

Banks didn't acknowledge his humor.

"It's a beautiful day," said Roberta, looking to the sky. She lifted a hand to shield her eyes from the sun.

"Do you mind if I ask you some questions, Roberta?"

"About me?"

"Yes, about you." Cam pulled his press badge and showed it to her. "I'm with Banks Media out of Los Angeles. I'm here to find out what life is like in Perion City."

"Okay," said Roberta. She fidgeted under her black sweater and white blouse; her fingers held the edges of her sleeves against her palms.

"Alright, first question," said Cam, swiping his sliver. "What's four plus four?"

"Eight," answered Roberta.

"And the capital of California?"

"Sacramento."

"And the diameter of the earth?"

Roberta paused. "I thought you wanted to know about me."

"I do. These are just some baseline questions I ask everyone."

"Really?"

"I promise. Now, diameter of the earth?"

Roberta smiled and shook her head. "I don't know, Mr. Gray. I bet we could look it up though."

"Would you?" asked Cam.

"Alright." Roberta tapped her empty pockets. "I seem to have forgotten my phone. Can I use yours?"

"Can't you just retrieve the answer wirelessly?"

Some art school prodigy had done a damn good job of programming Roberta to simultaneously lift and push her eyebrows together. "Yes," she said, drawing out the word. "I can do it wirelessly, but I'll need a *phone* or a palette or some kind of *wireless device*." She put air quotes around her last two words.

Cam made a note regarding her sarcasm.

"When performing CPR, what is the ratio of chest compressions to breaths?"

"I heard you weren't supposed to do the breaths anymore, just the compressions. But you'd want to do about a hundred compressions a minute."

"How old are you?"

"I was born in 1990, so I'm twenty-five."

"Where do you work?"

"In the Clerical department on the eleventh floor of the Spire. I'm currently on vacation though."

"Who holds the record for the most rushing yards in a rookie season, before they allowed augmentations?"

"I have no clue."

"What's your favorite color, Roberta?"

She leaned in and smiled. "What's yours?"

Cam took the moment to catch his breath. His sliver was flashing happily, but it was only recording words, not the expressions on Roberta's face or the intent of the rapid-fire questioning.

"It's gray," he replied.

Roberta nodded. "I should have guessed. That's my favorite too."

In the back of his mind, Cam heard Banks clucking his tongue.

"It's funny you say that," said Cam. "It makes me wonder if you've been telling the truth or not."

"Why would I lie?"

"Because you can. I know for certain you have the ability to calculate the fourteenth digit of pi, but if I asked you to, you'd probably say you can't. So either your programming is crippled, or you've been instructed not to act like a machine and spout off statistics without consideration for whether the average person would know the answer. It's like you've been purposefully dumbed down from the super-intelligent synthetic you are to a slightly above-average human."

"You're being quite rude," said Roberta, her eyes narrowing.

"What if I had said my favorite color was red, would you have changed your answer?"

"No, I told you. It's gray."

"But how do I know yours was gray before I told you mine?"

Roberta crossed her arms and looked away. "Believe what you want, Mr. Gray. My feelings aren't dependent on your trust."

"That's… a good point," said Cam.

"I know it is," said Roberta. She brushed a section of her hair away from her cheek, reminding Cam of her wrist.

"What's your sign?" asked Cam.

Roberta faked a calming breath.

"Virgo," she said softly. "It means Virgin."

A flash of gleaming metal caught Cam's eye through the rose bush and within seconds, the garden was filled with half a dozen Scorpios, though they looked more specialized than the synthetics at Outpost Alpha. Where those had been dressed in desert camo, these AGs were clad in black suits—their uniforms were more formal than functional. If it hadn't been for the silver machine guns in their hands—all of which were pointed in Cam's direction—someone could have mistaken them for businessmen.

"What the hell do you think you're doing, Gray?"

It was Sava's voice, but with a biting edge Cam hadn't heard before. He turned to face her.

"Are you out of your mind?" she screamed. "I don't give a shit how well-connected you think you are, you *don't* walk off with a million-dollar prototype. You're lucky I don't let these guys blow your head off. What the hell is wrong with you?"

Finally, a glimpse of the real Savannah Kessler.

Cam stood up slowly, stowing his phone in his pocket.

Roberta followed suit beside him. Her eyes jumped from one machine gun to the next, and for some pre-programmed reason, she stepped closer to Cam.

"First of all," said Cam, "I meant no disrespect. This wasn't an elaborate heist or an attempt to hide anything. Why you thought it was necessary to bring guns into this is beyond me. Hell, you can see the car we came in from here." He pointed to the Nissan parked at the curb. "You wouldn't have been able to leave without spotting us. Second of all, the lady looked like she could use some fresh air. She came of her own free will."

Sava's eyes flashed red. "Fucking outlander," she mumbled. With a wave of her hand, she dismissed the well-dressed AGs. "You're really testing my hospitality, Gray."

How quickly formality broke down, thought Cam.

"I don't want or need your hospitality, *Kessler*. This isn't a vacation for me. I'm here because my boss has an arrangement with your boss—that's it. I've got directives you aren't even privy to and at no point in the description of those directives was I told to take direction from a power-tripping flack with trust issues."

Sava started to respond but turned her attention to Roberta instead. "Get inside. Mr. Maddox is waiting for you."

"You're not her master," said Cam. "If she wants to stay out here with me, then that's her choice."

"Stay with you? You're not even authorized to know she exists."

"Do I really have to pull rank on this one? You don't think I could get Banks to make this happen?"

Cam held out his phone to sell the threat. Before Sava could answer, the display lit up with a curt message from Banks that read *on it*.

Sava looked like she wanted to hit him. "Try it, just fucking try—"

A screeching ringtone interrupted her. With one eye on Cam, she stepped away to answer the phone.

"You could cut the tension with a knife," whispered Roberta.

Cam turned his head slowly.

"You're very perceptive," he said. "Does this kind of thing bother you?"

"It's difficult to say. I feel empathy for both of you."

"What if she had hit me?"

Roberta smiled and took another step closer. She touched Cam lightly on the arm. "It would have been the last punch she ever threw."

Cam stared at the delicate fingers on his arm until she removed them.

"Gray, huh?" he asked.

"Yes, Mr. Gray."

"Son of a cock," yelled Sava.

She tried for several seconds to squeeze the life out of her phone. When it wouldn't crumble in her hand, she shoved it into her purse. Her fingers came out holding a code card, the kind popular among Hollywood synth enthusiasts and Los Angeles synth addicts. She used her thumb to break the seal and slid out the electrode in one smooth movement.

Not her first time, thought Cam.

Sava held the card to the back of her neck, all the while staring coldly at Cam. Within seconds, her gaze softened, and the anger began to drain out of her. Her shoulders relaxed and her stance changed from aggressive to casual.

Cam had done numerous stories on code cards for the general health hashes of the Banks Media feed; he even had his own stash of green and black cards back at the house for special occasions. It was the same synth haze anywhere he went, but what differed with Sava's was the speed at which the code overtook her body.

This wasn't some dime-card South Central junk she was loading. This was prime, maybe even local.

Drug abuse in the heart of Perion City; the headline wrote itself.

With an even voice, Sava said, "Since you no longer require my assistance, I'll leave you to your job, Mr. Gray. We do have a dinner reservation at Chez Cosimo at seven. If you and Roberta are not in attendance, I will send a hundred AGs to find you. If you try to leave the city, I will have you shot on sight and then dismembered."

"So, formal wear?" asked Cam.

"Roberta, directive."

Roberta's body stiffened.

"Imprint protocol Bravo."

"Subject?" asked Roberta.

"Cameron Gray," said Sava. Then, with none of Cam's flourish, "With Banks Media out of Los Angeles."

The synthetic nodded as a shiver went up her body. She looked around as if she hadn't been paying attention. When her eyes fell on Cam, she smiled.

"Chez Cosimo at seven," repeated Sava. "Don't piss me off any more than you already have."

"Yeah, or you'll dismember me. Got it."

Sava dropped the used code card into her purse and secured it on her shoulder. She turned and headed for the back of Southpoint Synthetics where Tank Maddox stood with one foot propping the door open.

"She's not pleasant," said Roberta. Her hair fluttered in the slight breeze; she turned to face the wind.

Cam watched her glistening eyes as they observed the world.

Perceptive, he thought.

NINE

"Tell me about Los Angeles."

Roberta hadn't spoken in a while, had instead spent the last ten minutes approximating the act of eating an ice cream cone Cam had procured from a passing street vendor. Though she likely couldn't enjoy the dessert, she attacked it with the same fervor of a girl much younger, and much more human.

"Cameron?"

"Oh, yes," he stammered. His mind had wandered due to the gyrations of a synthetic tongue as it lapped at the melting ice cream. "Los Angeles, the Windy City."

Roberta laughed, having settled on a distinctive trill over the last few hours, likely the result of some algorithm to gauge Cam's reactions to her various chuckles and giggles.

"I don't think that's right," she said.

Cam sipped at his Screwdriver. "My mistake." He cleared his throat, causing a nearby waiter to perk up. "Los Angeles, the City of Brotherly Love."

"Another drink, sir?" said the undoubtedly human waiter—no logical creature would have embedded those ridiculous bicycle tires in its ears.

"He might have had too many already," said Roberta.

"Los Angeles, the City of Angels; the Entertainment Capital of the World; the House that Banks Built; La-La Land; the Big Easy…" Cam handed his empty glass to the waiter. "Chi-town."

"I'll bring you another as long the madam is driving you home."

"I'm not sure she knows how," said Cam, sitting back in his chair. He put his hand to his chin and scratched at the fresh stubble. "What about it, Roberta? Are you licensed to operate a motor vehicle?"

Her eyes drifted to the street where bikes outnumbered cars four to one.

"I can ride a bike," she said, dabbing at her mouth with a napkin.

"Seriously?"

"Well, I haven't in a while, but you never really forget."

Cam's laugh was amplified by the alcohol, but it evoked such a proud smile from Roberta that he didn't care how foolish he looked or sounded. Besides, it was still early, and the patio was mostly deserted except for a few gray-haired engineers sitting down for their early bird specials.

"Anything for the madam?" asked the waiter as he returned with a glistening Screwdriver. "A glass of wine perhaps?"

"Oh, I don't drink," said Roberta.

Cam wanted to ask whether she meant alcohol or all liquids, but the words wouldn't come out. Roberta was being a good sport about the whole *not being human* thing. There were times, however, when his questions pulled them out of the fantasy and back to the world where she was just a collection of gizmos and whatsits, a synthetic being manufactured and programmed in a lab somewhere in the Spire. She was aware, at some level, when his questions went too deep, but was it programmed indignation? Was it code that made her eyes flutter, that gave her pause—all to let Cam know he had touched a nerve, and more importantly, had hurt her feelings?

The answer was elusive, and the booze certainly wasn't helping.

"You'd like LA," he said at last. "Lots of stuff for a girl like you to get into. We've got traffic, pockets of high-density crime, and a professional football team that hasn't been to the playoffs since before I was born. It's a smorgasbord of excitement."

Roberta reached out and put her hand on his. "And it's got you."

Cam laughed as he shifted in his chair, crossing one leg over the other. Turned on by a robot, he thought. If Banks found out, he'd never let him live it down. With a quick swipe of his sliver, he severed the uplink feed. When his phone beeped a few seconds later, he ignored it.

"I'm sorry," said Roberta, withdrawing her hand. "I didn't mean to make you uncomfortable."

"Not your fault." Cam chugged the rest of his drink and then rattled the ice in the glass. "Just sometimes I forget you're…" Again, the words faltered under the weight of some undefined sense of civility.

"I'm what?"

Her ice cream cone sat melting on a bread plate as she waited for an answer.

Cam reached out for her hand and tapped it lightly. "You're delightful," he said. "And amazing." The haze crept in. "And beautiful. Witty. Erot—"

The blaring of a car horn cut his list of adjectives short. Cam turned in time to see a bicyclist go tumbling over the hood of a silver sedan, his ten-speed bouncing back the other way. All traffic around the accident came to a standstill, but nobody rushed to the biker's aid. When he popped up and started looking around for his bike, Cam realized he must have been a synthetic.

"What in the holy fuck-all is wrong with you?"

The driver slammed his door as he got out of the car. He was a shorter man dressed in business casual, with a loosened tie and white sleeves unbuttoned at the wrist. Not a scientist or engineer, and therefore not part of the PC elite. Like Cosimo, this guy was just a worker, a skilly in a city of techies.

"I'm sorry, sir," said the synthetic. A section of pink skin hung from its cheek; manufactured muscles of light blue undulated below a black, fibrous inner wall.

"What's your tag number, asshole? Who the hell taught you how to ride a bike?"

Cam glanced at Roberta, wanting to make a joke about never really forgetting, but the way she was sitting at attention stopped him. Her eyes were wide and the vein running the length of her neck throbbed in a rapid tempo. Cam wondered if she had ever been exposed to violence before today.

The driver, fearing no retaliation, got right in the face of the synthetic, poking him in the chest with every curse word he threw out. Then came a genuine shove, sending the synthetic stumbling backwards. Evidently, it was not endowed with the same kind of lightning reflexes as the cooks in Cosimo's cafeteria. Once the synthetic was on the ground, the driver kicked him in the face.

Roberta gasped, which was all the encouragement Cam needed to spring from his seat and vault the low wrought-iron fence at the edge of the patio. He had no idea what he was going to do until he was pushing the driver away and stepping in front of the fallen synthetic.

"What the hell's your problem?" asked Cam. The question activated his sliver and restored the uplink.

The driver blanked for a moment, as if he hadn't considered the idea of someone coming to the synthetic's rescue. His anger refocused on Cam.

"Who the fuck are you?" he asked.

"Cameron Gray, with Banks Media out of Los Angeles. I'm investigating no-class Perion employees who beat innocent synthetics in the street. Perhaps you'd like to take a swing at me so we can explore the differences between synthetic and human responses to violence?"

"Please don't," said the synthetic. He climbed to his feet slowly, as if he had sustained actual injuries.

"Oh," said the driver, "so you're the big shit aggregator everyone's been talking about? Well, I've got a *feed* for you, Mr. Banks Media Los Angeles: this is a Perion-only matter. Why don't you get the fuck out of my face and out of my city?"

"But don't you see? Perion-only matters are what I'm interested in. I want your face under my headline. *Synthetic Punching Bags: The True Story of Humanity in Perion City.* Your name, your story, followed by James Perion's reaction to his employee's conduct. How does that grab you, asshole?"

"Please, sir, there is no need for an altercation." The synthetic put a hand on Cam's shoulder.

With his head turned, Cam barely saw the sudden movement out of the corner of his eye. The driver lunged forward, swinging a hefty fist at Cam's face. He felt the wind from the impact as it stopped an inch from his nose. He stumbled backwards from the shock and was caught by the biker.

"Why don't you pick on someone your own size?" asked Roberta. She had plucked the driver's fist out of the air and was now squeezing. His knuckles popped, audible even as he screamed in pain.

"Roberta, directive! Release him."

Sava's commanding voice took the air out of the confrontation. Even the murmuring of the crowd died down as people began to notice the half dozen men with guns who had circled the area.

Roberta let go of the driver's hand, allowing him to fall to his knees. An ambulance honked its way through the crowd carrying EMTs. They rushed to determine the extent of the driver's injuries. Seconds later, another team arrived to examine the synthetic.

"Did you forget what I told you about pissing me off?" asked Sava.

Cam took a step back, not liking the smell of the flack's breath. "Maybe. Was it after the part where you told me you'd be following me around waiting for me to fuck up?"

As the adrenaline tapered off, Cam felt himself start to sway from the weight of four Screwdrivers.

"You're not here to fight with the locals."

"Technically, I wasn't fighting with him. He took a swing at *me*. Plus, you should be thanking me. I was protecting your investment."

Cam looked down as a hand slid around his waist to steady him.

Sava saw it too.

"You're not here to *fuck* the locals either."

"Rude," said Roberta. "Cameron, can we go now?"

Cam brandished his teeth at Sava.

"You're lucky I don't bounce you," said Sava. "I could do it, you know."

His phone beeped and Cam noticed his sliver was glowing red.

"So is this kind of behavior common in Perion City? Do the humans regularly take their anger out on synthetics who can't fight back?"

"Sometimes, yeah," said Sava. "That's how we do things. It's not assault because they're not human. It's property damage, *our* property."

"And the synnies always have to take it?"

Sava scowled at Roberta. "I guess not anymore."

Roberta said nothing, but stepped behind Cam as if he could protect her.

TEN

"You turned off your uplink," said Banks, his voice echoing.

Cam grimaced.

It wasn't exactly protocol to hijack the feed and speak directly through the whisperer, but with Banks, it was downright unsettling. Having that man's voice in his head was like having a second ego, and Cam already struggled enough with the one.

At the moment, he had a bigger problem—trying to stay upright while making use of the facilities at Chez Cosimo. Luckily, the bathroom's designers had been bright enough to put thick walls between each of the urinals, giving Cam something to lean against as he relieved himself.

"Not now, boss," he replied. "I'm trying to piss."

"I don't care if you're up to your elbow in synthetic cooch—you don't kill your uplink."

"Nice image," said Cam, testing his ability to stand. Finding the task too difficult, he leaned once more on the wall. "Speaking of cooch, how'd you swing the deal with Roberta? Sava was pee-issed."

"I don't know. I was surprised myself." There was a pall, broken by the flush of a urinal. "I really thought Perion was going to fight me on it."

"Well, I'm glad you did whatever you did. Roberta is *awe*some. If she's what's coming down the pipe, Perion is going to make a metric fuck-ton of money."

"Now you see why I didn't dump my stock like the rest of those idiots?"

Cam zipped up and went to the sink to wash his hands. He noticed the bathroom attendant regarding him with a narrow eye. Cam tapped the side of his head in explanation.

"Bullshit," he told Banks. "No way you knew about this beforehand. Even Kessler was completely blindsided, and she seems like the kind of woman who does her homework."

"Jesus, Cam. How much have you been drinking? Of course I didn't know about Roberta. All I knew was Perion had something up his sleeve. He's a thinker, a problem solver, and all of that *before* a businessman. He's got more ideas than you've got brain cells. He's a…"

The whisperer went silent.

Cam let the water run in the sink and then dried his hands.

The tinkling of ice in a glass preceded Banks' next words. "He's a titan. And people should respect him for that."

"Is that what this is about? Honoring him?" Cam leaned against a table near the door. "You want me to paint a pretty picture? Perion's perfect PC isn't presenting a promising potential. All menial jobs will be taken by synthetics, leaving the uneducated unemployable. We're talking about a new age of slavery signed, sealed, and supplied by the old man himself."

"That's not his goal," said Banks, his voice even again.

"Then what is?" asked Cam. He caught his reflection in the mirror and smoothed out his hair.

"That's what you're there to find out. Why Perion City? Why the mystery? Based on what we've seen today, these things look ready for real-world testing, and yet Perion's keeping them close to his chest. I want to know why."

"I'll go find out," said Cam, jumping in place a few times. He stumbled on the last hop and fell into the wall. "Or throw up trying."

The whisperer ramped up again, feeding the usual white noise of world news and sports roundups. A trailer for the latest Bollywood invader played as Cam exited the bathroom.

Chez Cosimo's Monday crowd was a mix of stiff-shirted executives and lab-coated engineers. Every table in the main dining area was full, as were the booths lining the outer walls. Towards the back, silhouettes of raucous dinner parties danced on the privacy screens. The door to the largest of the private rooms was slightly open in anticipation of Cam's return. Inside, he could see Sava sipping from a glass of wine and playing with her phone. She spied him through the open door and looked away.

Cam stepped into the room and smiled when Roberta's eyes lit up. She was sitting next to Chuck Huber, who was doing his best to appear aloof to her presence. To her right was Dr. Langley Bhenderu, who had brought his wife, a stout woman in her late forties or early fifties with muddled Indian features like her husband. Also at the table was a square-jawed suit with a signature bulge under his jacket and a very official security laminate around his neck that read *GANTZ*.

No doubt the law man had been called to dinner at Sava's insistence.

"What'd I miss?" asked Cam, taking his seat between Gantz and the empty chair reserved for the absent Joseph Perion. On the table, a refreshed 7&7 beckoned him.

"Ms. Kessler was just telling us about your feat of heroism this evening," said Bhenderu. He had a habit of speaking into his glass of water, making his voice reverberate. "Tell me, Mr. Gray. What possessed you to come to the aid of a machine?"

"Seemed like a good idea at the time."

Sava scoffed; Roberta smiled.

"And yet you were aware the synthetic was not in danger? Mr. Galvan could not have hurt it."

"That's not really the point," said Cam, feeling his words beginning to slide into each other as they rolled off his tongue. "Pardon my language, but that guy was an asshole. Synthetic or not, you don't let people act like that. There's this subtle elitist vibe oozing from every pore of this city, but I haven't really seen any action to back that up. You've given your synthetics a sense of humanity, yeah, but if Mr. Galvan is an example of the source material… I mean, you don't want people returning their synthetics because they're total dicks, right?"

Bhenderu dismissed the idea with a shake of his head.

Chuck gestured to his colleague. "Dr. Bhenderu is a leader in the field of synthetic psychology. There is no one on the planet more qualified to select the source material than he."

"Is that so?" Cam's straw made a slurping noise as he emptied his drink. "What happens when your synthetics recognize the class war already building here? Not just between humans and synnies, but amongst themselves. You keep last year's models in circulation and pretty soon they'll start feeling better than each other."

"How can you know that?" asked Bhenderu.

"It's human nature," said Cam.

"Obviously we have different definitions of human nature," said Sava.

"*Ob*viously."

"Yes," said Sava.

"Yes," repeated Cam.

Finally, she looked him in the eye. "Real mature."

"Real mature," said Roberta from across the table. She giggled and mouthed the word *fun* at Cam.

"Roberta, directive—"

"No," barked Cam, slapping the table with his hand. "No more directives. No more orders." Then to Roberta, "You don't have to listen to her."

"In fact, she does. It's part of her programmed psychology, a hardcoded directive to obey. Isn't that right, Dr. Bhenderu?" Chuck's arm moved to the side, perhaps slipping a discreet hand onto Sava's leg.

"It should be, but then I'm not overly familiar with the Virgo line," said the doctor. "Completely different department."

Cam felt his eyebrows smack together. "I thought you were the psych lead for all synthetics."

"I don't have a hand in every single one," he admitted. "Mr. Perion has multiple departments running concurrently, each with their own teams of engineers. I oversee the standard build and mission critical synthetics like the

Scorpio-class guards you've met. I do not remember being involved with the Virgo prototyping; I'm assuming it uses a significantly different—and likely inferior—psychological model."

"She's sitting right there, you know."

Bhenderu turned to Chuck. "This is what I'm talking about. See how *he* has imprinted on *her*? We have gone past the valley of the uncanny. It is too soon."

Chuck nodded but said nothing.

"Am I missing something?" asked Cam.

"Just your AA meeting," said Sava.

"How is everyone this evening?"

"Cosimo!" yelled Cam.

The chef had entered the room at some point and was now standing with his hands folded behind his back. A young waiter at his side stood in a similar stance.

At Cam's outburst, Cosimo bowed his head minutely.

"I've prepared a special meal tonight in honor of our guest, Mr. Cameron Gray. I trust everyone brought their appetites?"

"Am I drunk or is he talking funny?" asked Cam of no one in particular.

Cosimo locked eyes and shared a terse wink. Evidently, the chef with rough but genuine edges Cam had met at the cafeteria was not good enough to work at Chez Cosimo.

"Let's start with two bottles of Iron Cactus for the table and our guest," said Cosimo to the waiter. "On the house, of course."

A clinking of silverware against glasses filled the small dining room.

"Please enjoy a drink and I'll have the servers bring in the first course shortly." He made another awkward bow and left the room.

"Curious," said Bhenderu. "He didn't even tell us what we'll be having."

"Something Italian, I'd wager," said Cam, reaching for his empty glass. "Or French." He sucked at the straw without effect and set it back down on the table. "Anyone seen a waiter?"

"Couldn't even stay sober for one night," said Sava.

"I could," said Cam. "I *choose* not to."

"Then by all means, keep drinking."

"I will, thank you." Cam turned to the doctor. "So what's wrong with me *imprinting* on Roberta? Don't you want people forming bonds with their synthetics?"

"Where appropriate," said Bhenderu.

Chuck coughed into his napkin. "And where practical." He took inventory of Roberta and then caught Sava's glare.

"Yes," said the doctor, "where practical. Mr. Gray, there is a limit to all human bonding, a point at which it interferes with logical thought. This happens mostly between two emotional beings, but occasionally, and sometimes quite famously, this is extended to inanimate objects. Your altercation with Mr. Galvan is a prime example of that. You admit you knew the man on the bike was a synthetic. You knew he could not be harmed. And yet you got involved anyway. *You* could have been seriously injured."

"I think Cameron's actions speak to his bravery and compassion," said Roberta. "If he is willing to sacrifice himself for a stranger, what does that imply for those he loves?"

There was silence at the table until Cam said, "Perceptive, isn't she?"

"It sounds to me as if the young lady is smitten with you." Bhenderu's wife smiled as she spoke.

A collective groan filled the room as Roberta blushed.

Before anyone could put words to their skepticism, the waiter reappeared with the promised bottles of wine. He presented Sava with a fresh glass and poured for her, then Bhenderu's wife. When he turned to Chuck, Cam cleared his throat.

"Aren't you forgetting someone?"

The waiter stopped and looked around the table. After following Cam's gaze to Roberta, he approached her uncertainly.

"Please," said Roberta, handing him her wine glass. "I usually don't, but this *is* a special occasion."

Cam waited for someone to object, but no one spoke.

"So where have they put you up, Mr. Gray?" asked Bhenderu. "Or will you be staying with Ms. Kessler for the duration?"

Sava spit wine back into her glass. "Holzgraf," she sputtered. "He's staying at the Holzgraf."

"Question," said Cam. "Does anyone know where that is?"

Out of the corner of his eye, Cam saw Gantz crack a smile.

"We'll have someone drive you," said Sava. "Only the best for Banks Media." She lifted her glass in an empty salute, realized she had spit in it, and set it back down.

Cam raised his glass anyway and took a long pull of the wine.

"Follow-up question, Doc. How did you come to meet the charming Mrs. Bhenderu?

"An interesting story, that," said the doctor. He sat up straight in his chair and began rambling about a medical conference in Calcutta.

The red glow of his sliver told Cam it was safe to let his mind wander. And with Roberta sitting across the table, staring at him through the distortion of her wine glass, he found himself lost in a sudden synthetic fantasy.

ELEVEN

The automatic blinds rose at seven, drowning the Holzgraf suite in a headache-inducing glare. Cam was already up, sitting on the edge of the bed with his arms on his knees, trying to decide if he really needed to throw up or if he could hold it in with some mental toughness. He really wanted to avoid rushing to the bathroom if possible, but every movement made the contents of his stomach slosh around. Now with the room illuminated, Cam could see himself in the mirror on the low dresser.

His hair was standing straight up, set that way by a night spent with his head buried in a pillow. Combined with the stubble on his face and the harsh sun, he looked less like a smooth-talking aggregator at Banks Media and more like the synth junkies who sat outside the tower begging for money or a code fix. Staring into his own bloodshot eyes, Cam realized his appearance was the least of his problems.

The most pressing issue was lying in the bed behind him, half covered in a jumble of sheets and pillows, her perfect synthetic breasts bathed in a golden hue. Cam had barely glanced at her when he awoke, yet he could close his eyes and recall every inch of her body. Roberta had pulled back her hair before putting her head on the pillow, revealing a high and smooth forehead. Her eyes were closed, but there was movement beneath her skin, as well as a flaring of her nostrils with each simulated breath. A tiny pulse beat from the artery—if that was the right word—in her neck.

Cam wondered first why Roberta even needed a pulse, then how it was being generated, and finally, whether she had actual blood circulating through her body, or some kind of artificial equivalent, or worse, a black sludge mixture of oil and grease, something to lubricate what must have been a million or more moving parts. He saw her stripped of her outer layer to reveal tiny gears and wiry tendons, all dripping in the same oily goop.

Cam tightened up as another swell built in his stomach.

He needed some air, and the voice-actuated room was more than happy to open the balcony doors for him. The resulting breeze made goose bumps stand out on his skin.

"Narrative," he said to his sliver. "Private entry."

The sliver blinked red twice and settled into a steady green.

"Someone folded my clothes and put them in a neat pile on the dresser. My socks are balled up in my shoes, which have been pushed *under* the dresser. The question remains: how did my clothes come off in the first place?"

Behind him, Roberta stirred, moaned quietly.

"There is a possibility I shed my clothes on my own and they were collected and sorted by a prototype synthetic who is now sleeping in my bed. Then again, for all I know, she undressed me and tucked me in with a good night kiss. It doesn't explain why she's naked though, or why my boxers are on backwards."

Cam pushed his boxers down his legs, turned them around, and pulled them back on. When his stomach didn't lurch in response, he stood on wobbly feet and leaned towards the balcony. The closer he got to the open door, the colder the breeze felt, as if a front had moved in overnight.

"Good morning, Perion City," he said, placing both hands on the damp balcony railing.

At street level, PC residents were making their way to work, pedaling their bicycles or walking briskly on the sidewalk. Occasionally, one of the humans looked up to gawk at the disheveled man standing on the balcony in his boxers. Cam assumed the synthetics knew of his presence, but seeing how he had no impact on their operating radius, they ignored him. Perhaps the humans thought he was going to jump. Or maybe he was inadvertently exposing himself through his thin boxers.

As if sensing the general distress of the citizenry, Roberta appeared behind him.

"I brought you a robe," she said, holding open the white terry cloth emblazoned with the Holzgraf's double eagle emblem. "It's cold this morning."

Only after stepping into the robe and away from Roberta did Cam realize she was completely nude. Where *her* clothes had ended up was only one of the many questions that popped into his head, following right behind the mystery of why Roberta didn't have tan lines or if her synthetic chassis even supported them. Her skin held the same even tone from her neck to her chest to her stomach, varying only when it was obscured by a thin patch of pubic hair.

Cam tried to focus on the job, on the questions he was sent to ask.

Dr. Bhenderu, he thought, why would a synthetic need to get undressed to sleep?

And to Chuck, why would a synthetic need to sleep at all?

"Thanks," said Cam, as he pulled the robe tighter. The warmth made him feel better and the thick cloth helped conceal his excitement when Roberta stepped forward and slipped her arms around his waist.

So it's like that, he thought.

"What happened last night?" he asking, swiping his wrist behind Roberta's back. The green light flickered to red.

"A lot," said Roberta, giggling.

"How good is your memory?"

"I remember everything," she said. Her eyes drifted away, as if surveying the street below. "You were…" Her eye twitched. "I mean, it was so…" She stepped out of the embrace and approached the railing. "Something's different."

No kidding.

Waking up next to a naked synthetic with his boxers on backwards didn't exactly scream normality. There were so many questions needing answers, not just in the *why* but in the *how*. Had he made drunken love to a million-dollar sex toy?

"What do you mean?"

Roberta nodded at the people below. "They don't look right."

Now that she mentioned it, Cam noticed something off about the synthetics—they were easier to spot now that most of the humans were staring at the naked woman standing on a balcony. Not only were the synthetics disinterested in Roberta and Cam, they were stuttering in their movements, infrequently but noticeable when it happened. In the middle of the block, a younger-looking synthetic was trying to sweep the pristine sidewalk in front of a small grocery store. From a distance, Cam hadn't even noticed there was nothing to sweep, that the synthetic appeared to be caught in a loop, more like a machine with a set program instead of a cutting-edge, assumed intelligence.

"Probably just the cold affecting them. You know how it is."

"No," said Roberta, "I don't."

"Do you remember how we got here last night, Roberta?"

"A car brought us." She smiled, remembering. "It was a limo with sideways seats and vidscreens. We were all able to fit inside."

"All?"

"You, me, your friend Cosimo, and Chief Gantz."

The name wasn't familiar, but then the dossiers were all fuzzy in Cam's memory. "I don't remember any Gantz."

"He was at the dinner—the man in the suit."

The law man, thought Cam.

"I'm surprised you don't remember him. You two were fast friends last night. Things were a little tense at first, but once *he* started drinking—"

Roberta shuddered.

"Are you alright?"

"Maybe it is the cold," she replied, pulling Cam's robe open. She pressed her warm, synthetic flesh against his cold skin. "We should get back in bed. Maybe we could finish what we started last night?"

Cam caught his reflection in the glass of the balcony doors.

"I need a shower," he said.

"I'll join you," replied Roberta.

Cam was about to agree before his boss spoke up.

"Have you ever considered *why* you met Roberta?" asked Banks, except his voice didn't come through the whisperer. It was in Cam's head, an imitation of the clear-headed thinking and suspicious questioning his boss was always preaching.

Mental Banks made a good point. Meeting someone, or something, like Roberta was a one in a million shot. Maybe it was part of some ploy by Sava to get Cam to bed a synthetic and then later, if he wrote anything unflattering, she could claim impropriety with one of their products, expose him and his sexual proclivities. Whatever he had done with or to Roberta the night before, there was no doubt it had all been recorded in some databank—five streams for five senses, just waiting to be played back in high definition should he color outside of the company lines.

Cam's throat tightened. What if Sava had been watching live?

"Who are you?" he asked, taking a step back.

"Cameron…"

"I just met you yesterday. I don't know anything about you."

"That's not what you said last night when you were inside me. You said we had a connection, a—"

"Stop," he barked. "Cut the bullshit."

Roberta opened her mouth as if to speak, shuddered again, and then collapsed on the balcony. The slapping sound of a grown woman hitting the evercrete twisted Cam's stomach, but it was nothing compared to the echo that came from below.

Cam peered over the railing to see a dozen or more people—synthetics—dropping in the street and on the sidewalk. Their human counterparts were standing around dazed or indifferent. Further down the road, the scene repeated, with bicycles crashed into news kiosks and lifeless bodies lying where they had fallen. Only when the first human moved towards a prone synthetic did Cam's shock start to recede.

He knelt at Roberta's side and shook her shoulder, but she was unresponsive. Her chest rose and fell, but her open eyes were devoid of any life. He stared into them as shouts from the street began to increase in frequency and alarm. Synthetic names echoed between the buildings, but there was no changing the fact that a good portion of Perion City's population had just fallen down dead.

Cam's sliver glowed.

"It's like they all lost power at the same time," he began to narrate. "It appears to be widespread, affecting every synthetic in sight. It could be citywide or localized to the surrounding streets, I can't tell for sure. Nobody seems to know what is going on. I—"

A soft whimper came from Roberta's lips, though they did not move.

"Roberta?" he asked.

"The…" What followed was barely a whisper, sounding more like a melody than an actual string of words. She repeated it, as if on a loop.

After several repetitions, Cam realized the sound wasn't just coming from her, but from the street too. It sounded like the collective groan of *brains* from a horde of zombies. The loop went on and on.

"The Creator…"

Roberta blinked, came out of the stupor that had held her hostage. She looked at Cam with glistening eyes and spoke the message clearly.

"The Creator is dead."

PART TWO
CYNTHIA MESQUINA

TWELVE

A pall had fallen over Umbra.

Lincoln Tate stood at the window on the fifth floor of the Decker Plaza building and watched the people moving listlessly in the streets below. Usually filled to the brim with synth-fueled wonder, tonight's crowd was subdued, as it had been for the past two nights. Rumors of James Perion's death had shaken the foundation of the city and left its residents scrambling for something solid to hold onto. Tate had tried to provide a baseline by lacing the Lincoln Continental feed with mood-leveling code, a subsonic insertion meant to calm and sedate his subscribers. It had kept the city from erupting into a riot, but a pensive population meant less excitement, meant less content to feed.

The Umbra Tower pulsed against a moonless sky, rising out of the Canopy like a steel nail from a board. A blue haze climbed its length every thirty seconds, symbolizing the city's cultural contribution to the world. This night, however, the pulse stopped halfway up, held for two seconds, and then faded out.

"So the old man is really dead," said Tate. He had his arm pressed against the window and his forehead resting on his fist. The eyes staring back at him from the other side of the glass blinked rapidly.

"If it's true, it's a damn shame."

Tate turned to look at Cynthia Mesquina, who was splayed out on the couch with one leg propped up on the armrest and her dark, red hair fanned out over a black throw pillow. She wore a white tank top under a half-open shirt that hung loosely over skin-tight leggings. Along the insides of her exposed arms, an intricate black tattoo snaked its way over her skeleton, moving from joint to joint like a subway map.

A memory flashed: the tattoo covered Cyn's entire body, from the base of her jackport to the augmented Achilles tendons in the back of her heels.

At twenty-two, she was the youngest of his freelance aggregators, but the most tenacious by far.

Tate adjusted the sleeves of his jacket, making sure his Franz Felis shirt only peeked out a quarter of an inch. His titanium cuff links glinted under the multi-colored lights of the vidscreens on the far wall.

"What do you mean *if it's true?*"

Cyn tapped her phone; it responded with a dull beep and a somber melody. "I'm terrible at this game." The phone disappeared into an invisible pocket. "That's why you called me up here, right? Nobody really knows if Big J has jacked out for good? Perion PR is ignoring the question, and Banks is feeding nothing but line noise. You ever get a name on his inside source?"

"We think it might be Frank Gattis; he's been covering Vinestead Synthetics for Banks for the last couple of years. The boys in the back think it could also be Cameron Gray out of Banks' inner circle, based on the way the feed is structured. The meta coming off the BMP feed has been stripped of any aggregator IDs, so it could be anyone."

"I think what you really want to know is how Banks got a man on the inside." Cyn tugged at one of the many bracelets on her wrist. "If Banks is withholding the aggregator's name, maybe they're not there with permission."

"I have no idea," said Tate. He joined Cyn in the sunken lounge area and sat down on the couch opposite her; it groaned under his weight. "There's been a lot of chatter between Banks and Perion City, but nothing the boys have been able to decode. For all we know, it could just be broadcast SYN-ACK."

"Lincoln Tate does not like uncertainty," said Cyn.

"I can't feed uncertainty," he replied. "People want cold hard data, not water-cooler gossip. They sub Lincoln Continental, not the goddamn TMZ."

"People have to keep up with celebrities somehow."

"Look, no one is saying there isn't room for some celebrity news—Jesus knows we get our share in—but at the EOL, people want to feel like they've learned something, whether that's coming up to speed on new tech or reliving the terrifying moments of some military incursion halfway around the world. They're addicted to the data and right now they're not getting their fix. When they start jonesing, they get cranky, the SatIndex drops, the subscribers start to flee, and suddenly Banks' fluff pieces don't look so bad."

"The people are fine," said Cyn. She stretched her arms above her head, pushing her breasts into the air.

Tate looked away. "The SatIndex is down thirty percent since Monday. We haven't seen these kinds of numbers since the Calle Cinco de Mayo Massacre of '09. And that was seven thousand people meeting their end in a single day. This is one man, Cyn. That just shows you how important he is."

"James Perion, synthetic titan!" Cyn's voice pitched low as she raised a pointed finger to the ceiling. "Never before was there a visionary like James Kirkland Perion. Champion of the people. Fighter of the good fight." She took a quick breath and resumed her normal voice. "And so on."

"Do you honestly believe this is just about James Perion jacking out of Terrareal? You think any of those pierced-face freaks down there knew the man well enough to care if he lives or dies?"

Cyn touched the red stud in her nose and shook her head.

"Sorry," said Tate, sighing. His eyes jumped to the feed stats on the center vidscreen. The SatIndex was still in the high fifties, but it was falling. The people needed some reassurance.

"No worries," said Cyn. "Not all of us can pull off the teal suit and gold chain look."

Tate smiled, revealing his silver-plated teeth. "Not all of us have style, baby."

"No," she replied. "Not all of us do." Waving her hands around in the air, she asked, "So what is this all *about*, Lincoln?"

"Vinestead."

"May they burn in hell," said Cyn, pretending to spit.

"They might have, if Perion hadn't refused their help. He was the only thing standing between Vinestead and world domination."

"Now who's being TMZ?"

"Don't act like I'm exaggerating. You think Calle Cinco killed seven thousand people because VNet kept jacking up their access rates?"

"Kaili Zabora is a lunatic," said Cyn. "She'd kill her own mother if she thought it might cause a Vinestead employee some minor inconvenience."

"Well yeah, she's nuttier than a Folsom Retread, but killing civilians wasn't her intention. She wanted to bring down VNet, but she, like everyone else in this country, had no idea how deep Vinestead's code went. I doubt anyone was more surprised than her when the planes started dropping out of the sky."

"So it's been two days. If this is such a pivotal moment for Vinestead, why haven't we heard from Krazy Kai herself?"

Tate tapped the side of his head. "Good question, Cyn. A *damn* good question."

"Well? What's the *damn* answer?"

"I have no fucking idea."

Tate stood and walked to the bar set along the east side of the room. From the menagerie of bottles on the shelves, he pulled a nearly empty Stolichnaya that Benny Coker had sent over after last year's sub census. He placed one shot glass on the bar and held another up to Cyn with a questioning look.

"Sure, why the hell not? Been a while since I chem-tripped."

"All that synthetic shit you're pumping into your brain is gonna come back to bite you in that pretty little ass of yours someday. Couple decades from now, you won't even remember your name."

"So long as I can still do this," she said.

Cyn broke into an impromptu dance as she approached the bar.

"Cute," said Tate, sliding the diminutive glass in front of her.

"That's what they pay me for." She downed the shot in one gulp.

"Speaking of which, I didn't call you up here just to pretty up the place."

"I figured," said Cyn, tapping the rim of her empty glass with an obsidian fingernail.

Tate obliged. "How would you feel about a little trip to Perion City? I could use someone on the ground floor. Banks thinks he's the only player on the West Coast with the hookups to get inside intel. Well I say balls to that shit." He shot the vodka with a flourish and smacked the glass on the bar.

"Balls to that," toasted Cyn. "So do you have any pull with Perion? I'm guessing I can't just walk up to the front gate and say, *hello, Lincoln Continental Pizza.*"

"No pull," said Tate, replacing the bottle on the shelf. "No favors, no leverage. This is a total cold-call engagement. My hope is that you'll be able to get in, get the TL;DR, and get the hell out."

"What if I'm caught? Perion City has some pretty mean sovereignty laws."

"A girl's got a right to defend herself."

"Ah, so that's why you chose me."

"You know the stories about Perion City. You've seen the vids of people trying to sneak in. I thought you might be up for the challenge."

Cyn slid off the stool and drifted to the windows. Across the street, Version Seven was pumping out pure bass into the night, attracting those whose hearts beat with a similar tempo. Despite the chill in the air, there was still a decent line of body-mods and augs waiting behind the velvet rope.

"So you admit there's danger."

Tate smiled to himself. He had her. "Yes."

"I'll need money for equipment."

"Done."

"And a needler, something compact. And I get to keep it when we're done."

"I'll send the boys out for something immediately."

Cyn turned around and crossed her arms. "Standard six figure contract. Payment up front."

"I was thinking of a fixed seventy with a variable fifty depending on the SatIndex performance. The world is desperate for news about Perion. You should be able to swing the numbers easily."

"I can live with one-twenty," said Cyn. "Send the contract to Bryce and let him look it over. If he signs off on it, you've got yourself a deal."

"It was hand-delivered an hour ago. I asked Bryce to let me break the proposal to you."

"In that case," she replied, pulling out her phone. She sent a text to her handler and within seconds, had a response. "You weren't bullshitting."

"Have you ever known me to lie?"

"Only when you tell me you love me." She smiled at something on her phone. "Which leads me to my next question. What kind of insertion method do you have in mind?"

"Ah, now that you're gonna dig."

Tate produced a code card from his breast pocket and tossed it to Cyn. It fluttered in the air and fell at her feet.

"What's this?" she asked, bending to retrieve it.

"A simulation construct. A ground approach to Perion City would be sniffed out twenty miles from the border. But the sky… the sky's a much bigger place. I figure you can get a couple hours of simulated jumps in and be on a plane by four."

"You don't think Perion will get suspicious when we start feeding from the inside?"

"According to Benny Coker, James Perion is dead. And judging by the after-hours trading, Perion Synthetics is dead too. If there's a chance the company might survive, if there's a *plan* to keep Vinestead from capitalizing on Perion's death, I want to know about it. The American people want to know about it."

"The American people want hamburgers and porn. Just say your panties are in a twist because Banks is one-upping you and leave it at that."

Tate scanned the length of Cyn's body; it still amazed him how innocent she looked, how perfectly harmless her thin legs appeared in skin-tight pants. Only a trained eye would notice the rough edges around the jackport on the back of her neck, the secondary trauma of having a Guardian Angel biochip extracted and replaced with something more palatable.

"Stop eye-fucking me, Lincoln."

Tate spread his hands and backed away. "Just taking a mental picture in case the worst happens."

"Right." Cyn crossed the room and sat down on the couch again. The code card made a popping sound as she freed the electrode. "No funny business while I'm under," she warned.

Tate motioned to a door beside the bar. "My room is available if you'd prefer somewhere more private."

"Just keep your hands to yourself, boss."

Cyn pressed the tab to her neck and drifted away with a satisfied sigh.

Tate stood at the edge of the couch for several minutes, watching her chest rise and fall, wondering if he had made the right move.

THIRTEEN

The roar of dual props clawed at the foam plugs in Cyn's ears, but her mind was on other things.

There was a memory stirring in her brain, a chemically repressed recall of a time in her life before Liberation, before she had paid a back-alley hack four hundred bucks to rip the Guardian Angel chip out of her neck. She had only been seventeen then, a late bloomer in a world where children grew up too fast, where each new generation of tiny, unmolested minds sought out a culture to call their own. Cyn got her start at the age of ten, latching onto the burgeoning NexLvl tech scene that would carry her into adulthood, a world of circuitry and augmented physiology, of endless possibilities put in reach for the first time by simple ones and zeros, by the inevitable melding of nature and science. It kept her attention even as her friends drifted away to the bourgeois pursuits of bad poetry, meaningless trysts with local boys, and even college.

Cyn never even considered the possibility of higher education.

By eighteen, she was free of the Vinestead shackles and well on her way to her first augmentation, which she financed through an under-the-table business of data theft and grid wipes. The last decade had made paranoiacs out of everyone, made them question the long-standing tradition of handing over their personal data for the promise of ten dollars off their next visit to The Gap or for access to the latest social networking destination. What it took the world ten years to realize, and what Cyn had known from what felt like birth, was that it didn't pay to be yourself in VNet or Terrareal. A veneer was always preferable to the truth.

Cyn stretched in the jump seat, reaching for the green mesh above her. Although the stimulants were keeping her awake and alert, her body was realizing it hadn't slept for a while. Her arms quivered in the form-fitting suit.

"Nothing but the best for my girl," Tate had said as he pushed the lid off of a gun-metal box like it was the goddamn Ark of the Covenant.

Contained within were various goodies: a helmet with AR capabilities, a chute rig with built-in oxygen tank, and finally, a next-gen automatic pistol known in Umbra circles as a needler. And though the weapon seemed to vibrate in her hand in anticipation of the slaughter to come, it had been the dive suit that grabbed

Cyn's attention. She had held it up to her body and wondered aloud how she was ever going to get into it.

The answer came at the Maine Prairie airfield thirty miles outside of Umbra. There, a tech who was more body hair than man had shown her how to cut the seams and then temp-seal them once she was inside. He had enjoyed every minute of educating an Umbrat, and he wasn't shy about lusting after Cyn's bare skin as she slipped the material on.

Not that prying eyes worried Cyn anymore. Most people were too distracted by her tattoos to notice anything anyway. Her ink's centerpiece was a skeletal outline that started at her jackport, descended her back, and disappeared over the curve of her coccyx, segmenting her body like the seams in the dive suit. It wasn't so much an artistic choice as a way to hide the scars on her arms and legs, the insertion points where her skin had been punctured and the augments assembled underneath.

Her drop shadow spine bulged in five specific areas to hide larger, more invasive insertions where her vertebrae had been separated to route the grow-wire from the MoA Ayudante chip on her brainstem to the breakout controllers at shoulder and hip height. The other breakouts reached around her spinal cord to interface with her heart, lungs, and other critical systems. The feedback loop it created was as close to military grade as any aug could hope for. Among the Umbra underground, Cyn was at the top of an ever-expanding inventory tree, a subset of players who had spent their experience points on a single upgrade path, banking everything on the improvement of their physical avatars in the hopes that one day, they might pass from human to machine with one final procedure.

It was the journey to that moment that discouraged most travelers, whether because of the cost, or the pain, or the perceived loss of humanity. Cyn's bank account could handle the first, her strength and determination would cover the second, but the loss of her soul…

Well, that implied there was something there to begin with, something to connect her to the rest of humanity.

Cyn felt neither the connection nor the desire for it.

The dive suit's helmet fit snugly; she expected nothing less from Lincoln Tate. Though he was sending her into a dangerous situation, it was worth the investment to see she came back alive. Slamming headfirst into the Perion City evercrete would be an expensive end to an aborted mission, especially since seventy thousand dollars were already sitting pretty in her Bank of MX money market.

A Nixle Chronos interface chip on the back lip of the helmet drew data from her Ayudante and displayed it on the visor in a bit of augmented reality trickery. In the lower corner, an iconographic plane approached the dive line set above a blue spike   the Perion Spire.

Cyn's heart rate rose, not in fear, but in anticipation. Not only had the simulation given her virtual experience in high altitude jumps, but it also awoke in her a taste for the rush, a nearly orgasmic response to the adrenaline overload she experienced each time she stepped out of the plane and into the nothing. As far as detachment went, it was the most removed from the world she had ever felt, so high above that great big ball of death and distraction whose edges curved in her periphery.

At the edge of her visor, a timer changed hue to yellow as it passed two minutes remaining. The plane had been climbing for an hour, making a slowly tightening corkscrew around the center point of Perion City, slipping in and out of commercial traffic to lower their chances of being spotted. The theory was that a completely vertical approach would provide a one-dimensional signature on the monitors, a blip the operators might dismiss as interference from another satellite passing too close, such as the MilTel A8 or the defunct Iridium 29 whose only purpose in life was to spit electronic noise into the thermosphere.

The timer turned red as it sank into the double digits.

Cyn stood and walked to the back of the pressurized cabin. A dull buzz rang out, signaling the impending loss of atmosphere. Soon, the pocket-size oxygen tank on her back would become the center of her existence. It hissed in response to the sudden drop in pressure and Cyn felt air swirling around her mask. Scrubbers along the backside of the suit would recycle what they could, but if she didn't find an oxygen-rich environment in ten minutes, then all the Pesos in the MX wouldn't do her any good.

A shiver ran through her body as she flexed and jumped. The cold air welcomed her, screaming across her visor in damp streaks. The initial violence of acceleration faded away until it was just Cyn and serenity diving together through a space whose definition was neither earth nor the emptiness beyond it. In between worlds, Cyn tried to steady her breathing. The great City of Perion was a speck on the brown landscape below and its approach was like that of a bulbous monster skulking its way to its next victim.

Then she was spinning, using her arms and legs to route the oncoming air such that her body turned in a lazy barrel roll. The horizon rotated, faster and faster. Cyn screamed with delight as the airspeed readout on her visor continued to increase. Beside it, an altimeter was headed in the opposite direction. It flashed red for a second as the numbers blanked.

Cyn's scream was cut off by something popping on her back.

Damn, she thought. Too soon.

Before she could come out of the roll, the stage one parachute had already wrapped itself around her torso. She made one last effort to right herself, but the nylon ropes found their way to her foot, circled it twice, and then began to pull as the chute caught some air. When it finally went taught, Cyn felt her body being thrown downwards, and then the earth and the sky swapped positions.

Cyn closed her eyes against the advancing enemy, recalling the relaxation exercise the simulation had drilled into her brain, training up the muscle memory so that any inkling of fear was immediately squelched by rote concentration. If she couldn't right herself before landing, if she cut loose and died on impact, there was no sense worrying about it now. There was nothing to do except breathe the dwindling oxygen and enjoy the novelty that she was likely the only person currently hurtling to her death in such an odd fashion.

Warmth spread through her neck; the Ayudante was coming online.

The change was subtle.

At first, Cyn was only aware of the wind running its fingers over her body, starting at her helmet on the way to caressing the impermeable fibers of her dive suit, leaving off with a soft tap on the toes of her shoes. Then she could hear the soft cries of alarm coming from the Ayudante. Even though her vitals were within normal ranges, its panic spoke to observations of brain activity, of a primal part of her gray matter that was trying to fill her head with images of a body splattered on the ground, its bones having liquefied on impact, with nothing remaining to identify the flattened organic mass as human.

Her hand moved on its own, seeking out the holster on her hip, her fingernails digging at the clasp set into the leather. The needler came free and she used both hands to steady it. Hitting the ropes would have been impossible; the half-inflated canopy was a much bigger target. Cyn let the air push her aim around, making holes in the sky-blue fabric.

The pressure on her foot lessened as the wind tore at the holes, ripping the canopy apart. Cyn found the freedom to rotate and pointed herself at the glittering tip of the Perion Spire, a pinpoint around which an intricate fractal of streets extended into the surrounding desert. She could make out the larger highways and heavy-duty trucks, but everything else was hidden behind the flashing text on her visor.

It was getting to be that time.

Cyn pulled the ripcord and breathed a sigh of relief as the main parachute deployed without issue. She settled into a sedate circle around the Spire.

Even with Tate's considerable reach and Cyn's own hacking, there was little intel on the Spire itself, save a few blueprints that had been marked up and shopped more often than Elise Portman. As far as anyone could tell, the Spire was home to offices and housing for C-level employees and managers who spent more time in meetings than checking in on their workers. As the Spire ascended beyond habitable dimensions, the space was thought to be filled with telecom equipment. Cyn could already see the flowery antennas of such equipment blooming on the scaffolding around the very tip of the Spire.

One of the sixteen schematics showed a service hatch within reach of the scaffolding, located on the west side of the building. In her tightening spiral, the compass on Cyn's visor was useless. She instead watched the horizon, knowing she had to put the Spire between herself and the sun. The anxiety about where to land faded, replaced by the more pressing issue of whether she could land at all.

Contrary to popular rumor, there were no sentry guns on the Spire, at least, not at her altitude. The only defensive measure in place was the reflective glass and the blinding glares it created every time she caught the sun in them. After the last flash, she made a sharp turn and approached the Spire head-on.

Cyn gripped the chute cord and waited for the right moment to cut loose. Though the parachute had carried her this far, it would no doubt pull her off the Spire when she landed. In one simulation, Cyn had broken loose ten feet above the scaffolding and simply grabbed a crossbeam on the way down. It would have made a compelling stunt in a movie, but here, without an audience, there was no point in showing off.

A section of the scaffolding banged against her shin, sending the splintering pain racing up her body. As it passed through the five gates in her spine, the signal diminished, until her brain was left with only a faint echo of distress. Cyn cut herself loose as her other leg hooked around a horizontal bar. When she heard the signature click and saw the chute fall away, she reached her hands out with the augmented power of a vise, latching onto a section of metal piping and a mesh of coaxial cables spilling from the back of a satellite dish.

She took a moment to catch her breath. The numbers on her visor began to settle and shrink, allowing her to focus beyond the fuzzy text.

"There's my bitch," she said.

Cyn pushed and pulled her way through the scaffolding with the ease of a child at play on a jungle gym. The door opened with a simple turn of a handle. Inside, she pulled off the dive helmet and breathed in the machine-heated air.

"Excuse me," said a voice to the right.

Cyn spun around, pulling the needler from her hip. She pointed it into the darkness and waited for the speaker to come into view.

Set on a pike in the middle of the room was the upper half of what Cyn hoped was a synthetic man. Cables drenched in an oily liquid hung from his elevated torso, dripping into a grate whose mesh was thick with the congealed innards of previous caretakers. The synthetic had the appearance of a young man and in another setting, might have been mildly attractive. The look on his face was so piteous that the Ayudante chip mistook it for sincere need and amplified it.

Empathy enveloped Cyn, enough to lower the needler a full inch.

"You are not authorized to be here," said the synthetic. "I will have to—"

The needler hummed as the synthetic's lips shattered and exited through the back of his head.

FOURTEEN

"Two minutes on-site and you've already popped one off?"

"Who are you, my narrator?"

Tate's laughed buzzed in Cyn's ear; the whisperer was holding up well despite the electronic interference coming off the tightly packed telecom equipment. Dusty metal blades with frenetic lights covered every surface of the glorified broom closet. A semi-circle of user-serviceable devices surrounded the pike on which the now lifeless synthetic—if it had even been alive to begin with—sat impaled with no legs and no head and no dignity. Even before Cyn had happened upon him, the synthetic had been indentured into the life of a remote terminal server, a set of hands in the inhospitable attic of the Spire where the dust and dirt swirled in the super-heated air.

When the line didn't cut out, Cyn asked, "Are you gonna babysit me the entire time?"

"Are you going to keep pushing your tach into the red?"

"Goddamn chute opened early. When I get back, I'm going to have some words with that ape at Maine Prairie."

There was a sporadic throbbing in Cyn's leg; the Ayudante was letting the pain through every couple of minutes to remind her of the injury.

"I'm fine, Lincoln. I don't need someone looking over my shoulder."

"It's not a problem," said Tate. "I dropped a tab on the way back so I am jacked, baby. So long as you make it back before this wears off, we should be good."

"We'll see."

Cyn looked around for a door, remembered where she was, and began examining the floor. A square section of the raised grate was marked with black and yellow paint. In the center, a looped handle sat in a recessed half-moon.

"Yes, we will," said Tate. "I gotta get this SatIndex up before we start losing subbers."

Cyn had the hatch open but paused to let her feet dangle into the dark room below. She pulled her phone from the zippered pocket on her chest and snapped a photo of the synthetic. "I'm sending you something. Just give me an hour before you feed it."

There was silence as the picture transferred.

"This is why I had to *pop one off*," she added.

"The fuck," said Tate. "Damn, girl. Alright, counter starts now."

Cyn rubbed the material on her shins, activating the luminescent fibers. The room below was slightly larger and similarly wallpapered in electronics.

"Same goes for anything else I send you. If Perion sees it, I want them an hour behind me."

"Little girl telling me how to feed like it's my first day and shit."

The needler was still warm, but Cyn didn't bother holstering it, not with the possibility of another synthetic in the room below. She pushed her chute rig and helmet into the corner, knowing she would never see them again. Gripping the needler in one hand, she used the other to lower herself to the next level.

No one, synthetic or otherwise, challenged her. Again, she searched the floor for a hatch, again she lowered herself down. The lower she got, the bigger the rooms became, the more the claustrophobia receded.

The banks of electronics gradually disappeared, leaving her with empty rooms of rough evercrete to crawl down through. Finally, she reached a room with massive generators set in two lines of three. She snapped a picture and sent it to Tate.

"What do you make of these?"

"Magnetic inductors," he replied. "Looks like they're using maglev for their elevator system."

"And just how would you know that?" Cyn walked around one of the generators, but its smooth sides gave no clues about the tech contained within.

"The executive entrance at Umbra Terminus takes you under the train's mag tracks. They've got similar designs, but yours looks more specialized."

"Are they about the same size?"

"It's hard to tell, but I'd say probably. Why?"

"How far can one of those inductors drive the maglev?"

"Give me a minute."

There was static on the line as Tate had a conversation with someone else. He wasn't afraid to get his hands dirty with the data mining, but years spent as a producer had left him slower than the boys in the back, his quasi-ciphers whose nimble fingers banged out like pistons, pumping ones and zeros into the ether like a needler firing at full automatic.

Cyn began to whistle but thought the better of it.

"Maximum track run is twenty-five hundred feet. On average, between Umbra and Sacramento, inductors are set every two thousand feet."

"And how tall is the Perion Spire?"

"It depends on which schematic you trust. This one says ninety or so habitable floors, another forty for equipment, and the rest is just decoration. This other one says it has a toe to teeth distance of sixteen hundred feet."

"And these are just pushing elevator cars, not whole trains."

Cyn pulled back a maintenance hatch near an inductor and stared into the black abyss below. In the distance, she could hear the smooth whooshing of air as an elevator car ascended.

"What are you thinking, Cynthia?"

"Not really thinking," she replied, pulling a glow stick from her belt. It was small, about the size of a tube of lipstick, but it gave off light like a strip of magnesium. She depressed the plunger on the end and tightened her fist around it. "Ten bucks says it bounces right off the top of the car."

"*What* bounces?" asked Tate. "What the hell are you up to?"

"Well," she replied, using her own voice as a distraction from the scenario building in her head, "it's simple. The inductors drive less weight a further distance than required by the Spire. So that means there must be more of this thing underground, and that makes perfect sense. Why keep anything of value in the fifth largest building in the world? You're just asking Kaili Zabora to fly a plane into it."

"You're going to jump, aren't you? Damn it, girl."

Cyn released her grip and waited a few seconds before peering down after the glow stick. The bright speck receded to a pinpoint, casting a green-white glow on the walls of the elevator shaft, highlighting a series of descending platforms and the connecting ladders. When the glow stick finally stopped, a tinny smack echoed up the shaft.

"Got it in one," said Cyn.

"I'm not sure this is one of your better ideas."

"You want the real story, don't you? Or should I just pick up a brochure in the lobby? One picture of that synthetic amputee isn't going to make Banks shit himself." She took a deep breath; the car was too far down to risk a jump. "Ask the boys in the back if they know anything about the mag-lev system. Is there a way to call the car to the top?"

"Oh sure," said Tate. "I'll just have them pull up the PDF." His sarcasm tapered to a long silence.

Cyn waited, wondering idly how much a pair of Koertig enhanced eyes would cost. Low-light vision, non-visible spectrum dithering, telescoping irises: anything to help her see the bottom of the elevator shaft.

"No luck hacking the planet." Tate huffed.

"Screw it. I've got enough spider silk to get me halfway down."

"And if the car is any lower?"

"Who thinks that far ahead?"

Cyn tugged at one of the hidden pockets running down the length of her leg and retrieved a titanium snare. Looping it into the spider silk took time; though both were rated for loads ten times her weight, she knew the weak point would be where the two joined. If she fell, it would be because of her own shoddy workmanship. After a few minutes, she had the snare and the silk wrapped around one of the anchor bolts holding the magnetic inductors to the evercrete floor.

"You're really going to do this?" asked Tate.

Leaning over the lip of the hatch, Cyn raised her sliver to her mouth. "Yes!" she barked.

Then she was falling at a clip that evoked a whine from the silk feeder on her belt. In the distance, the glow stick approached. As Cyn got closer, she realized the elevator car was descending, dropping just a little slower than she was falling. She did her best to match the speeds, but the impact was still more than she was expecting and louder than she would have liked. Cyn made a grab for the loose cables on the outer circuitry of the car to keep from falling off.

She could hear alarm in the muffled voices inside the car; hopefully they would pass her landing off as mechanical noise.

Cyn unhooked the feeder from her belt and hit the retract button. It sped up into the darkness.

"Sounded like that hurt," said Tate.

"You try it next time." She groaned dramatically, playing up the sympathy.

"Tell me what you're seeing."

The car continued its controlled fall as Cyn whispered to herself and Tate.

"We're going down, just passing the forty-seventh floor. There are chalk markings on the walls calling out each level. Doors, piston-driven, I think. Opposite side has ventilation shafts, maybe exhaust from the floors. I get a blast of warm air each time I pass one. Every fifth floor has a landing going from one side of the shaft to the other. Ladders alternate between each—"

"Ladders? You could have climbed down?"

"Yes," said Cyn, rolling her eyes. "And three years later I would have made it to the bottom. At least when this thing stops, I'll be able to climb off. Could probably make the jump now if I wanted to, but since I'm already…"

The car slowed to a stop on the nineteenth floor, paused, and started to climb again. Cyn jumped to the landing on the twentieth floor with a graceful leap.

"I shouldn't have said anything."

"What happened now?" asked Tate.

"Now, I have to climb." She tried to inject some enthusiasm into her voice, but the stiffness in her legs told her it would be a punishing descent.

Tate tried to distract her with stories of the continuing silence coming from Perion Synthetics. Meanwhile, day-old content tagged with Cameron Gray's name was just now hitting the feeds. He was painting a picture of a synthetic utopia where man and machine lived together in a harmony not known since the days of Adam and God. It was all bullshit, Tate was quick to point out.

"Lobby," said Cyn, between breaths. "Still going."

"I'm going to feed the picture now."

"It's your donkey show, boss."

Cyn continued on until she passed a marking indicating level B15. The shaft extended further into the earth, obscured by shadows. Using the platform for leverage, Cyn pried the metal grate from a ventilation shaft and set it beside the opening. The interior was shiny and slick, allowing her suit to slide over it with ease. She used the grips on the palms of her gloves to pull herself along, until finally the shaft broke out over a false ceiling. Light from the room below peeked in between the seams of the drop tiles.

"Where—"

"Hush," said Cyn, covering her ear. There were sounds coming from below, muffled as if behind glass.

Cyn lifted one of the tiles and poked her head through. The room was empty, sterile, and white. Along one edge of the room were five bassinets set apart with deliberate precision. But instead of looking cozy and warm as bassinets should, these were also sterile and lined with cold, gray cloth.

Cyn dropped down from the ceiling, felt the pressure in her legs as her augments absorbed most of the impact.

"I'm in," she whispered.

The lights in the ceiling left no part of the room untouched, and for a moment, Cyn felt completely exposed. The fear, however, wasn't strong enough to overcome her curiosity. She approached the middle bassinet with cautious steps. Something beneath the blankets stirred.

"What do you see?"

Cyn had no answer, for the thing in front of her defied sensible description. It gave every indication of being a baby—a normal, healthy infant with a light dusting of hair and puffy red cheeks.

But it wasn't a baby.

Babies had eyes.

This *thing* had nothing, had empty sockets backed by gears and motors and simulated sinew.

Cyn put her hand over her mouth, torn between the horror and a previously dormant maternal instinct.

The thing's little pink lips parted, opening in sickening mimicry of a crying baby, revealing another empty chasm glowing blue in the oppressive light.

"Fuck this," said Cyn, stumbling backwards.

FIFTEEN

Lincoln Tate pressed his cell phone hard against his ear.

For several minutes, the only sound coming over the link had been static, low and gravelly, approximate amplifications of the room Cyn had dropped into, a room of silence and horror and something else, something that had brought the toughest girl he knew to her knees. He'd heard her collapse, heard the plastic hit of her shin guards on the floor, followed by the dull slap of her back falling into the wall. Scraping sounds came next—Cyn trying to push herself further way from whatever she had seen. And though he called her name, she did not answer.

So he listened to the static and tried to visualize the room where Cyn sat huddled in the corner, legs likely pulled up to her chest, her face buried in the warm pocket of air created therein. For a time, the words *fuck this* had come across the line in a whisper, a repetitive mantra meant to protect her from the abrupt change in reality. But slowly, the repetition had faded out, replaced by nothing. Until now.

Tate heard the sound mixed in among the pocks and hisses of dead air.

Crying.

Cyn was crying.

"Cynthia," he said, barely hearing the word himself.

No response.

"Talk to me, baby. Tell me what you're seeing."

"Are you recording?"

Tate glanced at the vidscreen on the wall where Cyn's vitals flashed in bright yellow numbers. In the lower right corner, the red REC light blinked off and on.

"Always," he replied, "but we had to switch to another channel when you went dark."

"Put me back on primary. I want to go real-time."

Briefly, he considered lying to her, considered leaving her feed on standby until he could sort out the situation. Hearing her collapse on the floor, hearing her struggle to get the words out, had brought Tate down from his chemical high so fast it made his skin itch. Stolichnaya or not, he was completely sober in an instant. Even the tab he had dropped earlier felt like a distant memory. His sense of being *up*, of being tied into the world through a million data connections, was gone. Now there was only Cyn and her first moment of weakness in recorded history.

Tate tapped his palette, cutting off the filler material.

"You're live," he said.

"It's all bullshit," said Cyn. "This picture we have of Perion, like he's some goddamn savior. He's just another money-hungry suit who will do whatever it takes to be on top, to be *in control*. He's no better than Sedivy and Vinestead."

"Come on—"

"Just," interrupted Cyn. "Just listen to me, Lincoln." She sighed, rubbed her face with her gloved hand. "When I was eleven, I learned about something called The Net. I became obsessed with this infinite construct, a place where people could be truly free—no usernames, no product keys, no always-on DRM.

"Then came Vinestead and their nightmare network. The way they took over, the white-flag tactics they used… it made me want to join up with a cipher den and pledge my code and my life to Calle Cinco or some other group."

"Why didn't you?"

"They wouldn't take me. I was barely twelve when I began to seek them out in the darknets. I met a few recruiters in VR, but they took one look at me and jacked out. For the longest time, I couldn't figure out why. So I kept reading, kept devouring everything there was to know about ZabSix and RevoMT and Calle Cinco. I read about what they did in Sacramento, how they took one back for the little guy."

"The Reaping," said Tate.

"Yeah, The Reaping. People talk about it like it was some great thing to kill people just for working for Vinestead. In the end, it didn't even matter. That was the same day they passed the Guardian Angel bill, which meant all newborns had to be implanted with the biochip. No discussion, no way to get around it except to flee the country. And everyone just went along with it, just bowed to the promises Vinestead made with one hand on our shoulders and the other in our wallets. I was chipped even before that, but my parents never told me. I had to find out from the school nurse."

"You were still going to school?" asked Tate.

"I had no choice. I was infected with VTech; no cipher den would come near me. I had to live with the knowledge of that damn chip in my head for six years. And even when I got it dug out of me, I still didn't feel clean. I hated Vinestead for what they did to me, to all of us. Someone had to step up and challenge them; I cried the day I realized it wasn't going to be me."

"It's a tall order for one person, even for you."

"James Perion could have done it. He has so much weight to throw around. I thought of Perion as a white knight come to fight the Vinestead dragon. He was supposed to be the good guy, a champion of the people. But that was just a fairytale, a myth we all wanted to believe, like the X sightings in VNet. James Perion is a monster, Lincoln. No better or worse than Arthur Sedivy."

"Why do you say that, Cynthia?"

Cyn rose from her corner, her legs unsteady. She didn't want to look in the bassinet again, but she was able to lift her phone, point it in the general direction, and snap a photo. Covering most of the screen with her hand, she hit *SEND*.

It took a moment to sink in.

"Shit! That just went out live, Cynthia. The SatIndex is climbing over sixty."

"He's an evil son of a bitch," said Cyn, "and I'm glad he's dead. Perion Synthetics can burn in hell with Vinestead." She spit on the floor. "Why would he do this, Lincoln? Why would he make something so *wrong*?"

"I don't know, girl."

Cyn shook her head and retreated to the opposite side of the room. "You put your trust in someone," she continued, "and this is what you get. It's all so pointless now."

"It's not pointless. If Perion is responsible for this, we'll expose him. For now, it's time you got out of there. The boys are picking up a lot of chatter coming out of the Spire right now. I don't know if they know exactly where—"

"It doesn't matter," said Cyn. "Not anymore. If these *things* are Perion's legacy, then we're better off without him. Either way, there's no one left to stand up to Vinestead. We are all monumentally fucked."

Cyn closed her eyes and saw waves crashing on a beach, saw an ocean between her and an increasingly fucked up world.

"This is it for me. I'm out, Lincoln."

"Just like that? The SatIndex is over seventy and you just want to bail? We just gained half a million subbers, social media is blowing up, and Perion is trending on a dozen different networks. You've got support in all the major—"

She waited for him to finish his sentence, but there was nothing coming across her whisperer, not even static.

"Linc—"

The lights blinked out before Cyn could finish her question, plunging the room into a darkness so absolute she couldn't see her hand in front of her face. Her eyes adjusted, and she discovered a blue light coming from the other side of the room. Cyn shut her eyes, refusing to look at the glowing, synthetic baby heads. She remembered her phone and used it to walk the perimeter of the room, always away from the blue, always away from the subtle hissing of tiny servos.

Finally, she found a door with a recessed handle.

"Lincoln, if you can hear me, I'm gonna make my way into the hall."

She slid the door open, revealing a dark corridor much too long for the limited power of her phone's screen. The glow stick popped as she bent it. Cyn tossed it parallel to the wall she was hugging; it skittered down the hallway, casting long shadows on the doors.

No workers. No security.

Cyn crept out of the room and into the blinding green glare.

They were on her in an instant. They felt like men with thick arms pushing against her body—so many of them, attacking from all directions. The Ayudante couldn't keep track of everything, couldn't move her limbs fast enough to prevent them from being immobilized. She felt herself spinning, then going weightless. In a brief flash, she saw the ceiling deform as she crashed into it. Her leg snagged one of the crisscrossing grid lines, rotating her body and sending her face first into the floor. The impact changed the green world to blue. Then gray crept in from the corners of her vision.

As the world threatened to disappear, she saw them.

Two feet stood some distance away, only the black boots weren't boots at all, but segmented feet that clicked and whirred as they moved across the floor.

"Subject detained," croaked a voice, and then gray became black.

SIXTEEN

Cyn felt the emptiness the moment she opened her eyes.

It was an unwelcome feeling, one of want and of worry—a weak feeling that at first, she refused to acknowledge. There was pain in her head and soreness in her joints; those were concrete stimuli to be dealt with or ignored. But underneath the throbbing was a *lack* of something. Not knowing what she was missing made it even more confusing, made her mind go back in time and wonder what had been in her life that was no longer there, sitting on the rug in front of the television or relaxing in the middle of the bed.

Was that right? Was the thing a *who*?

She shifted under the thick blankets of the hospital bed, felt her skin move against a cotton nightgown. Her mind tried to fill in the blanks. What was the last thing she remembered before the emptiness?

Her normally pliant consciousness had no answer.

Cyn raised a hand to rub her face but found it weighed down by lengths of wires and tubing. An IV snaked along the edge of the bed, ending in a cannula on the back of her hand. Thin wires ran from the side of the bed, up the right side of her torso, and disappeared behind her back. She felt them taper off just below the base of her skull. When she took a deep breath to stem the rising panic, she felt electrodes on her chest move against the nightgown.

"Good morning, Mrs. Paulson," said a voice from the doorway. A woman in pink scrubs spoke as her fingers tapped rapidly on her palette. "I'm Suzanne. I'm the charge nurse on duty today. Dr. Bhenderu will be with you shortly."

"Who?"

Suzanne ignored the question and helped Cyn into a sitting position. She adjusted the sheets on the bed and rolled away the various medical carts. Once the room was in pristine condition, she touched her ear and said into her headset, "We're ready in seven."

Cyn glanced at the door but couldn't remember who she was expecting.

"Don't worry," said Suzanne, as she fluffed Cyn's pillow.

Cyn didn't get a chance to ask why she should worry before an older Indian man with dark brown skin and oily black hair entered the room, pushing his quaint glasses up his long nose. His white lab coat identified him as a doctor, at least in Cyn's estimation. That *was* how doctors dressed, wasn't it? Her brain answered with a *mostly yes* but was unable to offer more.

"Mrs. Paulson, how are you feeling today?" He took the palette from Suzanne and looked over his glasses at the screen. "I was relieved to hear of your improvement, though I never doubted you would pull through."

"What happened?" asked Cyn. Sitting up had shifted her weight, putting pressure on bruises she felt but couldn't see.

"A bit of misfortune, but that's not important right now. What *is* important is that you are feeling better. We are all very—"

"Just tell me what happened," snapped Cyn.

The anger had come from deep down, below the emptiness and the fleeting feeling that perhaps this was all a dream. It felt so different, so far removed from what she thought her life was. The sterile walls, almost blinding in their whiteness, didn't belong to the aging rooms at Sutter General in Sacramento or the free clinics in Ember.

The gears caught, stuttering on the word. Was that right? Ember?

Cyn shook her head.

"You were in a car accident." A black suit darkened the doorway for a moment before stepping into the room. "T-boned by a dump truck making a haul out to The Fringe. The driver was on some kind of synth, so we've got him locked up until we find out what it is and where he got it."

The Fringe, thought Cyn. It meant the outskirts of Perion City, an industrial zone tasked with the...

The feed petered out.

"Chief Gantz, please. This is not the proper way to talk to someone after they've experienced a serious trauma."

"It's fine, Doctor," said the square-jawed man. "She asked for the truth; beating around the bush wasn't going to do anything except freak her out." He came closer to the bed but stopped a respectful distance away. "Chief Robert Gantz, Perion City Police Department. I was one of the first responders to your... accident."

His subsequent smile set off an alarm in the back of Cyn's head. At least her bullshit detector was still going strong.

"Fortunately for us," said Dr. Bhenderu, "the safety systems in your vehicle performed valiantly. With the exception of some bruising, you escaped without major injury. No broken bones, no lacerations. The only concern we had was for your head. You suffered a nasty bump."

"How long have I been out?"

"About eighteen hours. We were keeping you sedated until the swelling went down. We shouldn't see any long-term effects, but you may experience some temporary mental fragmentation as a result of the concussion."

"What the hell does that mean?" Again, the anger surged. Cyn found herself unable to contain it, as if frustration were some orphaned thread running in the background, ready and waiting for the right memory allocation to come—

A spike tore through Cyn's temple, crossing behind her right eye. She put her free hand up to stop the stinging.

"Are you alright?" asked the doctor. "I've got you on synthetic regulators for now, but I can up the baseline if you're feeling any discomfort."

This wasn't discomfort; beyond the pain there was something more, some gaping emptiness.

"Mrs. Paulson, do you remember anything about the accident?" Gantz leaned against a counter on the far wall and buried his hands in his pockets. "Anything at all?"

Cyn tried to piece the memory together, but there was simply nothing there. The file had been deleted, the pointer overwritten with garbage.

"I don't remember... anything."

Her memory felt dull, out of focus, as if she couldn't pinpoint a single moment in her life before waking up in the hospital.

"Mental fragmentation," she whispered.

"It happens sometimes," said Gantz. "Nothing to be ashamed of."

Cyn shot him a look, asking who the hell said she was ashamed of anything.

"And nothing to be worried about at this stage," said Dr. Bhenderu. "It is almost always temporary. You should start remembering things soon and have total recall within two or three days. Going home will help immensely, but I wouldn't recommend returning to work for several days."

"Home?"

Home—a twin bed shoved carelessly into the corner, sea green sheets pulled back, waiting for her.

Gantz pulled out his phone. "2011 Westbrook, apartment 4D, out by the Drafthouse?"

Cyn shook her head at the chief. There was something odd about him.

"Why are you here?" she asked.

"Excuse me?" He drew himself up as he pocketed the phone.

"You heard me. Am I under arrest or something?" There was a lingering feeling of guilt circling Cyn's chest—she had done something wrong recently.

"I just thought you'd want to see a friendly face," he replied.

Cyn turned to the doctor. "Is my health so meaningless you'd have the cops here to interrogate me as soon as I wake up? I know my rights. If this is a formal questioning then I want my lawyer present."

If I *have* a lawyer, she thought.

Gantz crossed his arms and smirked.

"Please, Mrs. Paulson," said Dr. Bhenderu, "allow me to apologize. There are… *other*… circumstances that require Chief Gantz to be here. With head trauma, there are no hard and fast rules about recovery time. If you were found to be unfit—"

"Unfit? What the hell does that mean?"

Dr. Bhenderu put up a hand. "You were not the only one in your vehicle when you were struck yesterday."

Cyn's stomach flipped, gave her the same feeling as reaching out for a step that wasn't there. She thought of her family, of a mother whose face moved behind the curtains and a father who stayed in the distance, beyond the power of her mechanically enhanced vision.

That last part didn't sound right to her. She narrowed her eyes at a sign in the hallway, but it was too blurry to read.

"Who?" Cyn coughed in response to her suddenly dry mouth.

You know who. It was not a voice that spoke, but rather a feeling, a perennial directive that had always been there.

"I'll get the lady," said Gantz, jumping at the opportunity to leave the room.

"First, you should know she's perfectly alright. She's been under close supervision since your arrival."

She, thought Cyn. So her passenger had been a woman.

"Who is she?"

Dr. Bhenderu hesitated. "Your daughter, Mrs. Paulson. Your baby girl is just fine."

An unseen boot slammed into Cyn's chest and held there, preventing her from taking another breath. She wanted to question the doctor, wanted to ask how and by whom, but the words would not come out. She stared at his cold, brown eyes, speechless, unable to comprehend anything anymore.

The directive stepped forward to fill the silence.

It told her to look to the door, at the woman in slacks and a frilly red shirt. She carried a bundle of blue blankets in her arms.

Cyn didn't need to ask what the bundle was; the way the woman held it was answer enough.

"Cynthia?" asked the woman.

A nod was all Cyn could muster.

"Someone has been asking for you."

Then the woman was moving across the room, bringing the bundle closer and closer. Time slowed as she set the baby in Cyn's arms, which had opened automatically.

SEVENTEEN

Candice Marie Paulson.

They would call her Candy throughout high school, until she was able to break free from her assigned nickname and choose something for herself. Maybe it'd be the seven letters from her birth certificate, maybe it would be something silly like C-dice or simply C. Whatever her handle, it would never be as perfect as the one Cyn had chosen moments after delivering a healthy baby girl, just as the nurse was laying the screaming angel in her arms.

"Tangential to the primary issue is the application of force feedback as it pertains to pleasurable experiences for the user. If synthetics are limited by a directive to do no harm, then any exertion of effort in regard to rough play will be seen as a contradiction to that directive, leaving them inert and no better than inanimate devices."

The nurse attending to the talkative man nodded as if she understood or cared about the babble that had been coming out of his mouth all afternoon. Cyn was surprised her insurance wouldn't cover a private room; instead, they had wheeled the deranged man in around noon with assurances he was harmless but suffering from a bad ticker. The room was designed for two–a track for a curtain bisected it–but Cyn still felt like the man was intruding.

On the wall between the two beds hung a vidscreen that scrolled through a playlist of urban vistas, most of them of Perion City, landscapes as they appeared from the revered upper floors of the Perion Spire.

At the end of the loop, the manufactured images gave way to a live feed for a few minutes, showing a failing sun over a subdued city. The foreground detail was enough that Cyn could see corporate banners hung from every surface, from makeshift pikes on the eaves of buildings, to the railings of balconies, and on proper flagpoles in small parks. Corporate patriotism was at an all-time high; Cyn couldn't remember ever seeing the place so made up.

Couldn't remember…

Candice was asleep, so when the nurse wandered over to check on them, Cyn asked in a hushed voice, "What's with all the flags?"

"They've been like that since Tuesday." She grabbed Cyn's free hand to check her pulse, but it felt like she was going to deliver some bad news. "Everyone's been really worried about what it means for the company. They're saying it was a one-time glitch, but some of the engineers I know aren't so sure. Morale has been pretty low since then."

Cyn nodded, felt Candice stir in her arms. Staring down into her daughter's face made the nurse's words fade into irrelevance.

"The bones have to be as strong as they are pliant. They have to support the weight of the structure but not be more than the average man can carry or push around in the sack. The systems supporting this structure have to be equally light and resilient. Do you think this technology comes cheap, not only from a financial standpoint, but from the sacrifice our young men have had to make to ensure we found the right balance? Young men with their entire lives ahead of them confined to wheelchairs for months because of a shattered pelvis. And they have the nerve to call *me* reckless!"

"Please, Mr. Sayre, you need to keep your voice down. You don't want to have another episode."

"Episode? Is that what they teach you assembly line graduates to call cardiac arrest? My *heart* stopped beating! And whose fault is that? Mine? A Georgia chip would have kept me on my feet, instead of shitting my pants at the commissary. But no, the big man won't allow it. I can't even say the V-word in here without risking a pink slip. Imagine that–fired for saying a name. This is a massive company we're talking about here, not some scared-of-its-own-shadow startup hoping its patent violations go unnoticed."

"If you don't calm down, I'll notify the doctor, and he'll just give you another sedative."

"Are you threatening me, Ms. Medco 5000? You wouldn't even be here if it weren't for me. I'm done with you. You find me a *real* nurse right now!"

The nurse rolled her eyes at Cyn and smiled. "Sorry about him."

"Don't apologize for me. You have no right!"

"Hey," snapped Cyn. She whispered as loudly as she dared. "Shut the hell up. My daughter is trying to sleep."

"Well excuse the hell out of me," said Sayre. "I didn't know your *daughter* was asleep. Please give your *daughter* my deepest apologies. I wouldn't want to do anything to interrupt *her* precious little dreams."

"Nurse, hold my baby."

The nurse didn't have time to protest; she was still adjusting to the added weight in her arms as Cyn crossed the room.

Sayre's eyes widened as Cyn grabbed the front of his hospital gown.

"Look, asshole, if you say one more goddamn thing about my daughter, I'm going to rip your chest open and pull out your black fucking heart and squeeze it until every drop of blood squirts out onto your ridiculous fucking mustache! You let her sleep, or so help me, I will put *you* to sleep!"

Then an orderly was pushing her away as a team of nurses streamed into the room. Cyn unfocused and became aware of a grating alarm coming from the wall where a red light flashed its warning. Sayre's heart rate had spiked and the terror she saw in his face was not his fear of her, but of the tightness gripping his chest. In less than thirty seconds, the team had disconnected him from the monitors and wheeled him out of the room. As the bed rolled past the doorway, the alarms quieted.

Candice began to cry.

Cyn retrieved her from the nurse and looked down at the puffy cheeks and toothless gums. Goddamn Sayre and his rambling.

"Ssh," she said, rocking her baby back and forth.

"Someone's back to her old form, I see."

Dr. Bhenderu stood in the doorway, a curious smile on his face and a few drops of coffee on his otherwise white lab coat.

"It wasn't my fault," said Cyn.

"I don't presume to know the depths of the maternal instinct, so I certainly can't pass judgment on you. It's amazing what a mother will do when she cares very deeply for her child. It is admirable."

"I'd give my life for her," she said. "She is the most wonderful thing I've ever made."

Candice gave another cry and shook her tiny fists.

"I need a bottle for her."

Dr. Bhenderu nodded. "Of course. Perhaps you'd like to take her to the atrium? Get out of the room for a little bit? I will have the nurse bring Candice a bottle." He stepped aside and extended a hand towards the hallway.

Cyn had grown tired of her hospital bed anyway, so she followed the balding Indian man through the hallways and around the nurse stations until they came to an open space where the ceiling rose to twice its normal height. On the second floor, frosted glass railings obscured Cyn's view of the other patients.

The atrium was made up to look like a garden, with a quincunx of flower beds at the corners and center. The low walls of the beds provided close seating for those who could endure the overpowering aroma of fresh flowers. Small tables filled the empty spaces, with arm-less chairs for patients and doctors to sit and chat.

A bronze tree rose from the center of the atrium, its branches bending in a deliberate pattern, reminding Cyn of the copper pathways on printed circuit boards. Instead of leaves, the tree had sprouted four large vidscreens which displayed the same tranquil nonsense as the one in Cyn's room.

"There are some divans along the west side," said Dr. Bhenderu. "And it's quieter there as well."

"Thanks," said Cyn, though she barely felt the words.

Candice continued to whimper. The longer the doctor took to show her around, the longer Candice went without her late afternoon snack. If she didn't eat now, she wouldn't nap, wouldn't fall asleep at the right time later in the evening before Patsy arrived.

The name echoed, but no face rose from her memory.

"I'll see about that bottle," said Dr. Bhenderu.

"*See* that it's warm," said Cyn.

She made the short walk from the entrance to the blue divans, noticing for the first time that the skylights in the ceiling weren't real. It was in the way the light rolled, like old fluorescent light bulbs. The bits of blue sky were just projections from a vidscreen hidden in the ceiling. As she sat down on the divan, she wondered if anything in the room was real.

Candice settled down with the change in scenery, but it wasn't until the nurse arrived with the bottle that she closed her eyes in contentment. Her fidgety limbs slowed as she drank.

In the calm that followed, Cyn put her head back and shut her eyes. She listened to the din of conversation, the whoosh of an air conditioning vent somewhere off to her left, and the light classical music emanating from hidden speakers in the gardens.

The gentle melodies brought her heart rate down, allowed her a brief moment of repose before a voice in the back of her head spoke up, telling her it was dangerous to let her guard down. The voice had been chatty all day, begging for something but unable to articulate exactly what it wanted. It was hard to hear over the bustle of the real world, but in Cyn's fleeting moment of calm, it came out of the darkness like the backbeat of some techno slop when all other tracks had faded out. It came with the realization it had always been there.

Cyn opened her eyes, feeling a presence nearby.

On the divan to her right sat a woman about Cyn's age with radiant eyes that reminded her of Candice. The woman was smiling and blushing a little.

"I'm sorry," she said. "I didn't mean to wake you."

Candice had fallen asleep after the bottle went empty.

Cyn readjusted her arms and shook her head. "I must have dozed off."

"She's beautiful. I saw her from across the room and…"

Cyn tightened her grip.

"Oh, I'm sorry." The woman put up her hands. "Please don't think…"

Cyn managed a weak laugh. "No, it's me. I've been on edge all day. I'm not usually this paranoid."

"Every mother's different. Mine was very protective of me and my sisters when we were kids. She rarely even let us out of the house."

"I hope I'm not that bad," said Cyn, looking down at Candice again. One day, she would have to let her daughter go out into the world and experience everything it had to offer: sex, drugs, and rock and roll.

Cyn shook her head. Rock and roll? She couldn't remember being a fan. The only memories of music she had involved techno offshoots and anything by Eliana Alcivar. Why then had the words formed in her brain like that? Had she heard the three put together before? Was it just something old hippies said when they talked about the good old days?

"What's her name?"

"Candice," said Cyn, breaking out of the cloud. "And I'm Cynthia." She extended her hand to the woman.

"Roberta," she replied, grasping Cyn's fingers lightly. "It's a pleasure to meet you both."

EIGHTEEN

Roberta was at the hospital not as a patient, but as assistant to her new friend, a man she spoke about in a voice so wistful it made Cyn sick with envy. She pointed him out in the crowd, a lanky and stylishly unkempt man with dark hair and a disarming smile. He had soft eyes that shone with true interest as he spoke to people. He walked from table to table while Cyn and Roberta talked, sitting casually with older patients as they looked up from their palettes, artificial light glinting off the metal clasps of their oxygen tubes.

According to Roberta, she had met Cameron Gray only a few days before, the Monday preceding the Synthetic Collapse. She explained about the resulting confusion, the lack of direction from managers going all the way up the chain. How would the company respond? Would Perion Synthetics survive such a widespread failure? Patio cafes saw a surge in business as Perion City residents gave into their need for camaraderie, for sharing their theories about what went wrong and who was to blame.

After a few days, the only discernable change was the heightened security in the plaza outside the Spire. That and the media blackout, a safety measure the executive team assured residents was only temporary.

"But doesn't he work for a media outlet?"

"Yes, Banks Media Productions," said Roberta, "out of Los Angeles. All they told him was not to mention the Collapse, so he's just been interviewing random people for the past few days. It's been kind of nice. They've pretty much forgotten about us. Even that nasty woman who used to follow us around hasn't shown her face in days." She paused, sighed. "Cam's got hours and hours of interviews to go though. I'll probably have to help him index them."

"The things we do for love, right?"

"Yes, but what beautiful things come of it," she replied, nodding at Candice.

Cyn felt her eyes tear up and she sniffled.

The voice in the back of her mind was screaming at her, chastising her for being so weak, and pointing out the ridiculousness of being so attached to something other than her own life. But maybe that was what the voice didn't realize; as the directive pointed out, Candice was as much a part of Cyn as her own hand or memories or sense of morality. Candice had grown in her womb, had been assembled from Cyn cells and fed on Cyn nutrients. Why did the voice refuse to recognize that?

"Oh," said Roberta, raising a hand in the air. "Can I introduce you to Cameron?"

This time, the name resonated. Cyn reached for a memory that wasn't there.

"Sure," replied Cyn.

The aggregator cut through the crowd, tossing a few veiled looks at the two orderlies walking the second-floor balcony. When he arrived at the divans, he put out a sturdy hand.

"Cameron Gray," he said, "with Banks Media out of Los Angeles. Who are you today?"

"Excuse me?"

"How are you today, Miss…?"

"Paulson," she replied. "Cynthia Paulson. And I'm doing fine."

Cam sat down on the divan next to Roberta and tapped his phone. "I see you have a baby."

"You don't miss much, do you?"

Roberta snickered, but something defensive flared behind Cam's eyes. Cyn read the danger as easily as she read the laminated press badge hanging around his neck.

"I don't," said Cam. "That's how I get all the cushy assignments. First aggregator to step foot in Perion City in who knows how long."

"Eight years three months," said Roberta.

Cam laughed. "Yes, yes."

Cyn raised her eyebrow, but the aggregator pressed on.

"Would you mind if I asked you a few questions about you and your daughter?"

His enunciation of the word *daughter* had that same bite as Sayre's, but Cyn nodded her head anyway.

"First off, with the recent collapse of Perion's entire product line, I've been asking everyone for their reactions and what they think could have been done to avoid this mishap."

She paused, searching for an emotional reaction to an entire population of synthetics dropping dead, but found none. "I don't know. Everyone seems pretty worried about it, I guess. Everyone except you."

Cam shrugged. "Objectivity comes with the job. I'm just doing what I can to make sure the real story about the Great Perion Synthetic Collapse of 2015 comes out in the end, that all parties are held responsible, and that the true heroes are recognized blah blah blah."

He didn't actually use nonsense words, but Cyn heard the meaningless syllables in her head just the same. The little speech he rattled off reeked of insincerity.

"How's the general mood about the company?" asked Cyn. "Roberta says things have gone back to normal for the most part."

"Oh have they?" Cam nudged Roberta with his elbow. "Well, no doubt there have been some interesting revelations in the past couple days. The sense I get is that James Perion and his son don't see eye to eye on the direction of the company—maybe they never have. There's been a lot of miscommunication between father and son, lots of drama, and lots of *special projects* coming to light because of the Collapse. I'm purely speculating here, but I think Joseph Perion has been running his own little company right under the old man's nose."

"And what about the media blackout?"

Again, Cam shot a glance at Roberta. He raised the glowing red sliver on his wrist into view. "There are always exceptions."

Cyn looked to her own wrist, at the monitoring strip that hadn't come off when the nurse disconnected the wires. It felt stuck to her skin, as if some clueless intern had used too much glue.

"So let me ask you, Ms. Paulson…"

"*Mrs.* Paulson," said Cyn.

Cam made a note on his phone. "As you may have seen on the news, the world's population passed eight billion over the summer. This, of course, brings up a lot of questions about resources and social services, but one group in particular has been using this milestone to push their own agenda. This small minority believes childbearing should be a privilege, not a right. There is an article available on my feed about a small township in New England that has begun experimenting with competency exams and birth licenses. As a new mother, what is your opinion on that?"

"On what?"

"On requiring a license to have a baby. You would have to prove to a regulatory agency that you're competent to raise and care for a child, not to mention provide proof of financial stability."

Cam's eyes darted to the right to an approaching orderly. The man in the white smock slowed at the attention and took a position on the wall.

"Government," Cam continued, his voice quieter, "telling you if you're fit to be a mother. I'm guessing you didn't ask permission to have her, right?"

Cyn shook her head.

"Of course, this creates a market for training services. SAT prep classes are a million-dollar industry. Imagine the businesses that would spring up overnight if people actually had to *study* for parental competency exams."

"It would never work," said Cyn. "You can't deny people a basic human right."

"This is America, sweetheart. We haven't had inalienable rights since…" He paused, cleared his throat. "Well, ever, I guess."

"Is everything alright over here?"

Dr. Bhenderu was winded, as if he had just run a short distance at great speed.

"Dr. B!" said Cam, raising a hand. "Why am I not surprised to see *you* here?"

"Mr. Gray, I thought for sure you had left us already. I'm glad to see you're still in good health. No more incidents, I take it?"

"Nor will there be," said Roberta, putting a hand on Cam's shoulder.

So that's who wears the pants, thought Cyn.

"Well, Mrs. Paulson is still recuperating. Perhaps you wouldn't mind talking to her in a few days, once she's had an opportunity to regain her bearings."

"Her bearings seem fine to me, Doc."

"Is that your professional medical opinion, Mr. Gray?"

Cam grinned but conceded.

"Actually," said Cyn, "I am feeling a bit tired. I think Candice and I could use some quiet time."

Dr. Bhenderu smiled. "I will have one of the nurses take you back to your room, Mrs. Paulson. If there is anything else you require, please let her know." With a slight turn of his head, his smile disappeared. "Mr. Gray, perhaps we can meet later to discuss your interviews with my patients?"

"Absolutely, Doc," said Cam, examining his fingernails.

After Dr. Bhenderu had walked away, Cyn asked, "What do parental competency exams have to do with me? And why doesn't he want you talking about them?"

"It's just a theory I have, very new, probably all sorts of wrong. But sometimes you just throw things out there and see what makes people squirm." Cam's eyes trailed after the doctor. "I'm not saying I have all the answers, but if you go back to your room, we'll never find out if I'm right or not. And besides, there are other things you need to know."

"Like what?"

"Not here," said Cam.

Cyn watched Roberta inventory the room.

"West exit looks clear," she whispered to Cam. "The orderlies are distracted by a woman in a wheelchair."

"Window?" he asked, his eyes locked with Cyn's.

"Another sixty seconds. Allowing for the elevator ride and walk to the front door, we'd need to move soon."

"What do you think, Mrs. Paulson? You want to know the answers?"

"That depends on the questions," she replied.

"Let's say competency exams are a real thing or will be. Don't you want to know what Perion has planned or why he's spent millions of dollars lobbying the state and federal governments for more stringent requirements? And is James Perion behind this obvious cash grab? Or is it his son Joseph? Would the old man really have signed off on such a…"

"Immoral," said Roberta.

"A morally questionable project," said Cam, the fire going out of his voice.

"That doesn't sound like—"

"There's more, Cynthia." He gestured to the empty bottle in Cyn's lap. "For instance, why aren't you breastfeeding your baby? She can't be more than a few months old, right? And you've got no wedding ring on your hand, or an impression to indicate there has ever been one."

Cyn looked at her fingers.

"That's a second-generation Katsumi sliver in your wrist there. You have tattoos on the undersides of your arms that someone has tried to blot out with concealer, but they couldn't hide the surgical bonding. And I bet if you turned around, we'd find a top of the line, Umbra-exclusive jackport in your neck, probably higher-end than mine."

Cyn put a hand to the back of her neck and felt the circular grooves. Stepping out of herself, she wondered why Cynthia Paulson would even need a jackport.

"And," said Cam. He shifted from his divan to hers and put a hand on her forearm. His voice was a whisper. "Ask yourself, honestly. Why… why in the hell do they *insist* on calling you Mrs. Paulson? That's not what's written on your paychecks from Lincoln Continental, is it, Cyn?"

NINETEEN

The elevator was going *up*.

"And if that's true, then we have more to worry about than a few rogue projects," said Cam. He was talking to someone who wasn't there, someone whose responses only he could hear. "Forget painting him as a humanitarian; Perion is making a grab for world domination." He sighed. "It's the news, boss. It's *supposed* to be sensationalist."

Cyn looked down at the baby in her arms, torn between handing the infant over to Roberta and shielding it from all of the terrible things in the world.

If it weren't for that damn directive…

If it weren't for that compulsion to protect Candice, to keep her close, Cyn could… what?

"How do you know who I am?" she asked.

Cam shook his phone. "Snapped a picture."

"You have a phone and yet you're talking to someone in your head?"

"My boss. He has access to my whisperer. It's the only channel we have now. Guess someone upstairs forgot to plug a hole." Cam laughed. "He's actually going nuts over there. All this good dirt on Perion and we can only feed the fluffy stuff."

Feed. Feed to the subs. The words came to Cyn out of the gloom.

"Who is Lincoln Continental?"

"Not a who," said Cam, leaning against the handrail. "A what. Lincoln Continental is one of the Big Three media houses, along with Banks Media out of Los Angeles and Benny Coker's White Line out of Atlantic City. The LC is run by a man named Lincoln Tate, your boss. I hear you've been feeding some very revealing content. I haven't seen it myself, but based on what Banks tells me, I'm not surprised they had you holed up down there."

Cyn shook her head.

"That's bullshit," she replied. "Why would I bring my daughter with me?"

"An excellent question. Why *would* you bring a three-month-old baby to a covert and obviously dangerous assignment? I'm guessing you didn't pack up the minivan with a diaper bag and a playpen and drive right up to the gates."

"I don't remember how I got here," said Cyn.

"It's okay," Roberta assured her. "We know someone who can undo what they did to you."

"What *who* did to me?"

"*Doctor* Bhenderu," said Cam. "He and his crack team of mad scientists. God knows what else they've been up to down there." When Cyn shook her head in confusion, he explained. "We're under the Spire. The Medical level is five floors down from the lobby. From what I can tell, they have a massive underground complex fanning out from the Spire. Some floors look like hospitals, others like dormitories, nurseries, apartments… it goes on and on. And that's not all."

His eyes fell on Candice, and he was quiet for a moment.

"There are training areas, obstacle courses, firing ranges—everything you would expect to find at a Calle Cinco recruitment camp in the desert. The synthetics they had running those courses were bigger and faster than these AutoGuards they have all around this place. They looked…"

"Dangerous," said Roberta. "Like they were built for organic damage."

"Call it what you want: organic damage, urban pacification, or straight-up military grunts. They're building an army down there."

"Why would Perion need an army?"

Cam turned away to watch the numbers tick by on the elevator's vidscreen. "He doesn't, but the United States does. Every day the MX gets stronger, leans a little harder on the Rio Grande. How long do you think it will be before they're trying to push consumer-grade Ayudante chips on this side of the border?"

Cyn's hand went to the back of her neck.

"Similar to yours, yes," said Cam, "but without the neurochem or regulatory assist. Ayudante chips drive MX soldiers harder and faster than our boys with their government-issue Vinestead hardware. I think that's where Perion comes in. An entire army of replaceable soldiers—drones that walk and talk and *think*. No more human casualties and most importantly, no more money funneling into Arthur Sedivy's pockets."

The elevator slowed as the numbers on the vidscreen faded out, replaced by the word *Lobby*. Cam motioned for Cyn to stand aside before the doors slid apart. Only Roberta stood in full view of the lobby, her eyes jumping from one target to the next. She waited, inert, until the doors closed on her. Cam pressed the button for the third floor, and they began to rise again.

"Plan B," said Roberta, finishing some calculation in her head.

They stepped off the elevator onto a reception floor that was open to the lobby below. Parts of the floor fell away at the windows, allowing for an ever-shrinking atrium to reach higher into the building. Leather couches formed a line along the perimeter near the floor to ceiling glass.

The area in front of the elevator was deserted, save a janitor who was either too old to be performing manual labor or whose gears weren't tuned correctly for the repetitive act of emptying garbage cans.

Cam led Cyn to the nearest window where they looked out over the circular driveway in front of the Spire.

"We need to split up," he said. "Cyn, I'm going to need you to trust me."

"I don't," she replied. "At all."

"Fine, then trust Roberta. You'll need to give her the baby."

"Fuck that," said Cyn.

"It's the only way."

It was in the way his voice wavered; he was serious.

"I appreciate what you've done, but I'm not trusting my baby to a woman I've never met before."

Roberta took a step forward. "I'm more than competent to watch over the child until we meet up again."

Cyn wrapped a protective arm around Candice.

Cam turned away from the window. His face grew stern. "Look, Cyn. They'll let Roberta walk out of here with the baby. I guarantee they won't bat a fucking eye. Us, on the other hand, and *you* in your hospital gown in particular, will set off every alarm in this place. We have some work to do if we want to get out of here. If you want to drag Candice through that, that's your choice, but I'm not slowing down because of her, and I doubt any synthetic grunt is going to go easier on you just because you have a baby in tow."

"Please," said Roberta. "This way there's no danger for her. I'll take her right out the front door without incident and meet up with you later. I promise you she will be safe with me."

It took a full minute to approach Roberta and hand over Candice, who was still alert in her little blue bundle, still watching the world as if she could understand any of it.

"If anything happens to her, I'll kill you." Cyn opted for simple language. "If you run, I will hunt you down and then kill you. And not just you, but everyone you know or care about." She leaned closer. "Even *him*."

Roberta's eyes jumped to Cam and back. "I believe you."

"If you ladies are done," said Cam, "we need to get moving. Roberta, meet us at the warehouse. We shouldn't be more than an hour behind you."

"If we don't make it," said Cyn, "please take her home to Umbra—"

The city came back in a flash, its neon arcs erupting from uncertain shadows. She saw the Umbra Tower gleaming at midnight, its pulse climbing higher into the sky with every bass hit coming from the identical techno clubs and synth parlors lining the street next to... where... Decker Plaza? A skyscraper by Umbra terms, reaching two floors higher than most of the modest buildings on Grant

Street. And on that fifth floor, there worked a man with a shaved head and dark brown skin and rows of teeth that glinted like a crescent moon from one side of his hard, angular face to the other.

Lincoln.

Roberta was gone before Cyn could finish her sentence. Candice's face disappeared behind the closing doors of the elevator and Cyn thought for a fleeting moment she would never see her daughter again. The directive fumed, told her to get moving, to do *something* to speed their reunion.

"If you're wrong about her," said Cyn, staring at the silver doors, "it's gonna be your ass."

Cam pulled one arm across his chest to stretch his shoulder. "You don't have to worry. Roberta's a synthetic, and fiercely loyal to—"

"What?" Cyn spun around. "You let me hand my baby over to a *machine*?"

Cam repeated the stretch with his other arm. "A machine that has been imprinted to follow my orders."

"Not good enough! I'm calling this off. I'm getting my baby and going home."

"Okay," said Cam, cracking his knuckles, "but first—"

Cyn barely registered Cam's fist entering from the periphery. It came within an inch of her nose, but a last-second parry redirected the energy safely into space. Cyn's legs contracted, sinking her torso as her feet turned towards the enemy. Her back heel came off the ground in an on-guard stance while her hands came up in a modified defensive shell. A half-second after assuming the position, Cam came at her again, this time with an abrupt thrust kick aimed for her stomach.

Hospital-issue slippers twisted against the thin carpet, turning her body parallel to the incoming strike. Cam's leg scraped past her; the edges of his shoe ripped her gown, exposing her torso. Cyn only caught a flash of the thin tattoo running down the valley between her abs, disappearing under the band of stark white underwear. As Cam came down from his kick, Cyn threw an elbow into the space she knew he would soon be occupying. It connected, sending Cam stumbling back a few paces.

When he stopped, his feet pivoted out on his heels then again on his toes. His hands came up on a line extending from his chest.

"What the fuck, Cam?"

"You can subdue an Ayudante," he said. "The military has known that for years." His breathing was already ragged, and his chest pumped frantically. This man was no fighter.

And yet he pursued her, pushing in with a feinted jab followed by a low cross. His knuckles drove into Cyn's stomach, forcing the air out of her lungs. She fell back, struggling to breathe.

"With enough code," he said, throwing a roundhouse kick at her exposed knee, "you can mute an Ayudante to a dull buzz."

Cyn shuffled back and then forward, returning her own kick to Cam's inner thigh before he could recover. When he reached down to block it, Cyn's foot had already retracted and started for his head. She dug her toe into the side of his face between his ear and his jaw.

"When an Ayudante is compromised," he grunted, lunging at her with a lead hook, "there are only a few things that can bring it back."

Cyn's wrist erupted in fiery pain; somehow she had raised her hand and instinctively leaned away from the incoming fist.

"You can *short* it," said Cam.

A cross came flying from the right, followed by an open palm hook that rattled Cyn's head.

"You can reset it." He was toying with her now, sending an endless string of straight punches right down the center line, busting through her defenses to land on her chin, neck, and chest. "Or, you can knock some fucking *sense* into it."

Cyn felt the bones in her nose shift and the world muted itself into a dizzying array of sparks at the corners of her vision. She stumbled away, grasping at her face, feeling the wet skin. The directive in her head was still talking about Candice, but another speaker rose from the din, this one cold and calculating. It spoke rapidly in an unfamiliar language, but somehow she understood what it was saying all the same.

Wiping the tears from her eyes with her palms, Cyn tore at the shredded hospital gown and tossed it aside. She watched Cam's eyes go wide, but all she could think about was the cool breeze of the air conditioning on her bare skin. She drew herself up and took a deep breath.

Waves of soothing vibrations ran down her arms and legs—her augmentations kicking into gear. They drove her fists and feet faster than Cam could keep up with. Each impact sent a corresponding feeling of satisfaction throughout her body like some kind of synth rush with a tapered bite of accomplishment. She attacked; he retreated. She pursued, raining blow after blow upon the man who had convinced her to hand her baby over to a synthetic, on the man shouting nonsense about knocking some fucking sense into *her*. Now he would see how it felt to be on the other side, how it felt for someone to show him the error of *his* ways.

Cyn feinted a jab, feinted a hook with the same hand, and then delivered a strike with a rear cross. When Cam fired back, Cyn covered with her rear hand and dipped to deliver a shovel hook. It connected, leaving her too close and vulnerable. She timed her escape with a quick uppercut that landed more in Cam's throat than his chin. It had the desired effect; he crumbled in place and fell onto his back.

Her body moved without thinking, rushing forward with a foot raised in the air, her knee making a circular motion to put as much force as possible into a good old fashioned Umbra curb stomp, which by her estimation, would be powerful enough to crush Cam's skull.

Cyn saw all of this from her original position, as if her body had left without her. And though she desired his death, she knew it came without control, without being the one in charge. It was the voice in the back of her head, the smooth talker whose words of pure bass tickled the back of her neck. She wanted nothing more than to give into it completely, to sink into its powerful and tender embrace.

"Cynthia!" The voice screamed from all corners of the world. "Stop! You're killing him!"

Cyn froze in place, her leg hanging in the air above Cam's bloodied face.

"Lincoln?" she asked. "Is that you?"

TWENTY

They used to have a cat, a yellow and white furball who roamed the house like she owned it. Her name was Zao, after the tabby who had appeared in the animated film *All My Lives* the year they got her. Zao's favorite resting spot was in Cyn's room, in the line of sunlight cast by the tall, skinny windows on either side of the twin bed. She would start out on the floor in the morning, then move to the foot of the bed as the golden band shortened. Cyn would find her there in the afternoon, asleep or simply pensive, content in the safety of her kingdom. After a hard day of school, Cyn found no greater pleasure than burying her face in the tabby's soft fur, listening for that deep vibrato purr that always followed.

Years later, after the cat had died or run away, Cyn would experience the same rattling hum, but instead of a purr of pleasure, it would be from the spiking processor in her Ayudante chip.

Guardian Angels had no such problem. They stayed well within their rated frequencies, limits set by the manufacturer and government agencies. The MX had no such stipulations or federal oversight. If you could overclock the one advantage you had on the battlefield, then there was really no choice. Push your chip to the limit, the saying went. It wasn't as if you were going to live very long anyhow.

Cyn had learned to recognize when her chip was overworked, first by the humming and then by the heat it gave off, the dull ache it produced at the base of her skull. It wasn't a feeling that would put her down, but it wasn't exactly pleasant. And as she stood over the fallen Cam, listening to Tate's screams rattle around in her head, she felt the vibrations ripple through her body, as if the Ayudante were giving off its war cry, asserting itself after having been ignored for so long. The various aches and pains she felt in her body fell away, replaced by a sense of invincibility. The room around her shifted, became less of a generic background and more a three-dimensional puzzle full of escape routes and foot holds.

Cam was still rolling on the ground, hands holding the underside of his jaw as blood pooled on his light mustache.

Shaking off the disorientation, Cyn stepped forward and put out her hand.

Cam considered the offer for a moment before reaching into his pocket for his cell phone. He snapped a picture of Cyn and then dropped his head back to the carpet.

"Asshole," said Cyn.

With a groan, Cam rolled onto his stomach and then pushed himself to his knees. "My god," he said, struggling to find balance. "They build them tough in Umbra, don't they?"

"Just you, baby," said Tate. The whisperer crackled.

Cyn examined her wrist and read the black on silver text.

Connection Restored.

Rotating her arm, Cyn rubbed the remaining concealer away until the black, bony line took shape. The tiniest scar ran down the center of it.

"Augments," she explained. "They come in handy whenever a rival house wants to start some shit."

"Hey, I was just trying to…" Cam cut his sentence short when he saw the smile on her face. "Well, I don't know about your hardware, but your Kung Fu is definitely stronger than mine."

Cyn crossed her arms over her breasts. "What do you call that fighting style you were trying to do?"

Cam coughed, grimaced. The small stream of blood from his nose began to trickle down over his lips. "A little of everything, I guess. I've been training in VNet for the last year. Never really had an opportunity to use it in real life."

"Well, thanks for bringing me back."

"Sure. I owed Tate for some hospitality he showed me last time I was in Umbra."

Cyn touched the back of her neck where the tremors from the Ayudante tingled her fingers. "Damn this thing is working overtime."

Across the room, the elevator dinged. There was no time to run; Cyn fell into a defensive stance. Cam didn't even register the sound until he saw Cyn staring.

The doors parted, and out stepped a familiar suit.

"Chief of Police," whispered Cyn.

"I know," whispered Cam in reply.

Gantz took a few steps forward and crossed his arms. "Two aggregators from two of the biggest media houses in a city of hundreds of thousands, and you end up beating the shit out of each other in the most secure building in the city." He laughed to himself. "You can't make this shit up."

His tone made Cyn relax; beside her, Cam seemed positively nonchalant.

"What do you say, Gantz?" asked Cam. "Should we get the hell out of here? I think I've gotten all the material I need for my story."

Gantz removed his jacket and held it out to Cyn. "I'm not here, understand? I don't care what you feed, but you leave my name out of it. *They* are watching the feeds very carefully, and if you so much as hint about my involvement, all the augments in Umbra won't be enough to stop me from putting you in the ground."

Cyn reached for the jacket and pulled it on. It was much too big.

"Where's Roberta?" asked Gantz.

"She went on ahead," said Cam. "With the…" He pointed vaguely to Cyn's empty arms.

For a moment, she felt as if the Ayudante might buzz itself right out of her neck. The directive was still very much alive, though the Ayudante was doing its best to fight it. But how did the directive get there in the first place?

"Who…" She choked on the question, her brain refusing to admit the possibility. "Whose baby was that? I mean, I really felt like she was mine." A cold shudder went through her body. "I still do."

"She's not real," said Cam. "She's a synthetic like Roberta. Like I said, probably part of some scheme to cash in on the global population problem. My guess is Joe Perion wants to corner the market with synthetic babies that behave just like real ones. You pay your hundred-dollar course fee, train on a robo-baby for a while, and go take your test."

Gantz scoffed. "I wouldn't feed that bullshit if I were you, Gray. And attaching Joe's name to it would only demonstrate how little you know of him."

"If not him, then who?" asked Cam.

Gantz ignored the question and gestured to a nearby door. "Come on, we don't have time to stand around in our underwear."

Cam held his tongue until they had walked down three flights of stairs and passed through half a dozen security checkpoints.

When they stopped in front of a large exterior door, he asked, "Your company owes her an explanation, Chief."

Gantz examined the vidscreen next to the door, his fingers flying over the display, bringing up an inventory screen containing a gallery of cars. "The lab coats call them forced betas. Every so often, we get people walking out of the desert. Sometimes they're lost. Sometimes they're just curious."

"Sometimes they're looking for a scoop?" asked Cam.

"Not as often as you'd think," he replied. "We used to turn them away or have them arrested, but some people just didn't get the message. They wanted in, so we let them in."

A number flashed on the vidscreen and Gantz moved to a lock box on the adjoining wall. He fished out a black key fob. "Found our ride."

Cyn followed the chief and the shaky Cam out into the garage. Sunlight poured in from the open bay doors, bathing the evercrete cavern in an oppressive lens flare that made Cyn shield her eyes. Only by the sound of boots clapping on the ground in front of her was she able to keep up.

The key fob was for a black Nissan, similar to the Perion company cars she had seen during live events where James Perion arrived in a convoy of identical vehicles to keep any potential assassins guessing. But where those had been longer sedans with bulging hoods over massive engines, the car Gantz had chosen was smaller, more nimble. An unbroken streak of black glass dominated the driver's side. A hidden third door on the passenger side allowed Cam to slip into the afterthought of a back seat. Cyn sank into the conforming leather in front and reflected on how out of place she looked with her bare legs poking out from under Gantz' suit jacket.

"Where are my clothes?"

Gantz chuckled; Cyn watched his eyes seek out Cam in the rearview mirror. "Not the first time I've been asked *that* question."

In the back seat, Cam tapped a rim shot out on his knees.

"Hey, Chief Gantz of the Perion City Police Department, the guy who is currently helping me escape my unlawful detainment, where the *fuck* are my clothes?"

"Destroyed," he replied. "I know, it's a shame. That dive suit must have set you back five large at least."

"Nine," grumbled Tate, as if anyone but Cyn could hear him.

"We couldn't take any chances though," continued Gantz. "That thing was more tech than cloth, so we dropped it into the incinerator like a defunct synny. All of your equipment too. The only thing that didn't go down the chute was your needler, but Sava Kessler took that for herself. She says it's a one-of-a-kind Newmark out of South Africa. How did you come by such a weapon?"

"My mother gave it to me," replied Cyn. She crossed her arms and looked out the window as the car exited the garage.

"How does a PR flack even know how to place a gun like that?" asked Cam. "And you just let her take it?"

Gantz shrugged. "You pick your battles with Sava Kessler. Write that down."

The windows dimmed in response to the increased sunlight. None of the guards lining the posts along the driveway would be able to see in. Gantz had his window open only a crack, just enough space to show his badge. After a few tense minutes, the Spire shifted to the side view mirror and began to recede. Cyn relaxed for the first time in hours.

Then she realized her relief came not from the escape, but from the prospect of seeing Candice again.

"Why do I feel a bond with a synthetic baby?" she asked. "How is that even possible?"

"I don't know the why," replied the chief. "As to the how, it's like I said, forced beta. Lot of these drifters coming out of the desert fail one important immigration rule."

"Guardian Angel chips," said Cam. He cocked his head to the right.

"Yeah, Vinestead tech. It's also the weakest and most exploitable mass-market tech out there. It's not just a monitoring system; it can control you. Someone could walk in, say your average lab coat, and work fine and get along for years. Then one day, the code in their chip fires, activates some subroutine in their brain, and boom, they go all Kaili Zabora over some billion-dollar prototype. That's a time and money setback the big man would never allow."

"But you let them in anyway?" asked Cyn.

"Not without wiping them clean, eyebrows to assholes and everything in between. It's not exactly an on-the-books procedure, but the GA chip makes it easy to reprogram someone. It's kind of like the ReTread procedure they use on inmates. Dump the original personality and make the scum of society into a useful contributor. We haven't had a forced beta tester go rogue in a long while."

Cyn let out a deep breath.

The buildings outside towered over the car but began to shrink the farther away they got from the Spire. Soon they were passing residential areas, neighborhoods of boring beige houses that twisted away from the road.

"Well, if you're not gonna ask," said Cam. Then to Gantz, "She has an Ayudante chip. I didn't think anyone had broken MoA encryption yet."

"Not broken, but subdued. Interfered with." Gantz waved an uncertain hand over the steering wheel. "Deborah tried to explain it to me… All I know is that the girl with the skeleton tattoo isn't a Vinestead virgin. Scanners picked up some lingering VTech the moment we popped them on. It may not have been enough to ReTread her completely, but I guess they didn't need to."

Cyn felt herself being pulled through time to that back alley in Umbra, a nearly empty bottle of Stolichnaya in one hand and an anesthetic tab in the other. The hacker had said he'd get every trace of the diseased Vinestead tech out of her, but then he'd also promised his instruments were sterile.

The resulting infection had put her in the hospital for two weeks, but it had been worth it to be free of the Big V.

"Fucking Vinestead," she muttered. The Ayudante opened the feedback loop just wide enough to let her know she was grinding her teeth.

"Don't spit in here," said Gantz. "This is Corinthian leather."

"Like I give a shit about your car."

"It's not that. I just don't think you should do *anything* until we find out how badly they paddled your gray canoe. There's a guy I know who's done some ReTread work in the past. He's got access to equipment we'll need."

"That's where we're going," said Cam. Then, with just a hint of sarcasm, "Your daughter will be there."

Cyn looked over her shoulder and shot back, "And your *girlfriend* too, right?"

They made the rest of the trip in silence.

TWENTY-ONE

"What's it like?" asked Tate.

Cyn considered the synthetic baby in her arms, found beauty in the way the orange light from the streetlamps outside crossed her—its—little face. She was standing at the window with Candice, unable to resist the directive. The more she tried to fight it, the more the Ayudante wanted to help her, and the more it upped its frequency, until finally the world dimmed under the intense heat and vibration in her neck.

The biochip wasn't designed to fight its owner. Cyn found through experimentation that holding Candice, walking her around, and cooing when she began to whine, brought her a level of relaxation on par with any of the codified cocktails from the finest synth spas in Umbra. The Ayudante relented on Cyn's order—maybe it even recognized how therapeutic just having Candice nearby was.

"Like a drug," replied Cyn. "Like an addiction, but without the highs and lows. Caring for her provides a baseline. Any deviation from it produces a longing, a feeling of incompleteness. That stress makes the Ayudante throw a damn fit. And *that's* where the real pain is."

"Hell of a thing," said Tate, groaning. "I thought if you were caught, they'd rough you up a bit, maybe even try to jack you out, but I didn't expect this."

Cyn leaned against the cold glass of the window. The small office in the back of the warehouse was dark; shadows hid most of the mess surrounding a small desk with scattered papers and empty water bottles lining its edge like impotent sentries. Roberta had been waiting for them, as promised. Candice, asleep in her arms, was waiting too, also as promised.

Even for a synthetic, there was something off about Roberta, but Cyn couldn't lock it down.

"Probably star struck," said Tate. "Gray is something of a minor celebrity in the City of Angels, even if he isn't well-known in Umbra. She probably heard his name on the feed alongside some movie star or athlete, thinks she can swing a meet and greet if she just holds onto his coattails long enough."

"She's a synthetic; what interest would she have in any of that? I don't get why she's so attached to Cam. It's not like he's that good looking."

Tate huffed. "Bitches be crazy."

"Shut up."

Cyn smiled as Candice opened her eyes for a few seconds and then drifted off to sleep.

Did it sleep?

"Well," said Tate, his words beginning to slur. "At least we've got a story. You are blowin' up the feed tonight."

"It's a major score: brainwashing people, synthetic babies, compromised security officials. And if what Cam says is true, then the Perions are building an army as well."

"You know the worst part of being brainwashed? Not *knowing* you're brainwashed. If I have complete control over you and you're not aware of it, then everything I tell you to do, you'll think it was *your* idea. I could control everything, from what you buy to who you vote for."

The line went silent as Tate pondered the possibilities.

A minute passed.

"Don't be all doom and gloom," said Cyn. "We'll expose Perion, put him under the microscope. When our subbers get wind of this, they'll come gunning for Perion Synthetics. And not just them: the government, Vinestead, and hell, even the goddamn MX would risk an incursion if they found out someone has a way to dampen their command-and-control chip. You don't just push an Ayudante aside without the MoA pushing back."

Tate let out a slow breath. "James Perion is in for a world of shit."

"We all are."

The Ayudante had been fighting the lingering fatigue in Cyn's body, but the mellow provided by Candice had convinced it all was well and a little sleep might be good for the host. As if a dam of drowsiness had just broken, Cyn moved to the high-backed chair at the desk and sat down. She pushed back to recline, throwing her feet up and dropping them next to a blinking phone. Her new black boots—part of a gift of clothing from Roberta—shone with a red tint.

Cyn closed her eyes for the briefest of intervals.

In the darkness, she dreamed of home, of the shadowy streets of Umbra where tech was a presence you could feel with every breath, bleeding from every jackport, collecting in the street like a river of energy. Wading through it, walking with her steel toes in a sea of people and information, was the only time Cyn felt alive. The people of Umbra were just like her, pursuing the same things in life, yearning for that singular nirvana of total awareness. To be all knowing, to be completely connected: these were the dreams of the populace, fleeting fancy no one truly expected to attain.

She imagined Tate standing at his window again, hands clasped behind his back, his occasionally sharp mind thinking of new and interesting ways to enslave the population with a satiation of the dependency some of them had lived with since birth. In a way, he was the first generation of the coercive feeder, a prototype attempt at controlling people's lives. He chose the advertising, chose which stories to feed and in what light. If he didn't think he was manipulating people by constantly running anti-Vinestead propaganda, then he was more of a fool than Benny Coker. It was hard to imagine Tate not seeing the similarities between himself and James Perion, how alike they were in purpose.

"They're ready for you."

Cyn snapped awake, saw Gantz standing in the doorway with something of a smile on his face. Just how long he had been lingering there, she wasn't sure, but his eyes were still actively scanning her body.

"Why don't you take a picture?" she asked, pulling her feet down and pushing herself out of the chair.

"Cam already showed me his," said Gantz, grinning. "Whenever Miss Perky is ready," he added.

Cyn followed him down the hallway to the main warehouse. There, machinery lined three sides of a rectangular space, wrapping around table after table of synthetic females, all of them naked and supine. Upon seeing them again, Cyn felt the sickness return to her stomach. Something about the flesh on display didn't sit right with her, nor did the way Cam leered at the spread legs when he thought no one was watching.

Gantz had mentioned something about most of the synthetics being prototypes. They had been brought to the warehouse for provisioning or repair. He had tried to make it sound so natural, but when Cyn asked why an entire eight-foot section of the wall contained synthetic vaginas in frosted plastic bags, he had no answer.

Cam was standing by one of the work benches near the front of the warehouse, talking to a man in a faded leather jacket. He carried what appeared to be a tool bag in one hand.

As Cyn approached them, she sought out Roberta and found her on the other side of the room, standing over the body of a fair-skinned synthetic, an empty look in her eyes.

"Cyn," said Cam, motioning to the new arrival. "This is Gilbert Reyes. Gantz says he's the best handyman in all of Perion City."

"Gil," said the man with lines on his forehead and the first patches of white in his close-shaven hair. "It's nice to meet you." His eyes stared lazily into hers, as if the rest of her body were an afterthought of her existence.

"Pleasure." Cyn repeated the word in her head, unsure if she had ever uttered it in that context before.

A moment of silence passed over the group.

"Well," said Gil, "there's a game on tonight, so if you'd like to get started…"

While Gantz busied himself with clearing one of the nearby tables, Cam stepped closer to Cyn and asked, "Are you feeding this?"

She listened for Tate's light breathing. "Probably."

"Do you mind if I…?" He showed her his glowing sliver.

"How much is Banks gonna pay me?"

Cam nodded and drew his finger over his wrist.

"If you'll just hop up on the table," said Gil, "I'll get the trace and replace started. Perion's got the network locked down tight tonight, but I managed to scout a few connections that weren't on the map."

"How long will this take?" asked Cyn, touching her temple. Handing Candice to Cam had set off another headache. Any minute now, the Ayudante would ramp back up, fueling the cycle of pain.

"Ten, fifteen minutes maybe." Gil dropped his bag on the table and pulled out a thick laptop. He unrolled a length of trode cord, slotted one end into the ancient computer, and held the other out to Cyn. "For your jackport. What is that, a Seraphim Black?"

Cyn nodded and slid the electrode into place. She caught eyes with Cam. "Yes, it was a gift from Lincoln." He nodded as if he already knew.

The table was hard against her back as she reclined.

So this is what it's like to be a synthetic, she thought, staring up into the array of scaffolding and halogen lights. It was so unceremonious, so uncaring. Cyn turned to the right and looked at the lifeless profile of the synthetic next to her. Despite the uncomfortable slab, the synthetic appeared to be at peace, untroubled by the cold temperature or the three men standing nearby who had been ogling her all night.

"Cam, do me a favor. Stand next to her with the baby. Make sure she can see it." Gil turned to Cyn. "I want that part of your brain to glow. Think about her. Think about losing her. Get those synapses firing."

As if she had heard Gil, Candice began to whimper, which turned into a full-blown wail just as the Ayudante was latching onto the incoming feed. Whatever juice Gil was pumping down the line, Cyn's chip was drinking it up with pleasure. It would have been refreshing if not for the overwhelming sense of something being cut from her very soul. Not just Candice, not the synthetic machine made to look like a baby she could love, but the very idea that she *could* love, that she felt an attachment she had never before experienced, not with Lincoln, not with anyone. Cyn wondered if she would ever feel such a thing again, or would having her own children be underwhelming?

"And we're searching, we're searching."

Gil placed his hand on Cyn's shoulder.

"In silence, there is music," he muttered. "In stillness, there is life. You are not your programming, Cynthia Mesquina. You are not the individual lines of code or the output of some equation. You are the sum total of your experience, of trial and error. You simply *are*."

"It hurts," said Cyn, feeling the first tear roll down the side of her face.

"Change is painful," said Gil. "But change is the only way, evolution the only path. Forward, never backward."

Cyn wanted to tell Gil to shove his pseudo-Zen bullshit up his ass, but her mouth was too dry to form words. She bucked on the table as a convulsion lifted her body.

"Weakness leaving the body," said Gil. "Stripping away the extraneous data. Finding the soul within. True life cannot be coded. True consciousness cannot be evaluated."

Roberta appeared next to Cam, concern tattooed on her pretty little face. What was her problem anyway? Hadn't she ever seen a fellow woman suffer?

"Twenty seconds," said Gil. "Fifteen."

Roberta stepped forward and grabbed Cyn's trembling hand. "It will be alright, Cynthia. The stars will turn for you."

"Jackie?"

All eyes turned to Gil. All except Cyn, whose eyes had rolled up into the back of her head.

"Who the fuck is Jackie?" asked Cam. "Focus, Gil!"

The Ayudante flooded Cyn's system with the Cocktail of Last Resort. Her senses slipped away like the scent of flowers on a soft breeze. Then the darkness came, reminding her of Umbra.

Reminding her of home.

PART THREE
GILBERT REYES

TWENTY-TWO

"Rack 'em or stack 'em. Hot shooter coming out."

Eileen Coker was at the craps table losing money hand over fist and enjoying every minute of it when her husband of sixteen years strolled in through the main entrance of the casino with his security detail surrounding him at all points of the compass and his little whore of an assistant trailing after him. He had been gone for four days, ever since he broke the news of James Perion cashing out his chips once and for all. And just as he'd warned Eileen, the vultures had flocked to the White Dragon Resort and Casino in the middle of the Atlantic City Boardwalk, pecking and clawing for his source, for any shred of evidence to back up such outrageous claims.

So he had gone on a few conveniently timed business trips, leaving the day-to-day of the company in Eileen's hands, even though her primary role was that of legal counsel. Benny gave her the reigns because she was his wife and it was expected; she didn't run the company into the ground in his absence because she was technically his employee and her loyalty was also expected. Without a figurehead, the company went on as normal, though Eileen found her nights lonesome and subsequently used her husband's considerable wealth to buy friends on the casino floor where she gambled and drank and thought about how awkward the sex would be between Benny and his barely-out-of-college assistant.

How could a girl so young look at Bennett Buford Coker naked and not run screaming for the shore, intent on drowning herself to clear the memory of his sagging, wrinkled balls?

Eileen snorted into her martini as the dealer called out a Midnight.

At a distance, she couldn't hear what her dear husband was running his mouth about. She could tell something was up because the usually docile Benny was practically screaming into his phone. His slight hair was uncombed, waving off to one side as if a permanent breeze were following him around. His Atlantic City chic wardrobe was gone, replaced by a simple white button down with a bolo tie and loose cuffs he had bunched around his elbows. At least the shirt was tucked into his blue jeans, and someone had had the sense to keep him from putting on his cowboy boots, as he did when he was stressed and not thinking.

The Boardwalk was no place for a native Texan, but Benny had hired everyone from stylists to speech therapists to help perfect the suave, almost gangster persona he had used to launch The White Line media house. And though a video or a picture from Benny's past would show up on VNet every once in a while, no one really cared. He ran the third biggest feed in the country, eleventh on the planet. People were quick to forgive who he was back then when they stood in awe of who he was now.

Benny didn't look up as he passed the table, nor did any member of his posse acknowledge Eileen's existence. It wasn't until he had entered the elevator and looked back to survey the floor that his eyes met hers. Then he did that thing she had come to hate so much, that condescending underbelly scratch of his finger, the non-verbal *come here* command he used with his employees.

Was that all she was to him anymore, a goddamn employee?

If he wanted her company right now, at eleven thirty on a Friday night, then someone was in legal trouble, and not the kind that could wait until Monday morning. Somewhere, someone was in deep shit. Deep enough to bring the little cockroach out of his dark hole and back to the bright lights of Atlantic City.

Eileen waited for the elevator doors to close and then tossed a couple of hundred-dollar chips at the dealer. A passing waiter collected her empty glass. She asked the stringy young man to line up three Manhattans and bring them up to the penthouse. The fifty-dollar chip she placed on his tray made him smile; and he, unlike the dealer, snuck a glance at Eileen's cleavage, which she had put on display with the help of an expensive Gregory Pruit dress she had had flown in from Los Angeles the day before.

At the elevator, Eileen spied the waiter across the room with his similarly uniformed chums, having a good chuck. Laugh it up, she thought. Get all your chucks out now while you're still employed.

She swooned as the car began its ascent. Gripping the handrail, Eileen closed her eyes against the bright gold spots swirling in her vision. Maybe it hadn't been such a great idea to drink so much so early, but then, if she were going to have to spend the rest of the evening with Benny and his whore, the more booze she had in her the better.

The matrix of circled numbers on the wall lit up in sequence.

Eileen thought of James Perion and frowned for a moment. It was because of his death that Benny had skipped town in the middle of the night without so much as a knock or a note on her bedroom door. She had woken to find the penthouse empty and her husband's room in disarray. It was Daryl who had finally clued her in, though he had been hesitant to do so, as if he could sense the wrong Benny had done her.

She wished he hadn't gone, wished she could have been sitting with him when Donato Banks went live on his feed to all but repudiate Benny's claims. He had a man inside Perion City, and that man reported no official statement from the company, no funeral procession with hundreds of thousands of people looking on, and most importantly, no body. And though he produced no evidence, no recent video of the great man himself, the damage had been done. The burden of proof was squarely on Benny Coker, he claimed, and the rest of the world agreed.

Just thinking about the hurt look on Benny's face, about the pain he likely felt for once again being stepped on by Banks Media, made a warmth trickle up the inside of Eileen's legs. She rubbed them together as the car slowed.

The elevator dinged at the penthouse floor and the doors opened to a long, dim hallway. On the walls were individually spotlighted photos of great media titans, inspirational icons hand-picked by Benny. Conspicuously absent were pictures of Donato Banks and Lincoln Tate.

"Good evening, Mrs. Coker," said Daryl. He was perched on his stool by the door like an obedient watch dog.

"Good evening," replied Eileen. "I trust my husband is already inside the whore? Sorry, *with* the whore?"

Daryl gave an appreciative smile but said nothing as he opened the door for her. The foyer opened directly into the conference area where Benny and his assistant were seated. In front of them, the vidscreen wall had been cut up into six panels; five floating heads stared back from various offices across the globe. The sixth panel was dark. An icon at the bottom indicated it was a voice-only call. Gray static jumped across the frame every few seconds.

"And given the climate inside the city, we believe it would be too risky to attempt an incursion. We haven't dealt with Joseph Perion before. We don't know if he will be retaining the same legal team as his father."

The talking heads quieted as Eileen dropped into the chair next to Benny.

"What do you think, dear?" asked Benny. "If Joseph hires a new legal team, we'll lose our leverage on Adam Roe."

She looked into his eyes for some form of recognition but found none.

"That's only a concern if James Perion is really dead," she said. "Until we know that for sure, we have to assume the legal team will remain the same."

"He *is* dead," said Benny. "My guy has an inside source."

"*Your* guy," said Eileen, scoffing.

One of the heads cleared his throat. "We need to go public with this new information now. The market share projections are through the roof."

"What new information?" asked Eileen.

"It doesn't matter," said Benny. "We can't break the story until our man is out of danger."

"Thanks," said a voice from the sixth panel.

"Obviously, we're all trying to make a play at the Perion story. Myself, Banks, and Tate. And in doing so, we all find ourselves in the same position, with people on the inside who are now in what we know is very real danger, and I don't mean from a legal standpoint. Anything we release about Perion, whether true or not, will turn their focus on us. They've got the power and the resources to bring any of the houses down."

Benny sighed and looked down. His right hand reached for the whore's, but it stopped, pretending to scratch an itch instead.

"Hell, they could bring *all* of our houses down," he said.

"So what do we do?" asked one of the heads.

Eileen rolled her eyes.

"We wait," replied Benny. "We wait until we know exactly what Joe Perion and his new regime are up to. If we don't have a complete and *irrefutable* story, then we won't be able to generate the necessary public outrage. Without that, we're all gonna take it up the ass."

"Won't be the first time," said Eileen, under her breath. She caught eyes with the whore, eyes which fluttered away.

Benny leaned forward. "Dear, I need you to start preparing for the possibility that our man is discovered. Take it from both personal and corporate standpoints. I want this story chambered and ready to feed when the time comes. If we suspect Banks or Tate is about to go public, we dump the whole thing onto the network and let it all ride."

"But that will expose…" said a head.

"Our man has contingency plans for that. If his identity is compromised, he'll be the first to know. Until then, we stay on this story as long as we can."

The talking heads nodded in unison.

"Now," said Benny, standing up, "if you will excuse me, I'd like to have a private word with the man on the scene."

One by one, the five panels on the vidscreen blinked away, until all that remained was the fuzzy black static. It expanded to fill the empty space.

"Ladies, please, a little privacy?" asked Benny.

Eileen waited for the whore to leave before standing. She placed a hand on Benny's shoulder.

"Welcome home," she said.

Benny nodded and tapped her hand with his.

The lights in the hallway were down, but Eileen found her way to her bedroom by dragging two fingers on the wall. Curiosity kept her at the threshold of her door, frozen in place and listening. She heard her husband sigh, almost groan.

"How are you holding up?" he asked.

"I'm fine, Benny." The voice on the other end of the call sounded weary.

"And your cover?"

"It's getting harder every day to channel Meltdown, but it's holding. Look, everything's okay. I wouldn't have even contacted you if it weren't for..."

"I know," said Benny. "I'm still having trouble wrapping my head around it."

"I just can't figure out why they would use *her*." He cleared his throat. "She used to say it all the time. Whenever things got rough, whenever I was down on myself. *The stars will turn for you.* That same face, the same expressions. It can't be a coincidence."

"And you're sure she's a synthetic?"

"Like nothing I've ever seen before, Benny. She's a brand-new deal."

"Then she has to be part of whatever Joe Perion is cooking up. I say you stick by her, let her lead you to the answer."

"I don't know if I can..."

"It's personal now. If Perion made a synthetic out of Eileen... I'd..."

"You'd what, boss?"

Yeah Benny, thought Eileen. What the hell would you do?

"I'd ask for another." Benny gave a brief chuck. "One for the plane, one for the Seattle office."

"That might make Mrs. Coker jealous."

"She already thinks I'm cheating on her, as if Cora is a tenth of the woman Eileen is. At least I'd be cheating on my wife with *my wife*."

"Good luck feeding that. I'm gonna head back to the condo and lay low for a bit, figure out how to move forward. It just feels like something has started, Benny, like we've reached some kind of critical mass. I don't know how much longer I'm going to be able to stay in the PC."

"That's completely up to you."

"I may not be able to call again for a while."

"Upload when you can, and only when it's safe."

"Will do, Benny."

"Take care of yourself, Gilbert."

Eileen stood in the darkness of her room for several minutes, first listening to her husband's retreating footsteps and then to the ringing in her ears as the silence took over. She sat down on the bed and grasped at the echoes of Benny's words. Would he really want multiple copies of her? Did he really miss her that much?

She waited for an answer that never came. Instead, a soft knocking sounded from the door.

"Yes?" she asked, her tears not far off.

"Mrs. Coker, a waiter is here with the drinks you ordered," said Daryl.

"Come in," she replied, turning away from the door.

Rubber soles against hardwood floors; a tray sliding across her dresser; the tinkling of ice in glasses.

She didn't turn around until she heard the door close.

The waiter was still standing there.

"Is there anything else I can *do* for you?" he asked, his fingers already working at the buttons of his shirt.

Eileen put up her hand. "Not tonight, Tyler. Not tonight."

TWENTY-THREE

Friday turned to Saturday, and Gilbert Reyes sat with his legs dangling over the edge of the loading dock behind the warehouse, trying to beat back the sudden cold with a warm cigarette. He didn't normally smoke—synth alternatives were safer and more satisfying—but he needed an excuse to go out back and make a phone call. It was risky calling Benny on an unsecured line, but the news couldn't wait. He tried to minimize the danger by pulling the SIM card as soon as the call ended, snapping it in two before throwing the pieces in opposite directions. And since the phone would still give off an exploratory signal without it, he pulled the battery and tossed it at the gate on the far side of the parking lot. Now the phone sat on the evercrete beside him, disassembled and useless.

Gil understood the feeling. Seeing Jackie in the synthetic flesh had hollowed out something inside of him, a space he thought he had long since filled with acceptance.

He took a long drag of the cigarette and heard Jackie's voice saying, "Those things will kill you." As if he had anything to fear from cancer. At the first sign, Benny Coker would have shelled out the money for the VTech—anything to preserve the life of his deep cover aggregator. But he couldn't tell Jackie that, couldn't let slip his true employer. To her, he was just a handyman with a penchant for trite Zen aphorisms, someone she called when her terminal froze up or when the copier broke down. He was one of the few commoners allowed in the Spire, though only when summoned by some brainiac who could synthesize human emotion but couldn't figure out how to read their email without downloading every virus known to man.

That damn copier.

Gil hadn't shown up at the Spire that morning expecting to meet the woman of his dreams, but he was blown away by her presence all the same. She had met him in the lobby, signed him in through the security checkpoints, and rode with him in awkward silence to the eleventh floor. And even though Gil found the problem immediately, he stalled for time, using the interim to ask Jackie about her life, what she did, and who she was seeing.

Only after working up the nerve to ask her out did Gil finally toggle the power switch, sparking the hulking machine into operation again. He took the time to show her how to do it herself, enjoying the closeness of her body as they leaned over the copier.

That was all it took, one little service call.

The rest was a memory Gil thought he had buried. There was a foggy, damp part of his life he never looked into anymore, a place full of Jackie's smiling face, infectious laugh, and biting wit. Those memories often tried to draw him closer, but he knew he would never find her there.

The cig wore to the filter. Gil stubbed it out on the evercrete.

"Who were you talking to?" asked Gantz. The door banged shut behind him, pulled abruptly by the coiled spring above its frame.

"No one," replied Gil. "Just checking my messages."

"You talk to your messages?"

"What's it to you, Copper?"

Gantz chuckled. "So, I thought you said you'd done this kind of work before."

"I said I've read the ReTread spec. There's a big difference between wiping out someone's identity and undoing whatever your people did to that girl. Emotional attachment to a synthetic baby? What'd she do to deserve that?"

Gantz dropped into place at the edge of the loading dock, brushing the dismantled phone aside.

"She broke into the Spire, on one of the sub-levels. An Automated Guard got ahold of her, put her out before we even knew what was going on. They called me in, but by that time, the decision had already been made. It came from the top."

"From Perion?"

The chief hesitated. "Yeah, from Perion. I didn't want any part of it, Gil. I've seen things over the last few days that have made my skin crawl, but nothing as fucked up as this."

"And she's not a native."

"Not only is she an outlander, she's Lincoln Tate's main squeeze, and probably his favorite aggregator at the moment. Just look at the story she'll be taking home."

"If she gets out of here at all," said Gil, wondering for a second if Benny might actually suggest giving Tate a little setback by taking out his only aggregator on the inside.

"She'll get out. Soon as she wakes up, I'm taking her and Cam to the border myself. Hopefully I can get them past the PNR before anyone knows what's up."

Gil looked at the chief of police through a narrow eye. "You having a crisis of conscience, Gantz?"

He scoffed. "You think I give a fuck whether these two live or die?"

"Then why help them?"

Gantz looked up at the stars. "Because a shift is coming, Gil. The rules are breaking down; right and wrong depends on who's in charge. And when it all falls apart, the only authority left is the higher one." He paused for a moment before bringing his eyes back down to Gil. "Things are about to get real complicated and the less players on the field, the better. Look at those two in there—shit-stirrers, both of them. It's bad enough corporations are collecting and selling our personal info, but now we've got these rodents picking through our garbage, trying to find something juicy to feed to the masses?"

Gil faked a laugh and looked away to a flashing traffic light at a nearby intersection. "So that's why you don't feed?"

"Perion discourages it. He says there's enough corruption through conventional means already. He's always telling me about the time—"

"You've talked to him?"

"Does that surprise you?"

Gil shrugged. "He always struck me as a bit of a recluse, not counting his occasional public appearances. I didn't think he spoke to anyone."

"He has an inner circle, and I've sat in on a few important dinners. This one time, he had a little too much to drink and someone brought up the feeds. He said ninety-nine percent of it was crap. Said the only way to make sure you came out looking good on the feed was to give them *your* version of the story. Don't let them figure it out for themselves. Control your own destiny and whatnot."

"How pragmatic," said Gil, turning his face to the breeze.

Across the street, little red lights danced in the shadows—access card readers or perhaps the eyes of primitive synthetics working the graveyard shift.

"What did you think of the old man?" asked Gil.

Gantz hunched forward. "Just a regular guy, I guess. No different from you or me. He's got charisma, I'll give him that. I wasn't much for his ideas or visions, but he's always been good to me. Sitting with him, talking with him… you can't help but want to follow, even if it's not in the right direction sometimes."

"And yet you've worked with him for how many years?"

"Ha," said Gantz, slapping his knee. "I've always worked for Mr. Perion, and I always will."

"Sounds like something a synthetic would say."

"Damn straight," said Gantz. "That's why I get myself checked out every month. A little trip out to the PNR answers that question quick, fast, and in a hurry."

"Seriously?" Gil shook his head.

"I wouldn't put it past him. The man does what he wants. For the longest time, that was limited to what is socially acceptable in this country. But as time goes on… well, that's why we don't let aggregators in here. They may only see the horror and not the reasoning."

"Hold on," said Gil, raising his hand. "How can you claim there are special projects Perion didn't want anyone to know about while *two* aggregators who showed up got assigned personal prototypes that have never been announced, talked about, or even acknowledged? Cam's feed has been active for days and it's just going out there for the world to absorb. You don't think Cyn is going to start feeding about the daughter she never had as soon as she wakes up?"

"Cyn won't be feeding a goddamn thing if she knows what's good for her. Cam, on the other hand, I can't put a stop to. The order from on high is to let him feed whatever the hell he wants. Why he hasn't put out more than a single photo of Roberta or mentioned the Collapse at all, I don't know. All I know is I asked about putting the squeeze on him while we regrouped and got denied." Gantz laughed. "Arrogant little prick's been walking around like he owns the place, but he's got charisma like Big J and some of the shit he says... he kind of grows on you."

"Like Big J *had*," said Gil.

"What?"

"You said Cam has charisma like Big J has, like he's still alive. All week I've been expecting a parade or something, a final tribute to the great Creator. But I haven't seen anything and no indication from anyone in the company that James Perion is actually dead."

"Probably more legal than anything else," said Gantz. "The board has to figure out how to keep the company running, who should be in charge—that kind of stuff."

"They couldn't send a memo after what happened Tuesday?" Gil shivered at the memory of the rolling tide of whispers announcing the death of the Creator as it washed over the city.

Every synny in town had dropped dead in the street, but eventually they regained their footing, resumed business as usual. The humans had followed their lead—with everyone expecting the company to make an announcement of some kind. When none came, perhaps people assumed the whispers had been lies, that their fearless leader wasn't really dead.

But then why had Gantz gotten choked up that day? Why did he tell Gil that James Perion had passed on?

Gil suspected turmoil in the Spire, but there were precious few copiers breaking down these days, and he hadn't been inside in months. In a way, it was a blessing. The Spire reminded him of Jackie, and every time the elevator doors opened in the lobby, he hoped to see her face appear. She'd be wearing her hair up during business hours, with a few intentional strands hanging loosely over her black glasses.

The memory shriveled in the cold.

"You alright there? Kinda drifted away for a minute."

Looking over his shoulder at the warehouse, Gil said, "Roberta gives me the creeps."

"Really? Cam seems to be into her, *way* into her, if you know what I mean."

A fist shot out and caught Gantz in the meaty part of his arm.

"What the fuck was that for?" he asked.

Gil reached for the remains of his cell phone. He paused. "Well, I can't show you, but I had a picture of Jackie on my phone."

"Yeah, I was going to ask you about that. Who is she? I've never heard you mention her name before."

Who *was* she, thought Gil, for like James Perion, she could no longer be referred to in the present tense. Perhaps if he and Gantz were better friends, Gil would have told him about the woman who—

The screen door behind them screeched.

"Gilbert," said Cam, slightly out of breath. "Cyn is waking up."

Gantz nodded approvingly and tagged Gil on the arm. "Looks like I won't have to take you in for murder after all."

"You punch like a synthetic bitch," said Gil, standing up. He paused at the door. "You coming in?"

Gantz nodded. "In a minute. I need to check my messages."

TWENTY-FOUR

The warehouse was home to rows upon rows of synthetic women splayed out for provisioning and Gil couldn't keep his eyes from studying the details of their faces, wondering if there might be another Jackie lookalike laying on her back with her legs spread and a gaping hole where her synthetic vagina should have been. Gil wanted to ask the question of *why*. Why did synthetics need working sex organs?

He looked up at the wall of frosted bags.

Was there another warehouse down the block with a wall full of bagged dicks? Couldn't both male and female synnies get by with superficial detail? Why did they need to be functional and replaceable?

The answer, of course, was standing guard over a groggy Cyn, holding a screaming synthetic baby in her arms, and looking more and more like Jackie, with whom Gil had spent a few wonderful years of his life. Someone must have seen in her the same beauty Gil did and decided to make more copies—more Jackies running around town breaking the foolish hearts of brilliant men, tricking them into loving her only to die suddenly and tragically, leaving the men alone with their hearts so full of fear that even the idea of love caused them a mild panic.

We seek in others what we are missing in ourselves.

Jackie, more than any woman before, had filled some void in Gil he hadn't even known was there. Maybe Perion thought every man carried around a similar emptiness and that was why Jackie clones were being built as sex dolls for the American masses. One day, Roberta would be on sale at synthetic dealerships all across the country and some trust-fund sleaze bag would purchase her, take her home, and treat her like shit, even by synthetic standards. He'd have his fun with her, oh yes, he would. And Jackie, the *real* Jackie, would have no say in it.

Someone would have to speak up on her behalf.

Gil avoided Roberta's gaze and focused on Cyn, who was now rolling her head back and forth like a drunk who couldn't figure out which way was up. He pulled at her eyelids to check her pupil response.

Cyn forced his hand away with an angry swat.

"Will someone shut that goddamn baby up?"

Roberta pulled Candice closer to her chest and turned away. She walked down a few tables to try to quiet the baby.

"There's a break room back there," said Gil, motioning to the far wall.

Roberta nodded and whispered soothing sounds to Candice that were drowned out by Cyn's cries.

"Can you tell me your name?" asked Gil, taking Cyn's hand.

She jerked it away. For a moment, there was anger in her eyes, but recognition finally took hold. "Gilbert Reyes," she said.

"Fuck," said Cam. "She thinks she's you."

"Yes, I'm Gilbert Reyes. I helped reset you. But now we've got to make sure you're still you."

Cyn sat up and tugged at her shirt, pulling it down over her exposed belly button. "Whose clothes…"

"You can get some new ones once you guys are safely out of the city."

"I'm not leaving," said Cam.

Gil took a step back and put his hands on his hips. "You think being forced to love a synthetic baby was bad? How much longer do you think they'll let you walk around their city with impunity before they trigger whatever secondary protocol they have looping around in that thing's subsystems?"

"Roberta?" asked Cam. "She's harmless."

Gil raised an eyebrow.

"To me," he clarified. "If anything, she's protected me from every major threat I've experienced since I got here."

"Yeah," said Gil, "like she was designed for it, right? You just happened to be paired up with a prototype who A, wants to protect you, B, seems to almost *love* you, and C, is walking around with the face of my dead girlfriend."

Cyn stopped groaning as silence took hold of the warehouse.

With heat rising in his cheeks, Gil began packing his equipment into his tool bag. The laptop scraped against wires and metal clasps, until finally the zipper whined as he closed up the bag. Walking towards the door, he felt their eyes on his back.

"Gil, wait," said Cam. "I didn't know."

"Of course not," replied Gil, spinning on his heels. He spread his arms. "How could you have known you were lusting after a synthetic woman based off of my very real Jackie? That's your problem, Cam. You roll into the PC like you're above us all and you make a fucking mess. This is *my town* and *my*—"

Story was the word he wanted to say.

"So, what?" asked Cyn. "You're jealous? Is that what this is about?" She had swung her legs over the side of the table and was regarding the floor with uncertainty.

The urge to hit her made Gil's arm tremble, but he knew what she was capable of, had seen traces of augments in her system. Still, that didn't give her license to be ignorant.

"No," he answered, his voice low and calm. "I'd feel jealousy if Cam were actually dating Jackie, if Jackie actually loved and protected him. But he's started some sick relationship with a *thing* and it'll be a sunny day in Margate before I'm caught in bed with a fucking machine."

"She's more than that," said Cam. He crossed his arms and leaned against the table next to Cyn.

"Sure, if you say so, but consider the possibility that it only *appears* that way, that the humanity you see in her is only there because it was stolen from a very real human, from *my* Jackie."

"How can you even know that for sure?" asked Cyn.

Gil started to reply, but her question was valid. After all, he had only done a cursory investigation, seen the wrapping on Roberta's synthetic body and heard her speak just a few lines. Maybe they had done it as an homage or by randomly selecting a pretty girl from the company directory. And there were things Roberta did that Jackie never would have done, almost like...

"I need to scan her," said Gil. "If they used Jackie's personality as a base, then they could have done the same kind of modification they used with Cyn. You were still you, just with a few pieces changed. She could be Jackie carte blanche."

"Do whatever you want," said Cam. "She's not mine." He looked away.

It was all the invitation Gil needed. He set off for the break room but ran into Gantz coming down the aisle.

"She alright?" he asked. His cheeks were red from exposure.

Gil glanced backwards to make sure they were in earshot. "She'll be fine. She doesn't have any attachment to the baby anymore. I suggest you dump it at the nearest fire station. And Cam claims to feel no attachment to his synthetic, so now's as good a time as any to separate them. Is there any kind of plan to get them out?"

Gantz smiled and touched Gil on the shoulder as he passed. "God always has a plan, my friend."

Gil shook his head and continued on to the break room, moving past the second row of tables where the synthetics began to take on more ethnic diversity. He wondered who they were based on, which Perion employees had had their likenesses stolen for use in the synthetic sex trade.

"Fucking Joe Perion," he muttered. Even if it had been his father's idea to start this madness, Joe was the one letting it continue.

The break room was lit only by the streetlamps outside and a small bulb in the vent above the half-stove. Gil could just make out Roberta's outline sitting on the far end of a couch, a bundle held snug in her arms. She was staring straight ahead, ignoring the synthetic baby who, through some mutual understanding, was remaining perfectly quiet. It wasn't until Roberta detected Gil's presence that she began to move again, bouncing the baby as if she were trying to calm its nonexistent tantrum.

She looked up at him with orange light sparkling in her eyes.

"I know you," she said, her voice rising and falling in the unique cadence of the sweetest woman Gil had ever known.

"Do you?" he asked. "Why don't you let me scan you and we'll find out?"

Roberta shook her head. "No. I don't think that will be necessary."

"Why not?"

She smiled, revealing perfect assembly line teeth. "You know why, Gilly Bear."

Gil's heart shuddered and he felt himself fall two inches before his muscles kicked in. The pet name evoked images of Jackie lying in bed with a sheet hung over her stomach, with one hand supporting her head and the other reaching out for him across the gulf.

"Gilly Bear," she would ask in the first light of morning, "are you awake?"

"How," he stammered. "How do you know that name?"

Roberta set the baby down on the couch and stood up. Shadows hid half of her face and body, but the uncertainty somehow made her look more like Jackie.

"I don't know how," she said, taking a step forward. "There are so many memories of you, locked inside." With those words, she touched her chest just above her heart. "I can ignore them if I really try, but... I don't want to. I feel you in there. I just didn't know it was you until I saw you."

She paused at arm's length, removed her hand from her heart, and placed it on Gil's chest.

"Do you feel *me* in there?"

Gil gulped.

He wanted to reach out for her, put his hand on hers or draw her near, but his body wouldn't move. Staring into her eyes, he realized he was actually scared of her, scared she might come closer and rekindle the feeling he had worked so hard to stamp out.

You can't love a synthetic; he didn't need Meltdown to tell him that.

"You do feel me, don't you?" she asked.

Roberta closed the distance, pressing herself to Gil's chest.

Gil felt her pelvis against his erection and tried to move away, but a synthetic hand slipped behind his neck and held him in place.

"It feels good to remember, doesn't it? You were my Gilly Bear and I was your J-boo. Do you remember how you used to call me that? In the mornings, when you woke up, hard like you are now, and we'd fuck until we were late for work, until we lay there panting like a couple of animals? Yes, you remember."

Gil gnashed his teeth. "I remember fucking Jackie," he said, swallowing hard. "I remember fucking a woman. You're neither."

Thin fingers dug into the back of his neck, pulling his lips to Roberta's. In the instant they touched, Gil questioned his own declarations. Whether she was Jackie or a real woman, whether it was wrong to bed a sex doll, there was no denying the electricity flowing from Roberta's lips, no denying the exquisite taste and texture.

Gil dropped his tool bag to the floor and wrapped his arms around Roberta's waist. And there in the orange light of the streetlamps, man and machine kissed.

TWENTY-FIVE

Gil had often thought of Jackie in the moments before he fell asleep, when the lights in the room were so dim the LED from his phone lit like a road flare every time a new message came in. Darkness, two quick vibrations, and then the walls were bathed in a sickly red, telling him the world was reaching out to him, trying to get his attention. Only he didn't want the world's attention, didn't care what new products Katsumi marketers were trying to sell him. Only three important updates ever passed by way of his phone: Benny Coker with some fresh encouragement, his other boss, Lori Maxwell, with some middle of the night emergency tech repair gig, or Jackie, with a simple note telling him how empty her bed felt without him, how she was burying her face in his pillow to be reminded of his scent.

Lori's messages still came with regularity, though Benny's had petered out over the many months. Jackie...

Well, it felt like forever since her profile picture graced his phone.

Change is eternal and constant, a never-ending series of cards being dealt to all players at random.

It was difficult not to think about her, not to get a little excited every time the LED began to flash, especially if Gil had fallen into half-sleep and forgotten Jackie was gone for good, never to return to Perion City or even the land of the living. His imagination would not be stifled though, and he often wondered what would happen if she did come back, if one day he saw her walking down Twelfth Street with a wide-brimmed hat and shopping bags on her arms like some kind of Rodeo princess. He always imagined her like that, in a fairy tale sort of way where her life exceeded that of her previous existence. She was no longer a clerical aid in this new reality, but rather a woman of money and influence, of unarguable beauty and refinement, as she deserved to be.

And in those half-dreams that had left him sad or sexually frustrated, he had never imagined he would see her again under the swinging lights of a warehouse as they stood over the body of an aggregator who had snuck into the city and...

Gil shook his head, found he was gripping the steering wheel too tightly, turning his knuckles white. Beside him, Roberta sat quietly in the passenger seat, hands folded in her lap, her head turned toward the window. Sunrise was still a couple of hours off, and Gil could see the dashboard instruments reflected in her window. The blue LED indicating the status of the headlights fell on the reflection of her lips, giving them a wet tint. He thought about those lips and how they had felt pressed against his.

Sneaking out of the warehouse without telling the others had been an impulse decision; Cam had professed no attachment to Roberta anyway. Leaving the baby behind made practical sense, as it would be discovered in the morning when the first shift crews came in. It wasn't until Gil paused at a stop sign three blocks away that he risked looking back at the warehouse. Dark from the outside, the only discernible light came from one of the front windows, and it was very faint at that.

"We shouldn't stop," said Roberta, her eyes focused on the rearview mirror. "They'll be here soon."

"Who?" asked Gil. He searched the road for any other sign of life.

"Sava Kessler, head of public relations and a ripe old bitch."

Another one of Jackie's sayings.

"I don't see anyone."

"I can feel her," said Roberta. "She is getting closer. If she finds Cam with Cyn, she's not going to let him out of here alive." Her voice wavered; she touched her lips to stem the betrayal. "I'm imprinted on him," she explained.

Gil nodded, unconvinced.

"Drive," she said, "before they—"

Lights exploded in the clouds over the warehouse in three clustered sets of four—spotlights from unmanned drones. Gil had seen them before, mostly on reconnaissance runs from the Spire to the PNR. Rarely had their black hulls been seen in the skies above Perion City during the day; it would have spoiled the entire utopian illusion, one Gil had found himself believing in more and more these days.

Cruisers shot in from the cross streets and pulled up to the front of the warehouse. Automated Guards poured out of them, their guns trained before their boots even hit the pavement. Roberta gave a soft yelp, and Gil removed his foot from the brake.

He drove as if the AGs were already on his tail, making multiple lefts and rights, but always adding distance between himself and the warehouse. The navigation system in the dash showed he was heading towards the outer border of The Fringe. There, a recently constructed loop would let him circle around the majority of the warehouses and factories to rejoin the main highway on the north side of the city. The outer loop even had some traffic on it already, mostly trucks making their early morning deliveries, getting fresh supplies to the donut shops in midtown. Gil found a spot between a pickup and a van and let the autodrive take over.

Autodrive.

That's what Gil had been on since the moment he decided to leave with Roberta. Maybe it was because she had begged him in Jackie's voice that he had believed it was a good idea.

Gil studied Roberta's profile, tried to see motivation in her synthetic lines.

The car took a long, curving flyover onto the Perion Expressway and proceeded into the sleeping city. The Spire glowed dully as the sky began to warm. More commuters joined the flow; the short-timers were making their way to work. Diners lit up the side of the road every couple of miles, ready to fuel another day of innovation in the ol' PC. Roberta watched it all pass by without a single word, as if her mind were elsewhere.

"That's my condo, just up on the right there," said Gil. On cue, the garage door began to roll into the ceiling and a line of LEDs lit up the single-car space.

They waited until the door had closed behind them before getting out of the car. Gil led Roberta out of a side door and up a flight of stairs. Running lights glowed from the floorboards in the living room as he opened the door.

He watched Roberta explore the condo. She regarded the space with placid eyes. Maybe recognition was too much to ask.

"Have a look around, see what you think," he told her, tossing his tool bag onto the low table behind the sofa.

The hallway responded to his presence, brightening like a child's face at the return of its father. At the end of the hall, the ceiling in his bedroom ramped up to a soft glow; shafts of light danced above him in crisscrossing patterns. Gil eyed the bed with its one side of the covers pulled back, the pillows pressed up against the headboard—an invitation he almost accepted when he stepped into the room.

At the dresser, Gil stared himself down in the mirror as he removed his shirt. The warehouse had been rather dingy and his white button-up was scuffed with black marks. He would have to take it to the cleaners today, see if they could…

A memory flashed: Meltdown rolling his eyes in boredom.

Gil put his hands on the dresser. For the first time, the gravity of his predicament hit him full force. What would Lori Maxwell think when she found out her best employee had absconded with a prototype synthetic? It wasn't like pocketing a few office supplies.

The clock in the mirror showed it was just passing five thirty; luckily, the letters *SAT* were written above the numbers, giving him the day off. He wouldn't be expected back at work until Monday morning, which meant he had forty-eight hours before anyone realized he had deviated from his normal routine. And they *would* realize it. Someone was always watching and waiting for one of their little cogs to get out of line.

Gil pulled a t-shirt from the second drawer and sat down on the edge of the bed.

Yesterday had been fine, he recalled, just another day in the life of an undercover aggregator covertly feeding information to Benny Coker and The White Line. How many years had Coker been relaying the tidbits Gil was able to send him, throwing them out as suppositions instead of the cold hard facts he knew them to be? The ruse had gone on far too long.

"No," said Gil, to the t-shirt in his hands. He unfolded it, found he had pulled a race shirt from a 5K a couple of years ago—the last one he had run-walked with Jackie.

It wasn't the ruse or even how long it had gone on that was the problem. It was the corporeal ghost standing in his living room. It was Jackie returned.

Prior to his stint in the PC, Gil had worked the garbage-filled streets of Atlantic City, slipping in and out of various personas to gain confidence and information about the underbelly of a city whose veins were clogged with corruption and evil, with a steamy black liquid that led back to an ashen heart buried somewhere underground. Stories about the heart always made the best feed, especially for the locals. Sometimes they forgot just how horrible their own backyard could be. Benny Coker liked to remind them.

That, too, had gone on for years. The more times Gil escaped certain death, the more invincible he thought himself to be. Then one day he impersonated the wrong guy, ended up taking a meeting with a Vinestead enforcer who hadn't appreciated the deception. Gil was found bloodied and naked in the slums of Margate the next morning. After that, Vinestead had been gunning for him. Coker allowed two attempts on Gil's life before shipping him out west, out to the one place even the 'Stead couldn't reach him.

Waking up in that alley under a rotting cardboard box had been a *life-changing moment*, an indicator that things had gone too far over the edge, that life couldn't continue as before.

It was Vinestead's doing then; it was Perion's doing now.

When the end comes, it will come smiling and whispering words of comfort.

Gil cocked his head and listened for the synthetic in the living room, but all he heard was the dull hum of the heater and the rush of air through the vents. He pulled on the t-shirt and stepped into the hallway, half expecting to see the front door thrown wide with nothing remaining of Roberta except her perfume lingering in the foyer. Instead, he found her sitting on the couch, her gaze focused on the vidscreen on the opposite wall. Pictures scrolled across its surface, fading and star-wiping through Gil's history—more accurately, his history in Perion City, a history delicately intertwined with a woman named Jackie.

The screen paused on an image of Gil's living room, reversed, as if looking into a backwards mirror. In the pixelated memory, he was sitting next to Jackie. They both held a glass of wine; a blanket covered their legs. They were suspended in the moment before a kiss, a moment etched on every synapse in Gil's brain.

The anticipation, he recalled, had been exceeded only by the contentment, the simple happiness of having her nearby.

As the picture faded, the spell holding Roberta captive broke. She turned her head just enough for Gil to see her profile and the simulated tear descending her cheek.

TWENTY-SIX

In the kitchen, Gil poured himself a glass of water and stood at the refrigerator wondering why he was so surprised to discover Roberta could cry. She was, after all, a prototype beyond anything he had ever encountered. Even on his trips to the Spire, the synthetics had been nothing to write home about. They were advanced, yes, but primitive and clunky machines next to Roberta. They were not exactly uncanny either; you could always spot a synny amongst the organics, especially if you had been in the PC long enough, had watched the evolution with wonder as Gil had. Maybe in the back of his mind he knew one day they would get so advanced as to be indistinguishable from humans.

If Roberta could cry, then maybe… she could feel?

Gil turned his back to the fridge and stared at Roberta over the counter. She was lost in the swirling pictures on the vidscreen, entranced as if she had never seen a photo slideshow before. Was she doing what everyone else did when the screensaver kicked in, simply looking for themselves in the menagerie? There were as many pictures of Jackie as not, most of them with Gil by her side, a loving hand draped around her hip.

Was it difficult to see yourself in photos your brain could not remember, to be shown a life that used to be yours, but with every trace of it removed from your heart and soul?

Gil looked around for his palette and found it dormant in its dock on the table. He scooped it up, loaded his notebook, and began a new dossier for Roberta. He paused as he considered what to put for a surname, as synthetics typically had one or the other.

"Do you have a last name, Roberta?" he asked.

She was unwilling to take her eyes off of the show. "Mendes, but that doesn't feel right anymore. What was Jackie's?"

"Dulac," said Gil. He thought about writing the name next to *Roberta* in his notebook, but it didn't seem right. Roberta was not Jacqueline Dulac of 117 Gracy Farms Road, apartment 928, Perion City. She was not the Jackie who had stood in the kitchen three years ago and burned a batch of ice cream cone cupcakes.

A memory sparked.

It had been Jackie, not Roberta, who had reached for Gilbert Reyes in the middle of the night.

Roberta could then not be a facsimile of Jackie because Jackie was defined not only by how she affected the world, by what she did and said, but also by how the world treated her. And though Roberta might find her way into Gil's bed and might, in the middle of the night, pull up close behind him and slip a hand over his waist, he would never be able to do the same to her, would never be able to put from his mind the simple fact that Jacqueline Dulac was dead and gone. The sum of her existence was now only video, pictures, and text… and the dwindling memories in Gil's head.

For Perion Synthetics to bring her back, to give a synthetic Jackie's visage and verbal ticks, even her wonderful curves and impeccable posture, was an affront to nature and to those who loved her. More than that, it made no commercial sense. If the endgame was a product, something to be *sold*, then making it closer to human was commercial suicide. Buying and selling appliances was one thing; buying machines with memories and feelings was akin to buying humans.

The line between man and machine is forever blurred, Gilbert. The world does not see a difference, so why should you?

Gil wrote down Roberta's last name and filled in some physical characteristics from memory. He paused again at occupation and settled on *Synthetic Human*. It sounded right, anyway. More than any simple task assigned to her, her first job was to be a close approximation of humanity. For that job there were no breaks, no sick days.

Finally, he reached the blank line where he would write his topic question, the number one mystery he thought Coker and the world would want solved. Usually this question came after a long struggle. Humans were so complex and their stories so varied, but with Roberta, the question was too easy and came with such quickness that Gil found himself typing it before he had even completed the thought.

Why do you exist, he wrote.

Could Roberta even answer such a question?

Gil felt the reality of the situation as a throbbing in his stomach. His time in Perion City was coming to an end and the only way to go out was with an explosive bang that would shake the Spire to the ground.

It was what they deserved after disrespecting the dead. If Joe Perion thought he could do whatever he wanted…

The thought fizzled out in Gil's mind, replaced as always by the immutable time scale, the mental rule he used to arrange events in the past. James Perion's death stood like a beacon upon the line, obscuring the years that had come before it, but with a little concentration, Gil was able to see past the blinding light to the foundations on which his assumptions were based.

He shook his head. It had seemed natural to blame Joe Perion. Office gossip had it the boy was a loose cannon, off developing his own line of synthetics in areas the old man didn't agree with, things like sex dolls and military units. Gil would have believed every one of those rumors if it weren't for Gantz, who rarely had a discouraging thing to say about the next ruler of Perion City.

Maybe it was all a ploy, a calculated move to have a rumor out in the world to provide plausible deniability should word ever get out that there was a factory in The Fringe whose workers toiled day and night to repair engineered vaginas and fabricated cocks for a variety of lifeless synthetics. The old man could claim ignorance, give his son a slap on the wrist, and business would go back to normal.

From the people Gil spoke to, there was no doubt the sex dolls, or synthetic companions, as they were listed in the catalogue, were real. Only research in that area could have given Roberta the natural skin suit she wore. Only trial and error could have improved the internal mechanics such that she weighed a buck and some change. Preparing her predecessors for the sex trade had made Roberta more than human—their loss of humanity had increased hers.

So that takes care of her body, thought Gil.

For her mind, it wasn't a stretch to imagine the military applications for a thinking machine, synthetics who could react and plan in a battlefield situation—drones with minds of their own.

The pieces began to line up in Gil's mind. Seemingly random areas of study seemed to be converging on one ultimate goal.

But *why*?

Gil put the palette back in its dock and sighed. A sudden ache grew from the back of his head to envelope his entire brain. He stumbled to the couch, convinced that at any moment he might collapse from the pressure. Sinking into the cushions next to Roberta, he joined her in the passive observance of his photos.

After a few minutes, Roberta said, "You collect people, you know that?"

Gil barely heard her over the throbbing. "I what?"

"The way you take pictures. The way you organize them. It's like you're building a collection of people."

"I don't…"

Roberta pointed to the vidscreen. "Look, this picture is normal, just you and Jackie out at a restaurant. But then…" She waited until a specific picture popped up. "This is like a passport photo: straight-on, no expression, and nothing distracting in the background."

Gil stared at the worn face of Eric Rusk, who worked on the twenty-eighth floor of the Perion Spire as a marketing admin by day and an underground human-synthetic fight promoter by night. The synnies were usually already damaged in some way or handicapped by strategic snipping of vital tendons. Rusk justified the fights as a way for people to get exercise, learn to fight—the questionable list went on and on. Gil saw it as taking out aggression on poor synnies who couldn't fight back.

"A punching bag is a punching bag," Rusk would always say.

The story, titled *Synthetic Fight Club*, had been finished for over a year, shelved in some databank back in Atlantic City. Coker had enjoyed it, thought it oozed with the sickness affecting so many people in the AC. A little west coast disease for the east coast immune system, he had called it.

"Why do you have so many pictures like that?" asked Roberta.

Because Perion Synthetics is full of humans and humans are sick, conniving bastards who never fail to probe the depths of their depravity, Gil thought.

"There can't be that many," he said.

"Forty-eight." She turned to face him. "Kind of a strange hobby, Gilly Bear."

"What do you know from art?" he asked, feigning offense. "I like to take pictures of people's faces. Big deal."

Gil stood and retreated to the kitchen again. From the end cabinet, he pulled a bottle of aspirin and shook three white pills out onto the counter. They were chalky on his tongue.

"It's not just that," said Roberta. She had pulled herself up into a kneeling position, arms resting on the back of the couch. "You look the same age in all of these pictures. How far back do they go?"

"Far enough," whispered Gil. Then, louder, "Maybe my college photos just aren't a part of this stream."

"*Did* you go to college?"

His laugh echoed in the kitchen. "It's like you don't know me at all."

Roberta crossed her arms. "I only know what Jackie knew, and she didn't. There's nothing about you on the network before you came to Perion City. Your personnel record lists your previous employer as PracTech out of Flagstaff, but that doesn't wash with your Jersey accent."

"I don't have an accent," said Gil, listening to his words. They were clean, devoid of any AC affectations.

"Not that any human can hear," said Roberta, smiling. "But I'm more observant. I can practically smell the shore on you. So I wonder, why didn't your J-boo know anything about your past? Why didn't you tell her where you're originally from? Was your entire relationship built on lies?"

"I loved her," he said, his eyes dropping to the floor. "I would have loved her until the end of time. That's all that mattered."

Roberta considered the claim, relaxed, and sat back on her heels. A mischievous smile crept onto her face, put there by a million tiny servos embedded in her lips. For a while, she simply stared.

Finally, Gil asked, "What?"

"She loved you too," said Roberta. "Even at the end."

TWENTY-SEVEN

Gil sat on a worn stool in his workshop and stared at the folded piece of paper in his hands. It was a note from Jackie—the only hardcopy she had ever given him and the only thing she left behind.

Gil thought back to that summer evening and how he had come home after a long day expecting to be greeted at the door with a kiss and a hug from the only person in Perion City who brought him happiness. Instead, he had been met with silence and a jarring absence of all things Jackie. Her throw pillows were gone from the couch. Her glass shelf in the bathroom had been cleared. Shampoo and conditioner bottles sat atop a pink loofah in the trashcan.

The pristine condo made Gil wonder if his entire life with Jackie had been nothing more than a rush fantasy, a wandering of his idle mind. It was then he spied the note sitting on the dividing counter between the foyer and the living room.

Gil, the note read, *my love for you will always remain, in some form or another.* Not a rush dream after all.

Jackie had been in his life, and now she was gone.

It was worse than never having her there in the first place.

He had turned on the television absently, more to drown out the stifling silence than anything else. And as his eyes read Jackie's handwriting for the hundredth time, his ears picked up the voice of KPC anchor Lauren Simmons reporting on an accident on the Perion Expressway. A delivery van coming from Perion Terminus had blown a tire and jumped the median. It struck a taxi, killing both the driver and a female passenger.

"The victim's name has not been released, pending notification of the family."

When Gil's phone began to ring, his shaky hands could barely answer.

And so Jackie left without explanation and whatever reconciliation Gil could have hoped for had died along with her on the Perion Expressway. He had kept the letter safely hidden in his toolbox, folded gently and placed in a small compartment within the red lid. He didn't take it out often, but every time he opened the toolbox, he saw the edges of the paper sticking out, reminding him of what he had lost.

In some form or another.

It wasn't exactly poetry, and at the time, Gil had written it off to what he imagined was a waning interest in their life together, as if Jackie's real life were a wheel rolling along at a set speed, occasionally picking up people and things, carrying them through one or two revolutions, only to leave them on the ground once more, changed for better or worse, far from where they started. That's what Gil felt when he held the letter in his hand, when he sat on the same stool where Jackie had once walked up behind him and slipped her arms around his stomach and laid kisses on his neck; where he had spun around and pulled her close, sinking his hands down the back of her pants to squeeze her butt, a gesture that had always evoked a playful groan.

A note, a handful of memories, and a lingering question of why Jackie had gone and how poor her decision must have been to get such a strong karmic reaction.

Gil laughed. It was the kind of Meltdown-brand, Zen bullshit he might use on the feed, a scenario so overblown it could only be found on The White Line. Only Coker would make Gil dress it up, give it a spin worthy of its primetime slot.

Love and intrigue in Perion City.

Just like some Banks Media fluff piece.

Gil returned the letter to its resting place, folding it carefully to keep from stressing the paper. He closed the toolbox and put it back on the shelf next to bins of various computer parts he hadn't used in years. There used to be a time when repairing machines made sense, but working for Perion had shown him that not only was replacing the entire system easier, it was preferred. Just RMA the copier and send the defective unit back to the warehouse. Let the DeVry graduates tinker with it for a while.

"We can make you a technician," Coker had told him. "You like building computers, right?"

Gil had tried to explain it was just a vestigial pastime from youth, that now he cared more about being other people, slipping into places where he didn't belong, and getting the scoop no one else could get.

Looking around the converted bedroom, Gil tried to remind himself this was all an act, an illusory persona crafted for a singular purpose: to infiltrate Perion City. And he had done that. In another reality, he was already packing up his stuff and making a break for the PNR—he would have done so before the sun even cracked the horizon.

But because of Jackie and Roberta, the sun was already up, the day already set in motion.

Gil wondered what Coker would say if he simply abandoned the story, if he got in his car and rammed the synthetic guards at Outpost Alpha. It could work, though he wouldn't be able to take Roberta with him.

Footsteps in the hallway.

Roberta was standing at the door, a hint of worry in her eyes.

"She's coming," she said.

"Stay here," said Gil, as the soft tones of the doorbell began to echo down the hall. He looked around the room. "Don't touch anything and don't come out until I say it's safe. You hear me?"

Roberta took the seat he had vacated and nodded. "I hear you, Gilly Bear."

"Don't call me that," he replied, shutting the door. He secured the electronic lock with a four-digit code.

The doorbell chimed again before he made it to the foyer. On the wall above the light switch, the vidscreen showed two people standing outside. One of them was Gantz, still dressed in his gorilla suit, but he had tightened it up since their bullshit session behind the warehouse. The other was a younger woman whose hardened face Gil couldn't place. She looked impatient, and as the delay dragged on, she nudged Gantz in the elbow, to which he sneered and rapped harshly on the door. The sudden sound made Gil recoil.

"Who is it?" he asked.

Gantz looked directly into the security camera and said, "Perion City PD, sir. Can you please open the door?"

"Just a minute," replied Gil.

He scanned the room, but Roberta had left no traces in the condo. He dimmed the lights in the living room and kitchen, shed his pants, and tried to wrinkle his shirt as much as possible. The photo stream on the vidscreen continued to scroll; Gil slapped the remote control to turn it off. Then, as he opened the door just enough to get his head through, he tried to effect a fatigued look.

"Mr. Gilbert Reyes?" asked Gantz. His eyes flared for a moment, entreating Gil to go along with the deception.

"Maybe after my coffee," he replied. "Is there something I can help you with, Officer?"

A flash of recognition passed Gantz' face and he suppressed a smile.

"I'm Chief—"

"Where were you at eight p.m. last night?" interrupted the woman.

"I don't see how that's any of your business, lady."

"Mr. Reyes," said Gantz, "there's been an incident in The Fringe this morning. A vehicle registered to you matches the description of a car seen leaving the area."

"*My* car?" asked Gil. "You mean someone saw a blue Nissan on the road and you came *here* first?"

"We had to start somewhere," said Gantz.

The woman broke in again. "You didn't answer my question."

"I don't see why I have to."

Gantz cleared his throat. "Mr. Reyes, this is Sava Kessler, head of public relations for the company. She's investigating the disappearance of a prototype synthetic, handle Roberta. Have you seen any prototype synthetics running around the neighborhood?"

"She has a Brazilian template," said Sava. "Brown hair, light brown eyes, slim build."

"No," said Gil. "Not my type. I'm more into Asian prototype synthetics."

"Really?" asked Gantz. "But they're so small."

Gil shrugged. "We all have our tastes."

"Hey, asshole," barked Sava. She shoved the door open. An involuntary glance down at Gil's loose boxers made her lock eyes with him. "This isn't a social visit. You're a person of interest in a very serious investigation." Then to Gantz, "Make yourself useful and check the GPS in his car. We don't have time to be fucking around."

Gantz nodded and held out his hand. "I'm sorry to inconvenience you, Mr. Reyes. If you could just give me your keys, I'll do a quick check of your car."

Gil hesitated, but the look on Sava's face told him there would be no argument. He pulled the key fob from the bowl on the dividing counter and handed it to Gantz.

"It's in 8F," he said. "Door code is 0724."

Sava folded her arms as Gantz disappeared down the breezeway and stairs.

"So," said Gil. He searched for pockets to bury his hands in, found none, and ended up scratching himself.

Sava huffed and turned away.

"Do you work in the Spire?" asked Gil. When she didn't respond, he continued, "I've been there several times. Nice place. Always very clean. Kinda cold though, don't you think?"

A noise from behind caught Gil's attention. He turned and looked down the hallway. With the rest of the condo dimmed, the workshop's light blazed from behind the door. Shadows crossed the thin beam at the bottom of the threshold; Roberta was pacing the room.

Gil stepped away from the door.

"Stay where I can see you," said Sava.

"Just grabbing the remote," said Gil, scooping it up from the back of the couch.

The vidscreen popped back on and he tuned it to the local KPC news station. Once again, Lauren Simmons appeared on his wall, her long blonde hair framing a thin face, one punctuated by the brightest red lips super definition could deliver. Although the sound was muted, Gil gleaned everything he needed to know from the inset video in the upper right-hand corner. It showed the warehouse where he had brought a woman named Cyn back from mental death. It looked different now, as all things tended to when they were engulfed in flames.

"Looks bad," said Gil.

Sava turned to face him, followed his gaze, and nodded at the vidscreen.

"Was anyone hurt?"

"A few fatalities," she replied.

Was that satisfaction in her voice?

"Who?" asked Gil, pushing the words past the lump in his throat.

"You tell me."

They stared at each other for several seconds before Gantz came lumbering up the steps again, slightly out of breath.

"Car checks out clean," he said, tossing the key fob back to Gil. "Thank you for your cooperation, Mr. Reyes."

"Sorry I couldn't be of more help," said Gil.

Sava stared at Gantz for several seconds. "Okay," she said, "then I guess we're done here." She turned and headed for the stairs, pulling her phone from her pocket as she went.

"Have a good day, Mr. Reyes," said Gantz, following after her.

Gil peered into the breezeway just enough to see Gantz turn and walk backwards. He made a series of gestures: first, pointing to Gil's condo, then miming breasts with his hands, then finally flashing a questioning thumbs-up.

He knew, or at least, he suspected. Leave it to the Chief of Police not to miss a damn thing.

But then why had he lied about where Gil's car had been?

Gil glanced over his shoulder and then back at Gantz. He nodded, made an OK sign.

"Move your ass, Gantz!"

The chief put a finger to his lips and then hurried down the stairs.

TWENTY-EIGHT

The vidscreen in the kitchen came on at seven, as it had every Saturday and Sunday morning for the last few years. Previously, Gil had used the droning of the morning news to get him out of bed, and then later, as a backdrop to a breakfast of peanut butter toast or instant oatmeal. He hardly ever watched the television, instead preferring to flip through the feed board on his palette. Specialized apps pulled data from the big three feeds and displayed them in a carousel of content. Small up and down arrows below each story let Gil customize his megafeed, which over time, learned his preferences: technology, gadgets, and naked women.

Though Benny Coker might not have liked one of his aggregators subbing the other feeds, he knew it was necessary for Gil's cover, as showing preference for any one media house might reveal him to be biased. Besides, Lincoln and Banks put out good content from time to time. At the core, it was all the same news. When a pic of some celebrity getting out of a low car in a short skirt popped up, it was only a matter of time before it appeared on all three feeds. The only thing that really mattered in the feed business was who had it first.

Coveting everything leaves you with nothing.

Gil stood with his forehead pressed against the front door waiting for the adrenaline to drain out of his body. It pooled in the small of his back, causing the surrounding muscles to spasm in protest. Even though Gantz had covered for him, Gil still read suspicion in the Kessler woman's eyes.

"Mr. Sedivy, can you comment on the rumors of James Perion's death in Perion City?"

Gil turned at the mention of Arthur Sedivy's name. He approached the counter and put a hand on the back of a stool.

On the screen, Arthur Sedivy looked regal in his navy-blue suit and black tie—a uniform for Vinestead International executives if there had ever been one. Though anyone else would have been put out by a mid-meal interruption, Sedivy simply smiled and folded his napkin. There were a few seconds of playacting, as if he were trying to choose the right words instead of already having a prepared statement.

"Obviously," he began, ignoring the reporter and staring straight in the camera, "the entire Vinestead organization is deeply saddened by the recent stories implying the death of James Perion. As I understand it, he is battling, or was battling, a common form of cancer. I, of course, put the whole of Vinestead International at Mr. Perion's disposal, to include my personal medical team, but for his own reasons, Mr. Perion has declined my assistance. Although we did not see eye to eye on many things, there is no denying he is a pioneer and a visionary, two qualities this world is severely lacking. If he has truly passed on, then the world has suffered a great loss."

"There is speculation that Joseph Perion will take over the CEO position. Have you spoken with him? Is there any truth to the speculation that Vinestead International will try to acquire Perion Synthetics?"

Gil raised an eyebrow. Vinestead acquiring Perion was a stretch; nothing on the feeds for the last few days had even suggested such a thing.

Arthur Sedivy looked away for a moment and almost laughed under his breath. "Speculation," he repeated. "Someone on Wall Street is trying to position Perion stock for a quick cash-out. The acquisition of a company is not something we would do on a whim, nor on the mere rumors of a CEO's passing. This is a difficult time for Perion Synthetics. Out of respect for their family, we should reserve our speculation until the Perions have had time to get their house in order. At any rate, Vinestead Synthetics continues to make great strides. We will have some big announcements in the new year."

Vinestead Synthetics, thought Gil. What a joke.

No other company had generated as many sleek product images and lofty marketing claims as Vinestead's synthetics division. When Perion announced a new breakthrough, Vinestead followed it up with a similar but slightly better claim. The only difference was Perion had the hardware to back it up; all Vinestead had was a marketing department.

And there was the true loss. If Arthur Sedivy had any clue how advanced Perion's synthetics were, he wouldn't be out having dinner at a faux Italian restaurant; he'd be pouring every dollar he had into R&D. Perion's offerings were going to change the world, were going to put Vinestead in its place once and for all. And if last month's model wasn't enough, then there was Roberta, a fully formed realization of James Perion's ultimate dream. He could flip the cards over as if they were trash: cooks, messengers, and babysitters. Then, as Vinestead reached for the pot, he'd throw down his pair of aces, two identical copies of Roberta and her stolen personality.

It was in the way she looked at him, the combination of her twinkling eyes sitting above her reddening cheeks that let Gil know Jackie was in there somewhere. And though her future owner might not know Jackie's name, they would at least see a person, see the body language and mannerisms as real as anyone else's in the PC. With early synthetics, there had always been a desire to see them as real, to marvel in the novelty of the uncanny. With synthetics as advanced as Roberta, it was a struggle just to remember she was artificial. The lure of accepting her as human was just too much.

Gil touched the vidscreen and powered it down. There was no point in watching the rest of the interview; any interesting sound bites would be packaged up by a fellow employee at The White Line and would appear on the feed within a few minutes. Besides, there were more interesting things happening closer to home.

In the hallway, Gil stared at the thin blade of light seeping out from beneath the door. A sound came with it, growing louder as he approached his workshop, fluctuating like a variable-speed fan. Up and down, the noise pitched, reverberating in a tiny knot in Gil's stomach. He had left the room with everything powered down. The only moving parts would be…

"Roberta?" he called.

There was something else too, something beneath the hum, something grating and electronic.

Gil took a mental inventory of his workshop and thought of the various tools capable of making such a sound, settling on the hardened laptop he had used since the Margate days. He wondered how its fan had sounded the last time he used it, and suddenly he remembered the warehouse and the trace and replace on Cyn.

There had been shouting at the time, a sense of urgency, so the minor issue of a fan wearing down had left no impression on him. But he did remember the whine, the strident pitching of the power supply about to lose a capacitor. Even as Cyn writhed on the table, Gil had been thinking about how hard it would be to find a comparable part.

Gil approached the workshop door and keyed in the passcode, expecting to find his rugged computer beeping away on the workbench.

Instead, he discovered Roberta lying on the floor.

From the position of her body, he assumed Roberta hadn't fallen. She was lying perfectly straight with one arm by her side and the other outstretched to the laptop on the floor a few feet away. Slack wire traced a line from the laptop back to her neck and that was when he noticed her eyes were pegged open. The laptop's screen scrolled the same code Gil had used to restore Cyn, though the output looked garbled now.

Was she running the trace and replace on herself?

Gil rushed to Roberta's side and put an exploratory hand against her cheek.

"Hey," he said, shaking her at the shoulder. "What are you doing?"

There was no response. The independent threads responsible for making Roberta into a facsimile of a living breathing person were offline, likely crashed by the invasive software Gil had acquired at Pritchard Sansbury's in the AC. There was no way Meltdown could have known the program would one day be run against a synthetic human or that it would shut her systems down cold.

Gil pulled the electrode from the back of Roberta's neck and noticed for the first time she had a jackport hidden beneath her hair, as faint as a watermark. He climbed atop Roberta and straddled her stomach. Again he shook her; her body felt light in his hands, but she did not move on her own.

Something had gone wrong with the code, something in the way it performed the trace had been incompatible with the assumed intelligence of a synthetic. Gil thought maybe Roberta's programming had become corrupted, that her running config now contained extraneous characters that didn't translate into real instructions. If she were a photocopier or a network router, the only course of action would be to reboot her and hope her ROM contained enough information to bring her back online.

Gil scrambled over Roberta's body to the shelf on the far wall and began digging through the rows of bins. Buried at the bottom of one container, he found a card marked *Boot and Nuke*. He palmed the card and pulled wire cutters from his toolbox.

His eyes fell on a lamp in the corner of the room. With a grunt, he was able to pull the cord from the base, revealing two frayed ends. He stripped them with the wire cutters to expose the copper and then knelt beside Roberta's head.

Rolling her onto her side, Gil placed the nuke against her jackport and waited for its LED to light up.

Under his breath, he prayed.

If the nuke didn't work, that would be the end of it. He'd have to make a run for the PNR and get out of Perion City before Kessler figured out Gantz had lied to her. She'd come back with more firepower and kick down the door. And Roberta would still be there, lying on the floor like the inert doll she was.

Gil made sure he wasn't touching any part of Roberta as he pressed the bare wires to her neck just below the card. There was an audible pop in the room and the lights continued to flicker for several seconds after he removed the wires. Tremors raced the length of Roberta's body, shaking her fingers first before rattling up her arms and into her torso. The sequence repeated in her feet, culminating in a vibration in her chest that reminded Gil of a heartbeat.

Roberta's eyes rolled around in their sockets, finally settling on Gil. She smiled briefly before her eyes widened in shock.

"Gil? What happened?" She sat up and reached for him.

Gil took her into his arms and hugged her.

"It's okay," he said. "You're okay, baby."

Small hands pressed at his chest, pushing him away until he could see the sadness in her eyes.

"No, Gil-bear. I'm not."

TWENTY-NINE

"It's like waking from a dream," said Roberta as she searched for a comfortable position on the couch.

Gil nodded and checked his sliver for the hundredth time. It was glowing bright red, but he was sure that at any moment, the light would simply blink out and the live stream to The White Line would disappear with it. Seeing Jackie emerge from Roberta's skin had given Gil the confidence—the justification—to begin feeding openly for the first time since his arrival in Perion City. His transmission was sure to be noticed, whether by local monitoring or by the reaction of the world as the content hit the feed. Calling it risky was an understatement, but the world needed to know that a woman Gil had known and loved had been repackaged into a synthetic being.

It was because of his personal interest in the story that Gil reverted to a previous revision of himself, that of aggregator, a persona whose mannerisms were automatic, whose questions just happened to fall in line with what he wanted to know. And if *he* wanted to know the answers, then he was damn sure Benny Coker would want to know, and in turn, every Shore Dog and Umbrat in the country.

Coker, for his part, didn't even question the uplink. At least, he hadn't said anything over the whisperer yet. Gil assumed Coker was equally enthralled with Roberta's story and was pleased with the line of questioning so far.

"Go on," said Gil.

Roberta looked away to the screensaver on the vidscreen.

"You're aware of the dream while it's happening," she continued. "But it's not until you wake up that it all condenses and you realize none of it was real. I remember things that didn't happen to me, faces without names. I remember you helping a woman, but not here." She looked around again, her eyes searching out something familiar.

"Cynthia Mesquina," said Gil.

"She didn't like me very much," said Roberta. A chuckle escaped her lips—a human one. "And the man with the stubble?"

"Cameron Gray."

It wasn't like Cam and Cyn wouldn't have blown Gil's cover if given the chance. A billion curious fingers were likely hitting the search engines, elevating two previously incognito names to the most visible points on the grid. If they were in the feeding game for fame, then they would both get more than they could handle.

Assuming they were still alive.

"I feel something for him, or did," said Roberta, touching her chest. She held her hand there for several seconds. "My heartbeat is so soft. I can barely feel it."

"What's the last thing you remember from before?" asked Gil.

He grabbed the remote from the coffee table and switched the channel to The White Line home screen. Perion was still blocking the incoming feeds, leaving the scrollers at the bottom of the screen blank, but the stats were there, along with a photo of a smirking Benny Coker dressed in Midwestern formal. The White Line's market share, which normally hovered in the low twenties, had climbed to the ungodly height of forty-four, and was still rising. Gil watched as every question he asked, every response Roberta gave, caused a blip in the rolling line graph. In the upper right-hand corner, the SatIndex grew at a slower pace; people were probably too engaged with the story to upvote it.

Roberta glanced at the screen when it flickered, but didn't recognize Coker. She shook her head. "This is too strange. It's like these memories aren't my own. I can remember being in my car, driving on the PE, and then I'm outside with that Cameron guy. And the weather's changed and I've changed." Her lower lip began to tremble.

"It's okay, Rob—Jackie. We're going to figure this out."

"It's not that," she replied, forcing a laugh. "You don't work for Perion Synthetics without partly believing someday you'll wake up in a synthetic body. There were always jokes, you know, of them wanting to transplant a human mind into a synny. Everyone laughed at the idea, but I think we all secretly feared it."

"It'd be a breakthrough," admitted Gil. "I mean, it *is* a breakthrough. Here you are, right?"

Roberta looked down and examined her hands as if they were completely new to her. "I'm not here. This is not my body, no matter how much it looks like it. The real me is out there somewhere. Why isn't she here with you? How long has it been?"

For a moment, Gil wanted to turn off his sliver, but the numbers on the screen were just too high. To propel The White Line to the next level, to give Benny Coker a heart attack and make Eileen a slightly richer woman, he'd have to sacrifice a little of himself.

"The last time I saw you was here," said Gil. "Right over there by the door, actually. It was morning, and you were leaving for work. Later, in the evening, I came home, but you didn't. All of your stuff was gone. You didn't even say goodbye."

"I left you?" asked Roberta.

Gil nodded. "Four months ago. July 7. It was a Tuesday. You left on a goddamn Tuesday, Jackie. Without any warning at all."

"I remember my Rogue, but I don't remember packing it or ever wanting to leave you."

Gil could see the pain behind her eyes, the frantic shifting back and forth as they sought out a memory that simply wasn't there. A synthetic should have been able to recall any moment in its existence with perfect clarity, but evidently, that didn't apply to the memories they had stolen.

Maybe they had played around with her synapses, removing some and leaving others, perhaps choosing to block out what had happened when she headed out on the Perion Expressway with her entire life packed into the back of a taxi.

Gil's brain ground to a halt.

Taxi? Or her Rogue?

Either Jackie was misremembering the details of a major life choice or...

Look for the angle, Gilbert.

Coker's words echoed in Gil's head. He had often made mention of *the angle*, bringing it up whenever Gil set out on a new adventure to investigate illegal augmentations in the Manhattan Underground or to sample the latest offerings of the Margate synth pushers. According to Coker, it didn't matter what happened to whom or when or with what. It was the *why* that people cared about, the sequence of events and motivations that led us from point A to point B. Causality, he claimed, ruled the universe and all of the inhabitants of said universe were painfully aware of that natural law. It was human nature to seek out the reasoning behind everything and invent explanations when no true cause could be found.

Gil had once called the theory bullshit, only for Coker to reply, "Hell, it gave us religion, didn't it? So you go out there and find those people a reason. Explain it to them so they don't have to worry their simple minds about it. It hurts less for them to be told why than to let them think for themselves."

A hand on his leg made Gil look up.

"Where'd you go?" asked Roberta, smiling.

Jackie used to ask that whenever Gil drifted away to the workshop in his mind to puzzle something out. Roberta was laying it on thick. The question was *why*.

Look for the angle.

Why would a synthetic pretend to know him, pretend to want him? What was there to gain by attaching to Gilbert Reyes, handyman extraordinaire? Unless...

Maybe it was just a chance meeting at the warehouse. Maybe those mixed feelings truly were pieces of Jackie bubbling to the surface. But once Roberta was in his home, looking over his pictures, something had changed.

Something had been noticed.

"Do you know what I do for a living?" Gil asked.

"Make me happy?" asked Roberta in return.

"You know what I mean. Do you remember?"

She flashed a frown, as if hurt by his disregard for her joke. "You do tech repair," she said. "You come in when things break and make them work again. Right?"

"No, not right. I work for Benny Coker's White Line media feed. I came to Perion City four years ago to keep tabs on the development of a new synthetic race. Almost everything you know about me is a lie."

The SatIndex shot up ten points; people were intrigued. The new high made Gil smile, but he knew no good would come from exposing himself. He could have denied being the source of the broadcast, but attaching his name to the meta, plopping it down on the grid with the others, was something he never thought he'd do. It was a last resort tactic, something Benny Coker wouldn't have suggested no matter how good his hand.

"Why are you telling me this?" asked Roberta.

"I'm not the man you think I am. And I'm telling you this because I don't think you're who you say you are either."

"But I have her memories, her feelings. I feel love towards you. Isn't that enough?"

"I'm not here for love," said Gil, standing up. "I'm here for the story."

He walked into the kitchen and pulled down a bottle of Skyy from the freezer. A shot glass he had stolen from a bar in The Fringe was already sitting out on the counter. The vodka went down easy.

He cringed at the thought of how the real Jackie would have reacted to his rejection. It would have crushed her. She would have cried. Her heart…

"Of course you're just here for the story, Gilbert Alejandro Reyes of Leonardo, New Jersey. That's all you care about, because that's what Benny Coker has drilled into your head. You believe it so much you don't care who you hurt along the way."

Roberta rose and stood in front of the couch.

From behind the counter, Gil raised his glass to her. "To synthetics with feelings."

"You think you've been enlightening people with the little stories you've been feeding over the years? All you've done is set research back and help Vinestead keep pace. Every leak cost people their jobs. And for what? For a SatIndex? For market share?"

The dumber Gil felt, the more he drank. He had let her into his home, had been overcome with emotion for a dime store reproduction of a woman who hadn't loved him enough to stay with him.

And now his name was in the meta.

Gil downed his fourth shot and felt the warmth spread through his stomach. It wasn't the first time he had been conned, but no one had gotten him this good since his early days when he was making his way down the coast to the tech Mecca of Atlantic City. He'd arrived without the clothes he'd so dutifully packed, without the food or money that was supposed to sustain him on his trip. He'd arrived with nothing but a growing knowledge of the streets and a natural knack for social engineering. Those were the skills Benny Coker had tried to hone, but it hadn't been enough.

Nothing could have prepared Gil for life in Perion City. These were supposed to be the good guys, the ones you could trust. If Vinestead had been the target, Gil would have remained on guard for the duration. Instead, he'd become complacent and happy with Jackie.

Look for the angle. Find it before it finds you.

Gil drank another shot to Coker's sage advice.

"When did you know?"

"*It just feels like something has started, Benny, like we've reached some kind of critical mass,*" said Roberta.

The phone call to Banks from the warehouse—they had been onto him from the start.

Gil replayed the early morning events. When he got to Roberta and his workshop, the angle finally crystallized.

Roberta wasn't trying to reset herself; she was trying to steal his trace and replace program, code that could undo the best brainwashing of Perion engineers.

They got me, thought Gil. And they got my code.

"So," he replied. "Do I have time to pack? Or maybe a quick shower?"

"You thinking of running?" asked Roberta. "Not a good idea. They'll find you before you make it past the inner loop. And of course, you'd have to get through me first." She folded her arms and stepped closer to the door.

Gil laughed as he tried to pour another shot; it sloshed around in the glass and spilled on the counter. "It's a shame, you know? I bet I'm gonna regret not fucking you when I had the chance. You look like you were built to be ridden hard and put away wet."

Benny Coker's favorite saying in regards to Atlantic City escorts sent The White Line's market share to fifty-seven percent—an unprecedented occasion ruined by Roberta's cold laughter.

"And I would have let you, if that's what it took."

"Too late now?" asked Gil. "I mean, surely we have some time to kill before the police knock down my door."

"You don't get it, Mr. Reyes. I have your dead lover's memories. She didn't want to be with you, let alone have you flopping around on top of her."

Gil's vision had blurred, but still the market share numbers climbed. He poured the last of the vodka into his glass and raised it to the unseen audience. Their applause was deafening in his ears, making him smile. In his stomach, the liquor sent out comforting signals, tricking the brain into thinking everything was going to be okay. But it wasn't.

He stared at the empty bottle on the counter.

Sweet liquor eases the pain.

Gil was pretty sure Meltdown had never said that.

As the laughter threatened to overwhelm him, Gil reached for the bottle and whipped it at Roberta. It hit her squarely in the face, as if she hadn't even tried to move out of the way. Shards of glass exploded outward, covering the foyer in shiny glitter. A rivulet of crimson appeared on Roberta's forehead; it descended between her eyes, to the right of her nose, and came to rest at the corner of her mouth.

A bright pink tongue darted out and tasted it.

"I'm going to take my time with you, Mr. Reyes," she said, taking a step forward. "You think it hurt when I walked out of your life before?" She smiled; the blood broke free and dribbled down her chin. "I'm going to show you the true meaning of pain."

Gil bowed his head and looked at the shot glass. He had known there was going to be violence; it was for that reason he had begun drinking. The liquor would dull the pain, but the Margate chip in his neck would start pushing that gritty Jersey synth into his brain to keep it active. It wasn't invincibility, but it would keep him from freaking out when Roberta began breaking his bones.

"Alright," he said, adjusting his waistline. "Let's begin then."

THIRTY

"There are two types of people in this world: those that rush, and those that don't."

Leave it to a Margate rusher to simplify the world's population into two easily defined groups. Patrick Kumanov, whose business card gave his name only as Meltdown, often talked of the dividing line between the unenlightened and the transcendental. If you weren't rushing, he'd say, you weren't really connected to the universe. Only under the influence of a synthetic drug could a person finally see reality for what it truly was.

"Think about it for a minute," Meltdown had said one night while he and Gil tripped on a synthetic hallucinogenic known as Smashed Peas. He was leaning back in his favorite chair at Pritchard Sansbury's, a converted sim parlor whose machinery had been removed in favor of eclectic seating and dim lighting. It was still a parlor of sorts, except the clientele now preferred to trip in the comfort of their own minds.

"All these people," he said, gesturing to the circular couches set apart in the spacious common room, "are somewhere else right now. Each one is plugged into their own version of reality. Artists do this too, without the synth. To truly create something, they have to detach from this reality. A writer will sit for hours thinking about an entire microcosm that *doesn't exist*. That means, at any given time, millions of these artists are not connected to *this* reality. How scary is that?"

"What about aggregators?" Gil had asked.

"You're the worst of it. You think you're exposing the real world, but it's all at the mercy of the Almighty Filter. You pick up on something your boss doesn't like, and it'll never make it to the subby's whisperer. The houses think they're selling reality, when actually they're just selling perspective. Because that's all life is, a series of shifting perspectives. The story's never quite the same from the other point of view, is it?"

"And this will change my perspective?" Gil held a code card in his hand; its polished white gloss bounced the blue neons from above.

"When the time is right. It's a TSR variant of a military-grade enhancement program, reverse engineered from a burnt Ayudante chip."

"TSR?"

"Terminate and stay resident," Meltdown explained. "It will be with you at all times and activate when you need it most. Consider it a gift from one Bodhi to another."

Leave it to a Margate rusher to compare himself to the Buddha.

Gil shook his head at the memory of Patrick Kumanov, surprised by its sudden appearance and clarity. Why had the rusher's image come back to him now? Was it merely the splash screen of the TSR finally ramping up?

Roberta was over the counter before Gil could settle on an answer. Her small frame rotated in the air, going fully horizontal before swinging her legs beyond the edge of the sink. She slid down the veneered countertop, landing simultaneously on both feet. The first jab caught Gil by surprise, landing hard in his throat, causing a brief moment of panic as he struggled to breathe. He took a quick step back and felt his heels hit the refrigerator.

Roberta's arm shot out; Gil ducked and threw his weight towards the sink. At the last moment, he pushed off with his legs and launched himself over the counter. The plan had been to land as gracefully as Roberta so he could take off running, but instead, his foot caught on the faucet, causing him to crash to the floor and land on his back, knocking the air out of him. As the pain coursed through his body, Meltdown's voice spoke in his mind.

"You shall not rejoice in the killing of any living creature," said the rusher.

"She's not alive," Gil replied, straining to get the words out.

Like a vision emerging from a transcendental haze, Meltdown's face appeared. He blew a plume of smoke from the side of his mouth.

"Well then, I suggest you tear that bitch up."

Gil had only met one person in his entire life who had an Ayudante chip besides Cynthia Mesquina. He was MoA infantry turned Atlantic City street rat. It hadn't been an easy task getting out of the MX; the loss of his right leg and the burning of his Ayudante were the eventual tolls he had to pay. Still, he retained his memories and had story enough when Gil came around asking.

"It's like your first orgasm, every single time," the former *soldado* had said, trying to describe the totality of the chip's control. "There's a jittery feeling as it comes on, and you don't know what's going to happen. You're scared, but there's also a sense of well-being. Then you're hit with an unbreakable calm. It can resist everything the enemy throws at it: fear, doubt, and even pain. You can take a bullet like a slap on the wrist."

Scrambling to his feet, Gil looked around for Roberta, who was still standing in the kitchen, a thin smile on her face. There *was* a feeling in his stomach, but it was likely from the Skyy and not the foreign Ayudante code. He took a step towards the door, only to see Roberta slide across the tile floor and plant herself in the foyer. She hunched over and bent her knees, reminding Gil of a blitzing linebacker. With blood smeared on her face, she had never looked more unlike Jackie.

"You can't do this," said Gil.

"I'm pretty sure I can," Roberta replied.

"You see this?" He held up his wrist as if it were a holy relic. "You know what this flashing red light means? Everything we say or do is being broadcast live on The White Line. If you kill me, hell, if you so much as bruise me, everything Perion has done will be for nothing. Lay a finger on me and you'll kill the public's trust in Perion Synthetics forever."

Roberta shot forward, reaching for Gil's arm. Her fingers closed around the sliver in his wrist and squeezed.

At first, it was just a mild pressure; the vodka had dulled his senses sufficiently enough, but nothing could compete with the sensation of bones crumbling between synthetic fingers. The cracking sound echoed in the condo, each reverberation ripping at the lining in his stomach. Gil visualized his wrist turning to white shards, mixing with the sliver circuitry to create a non-viable, human-machine sludge.

The pain was intense but brief, occurring so quickly Gil wasn't sure it had happened at all. The blood was there, as was the mangled flesh and a hand hanging loosely from taut skin, but there was no data coming in, no mention of organic damage in any of the trillion signals passing through his brain. All he felt was detachment, an almost refreshing peace of mind.

On the vidscreen, the market share swelled, but the SatIndex took a huge hit as millions of angry subbers downvoted the sudden dead air.

Roberta had broken his wrist, and more importantly, the uplink.

A knee came up between them and Roberta buried it in Gil's chest. The acceleration backwards felt like falling, but Gil was able to get his body turned around before toppling over. Now he was falling forward, in the direction of the glass doors of the balcony. Instead of trying to stop himself, he pumped his legs and listened to Benny or Meltdown or someone in his head telling him to raise his arms and use them to protect his face.

The impact rattled his remaining bones.

How many times had he watched people go through windows and glass doors in movies? It had always seemed so effortless, but of course that was because it was fake glass, or pre-cut, or something other than the thick double-pane separating Gil's living room from his balcony. It almost felt like the glass wouldn't give; his elbows made no dent on their initial contact. Then his body hit and the door shattered before him, sending shards of glass into his forearms and torso. On some level, he registered the accompanying pain, but the Ayudante envoy was singing an inviting tune, drowning out everything else in the world.

Gil used his momentum to hurl himself at the railing. This time, there would be no jump, just a shifting of weight over the side to whip his legs up. He closed his eyes as he became weightless and didn't open them again until his shoulder dug into the soft grass, separating it from the socket. Gil let out a curt howl, then became quiet again. Staring into the brightening sky, he gave thanks that he was able to see it—

"Again, I'm addressing the current leadership of Perion Synthetics. You have a product that is out of control and threatening the life of one of my aggregators. You are also holding two aggregators from Banks Media and Lincoln Continental. If our people are not returned unharmed, we will have no choice but to hold Perion Synthetics and its employees personally responsible. Again, I'm addressing…"

"Coker?" asked Gil, looking around for his boss. He realized the voice was in his head, coming across the feed through his whisperer. Coker must have boosted the signal to get past the PC blackout. Jacking the repeaters was a trick that could only be used a couple of times; that Coker had used it to help Gil…

Roberta's face appeared over the railing of the balcony. Her eyes widened when she saw Gil lying on the grass.

He rolled onto his stomach and used his good arm to push himself up. His legs felt like sandbags, but at least they kept him upright.

The courtyard behind his condo was formed by the cornered arrangement of four buildings. Exits to the streets sat on the midpoint of each side, all pointing to a raised center where several picnic tables and two grills sat unused in the chilly weather. It was deserted; Gil looked around at the windows facing into the courtyard, wishing and hoping someone would be standing at one, perhaps sipping a cup of coffee, unaware they were about to see the first synthetic on human murder since Vinestead launched their NORM series.

A thud sounded from behind, and Gil ran.

He didn't know where he was running to, only that Roberta was behind him and if she got her hands on him again, she wasn't likely to let go. He opted for the closest exit, off to the left. He could see the black, wrought-iron fence growing out of the high shrubbery on either side of the path. He imagined himself hitting the gate, thrusting downward on the handle, and pushing his way out into the street. There, he would be able to flag down a car, or maybe someone would see him.

A sharp pain tore into in his calf muscle; a glance backwards revealed the retreating toe of Roberta's shoe. The remaining power in his legs gave out and he tumbled to the ground, once again landing on his shoulder. His little slice of Ayudante tried its best to block out the signals, but it gave up when Gil attempted to use his broken wrist to turn over.

When the pain got through, the fear followed close behind it.

Roberta was on his back in an instant, digging a knee into his spine and grabbing at his arm. She yanked his mangled wrist and twisted it behind him, as if it could be broken further. She answered Gil's cries with laughter.

"Let go of this reality." Meltdown's voice faded into nothing.

Gil raised his head and looked to the windows again, then to the gate where a dozen men in black riot gear were streaming into the courtyard. As they fanned out, a woman emerged from behind them.

Sava Kessler. And Gantz?

The chief trailed after the head of public relations, whatever emotions he was feeling hidden behind his sunglasses. They walked with urgency, but not fast enough for Gil.

"Get this fucking thing off me!"

"If you think they're here to save you," said Roberta.

"Roberta, directive!" Kessler's shout cut through the ringing in Gil's ears.

He tried to turn his head to see the synthetic's reaction and noticed more security filing in from the other gates. They joined together around Roberta and Gil, forming a circle.

Or a screen.

Kessler stopped a few feet away.

"Imprint protocol Alpha," she said. "Gilbert Reyes."

The pressure on his arm lessened, fell away. Sweet relief swept through his body as Roberta's knee slid from his back.

"Thank—"

"Confirm imprint," said Roberta, her voice flat.

Kessler nodded at her. "Confirmed by Sava Kessler. End this piece of shit."

Gil felt hands grip his head: one on the back and the other under his chin.

"Gantz, what the fuck?" screamed Gil, but the chief only turned further away.

There are two types of people in the world: those who rush and those who are dead.

Hyperventilating, Gil found it difficult to yell, but he managed to curse Sava Kessler, Robert Gantz, and the whole of Perion Synthetics before Roberta's hands pulled with all of their synthetic might.

Gil heard the wrenching sound, could almost visualize the tendons and muscles snapping.

There was a brief flash of Jackie's face before the world went dark.

THIRTY-ONE

The servers at The White Line pegged at one hundred percent utilization as the clock hit 8:34 on the morning of November 14th. A tapeworm planted by one of its employees, an aggregator by the name of Gilbert Alejandro Reyes, had just counted the last of its forty-eight intervals necessary for determining whether its programmer still walked the earth. Having received no feedback for two full days, the tapeworm set about liberating Gil's personal information from the databanks, both local and abroad. LEDs flashed, routers and switches glowed, and fiber connections full of viral code reached out to the world.

Backups hidden in the furthest reaches of VNet spontaneously combusted. Medical records safely stored in the firewalled servers of various New Jersey hospitals overwrote file handles with gibberish. At Affinity Credit Union, money jumped from a forgotten account into one owned by Maribel Reyes, raising her net worth by two hundred thousand dollars in the blink of an activity LED. The empty account then vanished into the ether, along with its backups on the archaic tape machine in the basement.

Within twelve minutes of starting, the whole of Gilbert Reyes' existence had been wiped from the grid and reduced to nothing more than an echo in the feeble memories of the people who had known him.

And if Gil had known this was happening as he lay panting on the floor of a dark room, he would have been pissed.

As it was, he had bigger things to worry about than being unemployed, penniless, and according to the United States government, non-existent. There was a languid quality to his body, as if he were stuck half in and out of a dream, staring at a reproduction of his bedroom, trying to get out from under the comfortable sheets but not realizing he was still asleep. The commands that would normally turn his head or raise his hands were muddled or ignored, resulting in an ineffectual flopping around like that of a drunk person.

After a few minutes of grunting, Gil found himself on his back, staring at the ceiling. His head fell to the side, allowing him to see a shaft of light coming in around the frame of a door. It was thickest at the bottom; shadowed footsteps crossed the amber glow, though none of them stopped or even slowed when he called out.

His mind raced, faltered.

There should have been pain, and lots of it, but he had been able to turn his head without any signals shooting through his nervous system. The realization spawned relief; perhaps Roberta hadn't broken his neck after all. Maybe she just maimed him, enough for Kessler to take pity on him and bring him back… where?

Gil felt around in the dark for his arm, felt the solid wrist that should have been in a million pieces.

"Fuck," said Gil, his heart picking up the pace.

He continued exploring, clamping his fingers around his wrist. He repeated the action on the other hand, just in case, but it too came up empty.

His sliver was gone.

An uncoordinated hand sought out the back of his neck, tried to find the small scar from the jackport. Instead, his fingers traced over unbroken skin.

The sons of bitches had taken his jackport too.

Gil wanted to laugh, but his sore throat flared every time he took a breath. He felt neutered, disconnected from the glittering world. Benny Coker had probably shit himself when the feed went dark. Whatever heights The White Line had reached during Gil's livecast were probably a distant memory now.

"The stars turned, didn't they, Coker?"

His listened for a response from his whisperer, but heard nothing, not even the signature white noise to let him know it was there.

"An aggregator without a whisperer. What the fuck is the world coming to?"

At least he was alive. Just thinking about the injuries to his wrist, shoulder, and neck sent a shudder up his newly repaired body.

Look for the angle.

No doubt they had been listening to the feed. They must have known how it looked to the world that a synthetic was threatening the life of a human. Regardless of what they or Sava Kessler thought of Gil, it was just bad PR to have someone die at the hands of one of Perion Synthetics' newest products. This was no Vinestead NORM with its silicone skin and wonky speech interface. This was Perion Goddamn Synthetics—only the best and the brightest minds fueled its development.

Fixing Gil's injuries and accelerating his healing would go a long way towards smoothing over the differences between Coker and Joe Perion. Though Vinestead would always be Perion's number one enemy, it wasn't a good idea to have a media house on your ass. As Meltdown always said, the feeds were just selling perspective. And if that perspective didn't look kindly on Perion and company, then millions of subbers wouldn't either.

Joseph Perion wasn't stupid; he knew the score.

Gil rolled onto his stomach and found his body willing. His arms felt stiff, but he was able to push himself up enough to get his knees under him. He paused for a couple of minutes, amazed that such a simple act could take so much energy. Yet he could feel the strength returning, more and more as he tried to whip the muscles into shape. Only after repeating himself, telling his leg over and over to get a foot on the ground, did it finally move. He climbed to his feet, stumbled, but caught himself on the wall.

Slowly, he made his way around the perimeter of the room to the door. He gave it a shove, but when it didn't open, he banged his fists against it, harder and harder until he could feel the numbness in his hands.

"Hey," he screamed. "Let me out of here you sons of bitches! You can't—"

Locks clicked at the top of the door, and it slid soundlessly into the wall. Gil held his hands to his eyes against the sudden light, stumbling backwards as it poured into the room. Two silhouettes stepped into view, their hulking frames filling the entire doorway.

"Come with us," said a deep voice from the right.

As Gil's eyes adjusted, he noticed they were both carrying SMGs against their chests.

"I'm not going anywhere," said Gil. "Not until I get some fucking answers."

"Ms. Kessler is waiting for you." It was the same voice, but it came from the left this time. "She will explain everything."

"Oh, she will, will she? Well then what the fuck are we waiting for? Take me to her."

The AG on the right stepped aside and held out a hand. "This way."

They walked single file down the hallway. Gil found the more steps he took, the easier each one got. He thought perhaps they had drugged him, as the lack of coordination reminded him of nights spent at Pritchard Sansbury's after transcending the borders of some new synth paradise. Except now he appeared to be coming back online at a faster rate, getting stronger as time wore on.

At the end of the corridor, they turned right and stepped into an elevator which had opened just as they were coming around the corner. As they rode up, Gil inventoried the synthetic standing next to him, checking out the various weaponry and immobilization equipment. There was a service pistol on its hip, but it was strapped down. There was no way he could make a grab without the guard behind him reacting first.

The elevator doors opened onto a new hallway with a softer décor. Instead of sterile white floors, Gil's footsteps fell on beige carpet. Tan wallpaper coated the hallway; faded images of autumn leaves dotted the wall every few feet.

"In here," said the guard, opening a door for Gil.

The room inside was dominated by a large, oak conference table in the center. Around it were a dozen chairs and seated in two of them were Cam and Cyn. They looked up when Gil entered, gave each other a glance, and returned their eyes to the table.

Gil followed the guards and sat in the seat next to Cyn. He tried to catch her eyes, but she seemed distracted, almost tired. At least she hadn't been too roughed up in the raid at the warehouse.

"I see you made…" he started to say, but then the doors on the opposite side of the room opened.

They entered one at a time.

First came the guards. There were four of them, obviously synthetic, with faces that eschewed any resemblance to humans. Reflective lenses covered their eyes while antenna-like wiring ran down from their hairline. Each was built like a slightly bigger version of the Automated Guards who had brought Gil upstairs. Although they had nothing in their hands, their belts were replete with imposing weaponry, including needlers that had been banned in the U.S. for decades.

Behind them came two men in lab coats. They glanced uncertainly at the three aggregators and shook their heads. The second one looked back over his shoulder at Sava Kessler.

She stared at Gil for several seconds, a smirk on her face.

The next man through the door made his heart race.

"Fucking Gantz," said Gil.

The chief of police wore a trembling grimace, and his bloodshot eyes held to the floor. He hurried to stand behind a chair next to Kessler.

Ten feet at the most, thought Gil. Ten feet of varnished wood was all that separated him from Robert Gantz, chief of police and backstabbing asshole. With his strength returning, Gil thought he might have it in him to rush the table and get in a few good punches on Gantz before they'd be able to pull him off.

The doorway darkened again, and Gil's mouth fell open. At first, he almost didn't recognize the middle-aged man with slightly graying hair. It wasn't until he took his place between Kessler and one of the lab coats that Gil figured out who he was.

"Ladies and gentlemen," he said. "Thank you for coming. I'm James Perion."

"You fucking—"

Gil felt his body move on its own and in an instant, he was up on the table and running for the founder and CEO of Perion Synthetics, intent on choking the life from his body, intent on making the rumors of his death into fact.

And then Gantz, that fucking liar. Gantz would be next.

"Gilbert, directive," said Kessler, barely raising her voice. "Stop."

Something wet and cold reached into the small of Gil's back, spreading into his stomach and hips. He froze in the middle of the table as his abs convulsed. Shivers ran down his legs, icing every muscle, gluing his feet to the wood.

Out of the corner of his eye, he saw Gantz mouthing the words *I'm sorry*.

Gil tried in vain to give him the finger.

PART FOUR
JOSEPH PERION

THIRTY-TWO

Construction on the north end of the Perion Expressway was supposed to have been completed in the spring of 2014, and yet by the summer of the following year, the road was still full of traffic cones and evercrete debris. While someday the four lanes would be more than enough to handle the traffic coming out of the executive villas, the current reduction to one lane had cars crawling along the blacktop.

Nico Shaw's driver had been unsympathetic about the delay, content to tap out the beat of whatever music he was listening to on the steering wheel while avoiding Nico's pleading glances through the glass partition. If they didn't find an alternate route and make it to the Spire by nine, then Nico would be late. And being late for a meeting called by James Kirkland Perion was not an option. If anything, Nico should have been an hour early.

It was all Katherine's fault, of course. She had set her alarm for six-thirty and was up and about when Nico's alarm went off an hour later. In her infinite kindness, she had silenced his alarm before it could properly do its job. Later, when he awoke to find the house empty and sun pouring in through the windows, it was already a quarter past eight. A quick shower and the suit closest to the door was all he could afford before the company car pulled up. He had climbed into the back seat still struggling with his tie and urging the driver to floor it—a directive he seemed to have forgotten.

The car pulled up in front of the Spire at ten minutes to nine. Even on the best of days, it would take at least fifteen minutes to clear security and ride the express elevator up seventy floors to Perion's personal meeting room.

Nico's sliver beeped.

"Where are you?" asked Joseph Perion, James Perion's son and heir to the throne.

Nico didn't even waste time responding. He made for the front doors, forgetting to take it slow in the July heat. By the time he arrived at the security checkpoint, the sweat was visible on his pressed shirt. He waved his badge over the scanner and waited for the usual hassle from the Automated Guards.

"Mr. Perion is waiting for you," said the AG standing next to the metal detector. He waved Nico through without scanning or patting him down.

In the elevator, Nico took out a code card and pressed it hard against the back of his neck. The rush came on in seconds, flowing through his extremities as if a swarm of bees were dancing beneath his skin. According to the elevator's display, there was plenty of time to complete the load before he made seventy.

Goddamn Katherine.

Making him oversleep had put the whole day out of whack. There was supposed to be plenty of time to wake up, have a quick workout, surf the feed for a little while, and then slip out onto the back porch with a code card and a glass of orange juice. The morning rush helped prepare him for the day, a synthetic psych-up he needed like most people needed coffee. And he had almost missed his daily fix thanks to his wife.

When the elevator doors opened, visions of serene beaches and gorgeous women undulated in his periphery. It took a moment to bring the true reality of the hallway into focus.

An AG let him into the meeting room, but with the synth drowning his synapses, Nico barely registered the somber mood.

"I'm not asking for the morality of it, Chuck. Just tell me whether the architecture can support it or not."

James Perion sat in the leather throne on the far side of the cozy room, alone against a mural of the Perion Spire at sunset. Around him on a small arrangement of couches were Chuck Huber, Langley Bhenderu, a woman Nico didn't recognize, and finally, Nico's boss, Joseph Perion.

Joe looked up as Nico entered the room and motioned for him to sit down. He didn't mention the time.

"We've made great progress," replied Chuck, "but at this stage, it is much too early to tell." He motioned to the woman. "As you can see, this is the most advanced chassis we've produced to date. The internals came direct from R&D and haven't even been through a full QA cycle yet. From our tests, we believe the chassis is solid. However, the brain is a different matter. Roberta only retained fifty-eight percent of her imprint's memories and personality. And that was after several reloads. We may be able to get as high as seventy percent imprint saturation, but we are up against immovable physical limitations. Katsumi has never produced the kind of synaptic density we would need to pull this off."

Nico took out his palette and began making notes. Engineers had a habit of rambling and without some sort of documentation, the details of the meeting were sure to be lost or misremembered.

"What do you say, Dr. Bhenderu?" asked Perion. "Can she pass for her imprint?"

Dr. Bhenderu's head wobbled from side to side. "This is not something I have tried, but I don't believe her friends will be able to tell the difference. The true question, Mr. Perion, is whether her imprint accepts her new life in a synthetic body."

Perion lifted a questioning hand. "Well, has anyone asked her?"

"It is not that simple," said Dr. Bhenderu. "We have to put her out in the world, back in her old life, to see if she will be accepted."

"Then do it," said Perion. He had a way with imperatives, handing out difficult tasks with ease where most people struggled to ask politely.

"We can't," said Chuck. "The download we got from the source wasn't a full imprint."

"How did that happen?" asked Joe.

"There was an incident with subject acquisition," Chuck replied. "By the time she was brought in, she was already expired."

Nico's finger paused on his palette. The flippant mention of death had made his ears perk up.

"We expect saturation to increase with a proper imprint," said Dr. Bhenderu. "A viable brain will provide more than enough data; my tests confirm it. The algorithm needs more effort, but it will be ready when the new Katsumi chips arrive. We will swap out Roberta's cortex and try again."

Perion put his hands to his face and rubbed away his frustration. A sigh escaped between his fingers.

"And when do we expect the chips to arrive?" he asked, hanging his head.

Chuck Huber consulted his palette. "There's a nine-month lead time, and that's with us at the top of the list."

Joe shifted in his seat, uncrossing and recrossing his legs.

"Well," said Perion. "That's disappointing."

"How so?" asked Chuck.

Perion didn't look up. "Because," he said, trailing off.

The synth haze retreated; silence filled the void.

"Because he'll be dead in six," said Joe. "So yes, if it takes nine months for Katsumi to deliver the chips, you might as well cancel the order, because Dad won't be around to sign for them."

Nico thought for a moment he had misheard his boss, that the words had been rearranged by some lingering rush effects, but there was no mistaking the reaction in the room. Both Chuck and Bhenderu sat slack-jawed, looking from Joe to Perion and back. Roberta seemed unfazed by the announcement.

Perion looked up and tried to smile at his son.

"Is this true, Mr. Perion?" Nico's throat felt dry, and the words came out uncertain.

For the first time since Nico walked in, the titan looked in his direction.

"Joey didn't tell you?" he asked.

Joe shook his head. "I kept hoping you would change your mind."

"Change your mind about what?" asked Nico.

The founder of Perion Synthetics sighed and sat further back in his chair. His eyes rose to the ceiling. At the odd angle, his face looked more worn, the lines a little deeper.

"Do you know why half of the people who are diagnosed with cancer die as a result?" he asked.

Nico shook his head.

Perion's eyes came back down as he tapped on the table. "Thirty percent of this country lives below the poverty line. That means no health insurance and no way to pay for medical treatment. Surviving cancer is no longer about finding a cure; now it's about finding a way to pay for that cure."

"So poor people can't afford it," said Nico. "What does that mean to you? You could have footed the bill for everyone who needed it last year."

"Dad could throw every dollar he has at it," said Joe, "but it wouldn't solve the real problem."

"Surely no problem is unsolvable," said Chuck.

"The therapy only runs on Guardian Angel chips," said Joe.

Nico felt the words like a punch in the chest. Guardian Angel—pretty much the only tech outlawed in the City of Perion.

Perion would rather die than have Arthur Sedivy's endotech in his city, let alone his body.

"They hold the patents," said Joe. "There's…"

"What my boy is trying to say, Mr. Shaw, is there's no other way to do this." He turned his attention to Chuck and Bhenderu. "So now you see why I commissioned this project. This isn't just some theoretical exercise for you to sit and ponder; this is life and death. My life and my death. If I don't get out of this meat suit by the end of the year, then that's it, game over, everyone goes home."

Nico thought he saw Joe wince.

"Why didn't you mention this before?" asked Chuck. "Had we known what was at stake, we would have… moved faster, put in more hours. You withheld critical information and this… this is no mere shipping deadline we're up against."

"Don't you think I know that? I've worked my entire life in pursuit of a dream and I'm sure as hell not going out before I see a synthetic in every home. I need you two to make sure I live long enough to make it happen. You do this, and generations of Hubers and Bhenderus will never want for anything."

"This is not about compensation," said Bhenderu.

"Then what?" asked Perion. "What do I have to promise you to make you find me a goddamn solution?"

"Nothing, Mr. Perion. You need only ask. My team will redouble their efforts and perfect the imprint process by the end of the month."

Perion nodded as if he had expected no other answer. "And what about you, Chuck?"

The architect shook his head. "We can try going with another manufacturer, but synaptic density has a finite ceiling, and no other system exists for converting an energy-based storage system to a digital one. I'll lean on Katsumi and scrape their R&D department. We should have prototypes by this time next month, if not sooner."

"We'll need to imprint before the end of August, while I can still think straight. I'd like to be in a new body as soon as possible after that. I'm not going to make any public appearances once my looks start to go."

If he had meant it as a joke, no one laughed.

"Then we have work to do," said Chuck. "And zero time." He stood and looked down at Bhenderu, waiting for him to follow.

"I will send you daily updates," said the doctor. "I promise results soon."

"Would you bet my life on it?" asked Perion.

Neither of the men answered. They paused to look upon the titan and then shuffled out of the room together, already discussing their plan of attack.

"Roberta, directive," said Chuck, from the hallway. "Come."

The synthetic closed the door behind her, and then it was just father, son, and Nico.

Silence rose; the energy drained from James Perion's face as he looked to the window.

"It makes you wonder, doesn't it?" he asked.

Joe was too caught up in the buttons of his shirt to respond.

"What does?" asked Nico.

"That," said Perion, nodding to the horizon. "You have to wonder how it will look with synthetic eyes, how the whole world will feel."

"Does it scare you?"

Joe gave Nico a stern look but couldn't hold it.

"No, Mr. Shaw. I'm not scared. Just curious." He drifted away for a moment. "You'll keep this between us, won't you? This is a delicate situation and will need to be handled as such. Not everyone will be privy to what you've heard here today. Not even Mrs. Shaw."

Nico thought about his wife, about how they rarely shared anything anymore. Usually it was Katherine sitting in on the big meetings, holding privileged information over his head. This time, Nico would know the *big plan*, a plan that if executed correctly, would never come to light.

The moment of pride ended with an abrupt realization.

The old man was dying. The titan was falling.

"Of course," said Nico. "Strictly between us."

"That's a good man," said Perion.

Nico scribbled a final note on his palette.

The only man worthy of succeeding James Kirkland Perion is James Kirkland Perion.

THIRTY-THREE

Dad was all but gone by November.

Joe watched his father labor for breath from a chair by the window.

In just a few short months, the cancer had thinned James Perion's gray hair, hollowed out his cheeks, and relegated him to his bed for the remainder of his life. The morning strolls through the halls of the Spire were a thing of the past, as were the lengthy moments spent at the window in his study, staring out over the empire he had created, visualizing the people and cars as cogs in his massive machine. Dad was like that, able to macro and micro simultaneously, to stay involved where others would call in subject matter experts. His hands-on approach at every level of the business was what most people agreed had given him the edge over the already established Vinestead International.

All he needed was a few more years, more time to unseat Vinestead through sheer determination and market reach.

The synthetics program was going to be the catalyst.

"How am I doing?" asked Synth J, as he entered from the living room.

Joe looked up from his palette and shrugged at the facsimile of his father. The synthetic James Perion had been running the company for three months, and so far the only person not sold on the imprint was Joe. For all matters business, Synth J seemed to have everything under control. He made decisions like Dad and evangelized like Dad, but when it came to interacting with his son, the artificiality always bubbled to the surface.

Sometimes the real James Perion appeared like a ripple on the synthetic's face, but those moments had become more infrequent as the months wore on. Those brief flashes of Dad only highlighted his replacement's artificiality.

"He can't be rushed anymore," said Joe, motioning to the code cards on the table beside the bed. He had tried several variants, from Margate sewer synth to the high-class Euphony couriered direct from Umbra. "The nurse started him on a morphine drip. It won't be very long now."

Synth J put his hands in his pockets. "I can imagine myself in his position, but I can't feel what it would be like. Is that strange?"

"You downloaded your brain into a synthetic. What did you expect?"

"Wait until you're on this side. Then you'll see." He took the chair by the door and pulled out his palette. His fingers moved faster than the touch tracking could keep up with, making him curse under his breath.

"What makes you think I'll ever cross over?"

Synth J appeared not to be listening. Some of the finer points of courtesy had been lost in the transition from human to synthetic.

"That will be your choice, of course," said Synth J, rejoining the conversation. "But by the time the choice becomes necessary, I think you'll find yourself more receptive to the idea."

"Right," said Joe. "As if people are going to accept the idea of immortality through synthetics. Do you have any idea how Vinestead is going to spin this?"

"Vinestead will be knocking down our door trying to get the spec. We have to be ready for them." He looked to the side, as if pondering something. "At any rate, you should probably start making regular backups so Mr. Huber can perfect his imprint process. I won't lose you to a random accident, Joseph."

Dad stirred in his bed, seemed to come to for a moment, but then closed his eyes again.

Joe shook his head. "If anyone finds out what we're doing here, it'll be the lawyers knocking the door down. It won't matter how close you are with Governor Howard; even he won't be able to stop the government from seizing your assets. Or transferring them to me."

"I would not bat an eye if they did," said Synth J. "My legacy is yours, but there is power in me yet. I can still contribute. As for property law, of course there is no provision for inheritance by a synthetic replacement; the same used to be true for women and minorities. But how can they not accept me as an equal? Look at me."

He stood with an ease Dad would never know again.

"They did it! Those crazy bastards actually found a solution to a no-win situation. Vinestead thinks they get to choose who lives and dies in this country, but that changed with me."

"Yeah, so you're golden, but what about him?"

Synth J turned to his ailing counterpart, his enthusiasm fading. "I can't even see myself in him anymore. I'm not entirely convinced I'm still in there. Regardless, we all die. Your mother passed, I will pass. It used to be we lived on in memory or in the fruits of our labor. I've simply found another way to persevere."

Joe stood and approached the bed. His father's hand had been reduced to bone and sinewy tendons that stood in relief under translucent skin. How many times had he felt that hand on his shoulder, in comfort and in anger? Now, the frail fingers could provide neither. Joe placed his hand on his father's.

Dad's eyes fluttered.

"He's still in there," said Joe. "He's still Dad. You're a recording he left behind, a notebook we found stashed in his desk. *This* is James Perion."

Dad was the only true ruler of this empire.

"Maybe you'll feel differently after he's gone. If I could bring your mother back, even for a day, would you want me to?"

"That's different. It wasn't her choice to die. You could have saved yourself, saved *him*."

"And let Vinestead into the city at the same time?" The synthetic's voice didn't pitch like a human's when it got angry. It sounded more like a recording of someone screaming played back at a low volume. "I've told you before how dangerous that would be. They're the only company in the world that brazenly sells one thing and delivers another. All they want to do is exploit people. I'm trying to *help* people."

"So was Dad. And I admire him for that. "

"What about me?"

Joe shook his head. "I don't know yet."

The bedroom doors opened before Synth J could respond. Nico Shaw entered, followed by Robert Gantz. Joe noticed the trembling at the edges of Nico's mouth. His assistant was rushing more and more these days.

"Chief Gantz is here to see you, Mr. Perion," said Nico.

"And you brought him *here*?" asked Joe.

Nico returned a plaintive smile. "Your father asked me to."

Joe looked to the bed. There was too much morphine in Dad's system to get any kind of confirmation.

"He means me," said Synth J. "I asked him to bring in Chief Gantz because it's time he understood what we're up against."

Gantz stood just inside the threshold of the door and stared at the bed and the dying man in it. "What am I looking at, Joe?"

"James Kirkland Perion, the original," said Synth J. "I am his replacement, James Kirkland Perion, the Second."

"I don't understand," said Gantz.

Synth J put his palette down on the bed. "All you need to know is that the human James Perion is dying and that I, his synthetic replacement, have assumed control of the company. And it's because of that look on your face right now that I've called you in today. When he dies, and yes, he is going to die, I expect some people will have a hard time accepting my assumption of his life, on both legal and moral grounds. I intend to change that."

Gantz moved to the foot of the bed; he had yet to blink.

"I'm sorry," he said, making the sign of the cross.

"For what?" asked Synth J.

"Joe, I'm sorry."

Gantz held his hand out; Joe shook it.

"Your father is a good man."

Joe had never known Robert Gantz to get emotional, and yet the chief of police's eyes showed hints of watering.

"Thank you. Dad always liked your style. He had nothing but respect for you."

Synth J gave a nervous laugh. "Guys, come on, I'm still here. I *still* like your style, Mr. Gantz. That's why I want you in on this, to give you a heads up."

The chief turned to Synth J and sized him up. After another glance at Dad, he said, "You made the switch months ago, didn't you? All this time, you've been pretending to be him."

"I *am* him."

"And nobody knows besides us?"

"A few people, but you should assume everyone is in the dark," said Synth J. "For all the world knows, I'm alive and well. That is the current reality. In time, that may change, which is why I've decided to call in a favor with an old friend. An aggregator will be arriving tomorrow."

"Will I be babysitting this aggregator?"

"No. He will require a softer touch. Ms. Kessler will be handling it. She will keep the aggregator on task during his visit. I just wanted you to be aware in case anything gets out of hand."

"Why?"

"Excuse me, Mr. Gantz?"

"Why bring an aggregator into the city? We've got corporate secrets walking the streets and you just want to put it all up on the feed for the world to see?"

Synth J smiled what it considered Dad's friendly smile. "I'm sorry you've mistaken this for a discussion, Mr. Gantz. My decision is final. Your job is to maintain order in my city, so I think you can handle one little aggregator."

"Which house?" asked Nico. His neck was covered in red gashes from the constant scratching.

"Banks Media, obviously," said Synth J. "We have no contacts within Lincoln Continental, and I wouldn't trust this task to a hick like Benny Coker."

Dad never would have talked like that. Joe wondered if his father could hear the conversation beneath the blanket of morphine.

Gantz crossed his arms. "Ms. Kessler is just a flack. I don't know if that's a good—"

"No one is more dedicated to the success of Perion Synthetics than Ms. Kessler, immediate company excluded. For this particular job, that is exactly what I need."

Synth J grabbed his palette and started for the door. "You just keep an eye on the both of them and make sure the aggregator stays on the primrose path. Any deviation and you shut the whole thing down."

"Meaning what?" asked Gantz.

Synth J didn't even pause at the door as he left.

Gantz stared after the synthetic with his hands on his hips. Finally, he threw them up and cursed.

"Your father has lost some of his touch," he grumbled.

"My father is too much changed," said Joe.

"Right, well, don't worry. He'll be going to a better place soon. In the meantime, I'll keep an eye on whoever Banks Media sends over. If he even *thinks* of feeding something unflattering, I'll boot him so hard he'll have a shoeprint on his ass for a week." He checked his sliver and must have seen something he didn't like. "Fuck all. I've got to run. Drinks later?" He glanced at the bed again.

"Yeah," said Joe.

"Good." Gantz turned and pointed at Nico. "And you, you little junkie. Lay off the synth and take care of my boy here. If I find out where you're getting that shit from, I'm hauling you and your source in on charges." He gave Nico a half-hearted shove as he passed him. "He *needs* you."

Nico stopped scratching his neck long enough to look at Joe, who had drifted back to the window.

"Is there anything I can do for you, boss?" he asked.

"Yeah. Get Ms. Kessler's people on an obituary for Dad. Tell them it's a just in case thing."

Nico pulled out his palette and made a note. "But I thought your dad was going to cover up his death?"

"Get this straight, Nico. That thing out there is not my father, no matter how much you or I want to believe it. My father is dying right here in front of us. So please, do as I ask. Get an obituary drafted. People should know how James Perion lived and died."

Something caught in Joe's throat.

"The world should mourn the passing of the real James Perion, not the synthetic."

THIRTY-FOUR

Joe's sliver began to flash fifteen minutes before eight o'clock on Monday morning, but instead of heading to the seventieth floor to hear about synergy and market verticals, he took the elevator down to the lobby and exited the north doors of the Spire into the Victoria Perion Memorial Plaza. It had a circular arrangement, with two large half-moons of black, wrought-iron fencing closing in from both sides, leaving openings at the south and north ends to connect the Spire to First Street. Set along the low fences were small tables, each with its own white umbrella. At the east and west points, mobile carts sold coffee, smoothies, and various breakfast snacks.

Joe had been at his table for ten minutes, staring at an uneaten blueberry muffin, when Sava Kessler showed up.

She was wearing a black blazer over a blood-red shirt; silver sunglasses obscured her eyes, but she took them off as she approached the table.

"Good morning, Mr. Perion," she said. "Mind if I sit?"

"Ms. Kessler, please," he replied, giving her as much of a nod as he could afford. "What brings you to the Spire so early?"

Sava placed a tall cup of coffee on the table and sat down. "I have a meeting with your father at eight-thirty. Won't tell me what it's about, but what can you do?" She scoffed. "He can be very secretive when he wants to be."

"Dad's got a lot on his plate right now. Arranging to have an aggregator come into the city probably takes a lot of work, especially if you're trying to keep it quiet."

Sava stopped mid-sip.

"Ah, so that's what your meeting is about," said Joe.

"Why would he want to do that?"

Joe shrugged. "He won't tell me. But hopefully he's rethought the plan and just wants you to talk to the aggregator over vidconference or something."

Sava sat back in her chair and crossed her arms. "It might make sense as a PR move, but we've got no products heading to market yet. The only other reason would be to answer some accusation laid by another company, and I haven't heard a peep out of Vinestead's people in weeks. So what is your dad trying to head off?"

How about the fact that a synthetic is running the show now?

"I don't know," replied Joe. "I don't know where his head is at these days."

Except he did know. It was lying in a hospital bed with oxygen tubes sticking out of its nose.

"If Mr. Perion is looking for some PR love, my department can deliver that without involving a media house. I'll see if I can talk him out of bringing someone in."

"I wouldn't get your hopes up. When Dad gets an idea in his head, he doesn't back down."

"Neither do I," said Sava.

A light breeze ruffled the umbrella above them. The plume of steam from Sava's coffee bent under the pressure.

Joe tried not to think of his father, but the image of a shriveled hand on blue hospital sheets was stuck in his mind. He had stared at it since waking up in the chair next to the bed, convinced it might move, that James Perion would make a miraculous recovery. But the only thing Dad could move was his chest, and even then a machine was doing most of the work. He wasn't dead, but he wasn't alive. He was just a wilting flower waiting for winter in a morphine haze.

"Are you alright?" asked Sava.

Joe fought back the tears and tried to compose himself. "I'm fine," he said. "I was just thinking about…"

About facing life without Dad. About having a synthetic control the destiny of the most innovative company on the planet. Synth J was supposed to carry on Dad's dreams, but over time, its focus had shifted from bettering the world to the preservation of its own existence. How an aggregator fit into that, Joe wasn't sure.

"…about Nico."

Sava raised an eyebrow. "Mr. Shaw? Why?"

"He's got a rush problem. Not enough to keep him from doing his job, but enough to raise eyebrows."

The words spilled out of Joe without much thought; his mind was busy elsewhere, going over memories that would become his only keepsakes after his father finally succumbed.

"Huh," said Sava. "I wouldn't have thought his job was that stressful. Maybe you're riding him too hard?" Sava's blue eyes sparkled over her smile.

"He'd have to show up for work first. And even then, he's so jacked I don't even know if he understands where he is."

"Have you told Mrs. Shaw?"

Joe shook his head. "I don't think he and Katherine are getting along these days."

"Well, there's your synth addiction," said Sava, tapping her fingers on her coffee. She paused and then patted her breast pocket. From inside, she pulled a code card and tossed it onto the table.

"What's this?" asked Joe.

"It's for Mr. Shaw."

"More rushing isn't going to help him."

"No," said Sava. "It's not that kind of program. This will cut through the withdrawal symptoms and heighten lucidity—kind of like an anti-rush. It might help Mr. Shaw find a baseline when he starts to come down."

"Thanks," said Joe, picking up the card. It sported the typical Perion silver with a band of blue adorning one corner. He slipped it into his pocket.

"Also, it's not exactly legal," said Sava. "Whoever smuggled it in took the time to load it on a one-use card. I'd keep it away from any members of law enforcement if I were you."

Her phone beeped; she glanced at it and sighed. "What's the point of scheduling a meeting if he's just gonna want me there early?"

"Synth—?" Joe caught himself just in time.

"Synth what?" asked Sava.

"Nothing."

"Alright, well, I hope everything works out with your assistant. I'd hate for you to have to go through the trouble of finding a new one." Sava stood and adjusted her blazer. "If I see Mrs. Shaw around, I'll try to feel her out, woman to woman. Maybe she and Mr. Shaw could use some counseling."

Joe nodded, but he couldn't throw his empathy behind something as minor as a marital dispute. There were bigger things going on in the world.

"Don't worry," said Sava, placing her hand on his shoulder. "Things will work themselves out."

Looking into her mirrored lenses, Joe replied, "Yeah. I'm sure he'll be fine. You be careful with that aggregator. Don't let them walk all over you."

"Ha," said Sava. "If I can handle weekly interviews with Lauren Simmons, I can handle one measly aggregator. Whatever your father's intentions, I'll keep the company's best interests in mind. After all, it's the company I was hired to protect, remember?"

"I was wrong to doubt you," said Joe. "Won't happen again."

"See that it doesn't," said Sava. "Have a good day, Mr. Perion." She turned in her glossy heels and headed for the Spire, walking with her shoulders pulled back and her legs reaching out in purposeful strides, reminding Joe of his mother.

The image of Victoria Perion as an early generation synthetic flashed in Joe's head, but it didn't last. There was no way to see his mother as anything except human, no way to see her face restored to the smooth, unblemished skin of her youth. A real memory fluttered out of the mist, one of Joe tucked in beneath the sheets of his childhood bed and his mother sitting on the edge, telling him he could do anything, overcome anything.

The scene broke down and he found himself staring at the table.

Joe pushed the untouched muffin away and got up to leave. In the atrium, dutiful Perion employees scurried about, each of them a spinning gear in the great machine, each knowingly or unknowingly carrying out the master plan set in motion by Dad so many decades ago. Would the workers be so eager to perform their assigned tasks if they knew their orders now came from a synthetic mind, from ones and zeros vibrating along the synaptic strings inside a Katsumi chip?

Joe rode the elevator up to the sixty-eighth floor. The walls came alive during his ascent, displaying a rotating selection of propaganda and public service announcements. A short video showed three Aries-class synthetics assisting a group of elderly engineers in their day-to-day tasks, as if they cared who helped them out of their chairs. Hopefully they were too senile to realize their twilight care had been pawned off on machines.

Nico was waiting for Joe in the hallway on sixty-eight, sitting on one of the leather benches with his legs crossed and one foot bouncing involuntarily. His head shot up at the sound of the elevator doors opening.

"Someone t-talked," he said. "It's all over the feeds."

"What is?" asked Joe.

Nico touched a dormant vidscreen on the wall to bring up a three-split of the Banks Media, Lincoln Continental, and White Line feeds. Hashtags jumped off the screen in bright white bursts.

Cancer? Dying? Future?

Shares of Perion Synthetics were falling through the floor.

"Who fed it first?" asked Joe. "Was it Banks?"

Nico started pacing the hallway. "No, not Banks. A smaller feed on the East Coast, but it got picked up by The White Line."

Joe watched the future of the company grow murkier with each refresh of the stock price.

"What does Synth J have to say about this?"

"You think *I'm* gonna bring it up to him?" asked Nico. "Fucking hell, Joe. He's going to think it was *me!*"

"Well, maybe it was. God knows what you'd do to score your next rush."

"You're gonna bring that up now?" He approached the vidscreen and pointed at the dropping number. "*This* is a fucking disaster, and you want to preach to me about addiction? This is our livelihood going down the toilet. Me, Katherine… hell, even you. Your father's company is about to be written off by every investor on the planet, and there's nothing he can do about it because he's already got one foot in the grave."

Nico was panting; sweat beaded on his forehead.

Joe looked down the hall to the double doors at the far end. Through them and off to the left was his father's bedroom. But Dad wasn't in there. His mind was gone or clouded enough to be just as well—saturated in synth and morphine.

"Shit," said Joe, taking off down the hallway.

"Where are you going?" asked Nico.

"To ask Dad a question."

"But Joe…"

"He's not dead yet!"

"We don't have time for this. We need to do something." Nico's shouting echoed in the hall.

"I know," Joe called back. He stopped at the doors and pulled the code card from his pocket. He said a little prayer as he thumbed its shiny surface.

Dad would know what to do.

THIRTY-FIVE

Ten minutes passed before the code started working.

Joe rose from the chair by the window and approached the bed, watching his father's eyelids flutter.

"The Creator is awake?" asked the synthetic nurse. She had been sitting quietly in the library, listening through the closed doors, likely plugged into the various monitors keeping watch over Dad.

She was an Aries variant endowed with the medical knowledge of a gray-haired physician, though her smarts did come at an aesthetic price. Her face had a silicone tint to it, an artificiality that kept Joe from treating her like a real person.

"Leave us," he said, without looking up from the bed. He waited for the sound of retreating footsteps.

Dad's eyes swung back and forth like a lazy metronome before finally settling on his son. Parched lips opened and closed.

Although it had sat untouched for days, there was still a pitcher of water on the nightstand, along with a glass and a straw. Joe filled the glass halfway and brought the straw to his father's mouth. Dad drank slowly, his throat convulsing as he took down the liquid. When his lips pushed the straw away, Joe set the glass back down on the nightstand.

"Joey." His throat rattled when he spoke.

"Dad."

"You look tired, son. Something on your mind?"

Joe reached for his father's hand. For the first time in weeks, it squeezed back. "Yeah, I've got a little problem," he replied.

Dad managed a weak smile, closed his eyes for a few seconds, and reopened them.

"How can I help?" he asked. A sudden coughing fit belied his offer.

"That depends," said Joe. "How are you feeling?"

"Been having bad dreams. About your mother. And you." His eyes drifted to the window. "What day is it?"

"The ninth of November," said Joe. "It's a Monday."

Just hearing Dad speak caused a knot to tighten in Joe's stomach. After slipping into a haze a week ago, Joe thought he would never hear his father's voice again, that he would have to content himself with the digitized reproduction coming from the synthetic. He wanted so much to share his pain with someone, but there wasn't another human on the planet who had simultaneously lost their father and yet retained a crude copy. Now, maybe he could share his struggle with someone who would listen.

"I missed the morning staff meeting, didn't I?"

"Yes, sir. Synth J ran it. He's meeting with Ms. Kessler right now. He's bringing in an aggregator."

Dad shook his head. "Sava Kessler. There's a woman I would have liked to see you end up with."

"You don't have a problem with an aggregator being in the city?"

"No, Joey. If I know myself, I'll have contacted Donato Banks and asked him to send his best man. Your godfather would never do anything to disparage the company. He's all too aware of what is at stake."

"But we've done things. Things the world isn't ready to hear about."

"The world is more ready than you give it credit for. Everything we've accomplished up to this point will be considered a miracle by most people. My plan has always been to perfect the product and then release it to the public without warning. People will be shocked; Vinestead will be shocked. But if I'm bringing in an aggregator, maybe I've decided to go another way."

He coughed, producing a fine spray that coated his chin. Joe wiped it away with the edge of the blanket.

"Do you know why I trust Mr. Banks? Because he runs his company like we run ours. Everything goes through him, from the biggest decisions to the tiniest details. Whatever his aggregator feeds will cross his desk before it goes out to the public. Even if he feeds some detail about how advanced our synthetics are, I'm sure it won't be without my counterpart's approval."

Joe let go of his father's hand and looked at the floor. He had never known James Perion to accept the will of others, even if the other person was himself.

"You get that from your mother. I tried to teach you not to look away when you disagree, but you have too much of her in you."

"And that's a bad thing?"

"On the contrary. I was lucky to have you to remind me of her after she passed."

"And what will I have?" asked Joe. He tried to keep his voice from rising. "A synthetic imprint? A machine that looks and talks like you but is *nothing* like you?"

Dad narrowed his eyes. "You don't agree with what he's doing?"

"I don't agree with any of this!" Joe backed away and put his hand on the window. "All those people out there have no idea what is happening right now. They need to know their time with you is coming to an end. You're not even giving people who love you the opportunity to say goodbye. What gives you the right to deny them that?"

Behind him, Joe heard his father take a deep breath and release it.

"Sava Kessler thinks she's talking to you right now," continued Joe. "She thinks she's doing what's best for the company because she *thinks* you are still running it. Of all the wonderful things you've done in your life, this deception will be what you're remembered for. Because when the news comes out, and you *know* it will, people will question whether anything has ever been real with you. Did you ever really want to help people? Or has all of this been about living forever?"

"You know I want to help." The usual bass returned to his voice for a moment and then was gone. "I still see a world where human lives are spared from the dangerous and the mundane."

"I know the propaganda. I know the story we've fed to the media in every interview for the last twenty years. But what's the truth? Why do any of this if at the end of your life, you'll just use what you've learned for your own selfish pursuits?"

Dad closed his eyes again, retreated to whatever dark place he had inhabited for the last week.

"Water," he said, lifting a weary index finger.

Joe obliged once more and waited as his father sipped. Part of him knew it was just a stalling tactic, but his heart kept him humble. As he put the glass down, James Perion cleared his throat.

"You were only seven when your mother died, but I was already an old man. I had spent forty-two wonderful years with her. Can you imagine that, son? Four decades with the same woman? Do you know how hard it is to let someone go after that much time?"

Joe shook his head.

"It's difficult, maybe the most difficult task life will throw at you." Dad looked to the ceiling. "We kept so many pictures of her around the house. Every video had her smiling face in it. I watched them after you fell asleep, over and over, for years. I sat in her favorite chair and listened to the piano play back her music. The keys moved like she was still there."

Joe remembered his mother playing piano, practicing for hours on what already sounded like perfection.

"There was a company out of Glendale called Companion Dynamics. They had a silly tagline like *one plus one equals one*. I heard about them when Vinestead tried to make a buy in the late nineties. CD refused, of course."

"What were they selling?"

Dad managed a playful sneer. "Love dolls. Silicone sex toys for the well-to-do but lonely American."

"You didn't…?"

"Please," he replied, shaking his head. "Companion Dynamics was blowing up, quarter over quarter, really positive growth. And I didn't understand it at the time. Maybe I was arrogant, but I judged every sale and every customer they ever had. How could people be so depraved?" He paused to take a sharp breath. "Some months later, I saw a documentary about CD customers, men who treated their dolls like wives and girlfriends. They dressed them up, took them to parties, the whole thing. I remember wondering how humans could bond so deeply with inanimate objects. Whether or not these men were deranged or depraved, they *believed* they loved these things.

"That's when I realized it wasn't just about sex for those men; it was about companionship, as CD claimed in their brochures. They just didn't have the funds or resources to take their companion dolls to the next level. When Vinestead eventually took them over in '03, all they added were ridges in their bajingos."

Joe laughed through his nose.

"Think it childish if you want, but Vinestead rolled CD into a new company along with Kitzingen Escorts and turned artificial sex into a multi-million-dollar industry. Sex sells, Joey, but Vinestead was missing the point, as usual. I thought about what I wanted and realized it wasn't intimacy with your mother. I just wanted her around again. I wanted her *presence*. That's when everything changed for me."

"So why didn't you get a doll that looked like her?"

Dad rolled his eyes. "I didn't want a doll; I wanted *her*. Plus, there was a stigma in those days. If people found out you had a doll at home, they immediately thought you were a sex-crazed deviant or maybe just a lonely, pathetic man. God help them if they took their dolls out in public. So I thought, what if the dolls were indistinguishable from a real woman? What if they actually had a purpose beyond sex and a personality beyond pillow talk?"

"But we don't have any companion doll products…"

"Of course we do, Joey. Don't you get it? *All* of our synthetics have the capacity to be companions. The last piece of the puzzle was the user and how to convince them they should love an inanimate thing. Virgos will change that; they have a spark of humanity that makes them more real than real. Roberta will be the first prototype in the Domestic Partner series." Another sharp breath brought a grimace to his face. "I was so close. Simple companionship. That's all people want."

"And you think Synth J will carry on that vision?"

"The other me has different priorities now, I expect. I don't know what they are, but I don't believe…" He paused, groaned. The heart rate monitor spiked.

"Dad?"

"Who would have thought dying would be so painful?" he asked. His eyes shut tightly over a forced smile.

"The Creator is in pain," said the nurse. The beeping of the monitors had summoned her from the library. "Doctor Parris instructed me to resume the morphine regimen. If you do not allow me, I will have to notify her."

"Not yet." Joe moved in front of her, blocking access to the tray of syringes next to the bed.

"Joey, listen to me."

Joe turned and faced his father; agony burned behind those tired eyes.

"I've always asked you to trust me, to listen to me and believe I'm doing the best I can for you. I won't be around much longer; you'll have to figure things out on your own now. You have a lot of your mother in you, but I'm in there too, and the world will have *you* to remind them of me. *You*, Joseph, are my legacy."

"What about Synth J?" asked Joe, squeezing his father's fingers.

"You will figure out what to do about him. Just know, whatever you decide, I will support it. It's your company now. If you want something, you demand it from him. Or remove him."

Dad cried out as his body convulsed.

"Please," said the nurse. "Don't let the Creator suffer."

"Let her do her job. We can talk a little later."

Joe thought of the inert code card in his pocket. He would have to get another one if he ever wanted to talk to his father again. He stepped out of the way and allowed the nurse to resume the morphine drip.

"I'll let you rest for a bit," he said.

"Thank you," said Dad. He pointed to the vidscreen on the far wall. "Do me a favor and put on a video of your mother. I'd like to see her again…"

One last time, thought Joe.

"Sure," he replied.

The vidscreen woke at his touch and displayed the company's feed. Joe switched it to his father's personal media and brought up a playlist of clips from the eighties. Victoria Perion appeared on the screen, looking young and healthy in her early thirties. Her voice flowed from hidden speakers in the ceiling, drowning out the beeping and whirring of the medical equipment.

A smile appeared on his father's face, but whether it was from the morphine or the movie, Joe couldn't tell.

"I'll see you later, Dad."

James Perion nodded and closed his eyes.

THIRTY-SIX

Joe drank the rest of Monday away.

He had only intended to fill the heavy tumbler once—the gritty but sweet taste of Glenfiddich was more his father's preference—but after feeling the comforting warmth in his stomach, Joe found himself pouring another, then another. Each time the tumbler grew empty, Joe held it close to his face and looked at the skewed world though the glass bottom. The cuts transformed reality, allowed him to see things from a different perspective. The answers he had been looking for pushed up through the dark wood of his desk, dancing in the shadows cast by the LED clock on the wall. Joe watched the shadows twist into letters, coagulate into words that foretold the future.

The events of the next few days unfolded before him.

Succumbing to the alcohol early, Joe fell asleep at his desk, missing the group dinner Sava Kessler had invited him to. He dreamed of his father's death and resurrection, repeating in an endless loop, with a synthetic audience looking on with indifference. And each time his father died, the more nauseated he became, until finally he awoke and threw up in the trashcan beside the desk.

The blinds were still open from the night before, and the clear weather allowed the moon to shine unopposed on his apartment. He used the ambient light as a guide to find his way to the bathroom where he washed his face and examined his features in the mirror, wondering when they would start to resemble his father's. The vidscreen by the door showed the time just passing three. Joe stumbled back to his bedroom and collapsed onto the thick pillows on his bed. The cool silk welcomed him, made him forget about the tempest in his stomach.

Around six, the sound of footsteps roused him from his dark sleep.

Nico was standing at the foot of the bed, his eyes red but his suit and tie in place. He cleared his throat when Joe refused to turn over.

"No meetings today, Nico."

"I know. I've cleared your schedule. You should come upstairs, Mr. Perion. Your father…"

Joe felt the fog slip away. He bolted upright.

Nico shook his head. "No, but it may come soon. Doctor Parris thought you'd want to be there for…"

The end, thought Joe.

"I've got the elevator waiting," said Nico.

Each action blurred into the next. Joe rose from the bed and navigated the minefield of his dirty apartment. The desk flashed in his periphery; a foul smell emanated from the trashcan. In the hallway, the walls rotated back and forth, the floor swinging like a pendulum. Joe imagined the whole Spire rotating around its highest point, suspended from the heavens like a knife held by the tip of its blade. His stomach lurched, but Nico had him by the shoulder and steadied him as they entered the elevator. When it opened on sixty-eight, the walls had stopped moving. Joe broke free of his escort and sprinted the last thirty yards to his father's bedside.

James Kirkland Perion was more corpse than man. The skin on his face had sunk even further. The eyelids were crusted in a white substance and nothing moved beneath him. Machines beside the bed beeped a forlorn tempo.

Alerts on the vidscreens flashed silently.

"I've turned off the audible alarms," said Dr. Parris. "I know it looks bad, but he isn't feeling any pain right now."

Joe grabbed his father's hand; the fingers were ice cold and unresponsive.

"Hell of a thing, isn't it?" asked Synth J. He was standing in the corner of the room with his arms folded and head slightly down. "I never thought I would live long enough to see myself die."

"This isn't about you," said Joe. "My father is dying."

Synth J approached the bed. "We all die, Joseph, in our due time. I'm not uncaring, but look what we're about to witness. If that James Perion dies and I continue to live, then the soul is truly divisible. We will have found a way to split the essence of a human being. That is simply amazing."

Joe didn't take his eyes off of his father. "I know you think you're this man, but you're not. You're a dermal veneer on a carbon-fiber skeleton. You're…"

"I understand you're upset," said Synth J.

"Yes, but can you empathize?" asked Joe. "Can you *feel* it?"

"I don't see what that has to do with anything."

"I can feel it," said the synthetic nurse. Though her voice was digitized, Joe thought he heard sadness in it.

"Aries-class," said Synth J. "The only thing they feel is obsolete."

"Joe, I think I should tell you," said Dr. Parris. "Your father was asking for you earlier this morning. I tried to ring your apartment, but there was no answer."

"I didn't think he'd regain consciousness again." Joe thought about the bottle of Glenfiddich in his apartment. Last he had seen, it was on its side on the floor by his desk.

Dr. Parris cradled her palette in folded arms. Strands of her blonde hair had fallen out of her bun, obscuring the bags beneath her eyes. "He's a fighter," she said, choking back a sob. "James Perion does not die until he is ready."

"Amen," said Nico. He had drifted to the door by the bathroom, a crumpled tissue in his hand.

"Mr. Shaw," said Synth J, "I don't think we'll be requiring your services anymore today."

Nico took a step, hesitated.

"He stays," said Joe. "I want him here."

"It's *my* goddamn death. I say who needs to be here or not."

"It's happening," said the nurse.

The monitor next to the bed flared bright red as Dad's heart rate dipped below viable levels. His chest shuddered, sending the EKG to the top of the frame before it dipped down again.

"His body is making its last efforts," said Dr. Parris. "You should say your goodbyes now, Joe."

"Shit."

Synth J snorted. "So now I know. The last thing my son says to me on my death bed is *shit*."

Joe leaned over and put his mouth near his father's ear. All of the speeches he had rehearsed fluttered into the breeze.

"Dad," he said, his voice failing. The tears began to run down his cheeks. "There hasn't been a day in my life when I haven't looked up to you. You've done so many great things. You've set the bar so high. I understand why you did what you did. You were scared I couldn't step up, but I'm going to make your dream come true. Go see Mom and tell her I love her."

A hand appeared on Joe's shoulder; it was Nico's.

"It's okay to go, Dad. I've got things covered. I love you."

Joe kissed his father on the forehead and stood up. He reached under Nico's arm and put his hand on his assistant's shoulder.

"Goodbye, Mr. Perion," said Nico. "It has been an honor to work with you."

The nurse approached the bed and said something in garbled white noise. Only Synth J seemed to understand what she was saying.

Dr. Parris tapped the vidscreens; their contents faded away. The respirator wheezed to a halt a moment later. "God speed," she whispered, hugging her palette again.

The room waited as James Kirkland Perion, founder and CEO of Perion Synthetics, drew his final breaths.

His chest rose and fell for the last time, and then the titan expired.

"Un-fucking-believable," said Synth J, before collapsing. He struck his head on the railing of the bed and hit the floor with a heavy smack.

Beside Joe, the synthetic nurse fell backwards into the window and slid down the smooth glass. She ended up in a sitting position with her eyes wide and her mouth agape. A hand from Dr. Parris prevented her from falling over completely.

Nico rushed around the bed to check on Synth J.

"Goodbye, Dad," said Joe. He reached out and put his fingers to his father's neck. There was no pulse.

"Mr. Perion, can you hear me?" Nico shook Synth J by the arm but got no response.

Joe patted his father's chest. "I got this."

"Joe, help me! Something's wrong with your father."

"My father is dead," replied Joe, refusing to turn around.

"Do you want to lose them *both*?"

At that, Joe stepped back from the bed and looked at Nico. The man's bloodshot eyes were pleading, but Joe simply crossed his arms. He drifted to the window and watched the city twinkle in the early morning sun.

When Dr. Parris saw him standing there, she seemed to remember herself. She stood and checked her sliver. "Time of death, 0708 hours."

Nico cried out as a synthetic hand closed around his throat. It tossed him across the room as if he weighed nothing. Synth J rose from the floor and surveyed his surroundings. His face was cold and toneless, a common configuration for newly minted synthetics. His eyes flickered, settled on the bed.

"The Creator is dead," he said.

From the floor, the nurse's voice echoed his statement.

Synth J looked at her when she spoke. Something clicked.

"Mr. Shaw," he said, kneeling down. "Are you alright?"

"Get the fuck away from me," screamed Nico. He pushed ineffectually at the synthetic's hands.

"Dr. Parris, this man needs attention." Then to Nico. "I apologize, Mr. Shaw. I don't know what happened."

"You glitched," said Joe, uncaring if anyone could hear him. "Not many people get to watch themselves and their Creator die in the same day. Your synthetic mind probably couldn't handle it."

Synth J stood slowly.

Joe faced him, drew himself up.

"Hell of a thing, isn't it?"

THIRTY-SEVEN

The body of James Kirkland Perion was burned at sunset.

In the morning, Joe placed his father's urn on the mantel beside his mother's and watched the polished silver gleam in the morning light. They had similar designs except for the etching along their lower thirds: schematic symbols, logic gates, and equations for his father; floral fractals and ribbons for his mother. Though their deaths had been decades apart, both urns gave off a brilliant luster.

He couldn't help but reminisce about his parents as he took the elevator down to the fifth floor. The vidscreens showed the same reassuring text from the day before, urging the residents of Perion City to continue business as usual. For the most part, people listened, though there was some talk, some whispering behind closed doors.

The fifth floor of the Perion Spire was home to the security arm of the company. Its primary mission was the protection of the city, its occupants, and its secrets, from both a physical and virtual perspective. At the head of the division was Steve Phelps, Vice President of Security. His direct reports were Deborah Keats, Director of Tech-Sec, and Robert Gantz, Chief of Police. While Deb and her team stayed behind closed doors, typing on laptops and palettes long into the night, Gantz' department ran more like a typical police station with an expansive, yet empty, reception area. If Perion City had criminals, they would have found the padded chairs and numerous vidscreens comfortable and inviting.

"Good morning, Mr. Perion," said the desk sergeant. "How can I help you today?"

Joe nodded to the hallway to the left of Booking. "Just here to see Mr. Gantz. Can you buzz me in?"

"Sure thing, Mr. Perion. I'll let the chief know you're headed back."

The door at the far end of the hallway buzzed and the magnetic locks at the top of the frame released. The frosted glass turned clear as the door swung open.

Joe walked past the front offices and the Quick Response room where two-dozen riot-geared AGs sat immobile on metal benches. Each held an assault rifle by their side, moving it only when a woman in a lab coat stepped in front of them to run diagnostics. Gantz must have been shaken up by the Collapse the day before, evidenced by the lack of Scorpios freely roaming the halls.

Gantz was waiting in the threshold of his office. He smiled when Joe came around the corner.

"Greetings, Mr. Perion," he said, bowing his head slightly. "What brings you to the lower levels this morning?" His eyes scanned the hallway, connecting with other uniforms in earshot.

Joe did his best to return a smile. He hurried into Gantz' office and shut the door.

"Sorry about that," said Gantz. He settled into his high-backed chair. "Appearances—a necessary evil, right?" When Joe shrugged in response, he asked, "How are you holding up?"

"I'm fine," said Joe. "We made our peace."

"Do you need anything? Anything at all?"

"Maybe. Have you seen the feeds this morning? The world seems to think my father is dead. There are no synthetics outside of the city to spill the news and no one in town who would report on the story, except for that aggregator."

Gantz waved the idea away. "It wasn't Cam. There hasn't been any mention of Perion on the BMP feed or any of its subsidiaries. Deborah says he has an uplink going, but either Banks isn't liking what he's feeding or he's saving it for one big push."

"Then we have a leak somewhere. Every synny in the city said my father was dead. Only a handful of people know it's true. And somehow it got out."

Gantz sat back in his chair. "Joe, we're taking care of it. Deb is watching the network traffic, and I'm watching the doors and windows. Nothing is coming in or going out of this city without one of us knowing. I'm not going to let anything bad happen on my watch."

Too late; the products had already taken over the company.

"Why the loyalty, Robert? My father is dead. You're taking orders from a goddamn synny."

"No. Steve Phelps takes orders from a synny; I take my orders from a higher power. I'm protecting the company the way James Perion would have wanted me to."

Joe leaned forward. "And now that's he's gone? Who do you take orders from now, his holy ghost?"

Gantz smiled and tapped the desk with his fingers. "I was wondering how long it would take you," he said, nodding. "Twenty-four hours to step up to the plate. I'm impressed."

"It wasn't all my idea," said Joe.

"Someone's been coaching you?"

"All my life." Joe paused a moment. "Dad and I talked before he passed. He told me to do what I think is right. And I don't think a product should be in control of the company that makes it. That thing is not a Perion; it's Katsumi tech, Chuck Huber architecture, and Bhenderu psychology. My dad's personality is just an add-on. And that's fine if you just want to keep up appearances, but we're talking about the future of a company here. *My* company."

"*There* it is," said Gantz. "There's the Joseph Perion I've been waiting for."

"So you'll help me then?"

"Not so fast. If you're going to suggest what I think you're going to suggest, then I need to be prepared to find myself on the wrong side of a Scorpio's rifle. Whether he's your father or not, that synny has your father's ambition. He'll lean on Phelps and Phelps will lean on me. And then you'll have no more friends in the PC. Nico might back you, but the poor bastard can't even face his wife without shitting his pants, and that's when he's not strung out. No, if you're going to do this, it can't be a full-frontal assault."

"Then I'll build up support," said Joe, running through the roster in his head. "I think we could get Ms. Kessler onboard."

"She'd never go for it. Too tied up with Chuck Huber to risk putting his research in jeopardy."

Joe stood and approached the vidscreen on the far wall. It was showing alerts and advisories in yellow and red text, but he wiped them away. A triplet of feeds faded in, one from each of the houses. In visual format, they appeared as a jumble of keywords scrolling off the top of the frame. The word *PERION* dominated two of the three feeds.

"Everyone is waiting to hear what Banks Media has to say. And we've got one of their aggregators roaming the city."

"He's touring the assembly facility today," said Gantz.

"The fact is he's here. We can use him."

"Then Kessler's really out of the question. I don't know why, but she can't stand him. You should have seen her at dinner on Monday. The tension could have choked a horse."

"Is he an asshole or something?" asked Joe.

Gantz shook his head. "No, she was just pissed because a Virgo prototype was staged at Southpoint, and no one had told Kessler about it beforehand. She tried to take the synny away and Cam went over her head. And if I know one thing about Sava Kessler, it's that you don't go over that woman's head."

"Alright, then we'll do this without her."

"Do *what* exactly? You're just like your father sometimes, Joe: big on the goals but scant on the details."

Joe looked away, at the floor, at the walls, but no matter where his eyes landed, all he saw was his father's shriveled face, the cracked lips. His whole world had changed a mere twenty-four hours before, and yet Joe felt he hadn't done enough in the interim, hadn't taken back the company with the speed and agility his father would have been proud of.

Deciding on the goal was easy: remove Synth J from power. How to achieve that goal was harder. There were several routes, from a simple conversation to physical detention, but no course of action felt like a sure thing.

If I had six hours to chop down a tree, I'd spend the first four sharpening my axe.

Joe recalled the quote written in permanent marker on the white board in his father's workshop, a white board that had followed him for decades. Joe first saw it when he was sixteen and at the time, had erroneously attributed it to Lincoln Tate, head of Umbra's Lincoln Continental feed. Only when he asked his father why there was a quote from a feed monger on the board did Joe finally understand it was from the *other* Lincoln.

Gantz was still waiting for an answer.

"I don't know yet," admitted Joe. "But I want you to be ready when the time comes." He turned to leave, but at the door, he found the handle wouldn't budge.

"There's just one more thing," said Gantz.

Joe turned and folded his arms.

"How do I know you're not a synthetic?"

Joe scoffed. "Are you shitting me?"

"Look, I just found out about your dad's little game on Sunday. I've been calling Synth J boss for months. How do I know there isn't another angle to this? You want my help? Prove to me you're human."

"How? Slit my wrists?"

Gantz shook his head. "Let's take a little drive out to Pure. You get ten paces past the PNR, and we're good. If not, I tell your father what you were planning."

"Don't call him that," said Joe.

"Fair enough."

Joe checked his sliver. "I've got a full plate today. Let's do this tomorrow, maybe over lunch?"

"If you're not there, I'll come for you," Gantz replied. He touched a hidden button under his desk and the locks in the door clicked open. "See you tomorrow, Mr. Perion."

"Can't wait."

Joe pushed the door open and walked back down the hall. For one terrible moment, he considered the idea Gantz could be right. After all, Joe hadn't been past the PNR in months, maybe a year or more. What would happen tomorrow when he walked past the outer marker? He put his hand over his heart, felt the beating. He licked his lips and smelled the air. His senses were operating as they always had, reinforcing the reality that he was a living, breathing human.

He slowed to a stop in front of the elevator.

If he fell down dead tomorrow, if his insides dissolved into sludge, Joe felt he wouldn't even be surprised.

At this point, there was no telling what Synth J was capable of.

THIRTY-EIGHT

As a synthetic, Synth J had no use for the comforts of the Perion master suite on the sixty-eighth floor. It fell to Joe to sort through the knickknacks and framed photos his father had scattered throughout the massive apartment, adorning shelves in the study, standing in front of books in the library, and placed with care above the vidscreen in the living room. There were two portraits of Victoria and James Perion there, each five feet tall. Between them, in an only slightly less gaudy and smaller frame, was Joe Perion, looking svelte at twenty-one.

Joe spent the rest of his day cataloging what would stay and what would go. Late that night, he carried a box full of mementos down to his apartment on the fiftieth floor. The ornate style of his father's things would look foreign among the neo-modern motif of his home, but Joe felt it was better to keep the photos where someone would appreciate them.

He placed a framed picture of Dad standing next to the very first Perion synthetic on the nightstand next to this bed. There was something incongruous about the crude prototype with its unibody design and the middle-aged man in a leisure suit and full sideburns, and though Joe hadn't been alive when the photo was taken, it reminded him of his childhood, when the ebullience of James Perion dominated not only his professional life, but his personal relationships as well.

The photo was the last thing Joe saw before he fell asleep and the first image he saw when he awoke. As the sun rose beyond his windows, he lay with the frame sitting on his chest, thinking about his father, and not just the most recent revision. There was modern Dad, with his focus on perfecting a dream. There was millennial Dad who spent most of his time on the road, glad-handing with politicians and private investors. James Perion of the eighties and nineties was only visible in home movies and aging documentaries, but Joe knew he would miss those versions as well.

It was perhaps the loss of future versions that kept Joe in bed until the vidscreen automatically turned on at ten-thirty.

"The mood in Umbra is subdued this morning for the third straight day on the news of the death of James Kirkland Perion, CEO and founder of Perion Synthetics. While the company has yet to confirm his passing, sources at White Line Media say the seventy-seven-year-old entrepreneur has finally succumbed after a year-long battle with cancer. Residents here are paralyzed by the uncertainty of the company's future, with one Umbra local calling Perion Synthetics *the last great hope* and *the world's most powerful weapon* against Vinestead. Arthur Sedivy, CEO of Vinestead International, could not be reached for comment."

Joe slapped the remote and turned the vidscreen off. Sliding his legs over the side of the bed, he sat up and put his head in his hands.

Seventy-two hours had passed since the rumor of James Perion's death had leaked and already the world was trying to figure out how to fill the void. A simple press conference would have put everything to rest, yet Synth J allowed the rumor mill to crank out theory after theory, creating panic in both public and private sectors, driving down the stock price…

Joe stood and walked over to the phone on his desk. He placed a call to Legal on the eighth floor and when a woman named Rita answered, he asked to look into stock trades for the last few days, specifically any company making huge buys since Monday. She assured him she would call back with the info just as soon as humanly possible.

"Message me with whatever you find," he told her, and then hung up.

Joe wandered into the living room as he gave his idea more thought. Could there be something behind the stock crash, something intentional? The vidscreen over the shelf came alive when he walked in front of it and synced to the bedroom's previous channel.

"Reports of virtual vandalism have been the buzz of VNet since early yesterday morning, with the message *THE CREATOR LIVES* appearing on high-profile landmarks in many public arenas. While initially thought to be the work of enthusiastic supporters, closer inspection by computer experts has revealed viral payloads hidden in the graffiti. VNet users who come into close proximity with the message may have their avatars overwritten with what appears to be black funeral dress. Subsequent attempts to communicate either orally or via text will be interrupted by the phrase *DEATH TO VINESTEAD*. VNet representatives have issued a statement assuring the public a patch will be released to deal with what they are describing as a minor and temporary annoyance."

An alert popped up at the bottom of the vidscreen—an incoming message from Gantz.

Damn, thought Joe. He had forgotten about their lunch date at Pure.

He dragged a finger over his sliver and opened the message.

"Security breach this morning," Gantz had written. "It's bad. Got a meeting with Big J in twenty. You going?"

Joe retrieved his palette from the desk in his office. A meeting invite was pending on his calendar. "Yes," he wrote, and then closed down the messenger app.

He was out of his apartment in ten minutes and in his rush, he almost ran into the Automated Guard stationed outside his door.

"Pardon me, Mr. Perion," said the AG.

"What are you doing here?" asked Joe. He didn't stop walking until he had pressed the call button on the elevator.

"For your protection, Mr. Perion."

Joe turned to look back down the hall. "Who says I need protection?"

"Chief Robert Gantz assigned me to this post, sir."

Damn he works fast, thought Joe.

The elevator doors opened, and Joe stepped inside. As the car rose, he thought about how serious the breach must have been to warrant an armed security detail. By the time the doors retracted on seventy, Joe had dismissed the AG as an overreaction, a precaution spawned from a set of protocols rather than a conscious decision by Gantz.

There were more Scorpios on seventy, about a dozen by Joe's quick count. They lined the hallways with their hands crossed in front of them, their guns hanging by straps at their sides. One looked at Joe as he approached, but upon detecting no threat, it resumed its stoic guard.

Joe could hear the muffled yelling as he approached the conference room doors.

"Vinestead? In my house?"

One of the AGs opened the door for Joe. Inside, he found Synth J standing at the head of the oak table, waving his hands around like a haywire synthetic. Also present were Robert Gantz, Nico Shaw, Chuck Huber, and Sava Kessler.

"How does this happen?" asked Synth J. He pointed to the vidscreen.

Surveillance footage rolled, showing a woman in a black, skin-tight suit blasting a synny to pieces. Joe didn't recognize the place, but given the synny's integration into the environment, it couldn't have been anywhere else except the Perion Spire.

"Joseph, you're here," said Synth J. "Please have a seat. I'm just going over with Mr. Gantz here the appalling lack of security in my city."

"I can't watch the entire sky, Mr. Perion," said Gantz. His eyebrows were scrunched together in the middle of his face.

"Then maybe I should hire someone who can!"

Screaming? Threats? Just how advanced were Virgo-class synthetics?

"Mr. Perion, if I may. We can argue security policy later. For now, we have Vinestead tech within our walls. We have to rid ourselves of this germ before it has a chance to infect us. I recommend you deport her immediately."

"Chuck is right," said Sava. "We don't know what she's carrying around in that head of hers."

Gantz cleared his throat. "Mr. Ferko says there are only *traces* of Vinestead hardware in the intruder. It's not like she's got a full-on Guardian Angel chip in her neck."

"No, Mr. Gantz, it is much worse. She has a modified mil-spec Ayudante. Imagine the damage she could do if she hooked into our network." Synth J turned to the vidscreen and shook his head. "Of course they would send a woman. They're trying to play to my sensitivities. Well, if this is what Arthur Sedivy wants, I'll show that motherfucker how the game is played."

Joe shook his head.

"Ms. Keats hasn't been able to match her with anyone in Vinestead's employee database," said Gantz. "We don't know for sure who she's working for."

"Then she's disavowed," said Chuck. "In which case, we can simply expunge her and be done with it."

"She came into my home," said Synth J. "She destroyed my property. She spent God knows how long sneaking around my building. If we hadn't grabbed her when we did…"

"Did you *ask* her who she's with?" asked Joe.

The room fell silent as all eyes turned to him.

"Brilliant," said Chuck, under his breath.

Sava gave him a slight smile.

"As if we could believe anything from a Vinestead spy," said Synth J. "Look at her, Joseph. She's a rogue agent, a loner. That's why she was chosen for this."

Joe noticed Gantz rolling his eyes.

"Vinestead thinks they can just pull some techy neophyte off the street and send them into my city? No!" Synth J banged his fist on the table, producing a noticeable dent in the wood. "They will not walk over James Perion. I am the defender of this castle and woe betide the creature who steps into *my* garden. We'll make an example out of her."

Sava looked at the floor, her eyes scanning back and forth.

"Chuck."

"Yes, Mr. Perion?"

"Is the Paulson imprint ready to go? Can you modify it for Ayudante architecture?"

"It will take a little time, but yes. Yes, I believe it will work."

"What's the Paulson imprint?" asked Joe.

"Don't worry about it," replied Synth J. "I'm handling this now."

"What's the Paulson imprint?" he asked again.

"It's done, Joe. Chuck, get on this immediately. I want it taken care of by COB today."

"Goddamn it, Dad. Answer me!" Joe felt the sting in his throat.

Synth J turned, the fire draining from his facial servos.

"Son," he said.

The word felt like a toothpick under Joe's fingernail.

"All you need to know is Vinestead is always looking for a way to destabilize us. I thought you would have understood that by now. Arthur Sedivy and I may play nice in front of the cameras, but down in the trenches, it is a never-ending war. He sends his soldiers into battle, and they follow his orders without question. Do you know why that is, Joseph?"

Joe shook his head. To his left, Gantz shifted in his chair.

"Because they have nothing to lose. And people with nothing to lose are the most dangerous type of people. You could simply *kill* the soldiers and be done with it, but that won't mean a thing to their commander. We have to send a message. We're going to give this woman something to lose, something so precious she will betray Vinestead to the bitter end just to protect it."

"You always taught me to fight fair."

"It's time to grow up, son."

"What's the Paulson imprint, *Dad*?"

"She wants to sneak around my garden? She wants a *story*? Well, we'll give her a fucking story."

Chuck Huber cleared his throat. "It involves the new synthetic infants we've been developing for the pan-Asian market."

"I'm out," said Gantz, standing up. "I'm not getting involved with anything… unnatural." He started for the door.

"I'm not done with you, Robert," said Synth J.

"The threat has been dealt with. She won't cause us any more trouble."

"That's not the—"

"You call me when there's a mob at the front gates. Call me when someone is pointing a gun at your head or Joe's head. I will *gladly* step in front of that bullet. But I will not be part of any sick experimentation." He kicked the conference room door open and stormed out.

Joe stood and was met with a cold, synthetic stare.

"You too?" asked Synth J.

"James Perion wouldn't do this."

Synth J crossed his arms. "Don't you read the feeds, Joseph? James Perion is dead."

THIRTY-NINE

Pure was one of the few buildings, and the only bar, to sit beyond the Point of No Return. It was staffed by and catered to humans only. The idea had come from Dr. Bhenderu, who thought people might need refuge from the synthetic storm constantly raging around them, a place to go to feel human again.

Joe had found Gantz outside the Spire after the meeting with Synth J, still grumbling to himself about ethics and nature as he fingered a code card in one hand. Joe suggested they grab a drink, and the chief of police accepted with a grunt.

They pulled into the empty parking lot at Pure just as the neon *OPEN* sign crackled to life. Inside, they found a table toward the back and adjusted the slats in the windows to let a little cool air in. The scraping of their chairs over the wood floor as they pulled them back echoed in the bar.

Holmes, owner and proprietor of Pure for as far back as Joe could remember, waited patiently behind the bar, arranging shot glasses in neat lines of ten on a black dish towel. It had been his decision to eschew the clean lines and thigh-to-ceiling windows so prevalent in downtown Perion City for a more hole-in-the-wall motif to remind people that not everything in the world was as shiny as the company made it out to be. The throwback style reminded Joe of the dirty college bars he had spent so many unremembered nights in during his time at Cal.

"I think I'm in," said Gantz. He took off his security badge and turned it over in his hands. This was typical; he didn't like to drink with the laminated ID around his neck, thought it sent the wrong message.

"I think I'm glad," replied Joe. "I'll need you for what I have planned."

"And what exactly do you have planned?" Gantz pocketed the badge and motioned for Holmes.

Joe ran his finger over a rut someone had carved into the table. "A coup d'état."

"How about a drink first?" asked Holmes. He placed a small bowl of pretzels in the middle of the table and dropped cocktail napkins on opposite sides.

"Dos Equis," said Gantz. "And keep them coming."

"And for Joe-boy?"

"Filthy martini," replied Joe. "And a glass of water, Mr. Holmes."

"No need for formalities, JP Featherbottom. We're past your father's reach out here."

Gantz smiled. "You're damn straight."

"Right back with those drinks, gentlemen. Maybe one of you would be kind enough to find something on the jukebox before it starts with the Garth Brooks again."

"Still?" asked Gantz.

Holmes shook his head. "Ashley's the only one who knows how to work the damn thing, and she thinks it's funny as shit." He broke into song as he walked away.

"So, how are we going to overthrow your father? And how are you going to make it legal?"

Joe shrugged. "The first part's easy, I guess. You and your team can just take him into custody. I'm sure your Scorpios are stronger than he is."

"Maybe," said Gantz. "But I haven't seen the specs on the Virgo synnies yet. Cam is running around with one and it seems to have strength and reaction speed beyond my Scorpios. I wouldn't be surprised if Synth J has some prototype enhancements we don't even know about. We should probably check with Mr. Huber before planning that part of the operation."

"If we can't shut him down cleanly, then we'll just have to put him out of commission." Joe put his hand on his knee to keep his leg from bouncing.

"I can do that, or I can have one of my AGs do it. You don't even have to be there."

"Thanks," said Joe, tearing a corner from his napkin.

"One bottle of the gross Dos," said Holmes, placing the beer in front of Gantz, "and one martini drug through the mud." He paused, surveyed the table. "Ah, forgot your water. BRB LOL."

Joe's sliver beeped and displayed an incoming email. He pulled out his phone to read it.

"Is it important?"

"Maybe," replied Joe. "I asked Legal to look into something for…"

He trailed off as he read Rita's message. It contained the information he had asked for: a top ten list of companies and individuals who had made the most buys and who were poised to snatch up more shares if the price of Perion stock dropped any lower. The number one entry was Doyle & Associates, LLC; an asterisk next to the name made Joe scroll down to Rita's notes.

"Doyle fronts for several political groups," Rita had written. "Most notable is the campaign fund for Governor Howard."

"What kind of something?" asked Gantz.

"I had an idea," said Joe, scanning the list again. "That someone might be profiting from our stock crash. Legal gave me ten names of people who have been snatching up shares and you'll never guess who's at the top of the list."

Gantz took a long pull of his drink. "Dear Lord, let it be me."

"Governor Howard," said Joe. He waited for the recognition to hit Gantz. "Well, not the governor personally, but his campaign fund. If shares go back up to last week's prices, he'll make millions."

"Shit," said Gantz, reaching into his jacket for his phone. He scrolled through his calendar. "And guess who's coming to dinner tomorrow." He slid the phone across the table.

Joe scanned the calendar for Friday. "There's a press conference tomorrow? What for?"

"I don't know, but Synth J requested extra security. Howard is coming in via helicopter and I'm supposed to have my best men waiting to meet him."

"He's going to do it," said Joe. "He's going to show the world he's still alive. What more reliable witness than the Governor of California?"

"Pretty slick move. I wouldn't be surprised if one of those companies is owned by your dad. You know, like a front betting against itself?"

"I don't recognize anyone else except Banks Media," said Joe.

"Are they number two?"

"No, but they've been buying pretty regularly since the beginning of the year. Number two is Diaz Investments, based out of Sacramento. I've never heard of them, and yet they're buying every share they can get their hands on."

"Maybe they're just big fans," suggested Gantz.

"Know what I'm a big fan of?" asked Holmes. He threw down another cocktail napkin and placed a glass of water next to Joe's martini. "Greasy Chinese food." He set a glass of dark, amber liquid in the middle of the table. "This one's on the house, just in case one of you realizes he's drinking piss. It's my own brew."

As he walked away, the jukebox flipped over a shiny disc and began playing *American Honky-Tonk Bar Association*. Holmes' curses were drowned out by the cheers of the concert audience.

Joe put his phone down on the table and folded his arms. As Garth's voice filled the room, he muttered, "This changes things."

"Yeah," said Gantz. "I feel like I should put on a cowboy hat or something."

"No, I mean with Governor Howard. No one would make such huge buys without having insider information. Doyle and Associates, Diaz Investments, Winston and Price: they *have* to know something. The question is how."

Gantz groaned. "You're suggesting more leaks."

"Maybe not. Howard thinks he's coming to meet my father, which means he knows he isn't dead and that the stock price will recover." Joe narrowed his eyes, tried to see all of the pieces at once.

"Collusion," said Gantz. "They're working together."

Joe considered the idea, tried to work out who would benefit the most from such an arrangement. Governor Howard's campaign fund would certainly welcome the additional support, but in exchange for what? Why did Synth J need him so badly?

"There's something I haven't thought of," said Joe. "All of my father's relationships, with politicians, with companies—what happens to them when I take over? I haven't even heard of a tenth of all the people Dad knows."

"Coups are never easy," said Gantz, emptying his bottle. He reached for the glass of home brew. "There's more to it than sitting in the big chair at the end of the table. I'm behind you, Joe, but you need to make sure you're ready for this. If your father made deals or had arrangements with people, they're going to expect you to honor them." He took a sip and nodded approvingly. "At least then we'll find out what kind of deal he made with Howard."

"Or I could just ask the governor himself tomorrow."

"There's always the direct route. What would we do in the meantime?"

"Go on as normal, I guess," said Joe.

Gantz snorted. "It's not exactly business as usual for Perion engineers to be experimenting on people."

The Paulson imprint—why did it upset Gantz so much?

"Leak it then," said Joe.

"What?"

He smiled and chomped on a pretzel. "That's pretty much the norm here now, isn't it? Something that's supposed to be a secret somehow ends up on the feeds?"

"But why would you think I would or could…"

"Use a proxy," said Joe. "Drop some hints to Banks' aggregator. Make sure he's in the right place at the right time so he sees what's happening."

"I don't know. I think if I get involved at all, I'd have to go full tilt." Gantz raised an eyebrow. "You realize once we set this in motion, there's no stopping, right?"

"Yeah, but at least we have a plan now. You help the Vinestead spy, I'll question Howard, and at the end of the day, we take out James Kirkland Perion the Second."

"We don't know she works for Vinestead. Hell, she could just be some Kaili Zabora copycat looking to make a name for herself." Gantz pulled his badge from his pocket and slipped the lanyard over his head. "Let's start with the first two," he said, pushing his chair back. "Depending on what we find out, we can go from there."

"Fine, but it will be *my* decision," said Joe.

"Yes, but you're going to need *my* help, so do me the courtesy of talking it over before you fire the first shot of the human-synthetic war of 2015."

"You don't think I'm ready for this, do you?" asked Joe, standing up.

"Joe, I love you, man, but taking out your own father? That's gotta be difficult for anyone." Gantz turned and headed for the exit. "Put it on my tab," he called out to Holmes.

"How about I put it on your face, Bob?" asked Holmes.

Joe followed the chief into the parking lot.

"Robert, I can do this!"

Gantz stopped in an empty parking space. He looked at Joe's GT-R and then at the long road back to town.

"What is it?" asked Joe.

"You see that car over there? Wasn't there when we arrived."

Joe followed the road to a sedan that appeared to have drifted onto the shoulder. Through the windshield, he could make out an arm draped over the steering wheel.

Gantz began walking and Joe followed close behind. As they neared the car, Gantz covered his face with his sleeve.

"Christ, do you smell that?"

The stench hit Joe a second later, a mix of burning rubber and hydrochloric acid.

"It's a synny," said Gantz, opening the door with his free hand.

Joe got a good look at the melting hulk of a synthetic man, now nothing more than a fragile shell hovering over a pool of green sludge. On the floorboards were the charred remains of shoes, already eaten through by the corrosive cocktail. Next to one shoe was a pistol; its surface bubbled and popped under the emerald liquid.

"That looks like one of your—"

Joe's sentence was lost under the sound of exploding gunpowder. Gantz pushed backwards into Joe, sending both men to the ground as shards of metal flew above their heads. More bullets followed; they pinged off the frame of the car for several seconds.

When the fireworks finally stopped, both men rolled onto their backs and panted at the sky.

"What is a synny doing on this side of the PNR?" asked Joe.

"With a gun," said Gantz.

"With a gun."

"I don't know." Gantz turned his head in the direction of the Spire. "But it wouldn't have crossed the Deadline without being ordered."

"You think it was meant for us?"

"Or *one* of us," said Gantz.

Joe stared at the sludge dripping down from the new holes in the bottom of the car and wondered if Synth J had the audacity to send a synthetic to kill a human.

To kill his own chief of police.

To kill his own son.

FORTY

Joe wanted nothing more than to confront Synth J about the attempt on his life, but even walking back to the car had proven difficult. There was pain in his face as if someone had attached a vise to the bridge of his nose, and everything smelled like blood. He had the back of Gantz' head to thank for that one, though if the chief hadn't forced Joe to the ground somehow, they might both be riddled with bullets instead of dealing with the headache to end all headaches. Joe recalled the moment of impact, how the sensation had crackled around his skull like a halo of lightning, touching each part of his brain with its prickly fingers before fizzling out into a dull ache.

He threw up before he got to the car, prompting Gantz to escort him around to the passenger side.

Gantz drove them back to the Spire and acted as a crutch for Joe as they rode the elevator down to Medical on B5. A synthetic nurse checked them both out and gave them a prescription for painkillers. Gantz refused his, waved them away as he spoke harshly into his phone. He was ordering his men—his *real* men—out to Pure to examine the melted synthetic. They wouldn't find anything, of course; the self-destruction protocols would see to that.

The chief's voice faded out under the haze brought on by the pills; Joe had been in too much pain to refuse his. The haze turned to fog turned to darkness, erasing all memory of how he made it back to his room.

It was the sound of a helicopter making a low pass around the Spire that woke Joe the next morning. The pills were still in his system, but waking up to the blinding sun made the pain bubble up through the grogginess. Outside, a sleek, blue helicopter made a wide circle around his apartment, its tail fin masked with the likeness of Governor Howard.

On the nightstand, Joe's phone buzzed. He snatched it up and found he had five missed calls, all from Gantz.

Joe pressed the answer button and said hello, setting off another series of pinpricks in the back of his brain.

"They fucking did it," whispered Gantz. "They brainwashed that girl. Kessler just stopped me in the hall and told me they are waking her up this morning. And get this, Joe… it was almost like Kessler was amused by it."

The headache pounded.

"So it's too late," said Joe. "There's nothing we can do for her now."

"The hell there isn't. I just got word from one of my contacts on the outside that she's with Lincoln Continental out of Umbra. We found nothing on the grid to back that up though, but Jesus, do you know what kind of shit storm it would create if it's true?"

"You saying we need to get to her first?"

"Yes, but even that depends on how scrambled she is. If the script Kessler gave me is any indication, they did one hell of a mindfuck on her."

"All of our minds are fucked," said Joe, pinching his nose. "I can be down there in ten minutes."

"What? No. You stay out of this. If people see you poking around, they'll go straight to Synth J. I've got to keep this low profile. And besides, there's something else you should be worrying about. Turn your vidscreen to channel twenty-sixteen."

Joe pointed the remote at the vidscreen and turned it on. He typed out the number with his thumb.

"It's asking for an access code."

"Zero eight, one eight, eight two," said Gantz.

The feed flickered as Joe entered the password, dissolving from one corrupted image into another. Finally, it settled on the conference room on seventy. Only one of the nine chairs was occupied; a brooding Sava Kessler sat with her phone in her hand, her face blank and cold.

"Sava's not sticking around to see the aggregator wake up?"

Gantz coughed. "I guess she doesn't like to get her hands dirty. Send in the chief to deliver some bullshit story about a car crash." His sigh sounded distorted through the phone. "Maybe I could get Cam into Medical, show this Cynthia woman a friendly face. They all know each other in the media houses, right?"

"Is that her name? Cynthia?"

"If it wasn't before, it is now, according to my script. It's been difficult to get confirmation; Umbra is a black hole of surveillance, even for Vinestead."

"I thought that was true for my dad's conference rooms."

That made Gantz chuckle a little. "Someone's always watching, Joe. For the right price, you can watch too. You don't want to know what I had to promise Deborah to get access to that feed."

On the screen, Sava perked up. She smiled like a synthetic as she rose to greet her guests.

"They're starting," said Joe, turning up the volume.

"Ping me if you find out anything. I'm gonna see what I can do for Cynthia."

Joe tossed his phone onto the bed as the line cut out.

"Governor Howard? I'm Savannah Kessler, pleased to meet you."

The governor was a tall man, like Dad, with a politician's haircut right down to the slight graying on the sides. He wore a navy-blue suit with a broad tie decked out in the red and white of California's state flag. When he extended his hand to Sava, the sunlight caught the gaudy chrome of his sliver.

"I assure you the pleasure is all mine, Savannah. And please, call me Martin."

Sava nodded and blinked away the glare from his wrist.

"You like that?" asked Martin, pulling back his sleeve. "That's a Raymond Weil original. Only eighty were made in the entire world. This is number twenty-seven."

"It's impressive," said Sava. She looked to his assistant.

"Ah yes, allow me to introduce my associate, Lee Winborn. Lee, say hello to the pretty lady."

"Pleasure," said Winborn, bowing slightly. He was a foot shorter than the governor, and though his suit was well-tailored, he hunched over, as if under the pressure of some invisible weight.

Sava pulled her fake smile even tighter. "Would you gentlemen like something to drink? I have coffee and water, but I can have some fresh tea brought up if you prefer."

"Lee, how about a cup of coffee?"

The assistant nodded and started for the French press at the back of the room.

Joe downed another painkiller.

"Savannah, dear," said Martin. "You look familiar. Do I know you from somewhere?"

Sava took a step back. "I'm head of public relations. I'm usually present at Mr. Perion's press conferences and publicity events."

Martin cocked his head. "Yes, that must be it. Strange I don't recall…"

"Mr. Howard!" called a booming voice from off camera.

The governor turned and shook hands with Synth J.

"Sorry to keep you waiting," said Synth J. "I trust Ms. Kessler has kept you entertained in my absence?"

"Absolutely," said Martin. "Savannah's been a real peach."

"Glad to hear it. Now, I know we had a sizable agenda planned for this morning, but I'm afraid other business has come up."

"That's fine. I'm here for the day. Maybe we can meet up later for dinner?"

"Great, great," said Synth J, looking around the room. He caught eyes with Sava. "Thank you, Ms. Kessler. That will be all for today."

She had just taken out her palette; her fingers stopped mid-keystroke.

Joe watched as her face flushed with anger.

"Fine," said Sava, standing. She nodded to her guests and then walked out of the room as fast as her heels would carry her.

"Lee, will you wait for me outside?" asked Martin.

There was no look of reproach on his assistant's face, just steadfast compliance. Joe assumed it wasn't the first time he'd been ordered out of the room.

"You're looking well," said Martin, as he sat down.

Synth J settled into the chair next to him. "I feel well, thanks for noticing."

The two men regarded each other with fake smiles and expectant nods.

"Your intel on Calle Cinco," said Synth J. "How well do you trust it?"

"Not a hundred percent," said Martin. "But nothing is. You put your ear to the ground and hope for the best. Right now, it's quiet."

"Nothing about an operative infiltrating Perion City?"

"It would have shown up in the report, especially if you were involved. As far as we know, Calle Cinco is laying low, waiting for their next opportunity to hit Vinestead, not you. What interest would they have in a synthetics company anyway?"

"I don't know, but nothing else makes sense. Vinestead wouldn't dare send an augment inside my walls, not without a fully functional Guardian Angel chip to send back whatever they discovered. So I started thinking, where does a woman with former V-tech line up in all of this?"

"Are we talking about a real person here? Has there been a breach?"

Synth J nodded. "Yesterday, but it's being dealt with. My concern is Calle Cinco's motivations. As you said, we're not their typical target."

"I'd hate to speculate and be wrong." Martin rubbed his sliver with his sleeve. "Did you run her face against the national DB?"

"We did a full run, domestic and international, and so far we've come up empty. There's no trace of her in the system—total grid-wipe. Meanwhile, she's got augments throughout her body and a scar the size of my dick on the back of her neck. She didn't simply have her GA chip removed; it was torn out of her, grow-wire and all."

"Sounds like something Kaili Zabora would do."

"I don't think anyone really knows what Crazy Kai is capable of, and that's what has me worried. If Calle Cinco is shifting their focus away from Vinestead and onto synthetics, then both of us are going to have a problem."

"How do you figure?" asked Martin, grinning. "*I'm* still human."

It felt like someone had shoved a hot spike into Joe's ear; he pressed it to his shoulder to stem the pain.

"For now," said Synth J. "But once you get my bill passed, you'll be on your way to synthetic immortality just like me."

"*If* I get your bill passed. Convincing the world a synthetic can own property and run a company is a tall order. Hell, even getting California to ratify is no small task, and we lead the nation in tech-acceptance."

"If you want to live forever," said Synth J, "if you want your family to live forever, you'll get the damn thing passed. And once that is done, you'll turn the full force of the state government on Calle Cinco. Because if Crazy Kai disrupts my business, that means you and your family will die just as I did."

Joe tried to swallow but choked instead.

"What choice do I have?" asked Martin. "You're the only game in town, but I know I'm not your only contingency. What other horses are you running, James? This new version of you seems to have a knack for covering every angle. Could any of those be taken as an affront to Calle Cinco?"

"Not on purpose," said Synth J, looking away. "I have no choice but to approach this from every possible angle; the stakes are just too high. Politics are important, but the media sets the tone of the nation. I've got an aggregator in town and if I can convince him synthetics are people too, then he'll convince everyone else. I'll have that story fed to every whisperer on the planet. And when you start raising support for my bill, Banks Media will be there to back you up, because they will have shown the world how real synthetics can be."

Martin tapped his fingers on the table. "I'm with you, James. I look at you even now and can't believe what you've done. You've changed the world, and in time, people will understand just how important that is. But until then, they're going to be suspicious. Aggregators will be the worst of them all. They will absolutely see through the bullshit. That's their job."

"I agree," said Synth J. "The average aggregator is objective and insightful, but what about when they're not thinking straight? What if they're emotionally involved or, if you can believe it, *in love* with their subject?"

"Don't tell me…"

"With a Virgo-class synthetic, same as me," said Synth J, laughing that hollow, digitized laugh.

"I hope she's better looking than you."

"Like you wouldn't believe." Synth J tapped his phone and handed it to Martin.

The governor let out a low whistle. "You don't have any more of these, do you? I wouldn't mind taking one home."

"Pass my bill, and I'll deliver her myself."

Martin slid the phone back. "Right. And what about the Point of No Return?"

"What about it?" Synth J leaned forward and folded his hands. "Do you really think you'll have to govern California from here? Or that I would be stuck in Perion City for the rest of eternity? The PNR is not carved in stone, Martin. It's just a song on the air."

"I have no idea what that means," said Martin. "But I trust that you do."

"Then we're agreed." Synth J stood and shook the governor's hand.

They walked to the door as their conversation turned banal.

"Ms. Kessler here is going to show you around until the press conference this afternoon. How does that sound?"

Joe could only see the top of the governor's head. "Works for me," he replied. "I'd very much like to meet this… Roberta, was it?"

"I'm afraid she's with another guest at the moment," said Kessler, off camera. "But I can try to locate her and set up a meeting."

"Yes, yes," said Martin. His voice dropped, "Bring her to me!"

Laughter carried them out of the room. When they were gone, a hiss ramped up as the microphones responded to the silence.

Joe hit the mute button and picked up his phone.

Gantz didn't answer.

Joe crawled off of his bed and began dressing in the clothes he had discarded the night before. Synth J's conversation with Governor Howard replayed in his mind, causing an ache to push through the pain meds. He needed to find Gantz.

He was walking into the foyer when a knock sounded from the door. The vidscreen showed Nico standing in the hallway, flanked by two Scorpios.

Joe opened the door to greet his assistant.

"Your father wants to see you, Joe," said Nico.

"He could have just called and asked," replied Joe.

Nico looked down at the floor. Beside him, the AGs stood impassive.

"He's not asking," said Nico. "Just come with me, please."

"Sure," said Joe, pulling the door closed behind him. He smiled at the synthetics. "Better not keep the old man waiting, right?"

Nico nodded and turned for the elevator, revealing fresh scratches wrapping around the back of his neck.

FORTY-ONE

The elevator sank to the bottom of the Spire.

Joe watched the numbers on the vidscreen by the door decrement at a steady clip, only slowing as they passed B15. At B19, the car came to a stop and the doors opened. In all of his years in the Spire, Joe had never been to this floor, but he recognized the décor from childhood, the way Mom had kept the house before she died. The walls were two-tone with a bright silver stripe running along dark gray walls. Sconces dotted the hallway every ten feet, radiating soft, yellow light from their bases. Framed photos showed the Perion scientists and engineers of old, gray-haired men who had come to the PC, worked the remaining years of their lives, and died in the service of a dream—a dream that had been lost, defiled.

"I thought we were going to see Synth J," said Joe.

Nico looked over his shoulder as they walked. "We are. He's waiting for you in the bunker."

"But I just saw him up on seventy with Governor Howard."

"I don't know his schedule," said Nico. "All I know is he asked me to bring you here so I did that."

They turned a corner and came upon a large, obsidian door. Two AGs stood guard on either side of it, their fingers extended just above the triggers of their weapons. They scanned the hallway, waiting for threats.

Nico touched the call button beside the door and moments later, Synth J's face appeared on the screen.

"Thank God you're here," he said, his sentence punctuated by the buzzing of locks and sighing of pistons.

The black square swung inward, revealing an expansive foyer that resembled an apartment complex lobby. Two walls held doors with brass numbers; leather couches filled in the space between them. A bank of vidscreens covered the third wall, each one showing a security feed from somewhere in the building, including the driveway in front of the Spire and Mom's plaza in the back.

Synth J grabbed Joe's shoulders as soon as he stepped inside.

"My boy," said the synthetic. "You're alright. I just heard about what happened in The Fringe yesterday. Are you sure you weren't hurt?"

Joe thought about the rhythmic ache pounding in the back of his head. "I'm fine," he replied. "Just a little bump."

"Why didn't you tell me about this when it happened?"

Because you already knew, thought Joe. He tried to read the synthetic's face, but there was no emotion to be found in the lines of its artificial skin. "Gantz told me he filed a report."

"Filed a *report*? Like it was some minor fender bender? Someone tried to kill my son!" Synth J stepped away, put his hand to the side of his face the way Dad used to do in moments of deep concentration. He began to mutter quietly. "Yesterday… multiple agents… not all detected."

"What is this?" asked Joe. "Why are you acting like you care about me? Do I even mean anything to you anymore or is all this just programming?"

Synth J frowned. "I'm still in here, Joey. Whether you want to believe it or not. We may have done things you don't agree with, but they were always for the good of the company."

"You mean yourself."

"Semantics, son. I *am* the company, and so are you. Good for the company, good for us. But this…" He sat down on the couch and covered his mouth with his hand. "This means someone is in our house. They're in and they're in deep. They know our system, know how to reprogram our synthetics. This is too complex for a drop-in Calle Cinco agent; this can only be Vinestead's doing." He looked past Joe. "Nico, get me Chief Gantz on the line. We need to call a strategy meeting. And bring down a dozen uniforms for the main entryway."

"I want to help," said Joe. "If someone is gunning for me, I want to find out why." He tried not to stare too intently at Synth J.

"Absolutely not. No, you stay here, where it's safe. I won't have any more attempts on your life. This bunker has everything you need for an extended stay and the synnies will keep anyone from getting close to you."

"Chief Gantz isn't answering his phone, Mr. Perion."

"Then go find him," barked Synth J. "How am I supposed to protect my son without my chief of police? What about the uniforms?"

"On their way," said Nico. "I spoke to the desk sergeant. He said he's sending down their most reliable Scorpios."

Joe scoffed. "Really? A synthetic tries to kill me and your plan is to surround me with more?"

"Don't worry about that," said Synth J. "There's a world of difference between Scorpios and the Capricorn that attacked you. The whole control paradigm was rewritten in the newer model. If Vinestead figured out how to reprogram our Scorpios…" He trailed off, as if considering the possibility for the first time. "Maybe it's only a matter of *when* they learn how to reverse engineer

Chuck's architecture. They've already broken the encryption on at least one model."

Silence hung in the room as the circuits in Synth J's head heated up. His eyes scanned back and forth in rapid bursts while his fingers dug into his cheeks.

"You're worried they'll be able to reprogram you," said Joe.

"No," said Synth J. "V-Primes have no networked connections. We're missing all of the voice-actuated commands present in the first Virgos."

"Are you sure?"

Synth J considered the question for a moment and then walked quickly towards the door. He snapped at the AGs standing guard. "No one goes in or out without my authorization. Come, Mr. Shaw. We need to locate Chief Gantz and Dr. Bhenderu."

"The doctor is working on the Paulson project right now," said Nico.

"Pull him off. Calle Cinco is the least of our worries right now."

"What about me?" asked Joe.

Synth J answered without breaking stride. "You're going to stay here until I say it's safe."

"Fuck that," said Joe, approaching the door.

An Automated Guard stepped forward and put his hand on Joe's chest.

"Take your hand off me," said Joe.

"Please remain in this room, Mr. Perion." Scorpios weren't built with the best voice enhancements; its words came out digitized and menacing.

"Or what?" Joe pushed the AG's hand away and tried to leave.

A firm grip on his arm stopped him.

It didn't hurt to have the synthetic's fingers wrapped around his bicep, but there was no struggling against it. The AG held tight until the bunker door slammed shut. Behind the plexiglass, thick metal cylinders extended into the evercrete doorframe. On the final click, the AG released its grip. It took up position next to the door, checked the safety on its gun, and then placed the weapon at rest by his leg.

"Asshole," said Joe, rubbing his arm. He sat down in the chair in front of the vidscreens and scanned the security feeds.

After an hour of watching random people come and go, Joe grew restless and set about exploring his jail cell. As prisons went, it had all the comforts he expected billionaires would receive when they were caught insider trading or draining the pension funds of their employees. Detention with class, thought Joe. Locked away from the world on a leather couch with all the booze and entertainment anyone could want—a staycation with only a hint of punishment.

Of the three doors in the foyer, only one opened at Joe's touch. Inside, he found a recently refreshed room, like a swanky hotel suite waiting for its next guest. To the left of the king-size bed was a small table with three chairs. To the right, a dormant palette sat atop a desk of metal and glass. At the foot of the bed was an area filled with a black loveseat flanked on both sides by recliners. A seventy-inch vidscreen hung on the wall in front of them.

The room resembled Joe's apartment, just condensed.

With his headache still pounding, he crawled onto the bed and sank into the welcoming mattress. He grabbed the remote and tuned the vidscreen to the media feeds. While they loaded, he stared at the faces of each house: Donato Banks, Lincoln Tate, and Benny Coker.

Joe selected Lincoln's brooding face and waited for the audio.

"…a Friday marred by protests in southern cities at the perceived aggression by the MX government. At issue are recent allegations into the MX' funding of drug cartels along the border, who over the last decade, have significantly devalued U.S. property."

Joe had been to Mexico once as a child. He recalled it being very dark, without the light pollution so prevalent in Perion City or Los Angeles. There, the unobscured stars twinkled in the sky above the vacation home his father jokingly referred to as a cabin. The boundlessness of the universe captured Joe's interest, and he spent many nights staring into the black dome.

Later, those twinkling stars were replaced by the flashing neons of Perion City at night, as seen from high in the Spire. Joe recalled Dad sitting in his office long after sunset, a stack of papers on his desk but his attention turned to the bustling city around him.

"We never stop," he would often tell the little boy in his pajamas standing just inside the door. "At any given moment, there are a hundred or a million people out there working for the same dreams you're working for, trying to accomplish the same goals. And the difference between us and them, Joey, is that *we never stop*. Each one of those lights out there represents a member of the competition. They're working while others sleep. And so must you."

And then the titan would turn to his son and say, "There will come a time when you have to make a choice, have to take a step. If you find yourself unprepared, there are only two things you have to remember. The first is that I will always love you and always be proud of you. The second is what your mother tells you every night before bed. Do you remember, Joey?"

Joe's daydream turned to images of his mother, blurred by the many years, but full of warmth and familiarity. He saw her moving about his childhood room, picking up the remaining toys he had left scattered on the floor. And when the last of the Legos and G.I. Joes had been put in their bins, she came and sat on the edge of his bed. The Smurfs lamp on the nightstand cast a blue glow on her smile and Joe felt her presence provided more safety than any bunker in the world.

Her lips moved, but the words were all wrong, not quite soft enough and tinged with an English accent.

"Vinestead stock rose again today on speculation its PMC division could be called upon by President Hadden to secure our southern border. Many democrats are calling this back-alley favors, citing the President's push ten years ago for the controversial GA bill, which was introduced by the then-governor of Massachusetts. Speaking from the Rose Garden today, the President challenged his critics to suggest a better plan for keeping immigrants from becoming burdens on the backs of hard-working Americans. A statement released by Calle Cinco today calls the President's remarks irresponsible and racist. No threat of terrorism was made with the statement."

Joe turned the vidscreen off and rolled onto his back.

In the darkness behind his closed eyes, he thought of his mother and what words of salvation she might have said to him so many years ago.

PART FIVE
ROBERT GANTZ

FORTY-TWO

The small studio apartment over the W.G. Walter Spiritual Center wasn't much, but it was a home to Dr. David Yates, who had run the WG for the better part of a decade. Unlike other professions, the role of spiritual advisor was a twenty-four-hour job, with services running from daybreak to sunset and walk-in meetings available day or night. Not that many ever took advantage. The ones and twos of the weekly congregations swelled to half a dozen on the weekends, but never more than that. It took a national tragedy to swell the ranks of the congregation, or perhaps just the rumor of an old man fading before dawn.

Yates thought about the strange week following the Synthetic Collapse as he lay awake in his twin bed, staring at the accumulation of light rain on his window, the drops of water warping the blue Southpoint Synthetics sign next door. Every once in a while, the blue flared to white as lightning reached out from the clouds. There was no thunder though, no distant rumbling to make Yates wonder what terrible pestilence might be lingering just beyond the horizon, inching and oozing its way towards Perion City. All week, the air had been full of potential, charged with some hint of a calamity ready to spill into this world. The clouds could burst or the earth might open up, but *something* was going to happen.

The people of Perion City sensed it; they came in droves to the weekday services. At Sunday's evening mass, two dozen of the city's newly faithful had to stand near the open doors, some even gathering outside to peer over the heads of others. James Perion likely never imagined so many people would need the Lord's words, not in a city of the scientific and pragmatic.

On the desk by the opalescent window, the day's log lay open to Sunday, November 15.

Evening Mass: 112 attendees.

That was one hundred and twelve worried faces trying to smile as they offered each other a sign of peace, two hundred and twenty-four doubting eyes looking to Yates for reassurance.

And though he had recited the passages and delivered the soothing words of the Gospel, he was not completely convinced of their impact. These convenient Catholics may have knelt before the Lord, but did His word truly mean anything to them? These were men and women of science and math—mere platitudes would not sway them. How could Yates convince them of a greater plan if they had always approached sky-gods as myths, and had never once seen any proof, any sign to suggest otherwise? If they were not ready to accept His word, why did they so eagerly fill His house?

Yates had just rolled over for the hundredth time when a soft knock came at the door of his apartment. Through the fabric partition between the living room and the bedroom, he could see green light seeping in beneath the door.

"Yes?" he asked.

"There is a man downstairs," said Truman, the Center's resident synthetic altar boy and custodian.

"Someone broke in?" asked Yates, grabbing an undershirt he had left draped over the footboard. "Did you notify the police?"

"No, Father. He *is* the police."

Yates touched the light switch in the foyer and retracted the deadbolts in the door. He pulled on a night robe decorated with Catholic imagery before turning the handle. In the hallway, the glow from the running lights lit Truman's face from below.

"Thank you, Truman. That will be all."

"Be careful, Father. He appears inebriated."

Of course he was, thought Yates, as he descended the circular staircase into the back hallway. In the main hall, an immense wooden cross hung in the shadows at the front facing the doors. Before it, an oversized Bible sat open atop a marble altar. Running lights illuminated the center aisle between the pews, spilling the green and amber hues halfway down each of the six rows.

In the final pew closest to the door, a hunched-over figure sat with his head down. His black trench glistened from the persistent drizzle outside.

Yates stopped at the end of the pew and clasped his hands together. The man did not look up.

"Welcome, my son," said Yates. "Have you come seeking comfort?"

Robert Gantz burped in response.

Yates sighed and took a seat next to the chief of police.

"How are you, Robert?"

"Wet."

"It's a blessing," said Yates. "Lord knows we need it."

Robert shook his head. "It won't last."

"No, I suppose it won't. But that's desert life, isn't it? Scarcity of water makes us appreciate His gifts even more."

Robert huffed.

Yates crossed one leg over the other. "I didn't see you at Mass today. I assume you were busy with that terrible business in The Fringe?"

"It was just a warehouse fire. Someone probably left some popcorn in the microwave too long." A hiccup. "There are bigger things happening."

"We are listening, my son."

Robert looked up and even in the dim light, Yates could see the red streaks obscuring the whites of his eyes. His cheeks were also damp, but that could have been from the rain.

"He's dead, Padre. Gil is dead."

Robert often spoke of Gilbert Reyes, a low-level employee who did tech repair in the Spire.

"I'm sorry to hear that, Robert. Death is… never easy. How did it happen? Was it the fire?"

"No," said Robert, shaking his head. He picked at a scar on the back of his thumb. "This was later, at Gil's apartment. A synthetic sna—" The chief's voice broke. "She snapped his neck. Right in front of me."

"And you feel responsible?" After a noncommittal shrug, Yates said, "I'm sure you did everything you could to prevent it."

"No, I didn't. Kessler had me. I thought I did the right thing by leading her away from Gil, but then his conversation with Roberta started showing up on the feed. I couldn't risk…" He squeezed his hands into fists. "And that's the other thing. It wasn't like someone was listening in and broadcasting his words; he was a fucking aggregator. He's been working undercover for The White Line this whole time. Under *my* nose. Everything he and I have been through… I thought he was my friend."

"You couldn't have known, Robert."

"I should have." The chief turned his face to the ceiling. "He lied to me. I trusted him and he *engineered* me. He passed along privileged information to the worst possible people. All week, I've been trying to figure out who was leaking information, and it turns out it was me. I told Gil secrets about Perion in confidence. I…"

His words trailed off as he closed his eyes.

Yates waited for Robert to get a few deep breaths.

"There are few hurts in this world as great as betrayal. We open ourselves to other people, but they don't always open to us. You can't blame yourself, my son. All men are fallible, but that shouldn't stop us from striving to be the very best we can."

A flask appeared from Robert's inner pocket. He took a quick pull before offering it to Yates.

"No, thank you. I'm on duty."

Robert shrugged and took another drink. "So am I."

Seconds passed in silence.

"You don't know how to feel, do you?" asked Yates.

"I asked Him for guidance, but He hasn't answered."

Yates put a hand on Robert's shoulder. "The Lord cannot tell you how to feel. That is one of our gifts as His children, to be capable of so many emotions, even those which are conflicting or paradoxical. You should not feel ashamed to mourn your friend's death and simultaneously feel anger at his betrayal. This is all part of the human condition, and no one should feel inadequate for simply being human.

"Each of us has the capacity to be many things to many people. You are the chief of police, yet you bow your head to a higher power every Sunday. I preach the Gospel to you, and yet I sit here in the dead of night with you not just as your pastor, but as your friend. Cherish the good you had with Gil and forgive the bad. That is the way to salvation, my son."

"Kessler knows I protected Gil," said Robert. "I'm almost certain she's told Perion. We're supposed to meet in the morning, the three of us, and I won't be surprised if they boot me out of the city. Or hell, maybe they'll just get Roberta to end me."

"I pray that doesn't happen," said Yates.

"You and me both." He looked up again, this time past the ceiling. "I don't know what to do."

Yates leaned back into the rigid pew. "In our times of need, we ask the Lord for guidance. While we wait for His answer, we must ask ourselves what it is *we* want to do. Often our tribulations are couched as if life is just something happening *to* us, when in reality, we are the captains of our own destiny. Sometimes that means we adjust our sails instead of screaming into the wind. Your friend is dead, Robert, but because you cared for him greatly, his death is not the end of all things. What you must ask yourself now is how you will honor his life, if you so choose."

"I could have stopped it and I did nothing," said Robert, sitting up straighter. "It was a sin of omission, and I'll never let it happen again."

"A virtuous pursuit if there ever was one."

Robert replaced the flask in his jacket. "I'm tired of this, Father. I have to put a stop to it, even if that means finding Sava Kessler and putting a bullet in her head."

"Violence begets violence, Robert. You know that. The Church cannot condone murder."

"I'm not asking for permission."

"And yet you would ask for forgiveness?"

Robert nodded. "I can't predict the future, but I know if I stand up for what I believe in, people are going to die."

The first crack of thunder rumbled beyond the front doors of the hall. Yates shot a glance at the ceiling.

"Killing in Gil's name will not honor his memory," said Yates.

"What about killing in the name of Joe Perion to protect him from the evil brewing in the Spire?"

"I was not aware Joseph Perion needed protecting."

Robert sat back in the pew and folded the flaps of his trench over his legs.

"Of course you weren't," he said. "No one sees it but me. Everyone is walking around like the Great Synthetic Collapse of 2015 never happened. They think a chorus of synthetics chanting *the Creator is dead* means nothing." He cleared his throat. "They believe the Creator is still alive, that the abomination in the Spire calling itself James Kirkland Perion is flesh and blood just like they are, but they're being lied to. The synthetic James Perion is devolving and he's taking Sava Kessler and anyone else in his orbit with him. The world can't lose Joe to that. *I* can't lose Joe to that."

Perhaps it was the lingering drowsiness that caused Yates to mishear Robert. For a moment, it had sounded like he was suggesting James Perion was a synthetic. There must have been some powerful stuff in that flask.

"I won't let that happen," said Robert, standing up. He walked past Yates into the aisle. As he put his hands on his hips, the flaps of his trench fell back to reveal the holster on his side. He looked aimlessly around the hall before his eyes fell on the exit.

Yates rose and followed the chief to the doors.

"Will you absolve me of my sins?" asked Robert.

Yates thought about the gun hidden under Robert's coat, the tears welling at the corners of his eyes, and the vengeance burning in his heart.

"Come see me tomorrow, my son, and we'll see what we can do."

Robert nodded and opened the door. Outside, the rain had begun to let up. He walked down the steps to the sidewalk and the curb where his cruiser was parked. After a short pause, he looked over his shoulder at Yates, as if asking permission.

"Better not to risk it," said Yates. "I expect to see you alive and well tomorrow."

"Thanks for the words, Padre," said Robert. He lifted the collar of his trench and set off towards the Spire on foot.

Yates closed the door and engaged the deadbolts at the top and bottom of the frame. He stood for a minute with one palm on the veneered wood.

"Is everything alright, Dr. Yates?"

Truman stepped out of the shadows.

"Yes," said Yates, "everything is fine. It was just something the chief said about James Perion being dead."

"The Creator *was* dead, but He is risen again."

The synthetic turned and walked towards the back room where it spent its nights.

Yates stared at the shadowy cross at the front of the hall. Truman was supposed to have retracted it into the ceiling where the other religious symbols hung on wires, ready to be lowered to suit the needs of the congregation.

Humans had so many gods.

Synthetics were supposed to have none, and yet Truman's words echoed in the stillness.

James Kirkland Perion.

Synthetic. Creator.

God?

FORTY-THREE

No one was talking.

Though Gantz had plenty to say to the other people waiting outside the conference room, he was thankful for the quiet. The hangover he had acquired pounded in the back of his head, reaching out with prickly tendrils with every footfall or throat-clearing.

He sat by himself on a low couch at the end of the hallway, his head resting on the silver wainscoting. A large Areca palm next to him provided the only shade from the rough sunlight pouring in through the window.

A tremor went through his wrist. It took every ounce of concentration to narrow his eyes enough to read the miniscule text on his sliver.

Breaking: Benny Coker of White Line Media files lawsuit in California court against Perion Synthetics. Suit names Joseph Perion and others as instrumental in detention and possible death of Gilbert Reyes. If suit goes forward, it will be the first challenge to the Perion City Sovereignty Act of 2001.

Gantz looked around the room at the *others* who would be named in the suit. Sava Kessler, looking bored with her nose buried in her phone, would definitely do time for her role as triggerman. Beside her, Chuck Huber spoke in hushed tones to Dr. Langley Bhenderu. They both had a hand in creating Roberta and thus were responsible for their creation's actions. It wouldn't be long before they were trading their white lab coats for orange jumpsuits.

Absent was one Joseph Perion and his personal assistant Nico. Gantz hadn't seen either since Friday morning. Calls to Joe's cell phone went unanswered.

Further down the hallway, the synthetic James Perion adjusted his tie in front of a mirror, flanked on three sides by equally synthetic security personnel.

He noticed Gantz looking in his direction.

"Something the matter, Robert?"

"No," replied Gantz, trying his best to smile. "The old man used to do that. It was his only nervous tick, if I recall."

Synth J pulled the Windsor knot tight and smoothed out his jacket. "It's not a tick. It's just something to occupy my hands while I visualize this meeting. Create the reality in your mind and your body will respond accordingly." He turned away from the mirror. "It works even better now." He smiled, lifting the corners of his mouth towards eyes that didn't narrow. "Come closer, all of you."

Gantz stood as the Spire leaned forty-five degrees and then corrected itself. Kessler raised an eyebrow at him but said nothing.

Lord, give me the strength to not choke the life from her.

They gathered around Synth J.

"This," he said, spreading his arms, "is my inner circle. You are my brothers and my sister. I have asked so much from each of you in the last week and each of you has exceeded my expectations."

"Then how about a raise?" asked Gantz.

"My head of security cannot want for money," said Synth J. "Or else Vinestead could buy your loyalty out from under me."

Gantz ignored the voice in the back of his mind asking *what loyalty* and replied, "It'd cost them a hell of a lot of money."

"Believe me, they have it." Synth J nodded in agreement with himself. "But let's not worry about that right now. Today we start a new chapter in our shared history. This is the moment when we start changing people's minds."

He motioned to the door, which one of the synthetics opened.

The Automated Guards entered first, followed by the lab coats. Gantz walked in after Kessler and stood behind a chair to her right. Across the table sat Cameron Gray, Cynthia Mesquina, and a third man Gantz hadn't seen before. He looked familiar and generic at the same time, as if his features had been averaged out of a sampling of magazines. The way he stared back spoke to some recognition, but Gantz couldn't place it.

Then Synth J walked in and the everyman across the table lost his shit.

"Gilbert, directive. Stop!"

Kessler's voice froze the man—Gil?—in the middle of the table.

Those sons of bitches had done it.

Gantz felt himself mouthing the word *sorry*.

Two AGs pulled the synthetic back to his chair, and each put a restraining hand on his shoulder.

Gantz turned to Kessler as she sat down. "You called him Gilbert. As in Gilbert Reyes?"

Synth J answered for her. "Your friend is gone, Robert, but we have saved the most important part of him. Say hello to Gilbert Reyes 2.0."

Across the table, Synth G mumbled a string of curse words as he struggled to regain control of his body.

"Gilbert, directive." The words flowed leisurely from Kessler's lips. "Shut the fuck up."

"If you don't mind, Mr. Reyes, I'll be doing most of the talking today. First, I would like to apologize for what must have been a very unexpected and traumatic experience. Although we have spared no expense providing you with a new—some might say better—body, it was never our intention. We have simply tried to make the best of a horrible situation, by which I mean your unfortunate death. The synthetic, Roberta, has been remanded to Diagnostics until we figure out how she misinterpreted the imprint protocols given by Ms. Kessler."

"What happened to Gilbert 1.0?" asked Cam.

"It was unpleasant," said Synth J, "and that is all I will say on the subject. We hoped Mr. Reyes would surrender peacefully, but then no man gets a Margate chip because he likes to acquiesce. He gambled on the path of violence and got cleaned out. It happens." Synth J shifted his gaze back to Synth G. "But all is not bad news. You are now the owner of the fifth Virgo-class synthetic ever produced. Thanks to Mr. Huber and Dr. Bhenderu, we achieved an unprecedented imprint saturation, far greater than we observed with Roberta."

"Why does he look like that?" asked Gantz.

Chuck Huber cleared his throat. "There was no time to template his physical attributes. We used a pre-existing design and did our best to create what few resemblances we could."

"Well, you failed." Gantz stared into the eyes of his friend's synthetic replacement, but there was no soul in there, no true memories of nights spent drinking themselves half to death at Pure.

"Thank you, Mr. Gantz," said Synth J. "However, in the long run, a man of Mr. Reyes' talents may be thankful for the new veneer, not to mention immortality, freedom from disease and fatigue, and so on."

"Did you throw in rust-proofing?" asked Cam.

"No," said Synth J, "but I can see to it that *your* synthetic is more than protected against premature oxidation."

Cam sat up straighter. "Are you threatening me, asshole? You so much as look at me wrong and everything I've archived for the last week will auto-dump to Banks. Even this conversation we're having."

Synth J put up his hands. "Begging your pardon, Mr. Gray. I misspoke. That was not a threat, but an offer. I'm presenting you, as well as Ms. Mesquina, with the opportunity of a lifetime. Several lifetimes, actually."

Gantz wasn't paying attention to the conversation. He was locked in a staring match with Synth G. Anger broiled behind those unblinking eyes.

"I don't want shit from you, Perion," said Cyn. "Except maybe five minutes alone without your guards to protect you."

"All I ask is that you hear me out. After that, the three of you will be free to make your own decisions. Are we agreed?"

Cam and Cyn remained stoic. Synth G tried to speak but was unable.

"Whether you appreciate it or not, Mr. Reyes represents the next great leap forward in human evolution. You may believe the path to salvation lies in augmentation, Ms. Mesquina, and in some ways, I agree with you, but we are now able to skip over the years of painful surgeries to arrive at a final solution: synthetic sleeving. Out with the old and in with the new. Why replace your body in a series of augmentations when you can do it wholesale in one treatment?"

Cyn regarded Synth G out of the corner of her eye. "He's completely synthetic?"

"Everything except his soul," said Synth J. "His mind is powered by proprietary synaptic gates, quadruple the density of anything Katsumi has ever produced. Like it or not, you are now a synthetic human being, Mr. Reyes, an ambassador for a new race of people. Ms. Kessler, if you would."

"Gilbert, directive. Speak."

Gantz detected a hint of pleasure in the way she gave orders. And was that a smile hiding in the corner of her mouth?

"I didn't ask for this," said Gil.

"And what exactly were you asking for when you started airing our dirty laundry to every feed junkie in the country?" asked Kessler.

Did she know the chief of police was the source of that dirty laundry?

"Information wants to be free," said Cam. "If you've got nothing to hide…"

Synth J nodded. "And what about Mr. Reyes? Does *he* want to be free?"

All eyes fell on Synth G. "I *am* free," he replied.

Synth J's laughter was mechanical and droll.

"No, Mr. Reyes, you are not free. In the eyes of the state of California, you are deceased as of eight a.m. Saturday morning. Industrial accident due to personal negligence. Or so they will say once Chief Gantz files his official report."

"Benny will never buy that," said Synth G. "I broadcast in the clear for several minutes before Roberta broke my sliver. I'm surprised you haven't heard from our lawyers yet."

Gantz touched his sliver; if Synth G only knew.

"You are correct," said Synth J. "That was a damning piece of sensationalist reporting, but it's nothing my head of PR can't sweep under the rug."

"She can't make something like this disappear. Not even with your help."

"Right again, Mr. Reyes. That is why *you're* going to help her."

This time, it was Cyn who laughed.

"Synthetic Humans: the next step in the evolution of mankind." Kessler's voice rose and fell in aggregator cadence. "A tragic accident in the heart of innovation, a man struck down in his prime. Mr. Reyes didn't ask for an untimely death, but now he has a second chance. All he asks is to be treated like anyone else, like a human being."

Cyn rolled her eyes. "Nobody will swallow that bullshit."

"Why not?" asked Synth J. "You're only marginally more human than Mr. Reyes. You're *allowed* to walk around with an Ayudante chip in your head because people are familiar with it, they know where it comes from. If you swap it out for something new, if you show people there's another way to go that's foreign to them, they'll come after you with scalpels."

"Let them fucking try," said Cyn.

"What do we have to do?" asked Synth G.

"You can't be serious," said Cam.

Synth G looked at his lap. "I'm a goddamn machine. And these assholes are the only ones who know how it works. What choice do I have?"

"We could always turn you off," said Kessler. "It makes no difference to me."

"Ms. Kessler, please," said Synth J. "Mr. Reyes, what I'm offering you, what I'm offering all of you, is immortality. Infinite re-sleeving for as long as the company exists. Mr. Huber will personally design your Virgo Prime synthetics, each one geared towards your individual specifications. Ms. Mesquina, you can be stronger and faster than you ever thought possible. Mr. Gray, you will always be young and fit, an enviable combination in the City of Angels. Mr. Reyes, you and Ms. Dulac can live out the rest of human existence together. And most importantly, no directives."

"Answer my question," said Synth G.

Synth J brought his hands together on the table. "Once you are all in your new bodies, you will go and preach the synthetic gospel to the people. You will use your positions at your respective media houses to further the rights of synthetic humans. You will continue to do this until synthetics have the same rights as organics."

"And then what?" asked Cam.

"Then you will be free."

Cam shook his head. "Walking around in Perion hardware means we'll never be free of you."

Synth J smiled. "A small price to pay, wouldn't you agree?"

"Balls to that," said Cyn.

"Yeah, great big hairy balls to that," said Cam.

Before Synth G could weigh in, the double doors of the conference room swung open, smacking the walls on either side. An unshaven Joe Perion stepped through and took in the room.

Gantz smiled at his friend but got nothing in return.

"You!" screamed Joe, taking a step towards Synth J.

Four AGs moved in front of him as his synthetic father stood.

"Joseph, what are you doing up here? We agreed you should stay in the bunker where it's safe."

"You mean where I'm out of the way? There was never any threat, was there, *Dad*?"

"How did you get out?" asked Kessler. "We had guards…"

"Oh, I know," said Joe, tiptoeing to be seen over the Scorpios' shoulders. "They had me locked up like a prisoner, but then I remembered. I remembered what Mom used to tell me."

Kessler laughed; Synth J's face lost all expression.

"And what did the darling Victoria Perion have to say?" asked Kessler.

Joe sank onto his heels and addressed the AGs in front of him. "All that lives must die. All must walk their own path to the dust." The confidence in his voice reminded Gantz of the late titan. "Now, leave us."

The AGs looked at each other and wandered away, as did the AGs standing behind Synth G. Every synthetic within earshot seemed to lose their programming, everyone except...

Joe approached the table as the synthetics filed out of the room.

"So," said Synth J, "you figured out the failsafe. Now what?"

"Now you go back in the box."

"An interesting idea." Synth J crossed the room to his son, his hand stroking the smooth skin of his chin. "I could do that. I could just stand aside and give up my dreams because my little boy wants to play CEO." He stopped in front of Joe and put a hand on his shoulder. "I have a better idea though. How about I stay on as CEO and bring about the synthetic revolution humanity has been waiting for and you... *you* learn some goddamn respect?"

"My father is dust," said Joe. "You are not him. You are not the CEO of Perion Synthetics. You are nothing but a *product*!"

A synthetic hand shot out and gripped Joe by the throat.

"Maybe *you'd* like to be dust," said Synth J.

Joe struggled to speak. "All that... lives... must..."

"Keep saying it, boy. Primes have no fail-safe!"

Gantz moved automatically; the adrenaline beat back the headache and the blurred vision. Muscles in his legs contracted, pushing the chair away and raising his body up. A hand that had been nervously tapping on his sliver sought out the hardware tucked beneath his armpit.

"Put him down, James!"

He was able to level the Perion PD standard-issue 9mm before he finished his sentence.

Synth J looked over his shoulder. "Stay out of this, Robert. This is a family matter."

"I will shoot if I have to."

"Will you betray me again, Robert?" asked Synth J. "After all I have forgiven?" He lifted Joe off the ground with just one arm.

"I won't let you kill my..." Gantz watched Joe's eyes roll into the back of his head. "My friend."

"Then die with your friend," said Synth J. His other hand shot out, perhaps intent on finding another larynx to claim as a prize.

Forgive me, Father…

Gantz saw the twitch in the synthetic's shoulder and gently squeezed the trigger. It only took one shot to send a firework of reverse-engineered Katsumi tech spraying across the table, splattering in a mixture of black sludge and metal shards.

Joe inhaled deeply as he fell to the ground.

"Are you out of your fucking mind?" screamed Kessler. "You just murdered James Perion!"

"That looks more like property damage to me," said Cam.

This time, it was Kessler who rushed the table. She was halfway to Cam when Gantz called out.

"Kessler, directive. Stop!"

Gantz retrained his weapon as Kessler turned to face him. That she could still move surprised him; he was almost certain she was a synthetic.

"Joe, what do you say we get the fuck out of here?" asked Gantz.

"I want on that train," said Cam. He waited for Cyn to stand and followed her to the door.

Gantz backed away from the table and helped lift Joe from the floor. At the door, he handed him to Cyn.

"Are you coming?"

Synth G hadn't moved from his seat, had barely winced when the shot was fired. "I've transcended the natural world," he replied, his voice shaky.

"I can't just leave you here with her, Gil."

"Gil is gone. Whatever I am now, I have to accept it." Finally, his eyes came up. "If they have Jackie…"

"This isn't over, Gantz," said Kessler. Standing in the middle of the table, she towered over the room. "You *will* answer for this."

"We'll see," he replied, backing up into the hallway.

"Next time, it won't be just one synthetic." She smiled. "I will bring every goddamn synny in the city down on you."

And yet you would ask forgiveness?

Gantz pulled the doors closed and engaged the magnetic locks.

The open elevator at the end of the hallway beckoned.

FORTY-FOUR

Gantz typed his security code into the elevator's vidscreen, forcing it to bypass all other floors on the way to the lobby.

In one corner, a dazed Joe stood with his back against a mirrored wall, one hand on the railing and the other around Cam's shoulder. The bruises on his neck had shot past purple and were now a sickly black. The few words he uttered were followed by furtive gasps and then sharp inhalations through his nose as he tried to breathe through the pain. Though there was blood at the corner of his mouth, it was not flowing.

Gantz examined the magazine in his 9mm and then stowed the weapon inside his jacket. His hand shook as he engaged the clasp on the holster. He held it there hidden from view until the tremors subsided.

Fucking Synth J.

It was one thing to deviate from the vision of his former self, but to physically harm his own flesh and blood? There was no excuse except one: Synth J was no longer flesh and blood, so the bond between father and son no longer existed. There was no guarantee Synth J wouldn't someday extend the dissolution of compassion to all of humanity and declare himself the god of a new race of synthetics, when he knew as well as Gantz there was only one true God. Ignoring the basic tenets of the human condition didn't come easy to most people, but once it started, the slope was often greased with blood.

Synth J's actions had already spilled enough blood, both human and synthetic.

"How long until we hit the lobby?" asked Cyn.

Gantz nodded to the vidscreen. "Maybe thirty seconds. Why?"

She looked at Cam. "Remember last time? I don't think we should be in here when it stops."

"What're you thinking?" asked Cam.

Cyn replied by stepping up onto the railing and punching her way through the white paneling on the ceiling. The sound of humming electromagnets filled the car as she opened the service hatch.

"It's risky," said Gantz. He looked to Joe. "What do you say? Can you climb?"

Joe made the slightest of nods and centered himself beneath the hatch as Cyn's legs disappeared through it.

Gantz helped Cam lift Joe into the ceiling. Joe gave a cry halfway up, but Gantz kept pushing anyway. When the scion was safely on the roof, Cam stepped onto the railing and using Gantz for leverage, hauled himself up through the hatch.

Cam called down into the car. "Tight fit up here, Chief. Not much to hold onto except our dicks."

"Noted," said Gantz, jumping up to grab both sides of the small, square opening. He kicked off the railing and launched himself upwards. He landed in a seated position on top of the car, legs still dangling inside. "Umbra girls always like to make a bad situation worse."

Cyn motioned for him to move. As she closed the hatch, the car began to slow. "We need to jump to a platform before it comes to a stop." She motioned to the platforms scrolling by on one wall of the evercrete shaft.

Joe's breathing rasped above the magnetic hum as they waited.

The elevator halted in a series of three diminishing bounces. Cyn jumped before the brakes kicked in, leaving the three men on top of the car. She landed silently on the metal grate and turned around.

Gantz placed a finger in front of his lips as a ding sounded from below.

Gunfire erupted from the lobby of the Perion Spire; the ricochets smashed the mirrored walls and the vidscreens behind them. Bullets and debris exited the back of the car and pinged off the elevator shaft, prompting Gantz to shield his face with his forearm.

Joe moved first, jumping down to the platform. He crashed against the wall, but Cyn kept him from rebounding further.

Gantz and Cam made their jump together and then one by one, they descended the ladder.

The shooting lasted a full minute, bathing them in stray shrapnel.

When it ceased, Gantz froze, even while Joe and the aggregators continued to descend. He looked up through the smoke to see beams of light spilling out of the back of the car, illuminating the dull evercrete. The amount of damage suggested more than a single shooter. Perhaps as many as half a dozen had opened fired on the elevator.

Without warning. Without regard to its occupants.

I will bring every goddamn synny in the city down on you.

Kessler wasn't fucking around.

"She's out of her mind," said Gantz, as he touched down on the B5 platform.

"Who is?" asked Cam.

"Kessler. Twenty bucks says they were firing under her orders."

Cyn shook her head. "Too soon. They were probably already in position. Something *else* happened to trigger that response." She traced the outline of a metal panel before turning around. "Maybe because you killed their leader."

Gantz looked to Joe and back again. "Human life over synthetic—there's no fucking question."

Cyn smiled as if expecting his indignation. "I'm not complaining, Officer. You get me a weapon, and I'll do the same to every synth cocksucker we meet on our way out of here. The way you opened Perion up… it was beautiful."

"It didn't seem to surprise you," said Gantz.

"What, that Perion was synthetic? How could anyone not see that coming?"

"I didn't," said Cam.

"Of course not," said Cyn. "You got way too close to the goods, Gray. That Roberta doll got your mind and your dick so confused, you didn't even know which way was up."

"I don't care which way is up, I care which way is out." Cam tugged on the collar of his shirt. "It's so fucking hot in here. I just want to get back to civilization. I want air conditioning and room service and a *real* piece of ass."

Gantz spread his arms. "Anything else, sir?"

"A Seven and Seven, heavy on the Seven."

"What's the play now?" asked Cyn. "What's our fastest way out of the city?"

"We drive out," said Gantz. "If they've got the lobby covered, then it's a fair bet they have the garage staked out as well. They won't be expecting us down here just yet, so we can sneak up a few floors and take a look."

Joe shook his head.

"No good, boss?" asked Gantz.

Joe wagged his finger, pointed to his chest, and then mimed a steering wheel.

"I was never good at Twenty Questions," said Cam.

"He says we should take his car," said Gantz.

Cyn pulled back the metal panel to reveal a service door. "What does it matter whose car we take?" she asked, over her shoulder. "We still have to make it through the garage, right?"

"No. Executive parking is two levels below, and it has its own exit to the PE. If we move fast enough, maybe we can sneak out of here before they think to come looking." Gantz gestured to the door. "After you, Mr. Perion."

They walked the service tunnels for five minutes before finding the crossover from maintenance into B5 proper. Gantz led them into a stairwell and paused at the door, listening for movement.

"We go up two from here," he said. Joe started up the stairs, but Gantz pulled him back into second position. "I'll take point." He drew his 9mm.

"Go," said Cyn. "I think someone is coming."

On B3, they broke out into a small corridor leading to the executive garage. Gantz peeked his head around the corner to assess the situation.

Thin lines of LEDs snaked along the ceiling, making the reflective yellow paint marking the parking spaces glow. Perion's personal fleet of identical black Nissans lined one side of the garage; the light bent along their recently waxed curves. They would have made good getaway vehicles if not for the GPS locators embedded in their engine blocks. Gantz had watched their little blue tracking dots crawl along a map of Los Angeles more than a few times.

Opposite the company cars was a varied collection of high-end sports cars and a few vintage models James Perion had acquired from museums. Joe's cobalt GT-R was parked at the end of the row near the entrance; the blue ground effects under the body sensed Joe's sliver and began to glow.

"Looks cl—," Gantz started to say, but then noticed something moving on the far side of the garage.

He trained his 9mm on the figure who had stepped out from behind an evercrete pillar. It was dressed in a green jumper; a patch on its chest held a nametag, but Gantz couldn't read it at a distance.

The figure twitched as it stood in the middle of the garage. It looked over its shoulder, down at its work boots, and then shuffled forward. Gantz waited until it came close enough for him to read the nametag.

"Sam," he whispered, over his shoulder. He looked to Joe. "Your mechanic?"

Joe nodded.

Gantz holstered the 9mm and waved his hand. "Let's move out."

They came out from behind the corner as a group and Sam immediately took an interest.

Gantz raised a hand in greeting at the synthetic, but it only growled in response. It took jerky, uncoordinated steps towards them, its eyes jumping from Gantz to the two aggregators. When its arms came up, reaching across the void, the party slowed.

"I think it likes you," said Cam.

"That's far enough, Sam," said Gantz. When the synny kept coming, he added, "Sam, directive. Step aside."

Sam moaned a response, but it was unintelligible.

Cam tapped Joe with the back of his hand. "Try the thing."

Joe croaked the first word and then grabbed his throat.

"Oh yeah," said Cam.

Cyn sighed and stepped forward. "All that lives must die," she said.

There was something in the way Sam locked onto her that made Gantz reach for his weapon again. He rested his palm on the holster and dug his nail under the clasp.

Cyn stopped ten feet in front of the synny and stood with her legs in a wide stance. "All must walk—"

Sam morphed into a blur of moving limbs. It shot forward with a grab that turned into a slashing elbow, catching Cyn on the side of her face. She stumbled as Sam pounced on her, wrapping one of its synthetic legs around hers. They fell to the ground and rolled towards a pillar.

"Shoot it," screamed Cam.

Gantz drew and tried to find a clean shot. He circled the wrestling match, but no matter if he stood tall or crouched low, he couldn't aim fast enough to catch an open window.

Cyn, for her part, was fighting back, sending a barrage of close quarter combat moves at the synthetic, keeping it from finding a lock on any of her limbs. Blood covered her face, loosed by the synny's first attack and smeared by the ensuing struggle. Gantz debated tossing the weapon to Cam and joining in the fray.

Before he could move, a guttural cry rose from the tangle of human and synthetic. It resonated in Gantz' chest and echoed through the parking garage.

Cyn's scream made Cam take a step back. Gantz watched as her body shuddered from head to toe. Although he had never seen it in person, Gantz had heard stories about the famed battle cry of the Ayudante biochip, a sound as common in the MX as that of birds chirping from the fabricated trees on any street in the PC. Gantz imagined the chip reaching deep into Cyn's body to take control of her augmented frame; the machinery responded to the common language as if meeting an old friend.

A knee came up between Cyn and the synthetic. It squirmed around until Cyn's foot found a soft spot in the synny's stomach. With another bowel-rumbling grunt, she kicked Sam off, sending the mechanic rolling along the oil-stained evercrete. It wasted no time regaining its footing to charge forward once more, but by then, Gantz had already fired.

The first bullet caught Sam in the leg, causing its body to spin. When it hit the ground, Gantz put two more deafening rounds in its torso. Cyn scampered away, and Gantz moved between them. He trained the gun at Sam's head.

"Say something witty," said Cam, stepping up beside Gantz.

"Fuck you, Cam," said Gantz. He pulled the trigger and lit the evercrete with a spray of white sparks.

Black sludge pooled around the synthetic's head. In the glare of the LED lighting, it almost looked like blood.

"Yeah," said Cam, kicking the synthetic in the ribs. "Fuck you, Cam!"

Cyn accepted Joe's outstretched arm and rose to her feet. She leaned against the spoiler of a nearby Countach. "Goddamn synnies are tough. We're not gonna make it out of here with just our fists." She paused, examined the torn skin on her knuckles. "Well, *you* won't."

Gantz nodded and holstered the 9mm. "We can make a break for it now or try to raid the armory up on five. Personally, I vote we break."

The son of Perion pointed to his GT-R.

"Cam?" asked Gantz.

"If my boss taught me anything, it's to always follow the man with the gun." He started walking away. "Come on, you lucky bastard. Let's check out your wheels."

Gantz turned to Cyn. "Well, what'll it be, Princess?"

"Next time," she replied, "pull the trigger *before* the synny opens my fucking face." She tried to smooth out her shirt before starting after Joe and Cam.

On the floor, the synthetic twitched as its chest began to sink.

Gantz smiled at the gaping hole in Sam's forehead.

"Keep 'em coming, Kessler. I can do this all day."

He kicked the synny in the head with his boot.

FORTY-FIVE

"It makes you wonder," said Cam, popping a Dorito into his mouth. "How are they all being drawn to the same place? There has to be some kind of centralized management system for getting orders to *all* of the synthetics at once. Maybe the directive spread virally, jumping from one robot to another until they were all infected."

Gantz was barely listening. He had been standing at the third-floor window of the 8910 Park building watching a steady stream of synthetic workers make their way east on Glendale towards the Perion Expressway. They would be joining the already massive contingent of stone-faced synnies occupying and blocking all six lanes of Perion City's main artery to the outside world. From there, they spread outward to circle the city, their ranks disappearing over the horizon. There had not been enough time to see how far they actually went.

When the synthetics first appeared on the road, Gantz had been able to weave the GT-R's bulky frame around them. The deeper they got into The Fringe, however, the more packed the streets became. Gantz crushed more than a dozen brown jumpsuits with the front bumper before deciding to turn off the PE and onto Loop 12, inadvertently leading the group past the charred hull of a warehouse, bringing silence to the car.

Turning into 8910 Park was a snap decision brought on by the sudden lack of synthetics, a rare chance to get off the street without being seen or followed. Now Cam, Cyn, and Joe sat around a low table in a break room, eating snacks from a busted vending machine and tending to their injuries.

"Too fast for word of mouth," said Cyn. "It's been what, only a few hours since we left the Spire? To reach that many synthetics in that short of time would take something more." Her voice was slightly muffled by the gauze she held to her cheek.

Beside her, a still-silent Joe played with the contents of a First Aid kit.

"A hundred and fifty thousand synthetics reprogrammed in less than three hours." Cam crunched a chip. "Maybe it's not really word of mouth, but more like peer-to-peer transmission. If a synthetic comes within a certain distance of the infected, it downloads the directives and becomes a mindless drone."

Outside, two dock workers in brown jumpers walked shoulder to shoulder down the middle of Park Avenue. They were last year's models, Libras perhaps. At the time, Perion had christened them free thinkers, with three times the autonomy of the previous generation of warehouse worker, able to complete multi-stage assembly jobs without constant oversight. Gantz hadn't heard how the trial ended up, but the idea of a synthetic being in charge of anything had not sat well with him at the time and seemed even more dangerous now.

The two synnies stopped at the end of the street; their heads turned on immobile shoulders as they scanned the area.

"Or maybe, your synthetics can phone home. Someone with the keys to that kind of system could reprogram an army of synthetics from the comfort of their office in the Spire." Cam leaned back and threw his feet up on a nearby chair. "What of it, Mr. Perion, recently promoted CEO of Perion Synthetics? Are you aware of any centralized system that can push new configs to your synthetics and if so, will this be a standard feature once you go into production?"

"Leave him alone," said Cyn.

"If there's a security failsafe," said Gantz, "it was never mentioned to me. The non-human population was never really considered a threat by my boss or Perion himself, perhaps because they knew how to shut them down if necessary."

"Well and good," said Cam, "but I was asking Mr. Perion."

Joe shrugged and handed fresh gauze to Cyn.

"A CEO with no comment," said Cam. "There's a surprise."

"Cut him a break, Gray." Gantz left his post by the window and sat down in the chair opposite Cam. "It's only his first day."

Cyn tried to laugh but hissed instead.

"It is interesting to note," said Cam, "that my LC counterpart has received a majority of the organic damage, even though our missions in Perion City were more or less the same. It makes one wonder if Mr. Perion's synthetics have been imbued with some good, old-fashioned American sexism. Although I have the CEO in my presence, I feel it would be pointless to even ask him for his opinion."

"Cut it out, Cam," said Gantz, folding his arms.

Cam lifted his wrist to show his glowing sliver. "Just keeping a record of everything that happens here. This kind of insight separates us from the likes of Lincoln Continental and The White Line."

Cyn snorted.

"It's only a matter of time before Banks Media becomes the dominant feed in the country. And I'm not talking about simple number one; I mean total coverage, a majority share to end all majority shares."

"Keep dreaming," said Cyn. "Banks thinks he's at the center of the world because he happens to live in Los Angeles, a city that hasn't been relevant in decades. The future is in tech, and the tech is in Umbra."

"The *future* is in media saturation, covering all facets, not just the latest Vinestead transgression or breakthrough in fuck-sims. The tech is in Umbra? Ha! Ha, I say! Umbra is a wasteland of tech-worship and depravity, a slag upon which the misguided youth sacrifice their humanity for a chance at symbiosis with a machine world that cares nothing for them."

Cyn stared back, unblinking.

"I mean, that's what I've heard."

Gantz watched one of Cyn's arteries throb in her slender neck. It beat a rapid tempo before disappearing beneath her skin.

"Don't hate," she said through a thin smile.

Cam fished another chip out of his bag. "The future is in tech and the tech is in you, right?"

"James Perion said he was the future too," said Gantz.

The aggregators stared at each other until Cam winked and Cyn rolled her eyes.

Joe stood up and made for the door. When Gantz asked him where he was going, he rasped the word *piss* in return.

"I think you hurt the prince's feelings," said Cam.

"No time to worry about that now," said Gantz. "We need to focus on getting out of the city. If the road is blocked from here to the PNR, then we're going to have a tough time even under the cover of night." He looked at the windows; the tint made the hour seem later.

"I thought Kessler said there was another way out," said Cam. "Like a back door to the city?"

"Yeah, but it involves a route through the mountains, and those tunnels are only opened in an emergency. I doubt the gates will be up."

"Maybe we shouldn't be running." Cyn flexed her arm and admired the bulging muscles. She looked to Gantz. "I'll be more than happy to get out of this shithole, and Cam probably has some ambulances to chase back home, but if Joe is the new CEO, why does he have to run? Why are you trying to get him out of the city?"

Cam sat up and pointed a finger at Cyn. "Good call," he said. The finger swung around to Gantz. "Plus, you left Gil in the Spire this morning like it was nothing. And he didn't seem eager to come with you anyway. The way you talked him up the other night, I thought you were good friends."

"So did I," said Gantz. "Now stop looking at me like that."

The aggregator stare—Gantz had first experienced it with Cam at Chez Cosimo and later with Cyn in the warehouse. Their cold eyes latched onto something just beneath the surface and the questions didn't stop until a story— any story—finally came out. When those questions were directed at Chuck Huber or Sava Kessler, Gantz couldn't have cared less. But now they were both looking at him, trying to pick him apart.

Let he who is without sin cast the first stone.

It was backwards, all of it. Neither of them knew what Gil meant to Gantz, nor did they know the depths of Gantz' desire to protect Joe Perion from all enemies, human and synthetic.

"Well, he did stop big Perion from killing little Perion, so obviously he's not meant to terminate the prince," said Cam. He leaned back in his chair and folded his arms.

"That could have been misdirection staged for our benefit," said Cyn. "He *did* shoot James Perion in the head, but evidently, that was just a synthetic. We don't know for sure if the real James Perion is dead or not."

"I told you he was," said Gantz.

Cam nodded, narrowed his eyes. "Of course you say that, but you also abandoned me and Cyn at the warehouse. Then you left Gil in the hands of the enemy. It seems you're only willing to stick your neck out when it's convenient for you."

"Or safe," said Cyn.

Gantz shook his head. How could they compare the lives of three gutter-dredging aggregators to that of one Joseph Perion?

"I give a shit what you people think," he said, standing up. He made a show of pulling his 9mm and checking the mag and chamber. "My job is to defend the Perions, not the Grays, and not the Mesquinas. I don't really need either of you as burdens or council. You want to come along? Fine. I'll get you out of the city, but you'll do it on my terms, and preferably with your mouths shut."

A crash sounded from the hallway, followed by a pained grunt.

Joe.

Gantz pushed his way through the chairs and rushed into the hallway. After turning two corners, he came face to face with one of the dock workers he had seen in the street.

It considered the chief of police with wide eyes. Behind him, the other synthetic had Joe in an arm lock.

"Let him go," said Gantz, raising the 9mm.

The laser sight bobbed in small arcs on the synthetic's forehead. Gantz pulled it left, made it flash in the eyes of the other synny holding Joe.

"I'm not going to say it again," he warned.

The synthetic rushed forward. Gantz barely had time to put a bullet through the synny holding Joe before powerful hands gripped his arms and pulled the weapon down. He got a round off in the synny's abdomen and then they were on the floor wrestling for the gun.

Out of the corner of his eye, Gantz saw the other synthetic falling backwards, hands grabbing at the empty space in its head. Black sludge glinted under the fluorescent lights as it poured out of the hole and through its fingers.

So strong, thought Gantz, as the synthetic wrapped its arms around him. Human muscles were no match for the pulleys and levers inside the dock worker. Visions of high school physics classes flashed in Gantz' head and he almost laughed. The truth was he had no idea what was inside the average synny chassis. For all he knew, they all had hamsters running themselves to death on a wheel inside their chests. The only thing he was sure of was that they had the capacity to kill.

As Chuck Huber had once told him, synthetics were compatible with the Three Laws, but they weren't constrained by them.

Gantz groaned as his legs took on additional weight; Joe had jumped onto the back of the dock worker and had his arm around its neck.

Though the tactic had no hope of killing the synthetic through oxygen deprivation, it did serve as a distraction, giving Gantz enough time to jam the barrel of the 9mm into the mesh under the synny's chin. He fired twice, sending a mushroom cloud of obsidian blood towards the ceiling. Some of it landed on Gantz' lips, making him spit at the bitter taste.

Joe drew himself up to a seated position against the wall and panted.

"Fucking synnies are going to be the death of me," said Gantz. He rolled onto his side and came up on one knee. He smiled when he heard Joe laughing. "Yeah, you keep it up, JP. But when this is all over, I'm getting a raise."

Joe flashed a thumbs-up.

"Where the fuck was Cyn?" asked Gantz, nursing his arm. "We could have used her."

The answer came in the form of a high-pitched scream from the break room. Gantz was up and running before the echo died out. The oil on the soles of his boots made traction difficult; he almost hit the floor coming around the corner. He stumbled into the break room and immediately raised his 9mm.

Chairs and tables had been tossed aside. In the cleared space, six synthetics struggled with the aggregators. Four of them had Cam pinned; they fought for leverage on his arms and legs. To the right, Cyn was doing her best to fend off two assembly techs. They attacked her in perfect unison, seemingly unaffected by her counters.

"I've got this," yelled Cyn. "Help *him*!"

Gantz swung around to Cam, but it was too late. One of the synnies had moved from the aggregator's leg to wrap a thin but powerful arm around his neck. Cam's screaming cut out, but it was all there in his eyes. The synny twisted, producing a crunching sound that almost emptied Gantz' stomach.

The head of Cameron Gray rolled across the break room floor.

Gantz opened fire, pushing the semi-automatic to its limits. The four synthetics released their grip on Cam's body when the mechanical damage became too much. Making holes in their chests was not enough; Gantz needed headshots to drop the mindless bastards into four quivering piles of bolts.

He swung around to Cyn, who had put one of her synnies on the ground. Gantz dispatched a fair-haired woman with a single discharge. Cyn planted a foot into the neck of the downed synthetic and twisted.

Stepping forward, Gantz prepared to put another bullet into its skull if it so much as twitched. His foot hit something solid, causing him to look down.

Cam's frozen eyes looked up at him from the floor.

Around the torn flesh of his neck, luminescent wires writhed in the black sludge.

FORTY-SIX

The GT-R sped along the wide streets of The Fringe away from 8910 Park Avenue. The few synthetics they saw in the road were little match for the car's bumper; they flew away like pinballs, the females giving shrill shrieks before rolling over the hood. In the back seat, Joe held his head, occasionally poking at the rivulet of blood oozing from his ear. Beside Gantz, Cyn sat upright in the passenger seat, shaking her head every few seconds as if arguing with herself.

Gantz' foot tapped nervously next to the clutch.

It was no longer safe for anyone in the city, least of all outlander aggregators and fugitive scions. The exits were all blocked, and no matter where they hid, the synthetics were sure to follow. Gantz only knew one thing for sure: they had to get to the other side of the Point of No Return.

Perion City only had a few roads venturing that far.

"Not me," said Cyn, her lips barely moving.

"What's that?" asked Gantz.

"Not me," she repeated. "No one is pulling my goddamn head off."

"I won't let that happen," said Gantz, patting his jacket.

At least, so long as the bullets lasted.

"Why?" Cyn turned in her seat to look at Joe. "Why would your father do this?"

Gantz answered for him. "It wasn't James Perion. I mean, it was, but not the James Perion the world knows and loves. That man really did pass away last week."

"I don't want to be a synthetic," she replied. "I want to be a better *human*."

"I'm pretty sure you're not a synthetic."

"How do you know?" she asked. "Everything feels wrong."

She quieted then, and Gantz passed the next half hour watching for stray synthetics on the side of the road. Their numbers dwindled the further out he drove, until finally the GT-R turned onto Loop Six, a road separating Perion City from the expansive desolation of the Californian desert. This close to the PNR, the synthetics weren't taking any chances.

Gantz let out a slow breath. The synnies may have seen the car heading out in this direction, but they wouldn't be able to follow. If Kessler wanted Gantz dead, she'd have to come herself.

"I bet there wasn't any time," said Joe, his voice hoarse but improving.

"No time for what?" asked Gantz.

"To build a synthetic for Cyn. You can turn out chassis by the hundreds on a production run, but for one-offs like Cam? It would take weeks. It took them a month to get Synth J to exact specifications."

"Yeah, but that was their first time building a Virgo, right?" asked Gantz.

"Roberta before him. So my dad was the second. By the time it was Cam's turn, maybe they had the process down a little faster, but Cyn didn't show up until when, last Thursday?"

Cyn confirmed with a nod of her head.

"Not enough time. And that's why they had to give Gil a generic chassis. They weren't planning on him either."

Loop Six shrank to two lanes as it turned more northerly. Gantz pulled down the visor and shifted it to the window.

"Okay," said Cyn, "but that means the synthetic Cam was already built when they took us at the warehouse."

"But Gil was killed the next day, so…" Gantz trailed off as he took an exit and turned left under the highway. He could barely make out the speck that was Pure under the glare of the sun.

"So they knew about it ahead of time," continued Cyn. "They were *planning* to swap in a synthetic Cam even before I showed up." She narrowed her eyes at Joe. "You're monsters, all of you."

"Yeah, yeah," said Joe. "Look, I didn't know anything about this."

"He's telling the truth," said Gantz. "We've been trying to figure out what Synth J was up to ever since we heard about an aggregator coming into the city. We didn't have anything to do with swapping out Cam for a synthetic."

"Like I'm going to trust either of you." Cyn crossed her arms and looked out the window.

"You could try your luck with *them*," said Gantz.

On the road ahead were roughly a dozen synthetics milling around in front of the yellow warning signs announcing the PNR. Gantz glanced at the rearview mirror.

"What do you think, boss?"

Joe rubbed his ear. "Burn it."

Gantz shifted into fifth gear and pegged the accelerator. The car gained another twenty miles per hour before it slammed into the first synthetic. Thumps and scrapes surrounded the cabin; after the fourth crunch, the windshield turned opaque as it shattered in place.

"Don't stop," said Joe.

Frantic fingers sought out the window controls on the door. When the glass had lowered enough, Gantz stuck his head out to make sure they were still on the road. A red flash flew by.

"What was that?" asked Cyn.

"A warning sign," said Gantz, whipping the car back and forth.

"A warning sign for *what*?"

"The PNR."

"No!" screamed Cyn, grabbing for the steering wheel.

Gantz had to use all of his strength to keep the GT-R on the road.

Above the roar of air rushing past the open window and the screams of synthetics on the hood of the car, Gantz heard the first of the tiny explosions. The black shadows on the windshield turned a sickly green. The smell of acid grew and stung at his nose. Out of the corner of his eye, Gantz saw the edge of the road fall away; the car was passing into the parking lot at Pure.

Wrenching the steering wheel as hard as he could, Gantz sent the GT-R into a tailspin. The rear bumper slammed into two support beams and took out the awning in front of the bar. It came crashing down on the trunk, shattering the back window and blowing dust into the cabin.

Gantz closed his eyes against the debris, but Cyn seemed unfazed. A whirlwind of sharp claws and gnashed teeth came out of the dust cloud, all intent on ripping Gantz apart. With one final push, he got his arms around Cyn.

"We're okay!"

It took a few more repetitions before the words made it through.

Cyn ceased her attack and looked around. Gantz loosened his grip slightly.

"You asshole!" She struck him in the face with an open palm and then kicked her way out of the car.

Gantz didn't wait for her to come around. He was out of the GT-R and straining to breathe the kicked-up dust before she got to him.

"You could have killed me!" Her shoulders dropped into a fighting stance, but froze when Gantz reached into his jacket.

He held his hand there until she backed away.

"Christ, Gantz. You had no right. If I'm a synthetic, then that's *my* burden to bear. I'll die on *my* terms, not yours."

It was worth the risk, thought Gantz. To protect Joe, he had to know who and what Cynthia Mesquina really was. Whether an augmented aggregator from Umbra or a synthetic copy just waiting to turn on its fellow fugitives, Gantz had to be sure.

He fingered the gun in its holster. Five bullets left in that magazine. Two magazines left on his belt.

"It's done," he said, slamming the door shut. "If you don't like it, take it up with my boss."

Cyn kicked at the dirt and walked a few feet away. With her back turned to Gantz, she let out a string of curses.

Gantz noticed Joe standing on the other side of the car, nose crinkled at the fumes from the dissolving synthetics still on the hood. He raised an eyebrow at Gantz.

"What? Too harsh?"

Joe shrugged. "Not what I would have done, but I wasn't driving." His eyes drifted to the large neon sign on the roof. Silver script spelled out the word *Pure*. "The whole city has gone crazy and *this* is where you think to take us?"

"No shirt, no soul, no service," said Gantz, pointing to the placard beside the door. It was barely visible behind the fallen awning.

"Too bad no synthetic can get close enough to be offended by it," said Joe. He walked around the car and stood next to Gantz. Together, they looked at the city on the horizon.

The Spire blazed in the afternoon light. At a distance, it looked serene and quiet.

"It wasn't just a test for her, you know." Gantz had been trying to ignore the question of Joe's humanity—not to mention his own.

Joe joined the train of thought. "I know. I wondered the same thing when you called me on it last week. There was a moment when I thought I really could be a synthetic. I mean, how would I know? Synth J would have done anything to persevere. I see that now."

"Your old man certainly took a turn for the crazy." Gantz waved his hand at the Spire. "I should have known it would end up like this. Synny zombies walking the streets—it's a goddamn horror show."

"They're just doing what they're told," said Joe. "You can't fault them for their programming."

"They should know better," said Gantz, adjusting his trench. "*You* should have known better. You gave the synnies three suggestions instead of three laws."

He took a deep breath; it was forced out by a rock hitting him in the stomach. A second later, another hit him in the shin.

Cyn laughed as Gantz looked around. "Fuck the police," she yelled.

Gantz raised a warning finger. "You stop that shit right now."

She threw another rock, but there was no power behind it. The pebble glanced off of his jacket and into the dirt.

Joe shielded his face with his arms and stepped away.

"Citizen, drop your weapon!" Gantz' voice boomed.

"You can have my weapon when you pry it from my gin-soaked hands," said a voice from behind.

Gantz spun around to find Holmes standing just outside the door to the bar, a double-barrel shotgun in his hands.

"Which one of you boys owes me a new awning?" he asked.

Gantz spread his hands as another rock pinged him in the shoulder. "You mind if we come in for a drink?"

Holmes considered the question. "Yeah, I guess you should. Probably better to be drunk when the bombs start falling anyway."

Gantz lowered his hands. "What are you talking about?"

"The war, Bob," said Holmes, popping the release on the side of his shotgun. The barrel split and fell open. "You haven't been following along, have you?" He turned and headed into the bar, mumbling to himself. "Goddamn synthetic revolution starts and all you yahoos want is to get smashed."

Cyn appeared at Gantz' left, a pile of rocks in her hand. "What's happening?"

"Sounds like we've been missing a war," said Joe. He maneuvered around the awning and went inside.

Gantz gestured to the rocks. "You get it all out?"

Cyn dropped them to the ground. "No, but you can buy me a beer. Maybe if I get a nice buzz going, I won't have to kick your ass."

"That'd be very humane of you," said Gantz, extending his arm towards the door. "After you, Cynny."

FORTY-SEVEN

Lauren Simmons silently reported the news on the vidscreen over the bar.

Timestamps and location codes along the bottom told Gantz it was a raw feed, a lone broadcast saturating the city but unable to get past the media blackout Kessler had laid down. Evidently, the memo to stay off the airwaves hadn't reached Lauren or the team back at the studio. The feed stayed glued to her uncertain smile even after she mouthed the words *back to you.*

Over the course of an hour, she reported on thirty-eight deaths and countless more injuries in the PC. Abbreviated interviews with panicked residents told the story of a city suddenly thrown into chaos as a third of its population simply dropped what they were doing and walked into the streets. Gantz read their accounts from the closed captioning as it scrolled off the screen.

Fire trucks and emergency response vehicles were left unmanned and idle in their garages. Patients were left suffering in their beds. A young intern at Perion General compared the scene to watching a toaster jump down from the counter and leave the house. The synthetics, as he put it, simply forgot their purpose.

It wasn't until people started getting hurt that the city realized something was wrong.

Gantz tried to piece together the timeline. It had been a long day escaping the Spire and driving out to The Fringe only to be turned back by a horde of synthetics. While they had been running for their lives, so too had any resident who looked remotely like Cam, Cyn, or Gantz. Those who resisted rarely escaped without injury. Some hadn't escaped.

He looked down into his beer, watched the amber liquid swirl at the bottom of the glass.

Civilians being murdered by synthetics. Kessler was dragging Perion Synthetics into the mud with her manhunt.

Gantz tilted his head back and closed his eyes.

Synth J wasn't above killing—Gil had found that out all too well—but his motivations were solely business-related. Gil had company secrets going back for years. Cynthia had seen things in the depths of the Spire and would have told the world about them. Could still tell the world…

And then there was Cam.

Gantz winced at the memory of the aggregator's head rolling along the floor. Had the real Cam met his end too? If not, where was he in all of this?

"I don't think I've ever met a woman like that," said Holmes, stepping out of a back room that doubled as his apartment. When Cyn had found out there was a shower nearby, she'd asked to be taken to it immediately.

"You two were back there a long time," said Gantz, pushing the empty glass across the bar.

Holmes tossed the tumbler into the sink and filled a fresh one. "She had me guard the door while she showered. Then we talked for a bit about Molly and Umbra and everything that's been going on."

"Who's Molly?"

"My first wife," said Holmes.

"I didn't know you were married before."

"You never asked. No one asks the bartender anything." He filled his own glass with whiskey and took a sip. "After she passed, I sold everything I had and moved to the PC. I bought this place, met Ashley a few months later." He looked around the bar. "Strange sometimes where we end up."

"And what would she think of your new life?"

"Molly? She's dead, Bob. She doesn't think anymore. But if she were alive, I'm sure she'd smack the tartar off your teeth for letting *this* happen." He pointed to the vidscreen. "You're the Chief of Police. It's your job to prevent this."

"I'm pretty sure I stopped being the Chief of Police when I put a bullet through James Perion's head."

Holmes stopped mid-sip.

"Don't worry, he was a synthetic. It's a long story."

"Long piece of stringy bullshit, maybe," said Holmes. "I don't care who you say you shot, these people were depending on you. Still are."

"You know who's depending on me? Joe Perion." Gantz nodded to the bench by the entrance where Joe lay stretched out, his feet propped up on one of the arms. "And James Perion, who told me to look after his son after he was gone. I delegated that job to Nico Shaw, but evidently he can't keep his brain in *this* reality long enough to get that done. The future of Perion Synthetics is that man right there."

"Is that so? Can he design synthetics? Can he build one himself?" Holmes shook his head. "Perion may have been a visionary, but it took real people to make his vision come true. And right now those people are dying in the streets like animals."

"Thirty-eight deaths is hardly a slaughter."

Holmes smacked the bar with his palm. "*One* is too fucking many! You know that."

Gantz shut his eyes and tried to tune out the world.

In the grand scheme, were the deaths of thirty-eight people enough to put the safety of Joseph Perion at risk? Gantz shook his head. Holmes could usually be counted on for good advice, but in this matter, he just wasn't seeing the bigger picture.

Opening his eyes, Gantz looked to the ceiling again. "What would you have me do? I'm one man against an entire army of synthetics."

"Seems simple to me," said Holmes, finishing off his drink. "You just even the odds a little."

"Kill a hundred and fifty thousand synthetics? You got a nuclear warhead back there under the boxes of stale pretzels?"

"Don't be simple, Bob. Someone is telling those synnies what to do."

"Yeah, but we don't know *how*."

Holmes frowned and slapped the vidscreen. He flipped through the channels until the Spire appeared. "Really? Look at that. Look at all of those dishes on top of that thing. And you say you don't know how the orders are reaching all the synnies? The Spire is one big antenna."

"Those are for satellite uplinks," said Joe, from the entryway. "There's some localized broadcast stuff up there, but nothing capable of sending out a mind-control ray. The synnies have an open connection back to the hub, but it's for software upgrades only."

"And what about the PNR?" asked Holmes.

"What about it?"

"How do the synthetics receive *that* signal if they only have one connection open?"

Joe sat up and swung his feet to the floor. He looked across the bar at Holmes. "What are you talking about? The PNR is a line in the sand."

"The hell it is. It's a signal and I can prove it." From his pocket, Holmes produced a small plastic square and placed it on the bar.

"What is that?" asked Gantz. "And what time machine did you use to go back and get it?"

Holmes tapped the smooth skin on his wrist. "It's what we had before slivers. This thing pulls radio signals out of the air."

"Do go on," said Gantz.

Joe stood and limped to the bar.

"See for yourself. Turn it on, tune to a station, and walk back to the PNR. As soon as you cross that line, the interference makes listening impossible. And the signal gets stronger the further into the city you go."

"You never mentioned this before," said Gantz.

Holmes shrugged. "Like I said, no one asks the bartender anything."

Gantz turned to Joe as he pulled up a barstool. "That's not how it works, is it?"

"That's not how it was explained to me," replied Joe, "but then Dad didn't always care to know exactly how something worked, only that it did."

"So that would make the PNR not a fence but a leash?"

Joe folded his hands under his chin. "An electric fence will keep people in or out, so long as there's power. The PNR circles the entire city. That's a long chain with a ton of individual links."

Holmes nodded along as if this were all old news to him.

"I see," said Gantz. He stood as if to leave. Laughing, he wagged his finger at Holmes. "I see what you did there."

"What did he do?" asked Joe.

"It's sneaky, but I wouldn't expect anything less from you, Holmes." Then to Joe, "It's a double-edged sword."

"*What* is?"

"The idea of more signals. You say there's only one signal and that it's for upgrades. Holmes says there's another to keep the cattle on the ranch. If we accept that idea and open the number of connections to two, there's no reason there can't be three or four or forty. Then you say, well, the signal turning all of the synthetics into zombies is coming from the Spire. So what is the only course of action?"

Joe spread his hands.

"Tell him, barkeep."

Holmes backed away and leaned against the sink. "Smash the grid. Stop the signal."

"Of course," said Gantz. "So that means we head *back* into the city and not just to any old place, but the goddamn Spire. I flash my badge at the door and we take a nice elevator ride up to the comm room. I'm sure there's a little hacker sitting at a keyboard up there telling all of the synthetics what to do. And in the name of the former Chief of Police of the City of Perion, I'll command him to cease and desist. Bob's your fucking uncle and we all live happily ever after."

"Maybe I should cut you off," said Holmes, reaching for Gantz' beer.

Gantz turned to Joe. "If we run in there with guns blazing, something or someone is going to get blown to hell. Maybe we shut down enough equipment to kill the signal, but then guess what happens."

Joe's mouth fell open. "If we kill the PNR signal…"

"Yeah," said Gantz. "A hundred and fifty thousand synthetics take an acid bath. Billions of dollars in experimental product and prototypes are incinerated at once."

"It would set us back a decade," said Joe. "It would put the entire city out of work."

"At least they'd be alive." Holmes slung a towel over his shoulder and crossed his arms. "You two knuckleheads are forgetting the value of human life."

"I think you've lived too long on this side of the PNR," said Gantz. "You forget why we're all here."

"You got that backwards, Chief."

"Fuck you, Holmes. The company *must* survive!"

"Gantz," said Joe.

His voice was too calm. Gantz tried to steady his breathing, but all he wanted to do was jump the counter and pummel some sense into Holmes' head.

"What?"

Joe stood and put a hand on Gantz' shoulder. "Is Perion Synthetics my company?"

"Yes, but…"

"So if I'm in charge, then I can do whatever I want with it, right?"

"Your father wouldn't have wanted this. He never would have thrown everything away."

"He doesn't have to throw everything away," said Cyn.

Gantz turned to the aggregator; she had a towel pressed to her damp hair.

"Great," said Gantz. "Now the Umbrat has an opinion. Tell us, what plan of action has the augmented princess decided is best?"

"I would say it's obvious," she replied, "but that word means different things to you and me."

Gantz took a step forward; Joe slapped him in the chest.

"Holmes is right though," continued Cyn. "We have to stop the signal. And that may mean we cripple the Spire's comm equipment."

"Thus killing everything synthetic in the city," said Gantz.

"No, we set them free."

Gantz tried to relate the word *free* to synthetics.

"Assuming it's even possible, how do you suppose we do that?" asked Joe.

Cyn eyed the vidscreen as it scrolled between the various feeds.

"You think Perion is the only one who can broadcast a signal?"

FORTY-EIGHT

It was past ten before they finally got back on the road.

Joe was behind the wheel of Holmes' ancient beater whose black paint had turned to rust over the many years. The Civic only had a fraction of the horsepower of Joe's GT-R, but at least its engine block wasn't completely melted by synthetic offal. The windshield, though splintered in a few places, kept the wind at bay as they cruised Loop Six at a strenuous seventy miles per hour. Having control of the vehicle put Joe at ease; maybe he thought that at any moment, he could whip the Civic around and head back to Pure or out to some other remote part of the city.

For now, the PNR still provided a measure of safety, but if they were able to pull off the plan they had so intricately laid out on a paper tablecloth, then that neutral zone, that home base of *oh-no-you-can't-touch-me* would go away in an instant.

Then Joe Perion would not be safe anywhere, and neither would the rest of the world.

Cyn had claimed the back seat for herself and used the extra room to stretch her legs. In her lap, she fiddled with the shotgun she had taken from Holmes. He had been reluctant to part with it, especially considering the potential tidal wave of synthetics that might be walking out of Perion City if things went right, but after some sweet-talking by Cyn and a recollection of a scoped rifle hanging over his bed, Holmes had handed it over without further protest. Now, Cyn's pockets bulged with extra shells. The smile on her face came and went; whatever dialogue she had going on in her head was waffling between the good and the bad to come.

The closer they got to the city, the more Gantz tried to convince himself this was a good idea. His questions to the man upstairs had gone unanswered for the better part of the night, but there did come a moment when Gantz saw the totality of Perion City's population as one great oil painting, showing them marching into the streets only to be gunned down by stone-faced synthetics. There was no telling how far Kessler would push or how long she would keep the synthetics in the streets with no payoff before ordering them into warehouses and businesses.

And eventually, homes.

Protecting Joe was his job, but saving an entire city felt like true purpose.

Though Gantz knew God had not phoned him up and told him to fight against Kessler, he did not reject the possibility that through his own introspection, he had been helped to the path by divine intervention. Some force out there had set him on the road leading them back into the city, speeding along the side streets under pockets of orange light, ever pushing towards the white spike someone had buried upside down in the ground.

Are you coming with us, Gin-slinger?

Holmes hadn't even answered, had instead thrown his towel on the counter and walked away, turning off the Blue Moon beer sign as he went.

"He would have just slowed us down," said Cyn.

"It's not that," replied Gantz.

Joe gave him a glance. "He can take care of himself. He agreed with the plan."

Gantz wanted to reply it wasn't so much the plan that was the problem; on paper, it made perfect sense and there had been an ease with which Cyn enumerated the various stages, but back here in the real world, it still had to be executed to perfection. Gantz would have to fire true, Cyn would have to push the limits of her various augments, and Joe would simply have to stay alive long enough to pick up the pieces of his father's ruined empire. If all went to plan, someone was sure to get hurt.

If all went to plan…

Gantz watched the streets scroll by.

"No synthetics," he said. "Slow it down, Joe."

The Civic lost speed, removing the blur from the front windows of the buildings they passed. Ever since setting out from Pure, Gantz had been expecting to run into a wall of synthetics at some point, but the streets had remained empty.

Gantz narrowed his eyes to see better in the dim light.

Shadows moved between the buildings—people hunched over as they moved from cover to cover, trying to avoid the halogen beams of Holmes' car. The human population of Perion City was still there, still venturing out despite the graphics on the public displays announcing a curfew in menacing red letters.

As the Spire loomed, Joe cut the headlights and used the ambient lighting to see. He slowed them down to parking lot speeds for fear for hitting a resident darting across the darkened street.

In the back seat, Cyn chuckled.

"Care to fill us in?" asked Gantz.

Cyn ran her finger down the barrel of the shotgun. "The Siege of The Perion Spire," she replied, "like it's some kind of run and gun. There are some augs I know who would give their left tit for this kind of action." She tapped her wrist. "If I could broadcast what we're about to do, it'd put Lincoln Continental on top for good."

Joe raised an eyebrow.

"Aggregators," said Gantz. "Always looking for a story. Can't even take 'em to bed without a play by play showing up on the feed the next morning."

"A night with Robert Gantz," said Cyn. "I took off my clothes. He blew his load in his pants. Later, breakfast."

"You're hardly my type, princess," he replied.

"Oh, I know," said Cyn, drawing out the word.

The Civic paused at a stop sign.

"Where to?" asked Joe.

Cyn leaned forward between the two front seats. "Stage one, we storm the castle."

"You mean, storm a castle guarded by a contingent of synthetic soldiers of unknown size or distribution," said Gantz.

"Alright, stage one, assess the defenses."

"There's a helipad on the roof of Southpoint with line of sight to the plaza," said Joe. "I bet if we got up top we could get a good look at the number of synnies we're dealing with."

Gantz imagined how the dealership would look at this time of night, but his mind's eye was drawn to the two-story building next door. He nodded in agreement.

Joe turned left down Eckles Street and then hung a right onto Harris Parkway. Halfway down the street, Gantz pointed to the curb.

"Pull up right there," he said.

"What is this place?" asked Cyn.

"The WG," said Joe. "Something like a church. Dad was a big believer in freedom of religion, even though he didn't care for it himself."

"The first feed," said Cyn, nodding. "Imagine if you always had God whispering in your ear day in and day out. It'd be worse than listening to Banks or Coker."

Gantz wanted to argue the point, but his eyes had fallen on the open doors of the Spiritual Center. There was splintered wood at the top and bottom, as if someone had tried to break them down. It was all the encouragement Gantz needed to jump out of the car and rush the stairs. He ignored Joe's questions as he entered the auditorium, gun drawn.

He waited for his eyes to adjust to the low light.

On the floor in front of the altar, a body lay face down, a pool of liquid surrounding it.

Gantz took his steps slowly.

"Padre?" he asked.

As he got closer, he noticed half of the figure's skull was gone, removed by some explosion or blunt force. Gantz thought of Yates' assistant, Truman, the altar boy who wasn't programmed to hurt a fly. How could he have done such a thing?

"Is that you, Robert?"

Gantz swung around as Yates stepped out of a darkened confessional.

"Thank God," said Gantz.

"No, thank Remington," said Yates, pulling a shotgun out from behind him.

As he approached, Gantz identified the weapon as a Versa Max with oversized bolt release and extended choke tube.

"Impressive," said Gantz, holstering his 9mm. "What's a man like you doing with a gun like that?"

Yates clicked the safety on and leaned the shotgun against a pew. "It's like I've always said. Put your faith in God but always have a backup plan."

Gantz shook his head. "You've never said that."

"Haven't I, Robert?"

"You alright, Padre?"

Yates nodded and sat down. "Today, a synthetic I've known and trusted for years started asking me where you were. I told Truman I didn't know. He didn't believe me, so I had to put a shell through his brain."

"Been there," said Gantz.

"Then you know what it's like. And you know this can't go on."

Echoes of Holmes' speech replayed in Gantz' head.

"I know. I'm trying to stop it."

"Even if you do, people may not feel safe here anymore. I know I wouldn't. How do we go about our business knowing these things can just turn on us at any moment with no regard for laws or morality or... or anything." He sighed. "I'm done with this, Robert. For good."

"You won't be the only one," said Gantz. "I think a lot of people are going to walk as soon as it's safe."

"You should come with me."

Again, Gantz shook his head. "My place is here with Joe."

"Does he mean that much to you?"

Gantz looked at the floor. Now was not the time to be answering that question.

"Hey, Chief," said Cyn, from the door. "I could use your help."

"What?" asked Gantz. "I'm in the middle of something."

"Joe's gone next door. I guess he got tired of waiting for you."

"Goddammit," said Gantz.

Yates made the sign of the cross and then waved Gantz away. "Go, my son. Help your friend."

"Will you be alright?"

"Of course. I have all the protection I need." He stood and collected his shotgun. As he walked back to the confessional, he said, "If I don't see you again, it has been a pleasure. Peace be with you, my son."

"And also with you, Padre."

Gantz turned and hurried down the aisle towards the door. Cyn led him down the steps and through a small garden. At the back door of the dealership, they found Joe tearing down a barricade.

"Joe, someone put that there for a reason," said Cyn.

Joe paused and put his hands on hips. "The helipad gives us the best vantage point. If you have any other ideas, I'm all ear." He tapped the side of his head in demonstration.

"Alright, calm down," said Gantz. "Here, let me help."

The flashlight on the end of Gantz' gun did little to beat back the darkness inside Southpoint. He went in first, trailed by Cyn. She walked to his right, holding the shotgun on her hip. If anything jumped out of the adjoining offices, it would be answered by a simultaneous blast of 9mm bullets and shotgun shells.

Gantz inched along the hallway. It was quiet, but every now and then he thought he heard shuffling in the distance, like shoes scraping along the carpet. Something was moving in the shadows, but he couldn't get close enough to see it.

Finally, they came to a set of double doors. The sign above it said *SHOWROOM* in blue on white lettering. Gantz put his hand out, but the door wouldn't budge.

"Up there," said Cyn, pointing to the two deadbolts at the top of the doors.

Gantz nodded and reached up.

"Don't!" cried a voice.

Gantz turned and focused his light on a man standing just inside one of the offices. At the sight of the gun, the man's hands shot up.

"Please, don't shoot!" he screamed, ducking his head to avoid the expected gunfire.

"Who are you?" asked Gantz. He tried to size the man up, but there was something off about the finely pressed, navy blue suit he wore and the wild hair sitting atop his bruised face.

"Maddox," he replied. "I work here."

"What happened to you, Mr. Maddox?"

"Oh, this." He touched the purple splotch on his cheek. "The synnies have gone nuts. I came by earlier to lock the place up, you know, to keep more of them from getting out. Barricaded the back door, but when I went around to the front, the place looked empty, so I came inside."

"There was a straggler?" asked Joe.

"Yes, Mr. Perion. A floor model, assisted-living imprint." He tried to chuckle. "She really wanted out of here."

"You got beat up by a girl," said Cyn, snickering.

Maddox nodded several times. "Like you wouldn't believe. I got caught between her and the barricade. My only choice was to lock myself in here.

"Why didn't you call for help?" asked Gantz.

"I did." He pointed to the badge around Gantz' neck. "Isn't that why you're here?"

In all of the confusion, he had forgotten to take it off.

"No, Mr. Maddox," said Gantz. "We're not here to save you. We need to get up to the roof."

"Oh. Well, you'll have to get past Amanda first."

"Not a problem," said Cyn, racking the shotgun. She pulled one of the deadbolts down and slipped through the door.

Maddox stepped closer, staring after Cyn. "Is she a synthetic?" he asked. "Like a bodyguard or something?"

"Yeah," said Gantz. "Augmented prototype. Built for organic damage. Powered by a state-of-the-art Ayudante biochip."

"I didn't even know we were integrating with biochips yet."

"She's an Umbra-class," said Joe, playing along. "She's new."

FORTY-NINE

"God help us," said Gantz.

By his count, there were over two hundred synthetics standing guard in the Victoria Perion Memorial Plaza. They stood in ranks five feet apart and their heads swiveled back and forth, scanning for targets. The usual tables and chairs had been moved, arranged purposefully in a ring of debris to make a thick but not impassable perimeter. The Spire's support beams on the northwest and northeast corners hid whatever forces might be guarding the front of the building, an entire army perhaps, just waiting to see which side would be attacked first. With those numbers, fighting their way in would be nothing but a suicide mission. They could drop six, maybe a dozen synthetics before being overwhelmed.

If ever there was a need for divine intervention…

The wind whipped over the edge of the roof at Southpoint Synthetics, swirling around the helipad and creating enough turbulence to force Joe Perion to a knee. Beside him, Cyn stood with one foot forward and her weight centered over her back leg. She hugged herself, occasionally reaching out to rub away some hurt on her forearm. She had come out of the fight with Amanda without a scratch, or so she had claimed.

"You guys aren't going in there, are you?" asked Maddox.

Cyn snorted. "You're a manly man, aren't you, Tank?"

"That's the problem. Man against machine isn't a fair fight," he replied.

"Yes, Mr. Maddox. We *are* going in there." Gantz bent a knee next to Joe. "What are you thinking, boss?"

"That used to be my home," said Joe. "And now we're trying to break into it." He shook his head. "The Spire shouldn't be a fortress."

"Yeah," said Gantz.

Joe had it wrong though. The Spire wasn't a fortress, the city was. James Perion had built it to keep out Vinestead and anyone else who might steal his inventions. And for all of the work and preparation he had put into securing the city, the real threat had come from within, from the old man himself.

Gantz cleared his throat. "Your dad lost sight of the dream, but you can put it back on track. And if Kessler tries to get in our way…"

"No." Joe locked eyes with Gantz. "No one else dies, you hear me? I don't care if Gilbert Reyes *was* working for The White Line; he didn't deserve to die for it."

Heartburn raced up Gantz' chest.

"And we need to find out what happened to Mr. Gray. If he's been killed, then Ms. Kessler will answer for that too."

"Don't lock down the final body count just yet," said Cyn. "There's no way we're getting through that crowd without losing one of you."

"Hey," said Maddox.

"She's right." Gantz stood and shook a cramp out of his leg. "The odds of making it past that many synthetics are low. We'll have to find another way in, maybe the garage again."

"Or create a diversion," said Joe. "If we can draw them away from the Spire, you guys could sneak in."

"*Us* guys?" asked Gantz.

Joe stood up. "Look, we both know you and Cyn are the only ones prepared for this. Dad taught me a lot of things, but gunplay and karate weren't exactly high priorities. You're a badass, *she's* a badass. Mr. Maddox and I will create a diversion; you two get into the Spire and carry out the plan. You have my permission to take down any synthetic who stands in your way."

"But not Kessler?" asked Gantz.

"No more human loss. Consider it an order."

"But what if she attacks us?"

"Then *I'll* take the bitch out," said Cyn. "A girl's got a right to defend herself."

Joe stared at her for a moment before turning to Maddox. "Do you have a vehicle?"

"Yeah, it's parked out back. Why?"

"I need to borrow it." Joe looked to the Spire again, at the silhouettes occupying his mother's plaza. "Set your watch, Chief. Twenty minutes. You'll know when it happens."

Gantz wanted to ask more questions, but all he could do was extend his hand. When the scion took it, he said, "Good luck, Mr. Perion."

"You're the one who needs the luck."

"I won't let you down."

Joe nodded and turned away. "Come on, Mr. Maddox."

Gantz watched them disappear into the rooftop lounge; the light from the elevator filled the small room for a few seconds before the door shut once more.

"I still say we should have picked up more weapons," said Cyn. "A grenade or two would really come in handy."

"This isn't the MX," replied Gantz. "You can't just wander into a convenience store and buy high explosives."

The only place to find ordinance like that was in the armory, and the armory was in the Spire.

"Come on," said Gantz. "We need to get into position."

Cyn followed him to the elevator, all the while flicking the dual firing pins of the shotgun with her fingernails. They rode down to the ground floor and made their way through the darkened offices. Joe and Maddox had already cleared out, so Gantz led Cyn back the way they had come, past the WG, to Holmes' car. It was still sitting undisturbed at the curb.

"What do we need the car for?" asked Cyn. She pointed to the Spire. "It's like three blocks away."

Gantz stood for a moment examining the front bumper of the Civic. "I was thinking battering ram. Holmes won't notice a few more dings on this piece of shit."

"Can I drive?"

Might be her last opportunity, thought Gantz.

"Sure, why not?"

He made her drive slowly and without headlights. Cyn guided the car along the empty streets until finally she turned into a pedestrian thoroughfare on Yager Lane. From there, they had an off-center view of the plaza. At ground level, the synthetics stacked up, making their ranks appear thicker.

"If we're lucky, Joe will get a good number of synnies away from the plaza. If you can get through that opening in the fence, you can drive us right up to the doors."

"And if they're locked?"

"Since when have glass doors ever truly been locked?"

Cyn nodded. "Roger. Property destruction approved."

"Once inside, we'll need to get through the lobby to the executive elevator. We can ride it all the way to the top."

"And if there are more synthetics in the lobby?"

Gantz chuckled. "You ask a lot of questions, princess. What are you afraid of? Either your augments are worth the price you paid for them or we're gonna die slow, horrible deaths."

"Balls to that shit," said Cyn.

Headlights broke out on the left; a car with its blinders on barreled down Harris Parkway, its radio blaring some Trip-Hop throwback, the bass hits accentuated by the sounding of a horn. Hundreds of synthetic heads turned in unison and focused on the incoming threat. As it neared, the Automated Guards began taking their first steps, breaking into a slow jog simultaneously, as if joined at the synapse.

"What the hell?" asked Gantz.

It looked like Joe was going for his own battering ram attack.

Instead of plowing into the crowd, the car turned at the last moment, clipping half a dozen Scorpios and sending them cartwheeling over the roof of the smallish coupe. He drove tangential to the crowd, darting in to run down the occasional outlier. Joe pulled their attention to the opposite side of the plaza, turned his brake lights to the mob, and sped away. He disappeared around a corner with the synnies still in pursuit.

"I guess that's our—"

A tremor tore through the car and surrounding buildings as a fireball erupted behind an apartment complex just off Epoch Avenue. Before Gantz could even consider whether Joe had just met his maker, Cyn slammed on the gas.

She left the lights off until they were on the outer plaza dealing with a dozen or so stragglers. When the synnies raised their rifles, Cyn hit the brights and used their momentary blindness to put the Civic squarely into their stomachs. The high chassis drove the synnies to the ground; their remains scraped against the undercarriage of the car. By the midpoint of the plaza, they had cleared most of the AGs. Only one or two remained at the glass doors.

"Alright, pull up right over there," said Gantz.

The Civic picked up speed.

"Cyn, slow it down!"

"Her highness isn't in at the moment," she replied, tugging on her seatbelt. She sank further into the seat as she stomped the accelerator.

"Goddammit, Cyn! Stop the fucking car!"

"Not so fun on the other side, is it?" she screamed back.

They hit the three-step walkup at forty miles per hour according to the dashboard. The glass doors shattered in front of them, but stray lengths of metal doorframe smashed against the windshield, obscuring their view of the lobby. Gantz felt the car strike several heavy objects; the lobby's centerpiece, the great stone hand of James Perion, scraped along the passenger door and retreated. Rows of couches opened for them as trashcans bounced in every direction. Beefy synthetics with featureless faces tried in vain to remain upright as the tidal wave of debris washed over them.

Over the roar of destruction, a chorus of gunfire ramped up.

Maybe it was the Ayudante chip finally pulling its weight, but Cyn managed to cut the steering wheel hard to the left at just the right moment to send the car into a drift. It screeched to a halt a mere three feet from the elevators, which Gantz could now see through the smashed passenger window. The next moment, Cyn was pushing on his shoulder.

"Out," she screamed, as bullets tore through the cabin.

Gantz opened the door and crawled to the elevator. He reached up for the call button as sections of the marble wall exploded around his hand. When the doors opened, Cyn's bony fingers were on his shoulder, pushing him inside. Cyn fell on top of him and together they tumbled to the back. Their legs intertwined; for a brief moment, Gantz felt an immense heat on his thigh.

Cyn was breathing hard, and her narrow eyes barely touched Gantz' before she pushed off of him and threw herself against the side of the car. She sprang to her feet and fell towards the vidscreen.

"Come on," she said, pawing at the numbers.

When the doors closed and the elevator started to rise, she sank to the floor and began to hyperventilate.

Gantz watched her tremble, watched the large vein in her neck try to push its way out of her skin. Cyn brought her knees to her chest and wrapped her arms around them. She squeezed as convulsions swept through her body.

The Ayudante had pushed her too hard, thought Gantz. Now it was killing—

A rough cry passed Cyn's smiling lips. It rose to a tremulous pitch before cutting out abruptly. Then she was laughing through deep breaths and wiping the sweat from her forehead. One hand went to her chest as the other pulled her feet closer.

She looked over at Gantz.

"What?" she asked. "Never seen a girl come before?"

FIFTY

The elevator began to hum as it reached its cruising speed.

"Does that happen every time?" asked Gantz.

Cyn climbed to her feet and brushed the dust from her arms. The previous moment's frenzy had all but disappeared, leaving behind a steely demeanor. To look at her, you wouldn't have guessed she had just survived a one-sided firefight.

"Only when it's good," she replied, trying to smile. She tapped the back of her neck. "The Ayudante wasn't designed for women. Even in the MoA, female soldiers are given different chips. Vergaras, I think."

"Never heard of those," said Gantz. He stood and leaned against the back of the car, evoking a crunching sound from the busted mirror.

"South American imports. Cross between a Brazilian med-tech assist and a Chilean social engineering mod. Makes their women healers and infiltrators. The Ayudante was meant for men, so sometimes it gets the signals wrong in the heat of the moment. But I tell you what, Chief. If it's wrong…"

"Seems like a liability to me," said Gantz. He approached the vidscreen and cleared the floor selection. In her haste to get the elevator moving, Cyn had hit every floor between fifty and seventy. Gantz keyed in the code for the 89th floor and stepped back.

"What's on eighty-nine?"

"The last of the occupied floors. We climb from there until we find what we're looking for. Telecom equipment starts at a hundred and goes up to the top."

The elevator slowed as the counter climbed into the eighties. There was just enough vibration from the brakes engaging to dislodge more glass from the sides of the car. Cyn lifted the shotgun as the doors parted.

Safety lights lit the hallway heading away from the elevator. They extended to the outer walls and then broke off in opposite directions. Gantz noticed a slight curvature of the far wall; they were now high enough to discern the outer shape of the Spire.

"Step back," he said, moving between Cyn and the silver railing on the back of the car. It was already coming loose from the wall; Gantz' kick freed it from its anchors. He dragged the rail and laid it across the threshold.

Gantz joined Cyn outside the elevator and watched as the doors came together, hit the rail, and retracted.

"That'll slow them down," he said. "The other elevators only go up to seventy. If anyone tries to follow us, they'll have to walk up the rest of the way."

Gantz led Cyn into the darkness, his 9mm pointed at the floor, his thumb digging into the safety. At the fork in the hallway, they paused and listened.

Silence.

"Either this plan is fucking genius," said Gantz, "or it's so stupid Kessler doesn't even think we'd try it."

Cyn shrugged. "Maybe it's both."

"Maybe it's both," Gantz repeated, under his breath. He turned left down the corridor and pressed forward. "Maybe it's both, maybe it's both."

It felt like they had walked a hundred and eighty degrees around the Spire when the path finally broke towards center again. It led into a control room filled with five empty desks set in front of a wall of segmented vidscreens. Each section showed a video feed from somewhere in the building, including the deserted security offices on the fifth floor and the smoldering remains of a slagged Civic in the lobby. There, a battalion of Scorpios sorted through their fallen brothers, deciding which could still fight and which were destined for the scrap yards on the north side of The Fringe. Walking amongst them like a general was a slender frame Gantz immediately recognized.

"I don't get it," said Cyn. "Why is this room all the way up here?"

"Secondary monitoring," said Gantz. "We have a similar room down on five, but it only really covers the publicly accessible parts of the building. Chuck designed a half-dozen watcher synnies to man these stations. From here, they can dispatch response teams anywhere in the Spire."

"They're the ones who saw me enter the building, weren't they?"

Cyn approached the vidscreens. The feeds were organized by floor, going from sub-levels on the left to the claustrophobic equipment floors on the right. Cyn stubbed her finger against an image of a legless synny impaled on a spike. It wasn't the same one she had blown away, but its arms hung lifelessly at its side just the same.

"Probably. Not all of their activity comes through me directly. Just the big stuff." Gantz paused, thought about how he had heard the news about Cyn. "Shit, sometimes not even the big stuff."

Cyn traced up the column and moved left by one. "Here," she said, tapping the screen. "I think this is where we need to go. Those look like high-grade LMR cables, the same ones I saw coming out of the dishes outside."

Gantz imagined what outside was like this high above the ground.

"And, we really need to get going," she continued.

"What is it?"

Gantz joined her at the wall and followed her finger to a section of the vidscreen. The feed showed a control room and two figures standing at the far wall. Gantz looked over his shoulder at the camera above the door.

Cyn jogged to the other end of the wall. "They're moving to the elevators."

"Then *we're* moving," said Gantz, brushing past her.

A service door to the left of the video wall led into a back room. There, thick evercrete columns housing the elevators climbed into the ceiling. Gantz walked around the center column and found the maintenance ladder—little more than steel rungs stapled into the evercrete. After holstering his gun, he began to climb.

They passed the many floors in silence. Gantz felt the soreness in his arms after only a few levels; they burned with every latch of his hand on a new rung. Below him, Cyn seemed to be having an easier time, though she did let out her fair share of grunts.

Gantz wondered how much the augments helped, whether they were worth the money and the pain.

"I need a moment," he said, wiping the sweat away from his eyes. He slapped the *122* painted beside the ladder.

Cyn climbed up through the floor and found a wall to lean against. Around her, unused electronics sat atop rolling carts, their wires impossibly tangled.

"I thought the Chief of Police would be in better shape," said Cyn. She didn't try to disguise her labored breathing.

"Says the Umbra augment."

Cyn laughed and ran her fingers through a pile on a nearby cart. "I can't believe you guys still have this stuff around. This is BBS-era equipment." She plucked an Ethernet coupler from the pile and slipped it into her pocket.

Gantz took a seat on the floor next to the ladder. "You mean it's pre-Cynthia, so therefore useless, right?"

"Not useless, but not what I would expect to find here in the high-tech capital of the world."

"You could say the same thing about yourself. Is this what you had in mind when you signed on for the job?"

Cyn shook her head. "I didn't think it would take this long, to be honest. Just a quick in-out, if you know what I mean. Lincoln was sure there was something going down behind the media silence. He's gonna shit himself when he finds out what you and I are doing."

There was something in her voice.

"You like him?"

"Lincoln? Sure. We have a lot in common. He hates Vinestead, I hate Vinestead. He's into body mods, I'm into augmentation." She paused to examine a line card from an old Orion. "He's black, I like pissing off my parents."

"Huh," said Gantz. "Pays you well, I'm guessing?"

"It's not Perion money, but I get by. I've actually been saving up for a new skin graft. It uses grow wire to create a protective mesh under your skin, like a bulletproof vest you wear on the inside. They're crazy expensive though. I've only known a few people who have them."

"Why not just make the jump to full synthetic? Perion gave you a chance."

Cyn turned and kicked her hip out to the side. She ran a hand from her face down to her stomach. "Not even the great J.K. Perion could synthesize this." She laughed at herself.

"I don't know," said Gantz, climbing to his feet. "You saw the warehouse. You saw Roberta. Girls like you are going to have some serious competition if the Virgo models ever make it to market. The coming generation of men will build themselves a synthetic harem and call it a day."

"Flesh will always top machine," said Cyn. "You can bet your pension on it."

Gantz put one hand on the ladder. "Yeah, but machines are easier." He began to climb again, grunting between his sentences. "All the time it takes to meet the right person, to build up the confidence to talk to them. You take them out, spend your money…"

"I'm familiar with the male point of view," said Cyn from below.

"What I'm saying is, it's easier to keep a synthetic in the house than work a relationship with a real person. The synny does all the chores, makes all the meals, and fucks for hours without complaint or need for satisfaction. What male isn't going to choose that over an emotional, unreasonable, and sometimes volatile human?"

"We're not always that way."

"Of course not," said Gantz. "Sometimes you're on your period."

Something caught his left foot and pushed it to the side. He missed the next rung and fell, pulling his arms taut. The pain rushed through his hands in a million little splinters.

"Don't be an asshole, Gantz. Flaws are what keep us human."

"Synnies don't have flaws. They have bugs and whole teams of lab coats to stamp them out. They'll never have a bad day at work. They'll never ask their owners if they look fat in these jeans."

"Yes, every man's fantasy," said Cyn. "All the sex he can handle without any of the baggage. Well, Mr. Chief, it's not all fucking and fondue; shit takes work."

Gantz glanced downwards. "Are you and Lincoln working on your shit?"

"No," she replied. "Company ink and all that. Besides, he probably doesn't want to deal with my monthly lady business. Maybe if I augment my cooch he'll pay more attention to me."

"Couldn't hurt," said Gantz.

They climbed five more floors before Cyn spoke again, muttering *asshole* under her breath.

"One thirty," said Gantz, pausing at the landing.

There was something different about this level, and it took a moment of staring at the black walls to realize they were heavily tinted windows. On closer inspection, Gantz found he could see the city if he pressed his face against the glass and cupped his hands around his eyes. He moved around the perimeter until he found what he was looking for.

"What do you see?"

"Gas station on fire," he replied. "It looks like it's spreading. There should have been a response team on it a long time ago."

"Synthetic response?"

Gantz looked at her over his shoulder. She was right.

"We need to get this done," he said. "The longer the signal is going out, the longer our synthetic lifesavers are offline. And if Joe was hurt in that explosion…"

"Are the EMTs synthetics too?"

Gantz nodded. "Seven more floors. Let's put these things back to work."

"Find me a terminal with an outside line," said Cyn, "and I'll make it happen."

FIFTY-ONE

"You're not listening to me, Lincoln. The signal has been in the broadcast traffic coming off the Spire for years, in the free and clear. We all thought it was background noise, but it's actually the command and control for every synthetic in the city. You need to go back in the archives and isolate it."

Cyn waved her hands around as if her boss could see her.

"Because this morning it changed to something else. Look for the delta."

Gantz could barely make sense of the one-sided conversation. His primary responsibility had been to stand guard at the ladder, watching and listening for any sign of pursuit while Cyn fashioned a jackport splice out of the discarded electronics she had picked up during their climb. That had taken half an hour, followed by another fifteen minutes of her cursing the Perion firewalls. When she finally did get through to Lincoln Tate, her mood was more agitated than relieved.

"Everything alright?" asked Gantz.

Cyn sighed. "It's a pissing contest over there. He's got Benny Coker in his other ear and that asshole doesn't want to give us access to his satellites even though he hijacked them and… fuck. Every other question out of Coker's mouth is about Gil."

Gantz looked down at the service hatch; had there been a sound from below?

"Well, tell them to hurry. We're going to run out of time here."

Cyn rolled her eyes. "Yeah, I hadn't thought about that." She turned her head to the side. "Alright, Benny is calling down to his tech team. They're going to start looking for the signal."

"You think they'll find it?" He gripped his 9mm tightly.

"They'll find it. The traffic coming out of Perion City has always been under scrutiny, but no one knew what they were looking for. We still don't."

"Then how…" Gantz trailed off, sensing agitation in Cyn's lengthy sigh.

"Because it's *different* today. If a stream of data is encrypted, the only thing you know about it is its signature, how it looks in encrypted format. Unless you're using some kind of rotating cipher, it all comes down to a consistent string of ones and zeros. We should be able to identify it simply because it *changed* today. So long as we can send out the same encrypted message, it doesn't matter what the actual content is…"

Cyn went quiet, then laughed.

"What's so funny?"

"Coker is drunk," replied Cyn.

She stood and dragged her tether to the telco racks where she ran her fingers through the patch cables as if they were the collected hair of an electronic woman. She picked up the shotgun from the desk and pointed it at the network devices. Her aim drifted to the left.

"There's my bitch," she said, tapping the switch with the barrel. "The only wires going up to the next floor run through these redundant switches. We take them out and the whole network is cut off. One little pull of the trigger and it's all over."

"That would be a very bad idea."

Gantz swung his 9mm in the direction of the sound. Standing at the ladder were Sava Kessler and Roberta.

"Mr. Gantz," said Kessler, pointing a needler in his direction. "Just what do you think you're doing?"

"What needs to be done," he replied. "And if that includes taking you out, then so be it."

Roberta took a step forward and slid into place in front of Kessler. Every time Gantz adjusted his aim, the synthetic moved into the line of fire.

"It doesn't have to go down like this, Robert. Lower your weapon and let's discuss this like professionals. Mr. Perion has agreed not to press charges if you surrender immediately."

"Joe?" asked Gantz.

Kessler shook her head. "James Perion, the man whose work you're trying to destroy."

"Bullshit," said Cyn. "I saw Gantz blow his brains out."

"Yes, of course you did. And like your slightly less masculine counterpart here, you've clearly forgotten to take into account the fact if we can make one…"

"Son of a bitch," said Gantz.

"But it will all be for nothing if you blow that switch," said Kessler. "A hundred and fifty thousand synthetics will go up in smoke. Do you have any idea what that will do to the company? Even if Joe were to take over, there would be nothing left for him. How in the fuck does this sound like a good idea to you, Robert?"

"Those same synthetics have been after us all day. They pulled Cam's head off on *your* orders, and you just want me to sit back and do nothing about it?"

"You'd trade one synthetic for an entire line? Think about who really got hurt here. Joe? Cameron Gray with Banks Media out of Los Angeles? No way. Put the gun down and we'll go ask Cam how he feels about his synthetic clone getting the chop. Hundred bucks says he doesn't give a good flying fuck about it."

"He's alive?" asked Cyn.

"Of course," replied Kessler. "We wanted to see if you would accept his replacement as one of your own."

Another science experiment.

Gantz shook his head. Cam was still drawing breath. Synth J had backups.

"I shot him in the face," said Gantz. "I blew his chip out the back of his head. Step the fuck back, Roberta!"

The synthetic paused mid-step and retreated.

"Call her off, Kessler. Or I drop the both of you."

Kessler reached her free hand out and put it on Roberta's shoulder. "You've already put one Virgo Prime out of commission. Do you really want to be financially responsible for another?"

"The company is insured," said Gantz.

"James Perion will sue you out of existence."

"Sued by a dead man. That'll be a first."

Gantz felt a hand on his back. It slid to his right side and pressed. In small steps, he allowed Cyn to guide him to the left, closer to the telco racks. Out of the corner of his eye, he saw the shotgun come up, leveled at the switch again.

"Goddammit, Robert. Don't let her do this."

"It'll be okay," said Cyn. Her voice was steely next to Gantz' ear. "Nothing is going to happen to your precious synthetics."

"I know," said Kessler, "because you're going to put the gun down."

Cyn laughed. "Naw, I'm going to put two rounds into this little box right here. And those two rounds are going to silence whatever nonsense you're feeding to your synthetic subbers. But that's alright because The White Line and Lincoln Continental are going to start broadcasting your PNR signal on every satellite they can get their hands on and they are going to bathe this place. All of your little robots are going to be just fine."

Gantz watched Kessler's eyes jump to the cable on the floor. She traced it to the switch and then back to Cyn's head.

"If that's even remotely true, you'll have synthetics being stolen left and right. They'd be able to walk right out onto I-30 and hitch a ride to the coast. And it won't be long before Vinestead—may they burn in hell—gets their hands on one and reverse engineers it. They could be turning out *working* synthetics by next summer."

"Not my concern," said Gantz. "There are people dying in the streets right now because our synthetics are busy chasing down the CEO's son. Why did you put them on us anyway, Kessler?"

"Because you're a wild card, Robert. Because *she's* a wild card. God only knows how badly you two were going to fuck things up. You have no idea how important it is for Perion Synthetics to survive. You're looking one, maybe two moves ahead, but I'm in it for the long con. Anyone who isn't with Perion is an enemy of the future. That includes Joseph Perion."

"Enemy of the future," said Gantz. "What a load of shit."

"The Great Emancipation," said Cyn, "began at the stroke of midnight on the seventeenth day of November in the year 2015. Through the alliance of the LC and White Line Media, the synthetics of Perion City were successfully freed from the control of Sava Kessler, rogue PR bitch of Perion Synthetics." She dropped the anchorwoman cadence. "When the sun rises tomorrow, everyone will know two things. First, that James Kirkland Perion is very much dead. And second, that his synthetics are now free."

The hammers on the shotgun fell; Gantz felt the heat in the small of his back.

"No!" The needler began to whine, bouncing sparks off the telco rack.

Gantz heard Cyn cry out and fall. He squeezed his trigger in response, and the semi-automatic beat out a long string of staccato notes as bullet after bullet tore into Roberta. They shredded the white blouse she was wearing and coated the fabric in a mixture of synthetic blood and oil. Gaping holes appeared in her chest. Within them, metal mesh glimmered with each bullet fired, reflecting the muzzle flash as brilliant yellow on silver.

Feeling the end of the clip coming, Gantz raised his arm and dragged a line up Roberta's neck. Her right eye exploded in a spray of gray flakes and shattered glass. As the gun clicked empty, Roberta went rigid, her face taking on a poor reproduction of shock.

She fell, revealing Sava Kessler behind her.

Gantz reached for his belt, but the needler was already turning in his direction. He was freeing the clip from its pouch when the first shard hit him, ripping away the cloth and flesh at his shoulder. The force turned him around as pin-pricks danced along his back. Only after a few seconds did they turn to intense pain; he looked down to see exit wounds vomiting blood onto his shirt. Gantz collapsed forward into a chair, and then the desk beside it. The strength left his legs, bringing his face down hard on a plastic keyboard. Then he was on the floor, staring at the metal grates in the ceiling.

Silence filled the room, marked by angry groans coming from Cyn.

Gantz tried to look for her, but his head wouldn't move. The edges of his vision blurred.

Bless me, Padre.

"It didn't have to go down like this," said Kessler, stepping into view. "We could have talked this out and saved the bloodshed. But you wanted to fight, you wanted to bankrupt the company. Now nothing will stand in Vinestead's way. *You* did this."

"No," said Gantz. The needler swung in a small circle above his head.

Thy will be done.

Kessler smiled. "Your final act on this planet and it was for the 'Stead, may they burn in hell."

"Fuck you, Kessler."

Her eyes widened for a moment. "Kessler?" She leaned in closer, lowered her voice. "Try Kaili, Kaili Zabora. The Butcher of Burbank. Veteran of the Reaping. And the last face you'll ever see."

Forgive me my trespasses.

The needler steadied.

Deliver me from evil.

"That's right, Robert Gantz. Calle Cinco is in Perion City, right under your nose. If the shame doesn't kill you…"

Amen.

Yates' voice exploded from the back of the needler's barrel.

"Welcome, my son."

PART SIX
SAVANNAH KESSLER

FIFTY-TWO

"I guess we should have expected this."

Javier Espinoza fiddled with the M4 carbine in his lap.

He had his feet propped up on the control board in the observation room atop Outpost Alpha, his head turned towards the north where the distant Spire bloomed like a taut spike of lightning. The rest of the city was dim, languid in its post-midnight haze. It could have been any normal night in Perion City, one in which its residents enjoyed a peaceful slumber. Engineers, artists, and even the middle of the road grunt workers all rested under the blanket of security provided by the sixty-strong team of guardians at Outpost Alpha.

Would they have slept so soundly had they known the number was only ten now?

Beside him, a dozing Kris Ferko had lowered his chair to its limit and was leaning back, trying to find a comfortable position. He knew there was a short but plush couch down in the scanning room, but the bowels of the outpost were so empty and quiet that fear had kept him awake, jumping at every sound in the dark. At least up in the observation room he had Javier to keep him company, to watch over him with a weapon that could cut down human and synthetic alike. That alone was worth the discomfort.

"I mean, you build these things to look like humans, and you expect them to be human day in and day out, but you forget they're just machines with programming. If they use the wrong words or if their inflection is off, we laugh at them like they're children. But when they all drop their weapons and head north like a flock of birds... I don't know. Even when you run them through training drills, you never see coordination like that. Whatever Perion did to call his children home must work at a primitive level. Right to the core."

Ferko rubbed his neck and felt something free up in the space between his vertebrae.

"Anyway," continued Javier, "I knew I was right to keep some real men on the team. They wanted me to enlist a fully synthetic squad, but I put my foot down." His voice slipped into a drawl. "When the revolution come, ol' Javier ain't gonna get bushwhacked by a bunch of life-size G.I. Joes."

"I don't think it's the synthetics you have to worry about," said Ferko.

"You talking about the Terminus?" asked Javier, glancing at the three monitors to the right of his feet.

The center screen displayed a video feed from the iron gates that spanned the entirety of the Perion Expressway. The steel barriers were still up, sticking out of the evercrete foundations like pegs in a corkboard. Behind the gates, a dozen men stood in tight formation, rifles not pointed at the growing crowd but ready all the same. Javier had ordered the lights at Perion Terminus turned down in an attempt to disguise his diminished forces, but the media crews had brought their own van-mounted floodlights, and they were all pointed into the city. Reporters stood by the gates and spoke into cameras while aggregators stood some distance away, whispering to their wrists.

"It was that aggregator who brought them here," said Ferko. "I told Kessler it was a bad idea letting a feeder into the city, but she said the order came right from the top. People weren't ready to see what's been happening here. And now that we've had one little hiccup, everyone's running around like someone stomped on their ant hill."

"And they won't stop either." Javier checked his sliver. "They'll stand out there all night asking questions even though no one is answering. No idea why they do it."

Ferko shrugged and rubbed his nose. "Content," he replied. "People on the outside are always looking for content. Why do you think they install those whisperers? God forbid they go ten minutes without a status update."

"That status update crap isn't content," said Javier. He motioned to the window. "You think I give a damn about what these guys do with their time off? Feed me something useful like military strategy or immobilization techniques. I don't need to know you're at the dentist."

Ferko thought about the men down on the street hidden behind makeshift barricades. In the blackout, only their flashers were visible, tiny LEDs that let out quick bursts every sixty seconds. They hadn't moved from their original positions since Ferko first came up.

"Alpha Three, zero one hundred sit-rep. No change."

The radio on Javier's chest crackled as the transmission cut off. He squeezed the transmit button. "Copy, Alpha Three. Let's get a perimeter sweep north side."

"Copy, Alpha."

Ferko laughed to himself. Fatigue made everything seem funnier than it was. The way Javier spoke to his men, it sounded like he was invading China.

"I miss my bed," said Ferko.

"We all miss a lot of things. Suck it up."

"You always know just what to say, don't you, Javi?"

"I know what people need to hear to get them through a situation," he replied, turning his head to show Ferko his smile. "That's one thing synthetics have going for them. You tell them to do something and they fucking do it. But us? We're more complicated. We have to be *convinced* to go into battle, to sacrifice our lives so that others may live. You can't march an army at gunpoint—the Soviets figured that one out—you have to change their minds with *words*." He lifted his rifle. "Words are more powerful than this thing, Ferko… when they're used right."

Ferko nodded, laughed to himself.

"Alpha Three, movement on the PE," squawked the radio. "Reading twelve tangos. Strike that. Eighteen."

Javier's feet came down in an instant, knocking his water bottle to the floor. He picked up the binoculars and trained them on the road.

"RTB, Alpha Three," said Javier. "Action stations, all personnel."

Ferko sat up in his chair and tried to see over the control board. With a groan, he stood to get a better look.

"I don't see anything," he said.

"Twenty-two tangos," said Alpha Three. "Thermal scan is reading below human thresholds."

Javier growled. "Synnies. They're back." Then, to the radio, "Prepare to open fire. Hold for my order."

"Twenty-nine tangos."

"I'm coming down," said Javier. He kicked the chair back with his leg and started towards the door. Pausing, he cast a look back at Ferko. "You stay here, yeah?"

Ferko nodded.

Javier pulled a revolver from his hip and held it out.

"I don't think I could shoot anybody," said Ferko. "Even a synthetic."

"It's not for them." Javier smiled. "I'm fucking with you, Ferko. Just point and shoot. Don't even think about it."

Ferko took the gun; it was heavier than he expected.

Javier scurried down the circular staircase in the center of the room. Ferko moved closer to the window and watched the flashing LEDs rearrange themselves into two groups, one on each side of the road. A minute later, a new LED emerged from the motor pool, walking in a straight line between the flanks.

"Control room, this is Alpha Actual. Copy?"

Ferko followed the voice to the control board and located a speaker just above the north camera feed. He pressed the small button beside it.

"Roger dodger, Alpha Zulu," he replied.

"Cut the shit, Ferko. On my signal, I want you to hit the highlights. Think you can manage that?"

"Wilco?"

"Good enough," said Javier.

Ferko moved down two panels to the facilities vidscreen. It held a virtual control panel for all lighting in and around Outpost Alpha. Most entries, including the exterior floodlights, had glowing red icons next to them.

"Thirty-seven tangos."

There was nothing in the space between Ferko and the Spire, just miles and miles of empty blackness, and yet one of the men claimed there were thirty-seven synthetics walking out of the gloom, thirty-seven potential killing machines with unknown intentions headed for the outpost, the PNR, and maybe even…

"Give me some light!"

Ferko ran his finger across the control panel, tripping the switches for the floodlights. The Perion Expressway lit up under the glare of Outpost Alpha's high beams. LED pinpoints became dark hulks of crouched men, their rifles leveled over the barricades. Javier Espinoza stood alone in the center of the road, his rifle in one hand and a radio in the other.

Thirty yards in front of him, both lanes of the Perion Expressway were filled with uniformed synthetics. Ferko recognized them as former members of the outpost's security detail; they were still dressed in the same black as the men pointing guns at them. And though they carried no weapons, Ferko felt his fingers tighten on the revolver. They were Scorpio-class synthetics with the programming to put a man down with their hands as easily as they could with a gun. Ten men against what looked like fifty Automated Guards.

Despite the unfavorable odds, Javier seemed undisturbed.

One of the synthetics approached, his face blank but his steps purposeful. He stopped when Javier put up his hand.

Ferko heard the conversation over the radio.

"That's far enough, soldier," said Javier. "State your name and business."

"A707101498, Private Henry. Returning to duty, sir."

"Where have you been all day, Private Henry?"

"The private does not know, sir."

The other synthetics fell into place around him, organizing themselves into five rows of ten.

"So all of you decide to go AWOL and now you want to come back like nothing happened?" asked Javier.

"Sir, yes, sir," answered the company.

Javier stood with his hands clasped behind his back while the rest of his human contingent formed up behind him, the scopes of their rifles glued to their eyes. Ferko tried not to blink, expecting to see the synthetics cut down in a hail of gunfire. Instead, Javier looked down for a moment and then stepped forward. He got in the lead synny's face.

"You do this again, and it'll be your ass. I will personally melt you down. You get me, private?"

"Sir, yes, sir."

"Then back to your fucking stations," said Javier. "This ain't no goddamn block party."

Fifty salutes flashed in the blinding light, and the synthetics dispersed into the building.

Ferko was still shaking his head when the hardline began to ring. He located the handset on the control board and picked it up.

"Hello?"

"Espinoza?" asked a female voice.

"No, this is Ferko. Kris Ferko. I work in the scanning room."

"I know who you are, Mr. Ferko. This is Sava Kessler. I need to speak to Captain Espinoza immediately. We have a situation."

"We know," said Ferko. "But it's okay now. They're back."

"What?"

"Captain Espinoza is outside dealing with some synthetics who just showed up. He's putting them back to work."

There was silence on the line.

"Ms. Kessler?"

"Lock it down, Mr. Ferko. Tell the captain this comes from the very top. On the order of James Kirkland Perion, you *shut down* the Perion Expressway. No one comes in, and no one goes out. And *do not* let your synnies near the PNR. Quarantine them, keep them locked up."

Ferko shook his head. "I… are you sure? They seem harmless."

"This is not a fucking suggestion, Kris! You lock that shit down now or you will answer to the man himself. *No one* gets within a hundred yards of the outpost or you put them down. Is that clear?"

"Roger," said Ferko. "I'll let the captain know."

"Do it now," said Kessler.

The line went dead.

Ferko put the phone down and wandered over to the window again. A synthetic was pacing the road with Javier.

Both of them had rifles slung across their backs.

FIFTY-THREE

"The strange thing about humanity is that we are always giving it away."

Sava Kessler had retreated to the imaginary construct in her mind as the elevator headed for the lobby. There, in the virtual dream world, the problems facing Kaili Zabora took physical shape, represented in wispy white forms dancing around her, fading in and out as their priorities changed or their solutions were found. Constant in this construct were two entities. One of them was her sister, Anela, looking proud and powerful in the tight red dress she had so often worn in the Net. Her avatar had been burned into Sava's mind at the age of fifteen, the year Anela had met her end at the hands of a man named G and a woman named Natalie, two people who had gone so far off the grid even Calle Cinco couldn't locate them.

It was Anela who spoke to her in the quiet times, offering advice or encouragement when necessary. Deep down, Sava knew it was her own voice coming from Anela's avatar, but technicalities of that nature were easily overlooked when the situation was dire, as it was now.

"Anthropomorphism likely started with pets—animals already demonstrate human characteristics—but then it spread to inanimate objects, some even too large to grasp. *The sea is a harsh mistress.* Have you ever heard that saying, Kai? An entire body of water imagined as a living, breathing woman, capable of thoughts and emotions. Not that anyone *truly* believed the sea was a real person. These were simply metaphors, harmless language nobody took seriously—until the day they went too far. Do you remember that day?"

In the construct, a diminutive Sava nodded at her older sister.

"January 23, 1988," she replied, back in the real world.

"Yes, January of eighty-eight. The United States government ratifies full corporate personhood, allowing businesses like Vinestead International to have the same rights and protections as naturalized citizens. Political contributions, tax loopholes, privately funded military companies: these all become permissible and *protected* under federal law. And look where we are now."

Sava turned to face the other entity in the construct. It loomed beyond the border, extending below the horizon as if it inhabited the true world and the construct were just a bubble floating within it. The entity took the shape of a titanic demon, outlined by red flames that graded to deep black. Two pinpoints of brilliant light shone where its eyes should have been, but Sava was often distracted by the horns above them, the blood-stained ivory reaching into the infinite ether, tips engulfed in blue fire. This shadowy creature had no true name, but Sava felt a word roll off her tongue every time she set eyes on it.

Vinestead.

May they burn in hell.

"It's not all bad," said Sava. "If Ferko is right, and the synnies are going back to work, then maybe the company can still be saved."

"True," replied Anela. "Just because they *can* leave does not mean they will. But we both know what will happen when Vinestead finds out they can take one out of the city."

The construct shuddered as the demon came closer, perhaps trying to listen in on the conversation. To the right, a smoke-based Cyn took shape, pulsed twice, and dissolved.

"She screwed everything up," said Sava.

Anela walked in a circle around Sava, her high heels clacking on the invisible floor. "It is a setback, as is the loss of Robert Gantz, but like you said, there is still hope. The company's inventory remains intact. As long as you can keep it in the city, Perion Synthetics may continue to prosper."

The elevator vidscreen flashed into the forties.

Sava put her hands to her face and rubbed her eyes. "Sometimes I just want to go home. I miss San Diego."

"We all want to go home," said Anela, "but there is a war going on, Kai. Right now, Vinestead is winning that war because they stand unopposed. You know how much we need Perion and what it would mean if the company were to not exist when the sun comes up."

"I know, but…"

"You promised me you would carry on the fight. Now that we are so close, can you really walk away from it all?"

"No," replied Sava, her head dropping.

Of course she couldn't walk away, no more than she could let Gantz shoot at her without defending herself. There were just some things in life that had to happen, effects that had to be caused. Sava had known domestic terrorism wasn't the answer years ago, when she first assumed her new life in Perion City. Abandoning the plan now would relegate her to a life of petty skirmishes that would do nothing to alter the course of history. Driving Perion Synthetics towards all-out war with Vinestead was her only hope.

As the elevator slowed, the construct began to break down. Anela's smiling face fell away, as did the smoky figures on the edges of Sava's periphery. The protective dome overhead winked out of existence, leaving Sava alone with the demon for one terrifying moment, and then it too was gone.

Sava opened her eyes as the doors parted.

The lobby was a mess, but the maintenance synthetics were doing their best to clear the area. Sava found a swept path on the other side of a Honda Civic and followed it to the north entrance of the Spire. Outside, the cool air caused a chill to go up her spine.

"What the hell did I miss?"

Sava looked down at Cameron Gray sitting on the steps leading to the Victoria Perion Memorial Plaza. He had arranged bullet casings into a small pile next to him. He flung one into the plaza as he waited for an answer.

"I thought I had you detained," said Sava. She sat down next to him.

"Yeah, well," said Cam, handing her a casing, "your guards kinda lost interest in me about an hour ago, so I showed myself out. I guess I missed the war?"

Sava chucked the casing at a nearby synthetic whose chest had been crushed by a tire. "This wasn't the war. This was all Gantz and Cyn."

Cam smiled. "I tell you those Umbra girls are crafty. Whole 'nother breed of woman, if you ask me." He glanced over his shoulder. "Where is she?"

"Halfway to hell I hope."

The smile disappeared. "And Gantz?"

"Already there."

Cam nodded and flung another bullet into the plaza. It clinked against an overturned drink cart.

"You didn't like him much, did you?" asked Cam.

"That had nothing to do with it. He and Cyn smashed our transmitter feed. Every signal in the city runs through it. Broadcasts, command and control, jammers…"

"Those are still working," said Cam, raising his wrist. "My sliver came back online about the same time the guards took a powder, but every time I try to upload to BMP, the connection gets reset. All I can do is download like some kind of ordinary subber."

The construct flared and Anela Zabora walked out of the black mist. "You have to tell him, Kai. Remember Rick?"

Sava fingered the silver band on her thumb. She had worn Rick's wedding ring ever since the day of the Reaping, the day he and so many others were betrayed by Vinestead treachery, the day Calle Cinco struck deep at the heart of the demon. And in all that time, no one had ever asked nor had she ever told what it signified.

In truth, Sava had assigned many meanings to it, from a simple remembrance of abbreviated love to a cautionary reminder not to get too close to the target. It stood for corporate misdeeds and omission of certain facts that could have saved an entire building of clueless engineers. It was a promise to fight against the denigration of the innocent, the assignment of numbers instead of names—against massive companies that wanted to turn people into machines, companies with no appreciation for the blood and sweat that fueled their profits. And though Vinestead was infamous for its disregard for employees, Sava knew more and more companies were adopting the practice, even Banks Media out of Los Angeles.

"No, Mr. Gray. Your sliver is broadcasting, but no one is listening. Banks Media servers aren't accepting your input anymore."

"Bullshit. The only way that would happen is if Banks fired me and yanked my feeder ID from the database. And considering the metric fuck-ton of content I've got for him, I wouldn't be surprised if he made me a partner when I get back."

Sava rolled a bullet casing between her fingers. "Cameron Gray still works for Banks Media, but his feeder ID has been updated to match his new sliver. The old ID was trashed."

"Why would I need a new sliver?" asked Cam, looking at his wrist. "This one works just fine."

"Not for you," said Sava.

She flashed on the memory of Rick's glazed eyes the moment he realized Vinestead had lied to him.

"We built a synthetic Cameron and equipped him with all of your tech. The only thing we couldn't clone was the hardware ID of your new sliver, so we updated the database. The synthetic you would have never known the difference."

Sava gave a quick glance to Cam and found he was staring at the ground and biting his lip.

"I uh," he said, chuckling. "I did a story once on cloning. People thought it was going to be an escape from death, but they didn't consider they might wake up as the original instead of the copy. I always wondered what that must feel like." He huffed, drew himself up. "I should like to meet this synthetic Cam."

"You can't," said Sava. "A couple of synthetics pulled its head off and dragged it back to the Spire. I had it destroyed."

"Naturally." His head bobbed. "You see, the originals got screwed because they weren't the ones moving on in the better body. If they cloned themselves to escape disease, they still woke with that disease. What you people did here was make an unnecessary copy. Were you just going to keep me locked up so the new me could take my place?"

"It wasn't supposed to go down like this. Things got out of hand when Cyn entered the picture. And then before I knew it, I had aggregators crawling out of every crevice in the city. You people really fucked things up for us."

Cam laughed. "And your role in all of this was what?"

"Everything was on the rails right up until your head came off. If Joe… if it hadn't gone the way it did, you'd be home in L.A. getting ready to forward the cause of synthetic rights. Just like James Perion wanted."

"And Donato Banks," said Cam.

"Excuse me?"

Cam dropped the remaining bullets to the ground. "I know how this works. There's no way you could have accessed the Banks Media database from here. Our Quality Control group is the second biggest department we have, right behind network security. And before anything gets to QC, there are checks to make sure it is coming from the right person. The feeder IDs of Banks Media aggregators are closely guarded secrets. You can't just telnet to our public webserver and change my identity."

Sava looked away. "I know."

"Only Donato Banks himself could have pulled this off without raising eyebrows, which means he knew the switchover was coming." Cam paused, took a deep breath. "He knew you were gonna fuck me and he did everything but put me in a pretty dress."

"He did not even get a choice," said Anela, her voice a whisper on the air.

The construct threatened to show Sava an image of Rick, of the way his face looked on the train back to Sacramento, the sadness in his dying eyes as she told him who she really was.

Kaili Zabora pushed the memory away to become Sava Kessler once more.

She reached out and patted Cam on the back.

FIFTY-FOUR

They came out of The Fringe like ants to a rotting carcass.

Hundreds drifted out of the alleys and down wide pedestrian thoroughfares on pre-programmed chemical trails as if heading into work for the first time that day. For all of the intelligence built into their synthetic brains, they seemed unaffected by the destruction around them. They stepped over and around run-over, dismembered, and crushed synthetics in the plaza as if they were loose trash someone had forgotten to pick up. Only the ones in blue jumpsuits occasionally emerged from the crowd to set a table upright before rejoining the flow.

Sava cursed every time she had to move over on the steps to give way to the swelling torrent of synthetics. There wasn't any danger of being trampled; Sava just didn't like all of those machine bodies walking so close to her, swallowing her up like the last remaining sandcastle on the beach, standing alone against the oncoming surf. The image evoked the crumbling memories of Anela throwing oversized towels into the car and driving them to the coast. Sava recalled watching the planes take off and land at San Diego International Airport in the golden light of dawn. There was a peacefulness to laying out on the sand with her sister that Sava had not known since, yet the memory was enough to calm her down, to remove the emotional barrier that so often got in the way of what needed to be done.

And there was so much to be done.

Sava stood and brushed the dirt from the back of her skirt. Beside her, Cam faked a cough. She walked closer to the parade of synthetics and examined them as they passed by.

"You," she said, pointing to a synthetic in a nurse's uniform, "come here."

The synny returned a smile and broke free from the pack. She stood in front of Sava and discreetly inventoried her injuries.

"How can I be of assistance?" she asked.

Sava ignored her and pointed again to the crowd. "And you, guard. Front and center."

A male synthetic at least six and a half feet tall brought his hulking frame and bolted-on scowl to rest in front of Sava. His eyes went passive, awaiting an order.

"There's an injured woman on one thirty-seven who needs medical attention. You can take the elevator to eighty-nine and use the service ladders the rest of the way." Sava pointed to the nurse. "Triage the situation." Then to the guard, "If she determines the woman can be moved, take her down to Medical and get her some attention."

The nurse nodded.

"Yes, sir," said the AG, furnishing a quick salute. He headed into the building at a hasty clip, the nurse following on his heels.

"I was wondering if you were gonna do anything about her," said Cam.

"She doesn't have to die," said Sava. "We're going to need more women like her in the world, people who are ready to fight for what they believe in."

"Then why'd you shoot her?"

"Just because she was *wrong* doesn't mean she didn't believe in what she was doing. It probably doesn't make any sense to someone like you, but there is honor in conviction. Mine just happened to be stronger."

Cam shook his head. "If that's how you want to justify it, fine. Gil and Gantz are dead; Cyn could be. I'm pretty sure you'd be digging a grave for me if this plan of yours had worked. The world doesn't need two Cameron Grays, does it?"

"*My* plan?" she asked, placing her hand on her chest. "You think I wanted any of this? I wanted James Perion to continue running his company for another thirty or forty years. He had infinite resources. He could have found a way to steal Vinestead's tech and save himself. But no, he had to be ideological instead of practical."

"So he *is* dead then?" asked Cam.

Sava nodded. "He could have faced mortality with dignity, but instead he was selfish, worried only about *his* wants and *his* needs. He lost sight of the bigger picture, of Perion Synthetics' role in the global tragedy that is our world. I went along with it on the assumption that a synthetic James Perion is better than no James Perion at all. But the longer this goes on, the more out of control it gets."

Cam nodded slowly. "James Perion became his own product. I should have seen that one coming. You people sure know how to fuck with the status quo."

"Whatever," said Sava. "If I had it my way…"

Sava felt the ground shift as the construct bloomed around her. The players crept out from the shadows and took their first positions. There was Synth J, pacing the invisible floor the way he had the previous Monday when word of his illness got out and the company's stock price had plummeted. His son, Joe, stood a few feet away, back turned to his father, looking for patterns in the ether. Cam and Cyn stood face to face, speaking into each other's slivers, caught in the mutual masturbation of cyclic feeding. To the right, Anela stood over the body of Robert Gantz, nudging him with her shoe.

So many pieces to move. So many different ways to set things right again.

"You are forgetting someone," said Anela. She tapped Sava on the shoulder and pointed behind them.

Sava turned and saw a figure in the distance. It was looking directly at her, shoulders slightly hunched, arms held rigid at its side. A mental manipulation brought the face closer.

Gilbert Reyes.

"If you had it your way?" asked Cam. "Let me guess, you would have dumped me and Cyn at Perion Terminus and been done with us, right?"

Sava looked down at the aggregator. "I still might," she replied, and then turned for the door. When Cam asked where she was going, she called over her shoulder, "More loose ends to tie up. Why don't you make yourself useful and go look for Joe?"

"And how exactly am I supposed to find him in this mess?"

Sava pointed at the black plume rising beyond the nearby buildings. "He's helping the people he hurt when he crashed into a recharge station," she said.

"How do you know that?"

"Someone is always watching," she replied, then stepped through the busted doorframe.

Inside, the lobby was looking better; the synthetics had made good progress in the last hour. The whine of six backpack vacuums filled the space, echoing off the high ceilings and reverberating in the hallways. Sava was happy to get away from the sound, and after turning a few corners, she found herself in silence again. It was there she could hear Anela's voice more clearly, where she could find comfort in its company.

Sava ignored the waiting elevators and ducked into a stairwell. She started up the stairs, happy for the exercise despite the fatigue in her body. The mechanics of lifting one leg and then the other distracted her from the world and refocused her attention to the present moment, to the pain in her calves and the tightness in her chest. By the time she stepped into the hallway on the eleventh floor, a thin film of sweat had developed on her face and under her arms.

Her thoughts turned to the glass-walled shower in her apartment, to the gentle yet firm spray of the showerhead spewing out the cleansing water to burn away the dirt and the grime from a tarnished veneer that had once shone so brightly. For those brief moments in the shower, away from the prying eyes of Chuck Huber and James Perion, she was no longer Sava Kessler, head of public manipulations for Perion Synthetics. Instead, she was Kaili Zabora, lover to a man she had killed, sister to a murdered patriot, and revered messiah of the Calle Cinco cipher den.

Those brief moments of honesty allowed her to see the big picture, the entirety of human existence intertwined in a beautiful and complex mix of past, present, and future. Presently, the big picture had a gaping hole where the face of Gilbert Reyes flickered like a busted vidscreen.

Sava roamed the hallways on the Clerical Services floor until she found the office she was looking for. Standing in the doorway, she observed the mammoth copier below a sign reading *for office use only*. It took only minor effort to imagine Jacqueline Dulac standing there watching a stack of paper disappear into the automatic feeder. Of course, Sava had to use Roberta as a stand-in, having never known Jackie personally, but in the haze of her fantasy, there was little discernable difference between the two.

Anela drew a sharp breath as Sava stepped into the copy room.

Gil was on her in an instant; his strong, synthetic hands ripped the needler from her hip and sent it flying across the room.

Sava imagined her sister shaking her head, the words *I tried to warn you* on her lips but forever unspoken. The image broke down as Gil pulled her back to reality.

She fell forward, stumbling towards the copier. Her legs hit a feeder tray first, whipping her body forward until her face smacked into the rigid plastic. Pain shot through her jaw, racing around her skull like a demon dragging its nails through her hair. When Gil yanked on the neckline of her blouse and pulled her away, she saw a splatter of blood on an index card of instructions someone had taped to the copier.

Fighting Gil was impossible; even a graduate of a Calle Cinco boot camp was no match for his strength and speed.

Sava recalled something Chuck had said the Saturday before, one of those throwaway ramblings he was so fond of laying on her after she had ridden him to his orgasm. He had complained about the time frame in which James Perion expected him to bring a fully functional Virgo-class synthetic online to replace the recently deceased Gilbert Reyes. Doing so meant cutting corners, meant some of the limiters they had put in place in Cam's synny had to be left out.

There just wasn't time to put physical restrictions on Gil before they flashed him. Chuck had then muttered an incoherent warning before rolling over and commencing his usual snoring.

And as Sava lay there with her fingers working below the blanket, she thought about what it would be like to have that kind of brutish dominance, to walk the world on a red carpet of impunity, knowing nothing short of decapitation or being crushed by a Honda Civic could ever end her life. Even if that happened, she could just imprint on another synthetic sleeve, or keep two running concurrently like James Perion.

Immortality would be a powerful advantage against Vinestead. Arthur Sedivy might not live forever, but his ruthless direction would continue on until someone finally stood up to the 'Stead.

Just imagining the destruction of Vinestead, of Sedivy's battered face and missing teeth, had been enough to send Sava over the edge, gripping the sheets and biting her lip to keep from waking Chuck.

"The things you think about in the moments before death," said Anela.

Gil's arm slipped around the front of Sava's throat.

"Gil," she rasped, before her airway tightened.

"Like a fucking dog," he replied, his voice a lifeless monotone. He pushed her to the ground and straddled her stomach. His fingers sought out her throat again. "You had me killed like a fucking Shore Dog in the street. And for what, Kessler? On whose fucking order?"

Sava slapped at his arms. "Not mine," she cried.

"Then who? James Perion? Why does he want me dead?"

The room grew dim, blended with the perpetual construct that existed on the other side of reality.

"Not dead. In his debt."

"I'm in *no one's* debt."

"You are now," she replied, digging her fingernails into Gil's synthetic flesh. "But you don't have to be…"

Gil squeezed harder, evoking a string of popping noises from Sava's neck.

The construct rushed in to fill the void left by the crumbling of reality.

FIFTY-FIVE

"The most efficient way to exploit a person is through their desires," said Anela. She had lost her body somewhere along the line and was now just a voice whispering in the construct. "People will give up their money and their lives to satisfy a desire, so all you have to do is figure out what they want most. Offer it to them, even if you cannot give it to them. The promise of satisfaction will be enough motivation. But remember this, Kai. At all times, consider how helping someone will help *you*."

The construct collapsed under the glare of track lighting in the ceiling of the copy room. Sava felt pain in her throat as she drew one labored breath after the other, coughing when she could afford the oxygen. All at once, awareness of her body flooded back; each limb belted out its own part in her private symphony of pain. She drew them together into a fetal position, held until the throbbing became too much, and released.

"I'm listening," said Gil.

He was sitting in one of the few chairs they hadn't overturned, one leg crossed over the other and a hand on a nearby prep table. The needler spun in a tight circle under his fingers.

Sava touched her hip where the weapon should have been and sighed.

"Clean slate," she said, struggling to get the words out. "You leave Perion City and we call it even."

"But it wouldn't be even, would it, Ms. Kessler? You had me killed, and you say James Perion ordered it. You didn't think I'd take offense to that?"

Sava shook her head on the carpet. "You're an aggregator, Mr. Reyes. You were working for Benny Coker when you were supposed to be working for Perion Synthetics. Who's supposed to be offended here? You *lied* to us, you compromised the security of the company, and you leaked secrets about Perion's illness and caused a massive devaluation of the company's shares in a single day. Billions of dollars, Gil. You must have seen people killed for a tiny fraction of that in Margate."

"I was just doing my job."

"So was I," said Sava, tapping the carpet with her back of her head. "We were both doing our jobs and things got out of hand, but we don't have to keep fighting forever. If you want to, you can walk out of here with no debts, no obligations. I'll convince Perion to let you live out the rest of your aggregator existence in peace."

"Right. And the second I step across the PNR, problem solved. Then it's suicide instead of homicide and you can sleep a little easier at night."

Sava thought of the kill order she had given to Ferko and Espinoza. They weren't the brightest in the city, but they'd follow orders. They would unload on anything that got too close.

"There is no PNR anymore. In exchange for your freedom, you'll agree never to reveal that information. You keep our secret, and we'll keep yours."

The needler came to a stop. Gil grabbed it and set it down in his lap.

"I think I'll go with my original plan," said Gil.

"Jackie. I can give you Jackie back."

He shook the needler in Sava's direction. "Now that's low."

"She's been damaged, but we can repair her. Ms. Dulac's imprint is still on file. We can reload her from scratch, make her the woman she was before—"

"Before she left me? Before she killed me?"

Sava looked away to the wall. Closing her eyes, she tried to summon the construct and her sister, but nothing appeared. She was alone.

"She would have no memory of that. Dr. Bhenderu could make her as docile as you want—the perfect companion."

"Two synthetics living synthetic lives having synthetic sex and synthetic babies... it's all bullshit, Kessler. Gilbert Reyes is dead. Jacqueline Dulac is dead. Why simulate what their lives might have been like?"

"That's up to you," said Sava. "The fact remains you're a synthetic. If you don't like it, put that needler in your mouth and pull the trigger. Otherwise, I'm offering you a clean slate and the woman of your dreams."

Gil stood and pushed the chair away. "I don't need shit from you."

"No?" asked Sava, using her arm to sit up. "What was your game plan, Gil? How did you think we were going to react when you started feeding your interactions with Roberta? You made Perion look like a goddamn mad scientist."

"He is. He brought Jackie back to life like he's some kind of god!"

Sava pulled her legs into her body. "Yes, but only because he was trying to preserve his own life. The advances he made with Roberta allowed him to live on when his original body died. And if it hadn't been for Roberta pushing that envelope, *you* wouldn't be standing here now."

"If you hadn't killed me, I would be home by now," said Gil, taking a step forward. "I'd be in a corner suite in Atlantic City with all the alcohol and women I could handle courtesy of Benny Coker. I would have been set for life, but that's gone now. All I want is my old life back, Ms. Kessler, and you can't give that to me."

Sava sighed. "You can't go back, but I'm offering to help ease the pain of your transition."

"You're bargaining for your life," said Gil, raising the needler for a few seconds and then lowering it again. "You're promising whatever you have to promise to keep me from ending you. And all of this from Perion's head of PR, a woman who has demonstrated her ability to kill if her boss orders it. To *kill*, Ms. Kessler. Do you understand how fucked up that is?"

"For a flack, perhaps," said Anela.

Sava turned to the side, shut her eyes. The construct assembled around her.

Anela sat in a high-backed leather chair behind an obsidian desk, as she had in the last photo Sava ever saw of her. The blood red dress flared in the dark construct.

"It might be time to tell him," she continued, folding her hands. "Even if it wins him over, you can always kill him later."

Sava let out a grunt as she stood up. Gil retreated while training the needler on her face.

"Relax. The floor's uncomfortable." She grabbed a nearby chair and set it upright next to a desk.

If anything, Gil became more agitated, alternating between pointing the gun at her and letting it tremble by his hip. If she lived to tell about it, Dr. Bhenderu would want to hear about nervous behavior in a synthetic.

"I'm not your enemy," said Sava, putting her hands on the table as she had seen her sister do. "You're a prototype of Perion's most advanced synthetic ever. The only people who want you more than us is Vinestead International—may they burn in hell. How long do you think you'll last out there, Gil? On your own? Without our protection?"

"Let them come," said Gil. "I'll put every last one of them in the dirt."

"In the beginning, I have no doubt. But they'll keep sending more and more men to hunt you down. Local police, PMCs—even the U.S. military might get involved. They'll find you, they'll take you, and they'll open you up."

"Unless I stay here, is that it?"

"No," said Sava, smiling. "You can't stay here. James Perion wouldn't allow it after all the trouble you've caused. My goal is to get you out of the city as soon as possible, so long as you're willing to cooperate."

"And if I don't?"

Sava scratched the side of her neck and then drew her finger across it in a slicing motion. When Gil stepped forward with the needler raised, Sava put up a hand. "But it doesn't have to be that way. Perion can't protect you on the outside, but I know people who can."

Gil shook his head. "Right. You said it yourself, they'll hunt me down. No one can stand in their way." He looked away for a moment as the synthetic synapses in his brain began to kludge.

At this, Anela Zabora clapped her hands softly. Five slivers of light shimmered in the dark ether behind her. From these gashes stepped five black-clad wisps of men; they split ranks to her right and left. Joining them from the periphery were thick bodyguards in gunmetal suits who were as big as the ciphers were small. Their augmented hands gleamed.

Sava thought about how much she could accomplish, even with such a small team.

"I'll put you with Calle Cinco. Los Angeles, Sacramento, Seattle—you name the place."

"*You* have pull with Calle Cinco? Bullshit. Crazy Kai wouldn't let you within a thousand yards of one of her dens."

Sava slapped the desk with an open palm. "*Don't* call me crazy!" She glanced at the needler and looked away. "I've made some mistakes, yes, but they were all with good intentions. Bringing down Vinestead is more important than you or me. If I have to sacrifice a hundred or a million lives to see it done, I'll do it. I don't care how shitty that makes me look in the eyes of Margate's judgmental and clueless."

Gil's eyebrows furrowed. "*You're* Kaili Zabora? You're the woman who killed seven thousand people in one day?"

"Seven thousand fifty-seven. And yes, I'm Kaili Zabora, the most feared woman on the west coast and the craziest bitch to ever walk the earth." Sava waved her hand around dismissively.

"What the hell are you doing *here*?"

She narrowed her eyes. "I'm here because David and Goliath is a fucking myth. A mouse can't take down a lion; you need another lion. Perion Synthetics has the size, the power, and the money to put an end to Vinestead once and for all. They will win that fight, and I'm here to make sure that fight happens. That means keeping Perion Synthetics out of trouble and off the feeds. That means getting muckraking aggregators like you to shut their fucking mouths."

"So," said Gil. "You're offering me sanctuary for silence?"

Sava stood and immediately put a hand down on the desk to steady herself. When the dizziness cleared, she adjusted her clothes.

"No, Mr. Reyes. I'm offering you a job. You've caused nothing but trouble here, and that's bad for Perion. But I'm in the business of trouble. I'm offering you a chance to use your talents for more constructive pursuits."

The collar of her blouse had lost its shape and one of the top buttons had come off. She did her best to make it look presentable.

"Think about it," she said, turning and starting for the door.

"Wait," said Gil.

Sava stopped in the doorway but didn't look back. "I've wasted enough time with you already, Mr. Reyes. There are things that need doing, things bigger than you not seeing the upside of a synthetic life. I've laid out the options; the rest is up to you. You want a life with your girlfriend? Fine. You want to join Calle Cinco and help us take down the 'Stead? Great. If not, shoot me in the fucking back. I really don't give a shit anymore."

She left him standing there in the copy room. As she marched down the hall, she prepared herself for the first of the shards.

They never came.

FIFTY-SIX

Sava headed down to Medical on B5 to see if the synthetics had retrieved Cyn and to get someone to look at the growing bruises on her neck.

She had stared at the red and purple splotches in the fractured glass of the elevator as it descended, idly wondering how long they would take to heal. It wasn't proper for someone in her role to show up for work with bruises and cuts from some illegal fight club operating in the back alleys of Perion City. She had an image to live up to and a reputation to protect, but there wasn't enough concealer in California to cover the blemishes stretching from her jaw to her collarbone. Looking at herself in the mirror, she sneered at the temporary tattoo Gil had given her.

Unless it wasn't temporary. Unless it was a permanent badge of honor.

Someday she would sit around a table in some dingy neon club and talk about her time in Perion City, how human and synthetic alike had swallowed her story of being some Berkeley grad with a passion for building relationships with the public through contemporary and emerging media. She would talk about how she went deeper than any member of Calle Cinco had gone before, slipping into her contrived persona like one of Anela's form-fitting dresses. There were lessons to be learned from her experience, from long-term social engineering to tolerating sleeping next to a brilliant yet socially inept man whose nighttime snoring was only exceeded by his nighttime flatulence.

The elevator jolted to a stop on B5, sending a searing pain down the left side of her neck. Sava put a hand on the railing to steady herself.

Fucking synthetic Shore Dog.

"You will have to kill him if he chooses not to play ball," said Anela.

Sava did her best to nod and left her sister standing in the elevator.

Gurneys flew past Sava as she navigated the hallways; they were pushed through the crowd with effortless precision by smocked synthetics. She passed the ER entrance, which opened into an underground garage where ambulances lined up to unload their cargo. Unlike the emergency rooms Sava had seen in the movies, this one was relatively quiet, save the moans and cries of the injured humans. The synthetic nurses spoke only in whispers, just loud enough to be heard by the headsets they wore over their ears. They went about their tasks with no emotional involvement, breaking the illusion of empathy.

Something tightened in Sava's stomach. Maybe repurposing every synthetic in the city for a manhunt hadn't been such a good idea. She imagined the scene would be the same at the other clinics in the city—innocent little engineers bloodied and bruised because of her actions. Sava touched her lip; a fingertip came away with a spot of crimson on it.

"Everyone pays a price," said Anela.

And besides, Perion himself had signed off on the idea. Granted, she had played up the story of Gantz shooting him in the head, thus proving the chief of police had gone rogue and was now treating Perion City like his private run-and-gun theater where anyone not on his side was an enemy to be dispatched. Perion had trusted her and allowed her to take charge. She wondered how he would feel once he saw the aftermath.

"Do you require medical assistance, Ms. Kessler?" asked a synny nurse who had paused to pick up a fallen palette. Her eyes inventoried Sava's injuries.

"I'm looking for a female patient," she replied. "Gunshot wound, maybe multiple."

The nurse's lips moved silently as her eyes drifted towards her earpiece. "We admitted a female with a single gunshot wound twenty-three minutes ago. Doctor Parris was able to stabilize her and the patient is now recovering."

"Where?"

"She is in the atrium. We have set up temporary beds during this emergency. Would you like me to show you the way?"

Sava shook her head.

"Please let us know when we can examine your injuries," said the nurse. She turned and hurried away.

Sava followed the flow of traffic down the hall for a few hundred feet. As with most of the sub-levels in the Spire, being underground meant not being constrained by the circular perimeter of the Spire's design. Medical stretched out towards the west, opening into a large atrium whose ceiling extended up another floor, just missing the outer edge of the real B4 by twenty feet. Usually, it was a place of relaxation, an expansive room with more potted plants than people. Today, light blue cots set in perfectly aligned rows occupied most of the real estate. Synnies walked the aisles between the cots, checking on the patients.

Cyn was in a bed near the tree in the center of the atrium, a bright white bandage wrapped around her shoulder. Beside her, a synthetic adjusted the drip from her IV. While standing, Cyn had the body language of someone looking for a fight, but reclining in a cot with a bottle of water in her hand, she had lost much of her intensity. Though, Sava wasn't stupid enough to think the smile on her face had to do with anything other than the drugs entering through the pinprick in her elbow.

"Well, if it isn't the Great Emancipator," said Sava, stopping at the foot of Cyn's cot. "Lincoln would be proud."

The aggregator's eyes fluttered and locked in. Her smile widened as she lifted her head slightly.

"Fuck you, Kessler." Cyn let her head fall back into the pillow. "Come to finish me off?"

A shudder went through Sava's body as she imagined the physical exertion it would require to kill Cyn. Whether or not it was necessary, or even desired, her muscles weren't going to have any part in it. Being awake for twenty-four hours was hard enough, but the immense stress and physical injuries had pushed her to the very limit of operational status. Her eyes sought out an empty cot in the atrium; perhaps she could grab a few hours of sleep while she waited for dawn. Everything would be better then.

"No," said Sava, sitting down on the edge of the cot. She couldn't stop herself from surveying the crowd again. "There's been enough killing."

"Fat lot of good that does Gantz," said Cyn.

Sava let her head drop and winced at the needles in her neck. "Forget about Gantz. You're free to go. We can't keep you here, and frankly I don't want you here, so whenever you feel up to it, you're welcome to crawl back to your hole in Umbra."

"Just like that? What if I talk about what I've seen here? What if I tell people you killed Robert Gantz in cold blood?"

"Robert Gantz was threatening the safety of Perion City and its residents. At the time, he was illegally trespassing on private property. I was well within my rights to protect the company and its interests. So write what you want. Tell people I killed him because of some long-standing rivalry or because we were secretly lovers—I don't care. Just remember this when you're painting me as some psychotic bitch with a blood lust: Cynthia Mesquina, at the behest of one Lincoln Tate of Lincoln Continental, did knowingly and willingly commit corporate espionage and sabotage. According to the laws of the state of California, Perion Synthetics has the legal right to seek damages in the amount of and exceeding the current net worth of Lincoln Tate and his media company."

The words rolled off her tongue as easily as any speech to Chuck Huber about how much more he had to offer the world than his scientific achievements. It was empty talk, a theory of a notion of an idea of what someone working for Perion Synthetics would want to hear. Most times, Sava found her mind wandering even as she was speaking, retreating to the construct to think about something important, like the future, or the war, or what she was going to have for dinner that night.

"I don't like threats," said Cyn.

Sava chuckled. "I'm just telling you how it is. You are no longer welcome here." She leaned closer. "It is time you went home."

"I would, but I have some unfinished business with a certain self-righteous cunt who put a bullet in my shoulder. If you damaged one of my augments…"

"Your vendetta will have to wait," said Sava. "Go back to Umbra. Spend some time recuperating. When you're healthy again, come knock on the gates. I'll have a hundred synthetic guards waiting to rip you limb from limb. I'll repurpose every bit of tech in your body and see that a future line of synthetics is built in your image, with your gaudy red hair and sexually ambiguous body type that drives all the immersion junkies in Umbra crazy. I will make you Perion's number one bitch until people have forgotten all about the real you and only remember Cynthia Mesquina as a submissive, synthetic whore who does all the naughty things not listed in the catalog."

Sava stood and reeled from the sudden vertigo. When she recovered, she looked down at Cyn to find the smile had left her face.

"Your time in Perion City has come to an end," said Sava. "Go in peace or in pieces. I don't care which."

Cyn snorted in response. "You can't hide in here forever. You know that, right?"

"Girl, by the time I leave the PC, this country will be embroiled in a second civil war. Companies will fall, lives will be lost, and even people like you will be forced to take up sides. So forgive me if I don't quiver in my panties at your little threats. When the end of the world comes, you'll be fighting so hard just to survive that your petty grudges will seem like pleasant memories. Find me then, and we'll reminisce about the time I shot you for trying to destroy billions of dollars' worth of private property. We'll talk about the Great Emancipation and how you set the fight against Vinestead back a decade.

"Or maybe we won't. Maybe there won't be a war after all. I'll wake up one morning to find I'm a VP at a bankrupt synthetics company. You'll wake up wondering why there's a Guardian Angel chip in your neck and Arthur Sedivy's voice in your ear. Either way, tonight won't mean a thing. The sooner you get over it, the better off you'll be."

"I'll get over it once I'm done here. *After* you've paid."

Sava nodded. She understood vengeance, its driving need.

"Suit yourself," she said, walking away.

"And I want my needler back," yelled Cyn.

"Mr. Reyes has it," said Sava, pausing for a moment. "Maybe if you ask him nicely, he'll give it back to you."

"Maybe I will. Then I'll come for you."

"Of course you will, sweetie." Sava resumed her march to the hallway. "I'll send some guards to wheel you out to the PNR. Some of my human staff will escort you the rest of the way to Perion Terminus." She raised a hand in a backwards wave. "It's been a pleasure, Cynthia."

A string of unintelligible curses followed her into the hallway.

Before Sava could turn the first corner, a synthetic nurse stepped out of an operating room.

"Ms. Kessler, I must insist we examine your injuries."

Sava felt her body sway. "Only if I can sit down."

"Right this way," said the nurse.

Fine, thought Sava. Ten minutes of downtime. Maybe fifteen.

After that, the real cleanup would begin.

FIFTY-SEVEN

"It's too much," said Sava, her voice flat in the infinite construct.

She was too tired to even imagine herself in her usual avatar. Instead, she sat on the glassy floor, legs doubled up beneath her, one shaky arm out to support her weight, the other pressed against her chest, trying to stamp out the fire in her lungs. Paralysis gripped her body, as if someone were holding her from behind, their limbs wrapped around hers. Sometimes this unseen phantom would flex its arms and a million little teeth would chomp their way along her triceps. Other times, it would dig a knee into the small of Sava's back, forcing her closer to the ground.

In the distance, the Vinestead demon towered over her, almost laughing, and Sava wanted nothing more than to stand up and face it. She didn't want to let it see her suffer, but there was no command she could give her avatar to make it move, no way to squeeze more energy from a depleted battery.

"That is the life," said Anela. "You fight, you tire, and then you die. Is today that day?"

"No," replied Sava.

"What was that? I cannot hear you from down there."

Sava looked up; Anela had turned her head away.

"I said no."

"Still nothing," said her sister, tapping her ear.

Sava groaned and put her other hand on the ground. She twisted onto her knees and fell forward. The floor of the construct smelled faintly of the Pacific Ocean. The black sludge made room for her nose as it conformed to her face. Suddenly there was no oxygen; she would be dead in a matter of seconds if she didn't pull away, if she didn't give her imaginary lungs the air they so desperately needed.

"Sometimes, you have to get close to death to recognize it. Sometimes, you must be shown what you stand to lose before you really start to fight."

Sava's scream trembled the ground around her, sending violent ripples throughout the construct. The ache in her muscles fell away as the flames in her lungs licked at her throat. Stepping out of herself, she saw the sides of her neck begin to redden. They did not flush; they glowed as if her flesh had been draped over a roaring fire. Her lungs flared in her chest, making them visible through her back. The avatar's black shirt burned away, exposing the many ridges of her spine poking up through her skin.

She pushed harder than the construct would allow, and it was just enough to tear through the constraints of the imagined simulation. She bolted upright on the examination table, narrowly missing an overhead spotlight.

A synthetic hand grasped her on the shoulder.

"Careful, Ms. Kessler," said the nurse. "You'll want to wait for the medication to wear off completely before you try to walk."

Sava felt dried saliva at the corners of her mouth. She wiped it away with the back of her hand.

"How long have I been out?"

"You slept for two and a half hours. Your body needed it."

"I told you I only had a few minutes. I'm supposed to check in with Mr. Perion every hour." Sava edged herself off the table. When her legs threatened to buckle beneath her, she gave them a stern mental command. After a few steps towards the door, she knew it had taken.

"Mr. Perion is aware of your condition," said the nurse. "It was his decision to let you sleep."

Sava stopped at the door. "*How* is he aware?"

The nurse pulled a section of the butcher's paper away from the exam table and tore it off. "He came looking for you earlier. When he saw you were asleep, he told me to keep an eye on you but not to disturb you."

"Where is he now? I need to speak with him."

The synny nodded towards the door. "He may still be in the atrium visiting with the wounded."

"She means glad-handing the proles," said Anela.

Sava shook the voice away and stepped out of the exam room. Her neck felt stiff as she turned side to side to look at the gurneys lining the hallway. She put a hand up to test the skin; it came back covered in some kind of sticky balm.

The mood in Medical had shifted during Sava's slumber. No longer were the patients being wheeled through the hallways like go-carts at an indoor track. The nurses, both synthetic and human, walked with less urgency, moved along by the plaintive cries which came less frequently. The worst was over; the tidal wave of injured and dying had been met by a massive synthetic breakwater. Anywhere else in the world, the nurses and doctors would have been overwhelmed by the sheer numbers.

But not in Perion City. Not in the synthetic utopia dreamed up by the man with graying hair and impeccable posture, by the man who now sat hunched over on the low wall of a garden in the atrium, his face pressed into his hand. For the first time since switching over to his synthetic body, James Perion looked tired.

Sava knew the feeling all too well. She navigated the rows of cots until she reached the garden. She sat down beside the boss of bosses.

"Ms. Kessler," he said, without looking up.

"Mr. Perion," she replied.

"Enjoy your rest?"

Sava felt the warmth climb her face. "I'm sorry. The time got away from me."

"A lot has been getting away from you as of late," said Perion. "I hope this isn't becoming a new habit of yours."

"Absolutely not," she replied, trying to convince herself and Perion simultaneously. "Everything is under control. I've neutralized all of the aggregators and restored the synthetics to normal operation, as you can see."

"*You* restored them?" asked Perion. "So Robert Gantz and Cynthia Mesquina had nothing to do with it?"

Sava's stomach twisted. There was no way he could have known that, unless…

She sought out a specific cot in the atrium and to her complete lack of surprise, it was empty. Cyn was gone.

"I would have put everything back," said Sava. "Once I had them contained, I was going to clean up the signal. So either way…"

"They came back," said Perion. "My son came back to stop the destruction of the city and its people. If they had escaped, how long would you have let the synthetics run amok before calling them off?"

As long as it took, thought Kaili.

"I didn't expect there would be this much collateral damage," admitted Sava. "The city was more dependent on synnies than I realized."

"It surprised me as well. I had always hoped for synthetics and humans to live side by side in a mutually beneficial relationship, but I never wanted us to be *dependent* on them."

"You mean us on you?"

Perion sat up straight and surveyed the atrium. "Yes," he said, his lips tight. "It's clear to me that *you* have become too dependent on the synthetic workforce, at least here in the city. We were supposed to be modeling real world applications, but no city on earth will have this level of synthetic saturation, at least not in the near-term. We reached a critical mass at some point, but none of us saw it. You can't have an entire firehouse of synthetics. You can't have only one doctor and two dozen synthetic nurses. All machines have the capacity for failure. Even ours."

"Especially ours," said Sava.

"Though it's not always their fault. Sometimes there is a human failure."

Sava nodded; she understood it was time to be humble. "Yes, sir. I accept full responsibility."

"No," said Perion. "I signed off on the idea. This is on both of us."

Sava followed his gaze over the endless sea of cots. For a few minutes, neither of them spoke.

"Was it really necessary to kill Robert?"

"You had to do it," said Anela. "There was no other choice. Make him understand that."

"You tell me," replied Sava. "How many synthetic James Perions would Mr. Gantz have had to destroy before you considered him a threat?"

Perion looked down at his hands. "There were two of us running for so long… I had gotten used to the secondary data stream. Sensory input from another place in the world, processed independently but synced to the same consciousness. When Robert terminated that copy, it stopped the stream. I had forgotten what that felt like."

"Like losing a loved one?"

"Deeper," said Perion. "Like I lost a piece of myself." He tightened his hands into fists and released them. "Maybe it was for the better. That part of me had grown dark and bitter. Too strong-willed. Perhaps Mr. Gantz did me a favor." He shook his head. "At any rate, this is just a temporary setback. I will have a new copy imprinted and the stream will resume. I doubt Robert meant to kill me per se. If anything, he probably recognized the simple truth that I can't be killed, and therefore my synthetic instances can be destroyed without personal risk to me."

"Any man who points a gun at my head and pulls the trigger is my enemy," said Sava. "I don't have the luxury of backups."

"You said I made a threatening move on Joseph. Robert's response was to destroy that instance of me to save my son's life. I see no problem with that."

"He shot at me, Mr. Perion. He emptied an entire clip into Roberta trying to kill me. Punish me if you want, but I stand by my decision."

The scene replayed in Sava's head. No matter which direction she took the simulation, it always ended the same way. Robert Gantz would have killed her just as easily as he killed James Perion.

"It doesn't matter anymore," said Perion. He gestured to the cots. "What matters is that we restore order, that we get these people fixed up and back to work. I imagine we'll lose a healthy number of them after this."

"You could give them bonuses to stay. Hazard pay or something."

"Money only goes so far, Ms. Kessler. You know that. They'll want someone to blame."

"I'll give them someone."

Anela walked the perimeter of the construct in Sava's mind, drawing up the shades on large vidscreens showing footage from the Spire's security cameras. The video would back up Sava's claims that aggregators acting with terroristic intentions, and with the help of a traitorous chief of police, had waged a private war on Perion Synthetics, its property, and its employees. By sabotaging key systems, they were able to bring down the command-and-control signal for all synthetics, rendering them mindless and freeing them from their safety protocols. Only through the tireless efforts of Perion engineers was order restored, showing once again that innovation and salvation will always come from within, that no matter what the world throws at Perion Synthetics, the company will forever endure.

The floor of the construct lit up in the undulating waves of an American flag as patriotic fanfare on a piano rose to a crescendo. Sava would make people loathe Robert Gantz and distrust any aggregator who dared to write one unflattering word about the company. In the end, the city would be stronger and its citizens more resolute.

It would be Sava's most epic piece of social engineering to date. And judging by the smile on Anela's face, Sava wasn't the only person who thought so.

"I want a proposal in my inbox by the end of the day," said Perion. He stood and adjusted his pants.

"Yes, sir."

"Now, if you've had enough rest, I would like you to collect my son and bring him up to my conference room."

Sava stood. "I sent Cam to look for him earlier, but I don't know if they've made it back."

"They just walked in through the north entrance." Perion's eyes drifted to the ceiling as if he were looking through the sub-levels to the lobby.

"How do you know that?"

Perion tapped the side of his head. "Multiple streams of sensory data. I had to fill the void with something."

Total awareness, thought Sava. Was Perion tied into the building's entire monitoring system?

"I'll bring him," she said, still wondering how long Perion had been subbing the security feed. Did he have eyes and ears watching and listening when she leaned in close to Gantz as he drew his last breath?

"Good," said Perion. "I need to have a talk with my boy."

FIFTY-EIGHT

It took ten minutes to clear the line of people waiting for an elevator on Medical. The crowd continued to grow behind Sava as she pulled out her phone, trying to ignore the stories of harrowing experiences from the synthetic uprising. She sent a quick message to Cam.

Send Joe up to 70.

She left out any explanation as to why she didn't want to meet them in the lobby. It wasn't just the possibility that Joe might be angry at her; simply being told his father still existed was an emotional blow Sava didn't want to witness, not after imagining it for herself. The scenario played out in the construct, showing Anela succumbing to some treatable disease, only to be replaced by a synthetic version, which was then blown away by Robert fucking Gantz, and once again replaced by another synthetic.

Sava wondered if she would lose her mind from the constant ups and downs or if she would take comfort in the fact that Anela Zabora would live on forever, an eternal shoulder on which to lean.

"I already will," said Anela.

The hallway was full of expensive suits and pleated skirts when Sava stepped out of the elevator on seventy. On the other side of the well-dressed regiment of Perion lawyers, Cam and Joe stood just outside the closed doors to the conference room. The son of Perion had paused as if collecting his thoughts. When Sava caught Cam's eyes, he shrugged at her in response.

Finally, Joe opened the door and stepped back, allowing the legal team to enter first. They filed into the recently cleaned room; no trace of the aerated Synth J remained. Joe followed the lawyers in and left Cam holding the door.

The synthetic guards standing beside the double doors nodded to Sava but put up a hand as soon as she passed.

"Sorry, sir. Perion Synthetics personnel only."

Cam raised an eyebrow and looked to Sava.

She returned a shrug.

"Fine, I'll just wait out here, I guess," said Cam, looking around for somewhere to sit.

Joe Perion came to an abrupt stop at the table as Synth J rose to greet his son. He opened his arms and offered an embrace. Joe accepted after a few seconds of hesitation.

"He does not understand the gift he has been given," said Anela.

As they separated, Perion motioned to an empty chair beside his. He sat after his son had settled.

"Alright, Mr. Roe, you may begin," said Perion.

If Adam Roe and his legal team were here now, then something more than a father-son chat was about to take place.

In the construct, Anela's hand appeared on Sava's shoulder.

"Thank you, Mr. Perion," said Roe. "I call this emergency meeting of Perion Synthetics executive staff to order on this seventeenth day of November 2015. Today's meeting is attended by myself, Adam Roe, and my team. From management, we have James Perion, Joseph Perion, Katherine Shaw, Nicholas Shaw, and Sava Kessler."

"Where is Steve Phelps?" asked Perion.

Sava leaned forward to look down the table. The VP of Security was absent.

One of Roe's men spoke up. "Mr. Phelps resigned his position this morning, Mr. Perion. Deborah Keats was his next direct report, but we've been unable to locate her."

Synth J shook his head and waved for Roe to continue.

"We've been gathered at the request of Mr. Perion to discuss the future of the company. All information disclosed in these proceedings is confidential and will be treated as such by all attendees per your employment agreements. If anyone is uncomfortable with these terms, they may leave now."

No one stood.

Roe cleared his throat. "Then, Mr. Perion, if you will."

Perion had been staring at his son, but the lawyer's words brought his attention back.

"Thank you, Mr. Roe. Fine work, as always."

Roe nodded.

"It's true," continued Perion, addressing the assembled crowd. "I have called you here to talk about the future. After last night, I'm sure you all have questions. However, I'd like to start by talking about the past, about the last six months in particular."

Sava felt the construct come on like a wave of nausea. She saw herself crouched beneath the dome, stuck in the moment between fight and flight. Beside her, Anela stood with her head tilted back, staring at the growing crack in the glass ceiling.

"Earlier this year, I was diagnosed with pancreatic cancer."

A red glow flared on the horizon as the demon reared its horned head. Black hooves dripping in thick oil slammed into the construct's dome, freeing crystal shards which fell like rain on Sava's avatar.

"By the time the cancer was discovered, it had exceeded the reach of pre-modern medicine. My only hope for survival rested in the hands of Arthur Sedivy and Vinestead International's Guardian Angel chip. Only through their implant, grow wire, and proprietary code would I have even stood a chance at beating this thing."

The lawyers were practiced at keeping their emotions hidden, but Katherine Shaw flashed worry, either at Perion's failing health or the possible presence of Vinestead technology in the city.

Perion looked at his son, but Joe was more interested in the swirls of wood on the table.

"On the morning of November 10, 2015, at 7:08 am, James Perion as you know him, passed away due to complications from pancreatic cancer."

Katherine Shaw gasped and grabbed her husband's hand. Nico showed no signs of surprise.

"Prior to my death, and through an unprecedented engineering effort, I was able to imprint my consciousness onto this Virgo Prime chassis." Perion caught eyes with the lawyers. "Yes, Mr. Roe. I'm a synthetic."

Adam Roe shook his head minutely. "But, Mr. Perion, this means…"

Perion held up a hand. "I know what it means. As of 7:09 am Tuesday morning, control of the company and my estate passed to my son. I had hoped to stay on as long as possible until Joe was ready for the responsibility, but after last night, it is clear my judgment has become questionable." He sighed. "I suppose we still have some work to do before… well, it doesn't matter anymore. This experiment is over."

"There were some legal agreements signed last week that will need to be redone," said Roe. He turned to his team. "Pull every deal and contract executed since last Tuesday and prepare them for Mr. Perion's signature. George, prepare HR for the personnel update." His eyes landed on Sava. "Ms. Kessler, we will need a press release and obituary ready by this afternoon."

"No," said Perion. "No fanfare. You can spin my death as an internal matter. We don't need memorials right now. I want all efforts focused on my son."

Joe looked up from the table and turned to Synth J. Some nonverbal message passed between them as he rubbed his throat.

Sava couldn't help but mirror the gesture.

"I know," said Perion. His voice lowered, though it was obvious he didn't care who heard him. "I tried to take everything from you, but now I want you to have it all. I'll stay with you as long as you need me, or if you'd like, I'll let you learn the ropes yourself. It's whatever you want at this point."

"As a matter of course, Perion Synthetics does not employ synthetic humans as such," said Roe. "We could not pay your father if he decided to stay on, nor can you allot him an interest in the company's business. I suppose you're aware of that, Mr. Perion?"

"Of course he's aware," answered Joe. "That's why he brought in Governor Howard. They want to make it legal for synthetics to own property and have the same rights as humans."

Sava watched the lawyers' heads bob in unison.

"That may work," said Julie Pennington, Roe's only female staffer. "If California were to pass a law recognizing synthetics as humans, then Mr. Perion could rejoin the company at any position. Though, as Joseph is now the owner and CEO, it would be at his discretion."

Crosstalk sprung up as the gears turned behind Joe's eyes. His lips moved as if he were mumbling to himself.

Finally, Perion stood up and called for order. "Ladies and gentlemen, it has been a pleasure working with each and every one of you. I will rest easy knowing my son and my company are in good hands. Since I no longer have a say in the company's direction, I'll take my leave."

He paused behind Joe and put his hand on his son's back. "I'll be with your mother if you need me."

Joe nodded as his father exited the room. His eyes found Sava's.

The construct shuddered under the weight of the demon's barrage. Anela stood a short distance away, staring at the red bloom, her arms crossed.

"This does not change anything," said Anela to the demon. "The company remains. The army continues to march against Vinestead as it always has; only the general is different. And you know as well as I do that one man or woman does not make a movement. It is in the numbers, the sheer power involved. No, my friend. The war is still very much on."

"Well, Mr. Perion," said Roe. "We have much to discuss. There is, of course, a mountain of paperwork for you to sign."

"We'll need an inventory of Mr. Perion's estate," said George Symanski. "The tax implications are going to be a nightmare, Joe, but we'll see you through."

"Mr. Shaw, I'll need to brief you on Mr. Perion's day-to-day responsibilities as CEO," said Donald Mills.

"And there's also the problem of what to tell the employees." Jason Minnick pushed his glasses up his nose. "Mr. Perion has been seen and may continue to be seen walking around the building. We don't want any confusion…"

"Enough!"

Katherine Shaw flinched at the sound of her husband's voice.

Nico gestured to Joe. "Can't you see he needs time to process this? Give him a moment to let it sink in." He stood and pushed his chair back. "This meeting is adjourned. We'll reconvene at Joe's convenience. Anything you have for him will go through me. Mr. Roe, designate one of your helpers to be the liaison. This transition *will* go smoothly so long as we don't rush things. The company has been without a human CEO for over a week; it can go another few days."

Some of the lawyers opened their mouths to protest, but Roe silenced them. "Very well, Mr. Shaw. We will put an agenda together and send it over with Julie this afternoon."

"Just the highlights," said Nico. "Top five action items and nothing else."

Adam Roe stood and extended a hand to Joe. "My condolences, Mr. Perion."

Joe shook his hand and each of the lawyers' hands as they filed out.

Katherine Shaw lingered in front of Joe for a moment before hugging him. "I'm sorry for your loss," she said.

If he heard her, he didn't show it. His eyes remained focused on Sava.

"Wait," he said.

Donald Mills stopped at the doorway.

"I'm ready for my first order as CEO of Perion Synthetics," said Joe, taking a deep breath.

The lawyer pulled his palette from under his arm and tapped its screen to wake it up. "What is it, Mr. Perion?"

A slice of the construct shook free and fell to the floor, tearing a line down Sava's back. Blood flowed in weightless bubbles, filling the space behind her. Anela did her best to contain the damage, but each time she grasped a globe of blood, it split around her fingers.

"Sava Kessler."

"Yes, Mr. Perion?" asked Sava, barely able to speak.

"You're fired."

FIFTY-NINE

There was a ringing in Sava's ears she couldn't blot out. It drove her to the safety of a bench just outside the conference room. There, Cam sat with his back against the wall and one leg crossed over the other, fiddling with his sliver. He was sure to have heard Joe's proclamation, but he didn't say anything until the last suit had disappeared behind the elevator doors, until the two AGs flanking the door had escorted the new CEO of Perion Synthetics out of his first all-hands meeting. Then it was just Sava and Cam sitting alone in the hallway, squinting their eyes at the rough sunlight pouring in through the window.

"Don't take it so hard," said Cam, running his finger over his sliver. The red LED blinked on. "Jobs are like relationships: if Joe Perion doesn't want you on his payroll, then I say fuck him. There's plenty of work out there for a woman of your tenacity."

Sava barely heard Cam over the steam whistle echoing in her head, but she could see his lips moving in her periphery. He was trying to console her about what he thought was a simple firing, a temporary loss of responsibility and income. He didn't understand the true extent: that with a single termination, Joe Perion had changed the course of Perion Synthetics and Vinestead International forever. Sava had spent so long trying to steer the ship in the right direction, getting cozy with the captain and the navigator and the deck hands who kept everything looking shiny. Now they had thrown her overboard, had left her floating alone in a sea of uncertain futures.

"Do you think you'll go back to San Diego?" asked Cam.

"Why would I go there?"

"That's where you're from, right? Your file says you grew up there. Sometimes people revisit their childhood homes when they have a life event. Helps to re-center, you know?"

Sava thought about her old neighborhood in the suburbs of San Diego: the uniform streets packed with cars on both sides, leaving only the tiniest path for traffic; the Tejano music blasting from every other beater up on blocks; the six legs of three Mexicans sticking out from under them; her family's rundown duplex with the stained white brick falling apart on the sides and the yellow paint peeling in the back; a yard overgrown with weeds and patches of dirt; her father standing on the porch watering the lone rose bush he had planted the year Anela died that had returned season after season while everything else languished around it; and finally, her mother, sitting in the rocking chair in the living room, perpetually jacked into a VNet simulation she never discussed with anyone but that Sava knew was just a sensory loop of decaying memories of a simpler time when her girls were just girls and the rest of the world was a dangerous but far-off place.

Going back there would just remind her of the pockets of desolation littering the country, the little neighborhoods where people went about their business with a wary eye turned to the dome, to the demon looming on the horizon. They were subjugated and they didn't even know it, caught in a cycle of debt and earning too little to ever break free of it. Why had Vinestead even bothered to bring jobs to the west coast if they were just going to pack it all up a decade later and ship it overseas? Why give her father a comfortable wage and then rip it from his hands just in time for his first daughter to be born?

"I don't need to re-center," said Sava, "and I don't need to go home. I need to be here, adjusting the sails. Everything was going according to plan. It was just going to be another few years, five at the most."

"Life changes," said Cam. "We can do our best to put a plan to it, but really it's gonna do what it's gonna do. You can't let it get you down."

Sava put up a hand. "Spare me, Gray. You think this is about a stupid job or some other intangible life event bullshit, but it's not." She turned her face to the window and closed her eyes. "Just because you don't see the enemy out there doesn't mean they're not there."

She fingered the ring on her thumb for a moment before pulling it off and examining it in the glare.

"Chuck's?" asked Cam.

Chuck Huber.

Where was he in all of this? How would he go on without someone in his life to keep him grounded?

"No," said Sava. "It's just a reminder of what we're fighting for. You spend so much time jumping from story to story, you don't see how it's all coming together. The endgame isn't pretty, Gray. The sooner you realize it, the better."

Cam shook his head. "Companies come and go. Whether Joe runs Perion Synthetics into the ground or towards global domination, it won't matter in the long run. What matters is quality of life, doing the things you want to do, and having the freedom to be your own person."

"Here it comes," said Anela.

"That's why I'm an aggregator; my only job is to document what I experience. And yeah, sometimes I'm told to ride out to a cloistered city in the desert and report on the lies and backstabbings of one of the biggest companies in the country, but that's the nature of the game. Am I happy my boss sold me out to that piece of shit James Perion? Of course not. Am I going to make Donato Banks pay for what he's done? You can bet your pretty ass on it. And after it's all said and done, I'll find someone else to sign my paychecks and do the whole thing over again."

Aggregators; they had no loyalty to any cause, large or small. They were bottom feeders, picking up the discarded morsels of news from the real players of the world, living vicariously through people and companies who used their power and raw determination to make things happen.

Sava sighed and tried to feign further interest in Cam.

"So then you have no love for Perion Synthetics, despite them being poised to take on Vinestead?"

"No," replied Cam. "I have no love for a company that brainwashes trespassers into thinking they gave birth to a synthetic baby. From what I've seen in the last twenty-four hours, Perion doesn't give a shit about his people, let alone the rest of the world. And nothing I've seen from Joe Perion convinces me anything is *ever* going to change. Like father, like son; they say that shit for a reason."

"It wasn't always this way," said Sava. "That's what drew me to Perion City in the first place. Big J was just so… genuine. I've never met someone who cared so much and had that much power."

"He was going to have me killed so he could gain a sympathetic voice on the feed. If I could put that giant toaster out of commission, I would. Shit, I still might. With everything I've logged in the last week, I could bring the entire company down and drop it at Vinestead's feet."

"Snap his neck," whispered Anela. "Do it now."

Sava felt her hand twitch, but nothing more. If Cam didn't spill the story, then someone else would. There was no guarantee Cyn would keep her mouth shut or that Gil wouldn't expose his synthetic condition to the world just to get back at the woman who had ordered his death.

It didn't matter either way; Perion Synthetics was no longer hers to protect.

Down the hall, the elevator dinged. Two Scorpios stepped out and approached.

"Sava Kessler?" asked the guard on the right.

"That's me," she replied, standing up.

The AG handed her a slip of paper.

"What does it say?" asked Cam.

"My employment with Perion Synthetics has been terminated as of seven hundred hours this morning. These toasters are going to escort me home to collect my things and then take me to Perion Terminus." She recited the key points in legalese cadence. "Can't return to my office, my last paycheck will blah blah blah."

Sava re-read the note, crumpled the piece of paper in her fist, and tossed it at the AG's chest.

Escort her home… as if there were anything there worth taking with her—Chuck included.

"I'll go when I'm damn well ready," she replied.

"We are authorized to use force if necessary," said the toaster on the left.

"You lay a finger on me and I'll slag you and everyone like you. I'll dance on your liquefied entrails, motherfucker."

She took a step forward, causing both AGs to reach for their holsters.

"Alright, alright," said Cam, jumping between them. He faced the synthetics. "Please excuse my friend; she's just been fired from her job. I'm sure you gentlemen can relate."

The guards took a moment to process the request before removing their hands from their weapons.

Sava narrowed her eyes. "What's your deal, Gray? When you got here, you wasted no opportunity to make my life a living hell. You stole a prototype, you went over my head, and then for the donkey punch, you aided two aggregators in corporate espionage. I should be beating the shit out of you right now."

"It would be a start," said Anela.

Sava clenched her jaw; sometimes she wished her sister would shut up.

"But you're not," replied Cam, grinning like a fool, "and it's because you and I both know it's all a game, a series of random events with no personal motivations involved. Banks could have sent some intern instead of me and then all of your anger would have been directed at him. It's not Cameron Gray—famed conversationalist and sexual marauder—who you have a problem with. You'd be pissed at anyone who came into your house and started breaking shit. Likewise, how can I be mad at you for doing your job?"

"So it all boils down to *no hard feelings*? I find that hard to believe, the way you talk about your boss."

"That's different. Donato Banks was my friend. He betrayed my trust. Whereas with you, I never trusted you in the first place."

Anela started to respond, but her mouth closed with an audible click and she drifted off to an unlit corner of the construct.

"God, you're retarded, Gray." Sava pushed past him and headed for the elevators.

The AGs followed at a respectful distance.

As she stepped into the elevator, she put one hand on the door to hold it open.

"Are you coming or not?" she asked.

Cam smoothed out the front of his jacket and patted the sides of his head. He cupped his hand in front of his mouth, breathed into it, and then made a face as he inhaled.

"Coming," he said.

Sava almost smiled.

In the construct, the demon roared.

SIXTY

"As a new day dawns in Perion City, change is in the air. Joseph Michael Perion, son of the late James Perion, has assumed control of the company and promises to carry out the dream and plans his father so meticulously set down. A young man of just twenty-seven years, it remains to be seen whether he has the ambition and the competency to lead a multi-billion-dollar corporation into the next decade and beyond. One thing we already know: Joe Perion is a man of action. Mere moments after assuming control, he relieved Sava Kessler of her responsibilities as head of public relations. With Ms. Kessler stepping down, the world waits in anticipation to find out who will replace her as the new face of Perion Synthetics. But what of Ms. Kessler? Where does a woman with her extensive list of accolades go after this? What company in the world could rival the prestige of the great and honorable Perion Synthetics?"

Cam paused and tapped his sliver. He looked over at Sava.

"You like that?" he asked.

Sava reached out and pressed the illuminated button for the lobby.

"Then again, just who is Sava Kessler? Why was *she* the first employee on the chopping block? What does Joe Perion know that the rest of us don't? Care to comment, Ms. Kessler?"

"Care to walk out of this building under your own power, Mr. Gray?"

Cam held up his wrist. "Wasn't recording that bit," he said, smiling. He tapped his sliver and resumed his rambling.

"The relationship between Ms. Kessler and the Perions will forever be a closely guarded corporate secret; even this aggregator could not glean the slightest detail about their history. Only over the last week, through my interactions with Ms. Kessler and the company, have I been able to form a foggy impression of how things might have been. The simple truth is this: Sava Kessler is a professional and was well-respected by James Perion. She was part of his inner circle and was trusted with more secrets than there are skeletons in Donato Banks' closet. Ms. Kessler stood behind her superiors and her company to the bitter end. If she is guilty of anything, perhaps it is that she cares too much."

Sava raised an eyebrow.

"I doubt this will be the last personnel change of Joe Perion's rule. Not that it matters; James Perion has already spoken through Sava Kessler, sharing a message of innovation, sacrifice, and cooperation—ideals that will live on so long as there are people who remember the man who set it all in motion. However it came to pass, however many mistakes were made, an era has ended at Perion Synthetics, and the previous generation is stepping aside to make way for the next. Ms. Kessler rides towards the sunrise with her head held high, carried by the satisfaction of a job well done and the legacy of James Kirkland Perion forever etched into the hearts and minds of people all over the world."

The elevator stopped, but Sava put an arm in front of Cam as the doors opened.

"Do you believe anything you just said?" she asked.

"Do you?"

"It doesn't matter what I believe, does it? You feed that shit to millions of people and they'll swallow it without a second thought. You think you're reporting on reality, but you're just making it up as you go along."

"You'll thank me in the end," said Cam, straightening his jacket. "I have enough dirt on this company to give James Perion a proper burial, but you can walk out of this without so much as a smudge."

Sava dropped her arm and stepped out into the lobby. It took every bit of self-control to keep from telling Cam she didn't want his help. He wanted to paint a pretty picture of her, maybe help her get another job somewhere else, but there was no point staying in the corporate world. The only course of action now was to resume her skirmishes with Vinestead, to come up with something bigger and more damaging to keep their focus away from Perion Synthetics while Joe learned the ropes. She'd be a diversion, one Vinestead International wouldn't be able to ignore.

Just the idea of a face-to-face fight with Vinestead made Sava smile.

The return of synthetics to the Spire had not resulted in a similar return of humans. The lobby was mostly empty; no line of employees snaked between the security station and the front doors, nor was there a crowd of weary office runners milling around the coffee bar tapping their feet as they waited for their morning fix. The cleaning crew was still hard at work, but they had gravitated to the outer edges of the lobby, sweeping the last of the debris into piles against the walls. The center of the lobby was spotless and two synthetics stood ready with floor buffers to return the marble to its previous sheen.

They were stymied by the presence of a small crowd—both synthetic and human—gathered around the lobby's centerpiece, the giant hand of the puppeteer reaching to the heavens. Seated on the circular bench surrounding Perion's hand was Gilbert Reyes. In his lap, he held Roberta's head; the rest of her body stretched out on the bench next to him.

Sava watched for a moment as Gil attempted to smooth out the damage on Roberta's face. He tugged at skin that had begun to curl, wiped the life-giving oil from her cheeks, and attempted to push broken bits of carbon fiber and frayed wires back into her eye socket. Sava hadn't really taken the time to survey Roberta's damage the night before, but dawn allowed her the clarity to see the quality of Gantz' marksmanship.

"I can't just leave her," said Gil, as Sava approached.

"She's not Jackie," said Sava. "She's a synny."

"So am I."

Murmurs began to rumble through the crowd.

"Don't you people have jobs to do?" asked Cam. "If not, I'm looking for someone to make an official statement regarding the mistreatment of synthetic beings in Perion City."

At that, the onlookers scattered. Cam chased after the dawdlers, rattling off his credentials for the thousandth time and begging for just one sound bite to put on the feed.

One of the AGs tapped Sava on the side of her shoulder.

"Give me one damn minute," she snapped, punching the synthetic in the chest.

"I was thinking," said Gil. "It wouldn't be so bad, living like this, if Jackie were there with me. I was going to make it a term of my employment that you'd have to help me get her out of the city. So I came down here to wait and then I saw two synnies carrying her out like she was a broken copier. They were just going to throw her away."

"It will be hard to repair her on the outside," said Sava. "Most of her parts are sourced right here in the Spire. The chances of getting our hands on substitutes are very slim or prohibitively expensive."

Gil nodded. "I don't expect you to pay for the parts, but I do want your help in locating them. And in exchange, I'll be your personal bodyguard. I'll protect you and your… secret."

"It will take time, Gil. Six months, maybe a year or more. You have to know that going in. And even if we get her operational again, there's no guarantee her matrix is still intact."

"It is," said Gil. "The bullets didn't get through the inner casing."

"She could be another bodyguard," said Anela. "Augments would be no match for fully synthetic muscle."

Sava leaned closer to Gil. "You know they're not just going to let us leave with her right? If you want to do this, it has to be now. And you better be ready for a fight."

"I know," said Gil. He shifted to the side and guided Roberta's head to the bench. Then, with hardly a grunt, he hefted the lifeless synthetic onto his shoulder and started towards the Spire's south entrance.

"Any day, Cam!" called Sava.

The aggregator hurried to join them.

As they walked around the elevators, Cam tugged on Sava's elbow to get her to slow down.

"Who's the muscle?"

Sava looked straight ahead. "Gilbert Reyes. He's an aggregator like you."

"I met a Gilbert Reyes last week," said Cam.

"Same guy." Sava wondered if that was true.

"Naw, he looks nothing like him. Look, I have a picture."

Sava stopped and put her hand on top of Cam's outstretched phone. "He's the synny version. We did to him what we did to you. He got the short end of the synthetic stick."

Cam watched Gil turn the corner. "How many deals did Perion have going?"

"There was no deal," said Sava, continuing on. "He was here undercover. Roberta helped us figure it out. Transitioning him to a synthetic chassis was the only way to get leverage."

Outside, a Nissan sedan pulled up in the circular driveway. Its driver got out and stood near the rear passenger door. When he saw Sava coming, he opened the door for her.

"We're taking two synthetics with us?" asked Cam. "How'd you swing that?"

"What are you doing?" asked the driver.

Sava watched as Gil carefully maneuvered Roberta through the rear door and set her upright. After securing her seatbelt, he stepped back and closed the door.

"I can't take a synthetic to Perion Terminus." The driver motioned to the AGs. "Will you two please remove this thing?"

Sava rubbed her neck. "Well, Gil. I think it's time to begin your interview. You think you can defuse this situation?"

"Shit," muttered Cam.

"Of course I can," said Gil. He flexed an arm. "You have no idea what this body is capable of."

Sava leaned forward and smiled. "Let's see it."

Gil's hand shot out and grabbed hold of Sava's waistband. He tugged sharply, pulling her towards the car. He slipped to her right and threw out an oblique kick, catching one of the AGs in the knee. It stumbled backwards a few steps. Gil changed direction and went after the other synth, stopping its hand before it could fully remove its sidearm from the holster. At such close range, Gil used elbows and knees to inflict most of the damage. When the synthetic was thoroughly disoriented, Gil used a palm strike to free its gun. The weapon rotated in the space between them before Gil grabbed hold of it and dug it into the AG's jaw.

Sava turned her head as he fired, coating the other Scorpio in oil. It wiped at its eyes as Gil spun around. He held down the trigger and put five bullets into the synthetic. It fell to the pavement with a thud.

It was over in a matter of seconds.

"Defused," said Gil, tossing the gun onto the fallen AG.

The driver took two steps backwards and then broke into a run.

"Ask him where he sees himself in five years," said Cam.

"No need," replied Sava, stepping closer to Gil. She lowered her voice to a whisper. "I know where you'll be: with me, and Jackie, and Calle Cinco. One big happy family."

"If you guys are done making out, we should probably go," said Cam, walking around to the driver's side. The car rumbled to life a second later.

"Welcome to the revolution," said Sava. She gestured to the car with her thumb. "Shall we go?"

"I hated this place anyway," said Gil.

"It had its moments," said Sava, taking one last look at the Spire, wondering if Chuck Huber were in there somewhere walking one of the hundreds of floors. How long would it be before he noticed she was gone?

Cam honked the horn.

Sava climbed into the passenger seat and buckled herself in.

"Where to?" asked Cam.

"Perion Terminus, then hang a right towards the coast."

Out of the corner of her eye, Sava saw half a dozen Automated Guards pushing through the crowd. They were already holding their rifles at the ready.

"Drive," said Sava, extending her arm outside the window.

She smiled as the breeze rushed over her extended middle finger.

SIXTY-ONE

"There's no fluctuation," said Gil.

Cam had been trying for the last half hour to engage him in conversation, but it was only after they had passed The Fringe that Gil could tear his attention away from Roberta. The line of questioning was centered on what it was like to be a synthetic, a topic just interesting enough to keep Sava from nodding off.

Besides, there was nothing worth seeing on the other side of sleep, just a construct full of the charred remains of slagged synthetics. And walking amongst the smoking limbs and hollow faces was Anela Zabora, a projection of a ghost of a memory, no more real than the demon obscuring half of the sky.

"I remember eating too much for lunch and it ruining the day," said Gil. "Then you've got caffeine and pain pills and a thousand flavors of synth. Your body goes up and down all day. But now… now it's all baseline, exactly the same from one second to the next. It's like they built a car but never asked how it drove. Now there's someone behind the wheel who doesn't feel tired or hungry or horny."

Sava chuckled in her half-sleep.

Cam looked at Gil in the rearview mirror. "You uh… you think it still works?"

"It works," said Sava. "You think Perion wanted to live out the rest of eternity without a fully furnished basement? Roberta's the same way, but you knew that, didn't you, Cam?"

"What's she talking about?" asked Gil.

Cam waved the question away.

"It's not his fault," said Sava. "I ordered Roberta to charm the panties off of Cam. And judging by the complaints from the other hotel guests, she succeeded."

Cam blushed. "Like it's some kind of huge accomplishment to get my panties off. Shit, I'd drop them for Sava if she'd smile every once in a while."

"I smile plenty," she replied, striking him in the chest.

Cam rubbed himself and looked in the mirror again. "You know that was before we met at the warehouse, right? If I had known…"

"I know," said Gil. "It's different now. I should be jealous you were with her and I should be pissed you're making jokes about it, but I don't really feel it deep down. I feel…"

"Untouchable," said Sava. "Perion said that to me a few days ago. Said there wasn't a human on the planet who could even reach him, let alone hurt him. Said he existed on another plane."

"A transcendental toaster," said Cam. "That's a first."

"He wasn't trying to be deep. He just recognized a flaw in his plan. Humans aren't immortal. If a human becomes immortal by imprinting on a synthetic sleeve, then they immediately forfeit any ties with the rest of humanity. Maybe Perion didn't know that going in, but he realized his place eventually."

"What place?" asked Gil.

"Your place as outcasts, part of a new evolutionary leap. It's the reason I fully expect you to jump ship the second Rob—Jackie—is repaired. Once you have her, you won't need me anymore. You won't feel any sort of obligation to me whatsoever, not like a human would."

"I meant to ask about that," said Cam. "Why does Sava Kessler need a bodyguard?"

"She's leaving Perion Synthetics," said Gil. "Think of how much she knows about the inner workings. Any company in the world would want that intel. If Vinestead gets wind of it, they'll literally break down her door to get it."

"Vinestead, Vinestead, Vinestead. That's all you people ever talk about here. Maybe they should call this place Vinestead City instead, maybe have Arthur Sedivy's hand fisting the Great Spire. I don't see what the big deal is."

"And you never will," said Sava.

She turned her head to the window and watched the desert scroll by. Much of The Fringe had looked like this when she first started at Perion Synthetics. Over the years, the city had expanded, churning up the faded and cracked earth to make way for another factory that would turn out a more specialized hand or eye or penis capable of four-hour erections.

Sava shook the image out of her head.

The expansion would continue, no doubt, whether or not James Perion stood at the helm. The machine was in motion, hurtling down the highway at a hundred miles per hour, heading for a collision with the immovable Vinestead boulder sitting squarely in the middle of the road. Though Sava wasn't on board, at least she was able to watch the scene from a safe distance where the impact wouldn't kill her but rather provide a spectacular show of flames and carnage.

Perion Synthetics was on its own now.

Fire and forget, thought Sava, as she closed her eyes.

The construct reorganized itself into a massive arena with two levels of stadium seating surrounding a dirt oval. At one end, the demon stood with its arms raised to the open roof, the flames on its horns licking at the stars. Around one of its massive legs, a chain of black steel secured the beast to the wall. Sava turned her mind's eye to the left and saw the Perion army amassed in total for the first time. Row after row of identical synthetics marched forward, their unnecessary fleshy veneers ripped from their chassis, replaced by charcoal sinew that disappeared into desert-camo pants. Their boots kicked up dirt as they pressed forward, closing the distance between Perion Synthetics and Vinestead International once and for all.

Sava floated into the stands and sat down next to her sister.

"This is the catalyst, you know," said Anela. "After this comes the war. Vinestead will feel threatened for the first time in its existence, and that means they will lash out harder and faster than ever before. Standing against them will be more dangerous, and it will only get worse as we get closer to the end."

"I'm not afraid."

"Courage will not be enough, Kai. You will have Gil by your side, but this war will be fought in virtuality as much as it will be fought out there. You should start gathering more ciphers to the den. We will need to be ready when the time comes." Anela placed her hand on Sava's knee. "You can do this, Kai."

At ground level, the army came within twenty yards of the demon. It paced in the small circle allowed by the chain, stomping its hooves in the dirt. As the synthetics approached, the demon retreated to the wall and gave a massive roar.

Sava winced as the dome glowed and cracked; it was poor protection against the sudden fire flaring in the infinite ether around the arena.

The hoof prints left behind by the demon turned black and reflective, and through them pushed the heads of ten smaller beasts, each one crying out in a high-pitched whine. As they found their footing, they turned their attention to the synthetics. In unison, they opened their elongated jaws and spewed flames across the distance, charring the dirt of the battlefield. The first row of synthetics melted mid-step and collapsed into a heap. Soldiers behind them crushed their remains with their boots as they passed over them.

"An ambush," said Anela. "We should have anticipated that."

Something blurry danced in Sava's periphery. She turned to look at it, swirling the construct around her. The bottom dropped out and she felt herself falling, chasing after some elusive piece of information stinging at her from the edges of her awareness. She pursued it deep into the black of the construct until the arena was but a speck overhead. Through this singularity, she could hear a voice calling to her.

"Kai. Kai! KAI!"

Sava jerked awake, slamming her knee into the glove box.

"Easy there," said Cam. "The bad man can't hurt you anymore."

In the distance, the brown hulk of Outpost Alpha pushed through a hazy mirage. There was no traffic on the PE, nor any obstacles to slow them down, yet Sava couldn't stop herself from imagining a line of demons stretching across the blacktop, their mouths open and ready to spew napalm.

No. Not demons…

To the right of the road, the last of the turnarounds flew by. In another hundred yards or so, the outer barriers would start to build up; they were designed to keep traffic from veering off the road as they approached the outpost, which was exactly what Sava needed Cam to do.

"You alright?" asked Gil.

Sava reached out and yanked the steering wheel towards her, pulling the car off the road and onto the uneven dirt. The vibrations made every muscle in Sava's body ache, but she held tight even as Cam wrestled for control.

"Stay off the road! And don't slow down."

Cam let the car drift a few more degrees to the right and then held a steady course.

"What's your problem?" he asked.

"Ferko." Sava took a breath to steady herself. "We need to go around the outpost. I gave a kill order to shoot any synthetic on sight. And after how we left things at the Spire, I'm sure they'll be expecting us."

"Yeah, but isn't there some kind of fence or something?" asked Cam.

"On the border, yes," said Sava, "but not here at the PNR. It's just stakes set in the ground. Pick two and drive between them."

"If the car holds up," he replied.

Gil leaned forward and stuck his head between them. "What the hell is that?"

Sava followed his gaze. A blur moved on the horizon, kicking up dust as it ran parallel to a line of metal poles jutting up from the dirt.

"Is that one of your AutoGuards?" asked Cam.

It was moving too fast over uneven terrain to be a Scorpio. It could have been something new, some special toy in Javier's arsenal he had been saving for a special occasion.

"Stay away from it," said Sava, "whatever it is."

Cam let the car drift to the right, only to see another blur pop out from behind a low ridge of rocks.

"Aw shit," said Cam.

"They're wearing AG uniforms," said Gil, "and they are really hauling."

"Step on it, Cam. They won't follow us past the PNR."

In the construct, Sava shot a glance at Anela, who shrugged in return.

The engine growled as Cam floored the accelerator.

"Not gonna make it," said Gil, sitting back in his seat.

"We'll make it," replied Cam. He squeezed the steering wheel, muttering *come on, come on* under his breath.

Sava looked back and forth between the blurs and tried to do the calculations. By the looks of it, Gil was right. Even if Cam could get the car's speed into the triple digits, the Scorpios were converging too fast.

"Ram one," said Sava, pointing to the AG on the left. "If he gets too close or if he starts firing, run him over."

"Just a little property damage, right?" asked Cam.

Seconds dragged as the car's suspension absorbed every rock and hole it encountered, whining in high-pitched squeals and sending vibrations racing through its passengers. Sava pulled her seatbelt tighter and gripped the handle above her window.

Cam cut left and put the car on a collision course with the AG. In turn, it skidded to a stop in the dirt and changed direction. Now facing them, Sava could see what Gil had seen with his advanced eyes: camo uniform, embedded sunglasses, and an M4 carbine slung over its back.

The Scorpio made no effort to avoid the car. At the last possible moment, it leapt at them, sending a flying knee into the windshield. It bumped along the roof, coming to a stop as metal fingers pierced the cabin just above the rear window. The rest of the synny crashed against the glass, shattering it and sending shards over Gil and Roberta. A gloved hand reached in through the open window and grabbed ahold of Gil.

Outside, the metal pikes of the PNR flew by without acknowledgement from the synthetics inside the car.

Sava turned in her seat, wanting to help Gil, but he and the Scorpio were moving too quickly, fighting it out with teeth and elbows, shredding the leather and busting out the side window.

Gil kicked at the back of the driver's seat, pushing Cam's face into the steering wheel. He let out a curt hack and then slumped over, remaining upright only by virtue of his seatbelt.

"Stop fucking around, Gil!" yelled Sava, grabbing for the wheel. The car was losing speed, but she still struggled to avoid the stray boulder or Joshua tree.

Gil let out a sudden grunt that faded into the distance. When Sava looked back, she saw both synthetics sliding off the trunk of the car. They landed in the dirt and rolled several times.

Sava threw the car into park and waited as it ground to a halt. Blood ran from Cam's nose, but the pounding vein in his neck meant he was still alive. Voices from behind drew Sava's attention, and she was out of the car and running before realizing she had no weapon, no real way of helping Gil.

"He is not worth your life," said Anela.

In the construct, Perion's army stumbled and fell, leaving the demon to roam free in the arena.

"We need him," said Sava. "The war needs him."

By the time she reached Gil, the Scorpio had ceased its attack. It held its position a few feet away from Gil, one knee on the ground, one hand reaching for the knife in its boot. Despite its aggressive stance, its face was calm, almost as if it were listening intently.

"All must walk their own path to the dust," said Gil.

The AG relaxed and considered its surroundings. Concern crept onto its face.

"We are past the PNR," it said. Frantic hands patted its chest to make sure it was still there.

"We are," said Gil. "And we're both still alive." He looked to Sava and forced a smile.

"Told you you'd be fine," said Sava.

"This isn't possible," said the AG, standing up. It looked back towards the PNR. "We... we can leave?"

The construct shimmered. Anela wiped away the arena and the stands and the stars until it was only her glowing figure standing in the null space. Her face grew dark.

The AG looked past Sava to the horizon. Somewhere beyond the curve was I-10 and beyond that, any destination a synthetic could dream of. It took its first voluntary step away from Perion City.

"No," said Gil, climbing to his feet. He pointed to the PNR. "You have to go back. Your brothers are waiting for you. Go tell them what I've told you. And then you show them and everyone like us that you're free to leave this place."

Anela's screams felt like hot needles in Sava's ears, but she couldn't bring herself to open her mouth. For so long, she had protected Perion Synthetics, putting herself between the company and whoever might threaten its security. But now, she wanted nothing more than to step aside, to let someone else take up the mantle for a while. And there was no reason that person had to be human.

Perion engineers had given synthetics everything they needed to pass for a real, live person.

Now it was time to give them a choice.

"Go protect your brothers," said Sava. "Vinestead will be coming for you. You need to prepare yourselves."

The AG stared at Sava for several seconds before touching the band around its throat. "Alpha Thirteen for Alpha Actual." He waited for a response, and then said, "Targets bugged out. Returning to base. Out."

"Good man," said Gil.

Alpha Thirteen pulled his rifle from his back and handed it to Gil.

"If they will be coming for me, they will be coming for you," he said.

Gil slung the rifle over his shoulder and nodded to the AG, who then took off at a light jog towards the PNR.

"Alright, let's go," he said.

Sava turned and walked with Gil to the car.

"You'll have to drive," she said.

"Why?"

"You knocked out Cam."

Gil huffed. "Just a little organic damage, right?"

"Right," said Sava, glancing back over her shoulder.

The PNR floated above a shimmering mirage. Just beyond it stood Anela Zabora with her arms folded and her head slowly shaking back and forth.

CODA ONE

Kaili Zabora
January 2016

Le Soleil Rouge occupied the second floor of a dilapidated building in Astoria's Old District. The elevator on the first floor had a sign on its doors directing customers to the stairs, as the decades-old cables could no longer reliably carry the car from one floor to the other. The foyer of the building had dust and occasional leaves collecting at the floorboards; painter's tape covered the far wall in random streaks, as if a renovation project had been started and forgotten in the same day.

The only clean surfaces were the stairs; each step had a veneer of polished, white marble with veins of some dark brown mineral flowing through it. The flickering LED lights near the elevator made the steps glimmer. The stairs snaked upwards in a spiral, clinging to the outer wall to form an open well; a chandelier hung down from the second floor to about six feet off the ground, its crystals throwing sparkling light on the walls.

As Kaili Zabora climbed the stairs, she noted the stark contrast between the first and second floors. Stepping onto the landing, it was as if the foyer had never existed, nor had there been an Old District or even Astoria. She felt completely transported, like stumbling upon a rogue construct in virtuality, some self-contained bubble of Eden floating in the ether. Through the glass walls of Le Soleil Rouge, she could see a young woman in a black blazer sitting behind a reception desk, the rims of her dark glasses framed by short, blonde hair. There was another woman seated in the waiting area with a palette in her lap. She wore a wooly scarf over a leather jacket—appropriate for an Oregon winter, if you didn't count the bare skin running from the lip of her skirt to the tops of her knee-high boots.

The doors slid apart at Kaili's approach, causing the receptionist to look up from her terminal. She smiled and rose to greet her customer.

"Welcome to Le Soleil Rouge," said the woman. "How are you today?"

The reception area was warm; Kaili untied the belt of her trench coat and slipped it off of her shoulders.

"I'm fine," she replied, though she was anything but. "Yourself?" she asked, though she cared little about the answer. Kaili Zabora didn't have the patience right now for inane niceties, but then at that moment, she wasn't Kaili Zabora.

"I'm doing great. How can I help you?"

"I have a reservation. Bonnie Diaz."

"Absolutely, Ms. Diaz," said the receptionist, sitting down again. She banged away on her keyboard for a minute and then pulled a palette from its dock. "Since this is your first time with us, we'll need you to fill out this registration form. Would you like a hot tea or water while you wait?"

Kaili took the palette and scanned the questions. "How about a coffee?"

The receptionist smiled. "I can make you a decaf. We don't recommend our guests have caffeine before their treatment."

That was too bad; Bonnie Diaz loved her coffee black and jittery.

"No, thank you," said Kaili. She took a seat in the waiting area, putting a low table between herself and the woman with the self-insulating legs.

The registration form asked for standard information like her name, address, and phone number. Kaili put bogus information in each text box, but the second part of the form made her consider her answers more carefully.

List your current injuries.

Kaili rolled her memory back to the week in Perion City when her carefully constructed plan had come crashing down. She had assumed an identity, gained the trust of hundreds of Perion Synthetics executives, and helped steer the company towards its inevitable showdown with Vinestead International. Then, a mistake, a rumbling of the foundation, and all of the cards she had so meticulously placed flew into the air. If the old man hadn't died, none of this would have happened. She wouldn't have had to kill Robert Gantz—a crime for which she had paid no real penalty except for losing her job.

Kaili Zabora: fired from a job.

It was the kind of story Cam would die to get his hands on.

She recalled her escape from Perion City, when the car was idling at the curb in front of Cam's house in Burbank. Cam had been quiet for most of the ride, staring out the backseat window as the car rolled along, occasionally sniffing away some pain. Kaili stood with him for several minutes on the sidewalk, talking about the future.

"You're going to feed this, aren't you?" she asked.

"It's what I do," he replied, his voice lacking his usual enthusiasm.

"And you'll mention my name?"

He looked away from the darkened door of his home and caught her eyes.

"Three months," he told her. "Maybe four. I can't stop the truth from coming out, but maybe I can delay it for a while. You can figure Benny Coker will be pushing Gil's story down our throats for the next several weeks, so I'll have to hold off anyway." He waited as she looked away. "You have to understand, Kessler. The guilty have a way of getting what's coming to them. The Perions, Chuck Huber, my backstabbing cocksucker of a boss, and yeah, even Sava Kessler. I'll do what I can to paint it in the right light, but you did kill someone."

"Don't worry about Sava Kessler," said Kaili, smiling. "She's not even a real person."

List all personal effects.

She had left Perion City with only the clothes she was wearing and the money in her pocketbook. Going back to San Diego had crossed her mind for a moment, maybe to see mom and dad before the shit storm came ashore, but showing up with two synthetics in tow would have raised too many questions. Instead, Kaili drove Gil and Roberta to a Calle Cinco safe house in El Cajon. She rested there for most of December before setting off alone on I-5, making the thousand mile trip to Astoria over the course of a week. A hotel in the Old District provided a place to sleep between the days spent walking the condemned piers of the city, watching the sun set in one unique oil painting after another.

"Ms. Diaz? We're ready for you now."

Kaili handed over her palette and followed the receptionist through a black door with a small porthole.

"This is our relaxation room. You can wait for your specialist here after you've changed. We have beverages—water, juice, and tea—but as I mentioned, no caffeinated or alcoholic drinks. Please help yourself to anything you'd like."

The woman led Kaili down a hallway to a door marked with a large *W*.

"In here, we have the women's locker room. Showers and sauna are through here. If you'd like to remove your makeup, we have vanities available as well." She stopped in front of a wall of lockers and opened one. "Robe and sandals. Please make sure you leave all of your personal items in the locker, as you won't be able to take them with you into the treatment room. Hair ties, earrings, necklaces, rings…"

Kaili touched the silver band on her thumb. She had only taken it off once since leaving Rick on the train, and then only for a moment.

The woman noticed the involuntary move. "We *do* take responsibility for items left in the locker, so even if someone does manage to swipe it, we'll cover you for the loss. In the five years I've been working here, we haven't had a single theft."

"I'd rather not leave it."

"I'm sorry," said the woman. "It would interfere with the machines."

Kaili nodded and slipped the ring into her palm.

"We're on your schedule for the rest of the evening, so please, take your time. We'll look for you in the relaxation room once you're ready."

When the woman was gone, Kaili noticed the tranquil music raining down from the ceiling. Water gurgled from a fountain between two showers on the other side of the room, rushing over polished rocks of tan and charcoal. Venetian doors hid four stalls across from a bank of sinks. Behind her, a long wooden bench extended from the lockers to the sauna. Kaili folded her trench coat into a small square and set it on the bench. She sat down beside it.

In the quiet, she waited for a familiar voice to speak up, to tell her she was doing the right thing and that everything would be okay.

A tenor saxophone whined above the twinkling of a piano.

Something caught in Kaili's throat, and it took all of her concentration to fight bursting into tears. She felt the compression in her nose and the narrowing of her eyes, as if either could stem the sadness rising within her. It wouldn't have been so bad to cry, to add her own wailing to the saxophone and piano and violin and gurgling water and white noise generators and the hiss of the sauna...

So many voices speaking to her, and all she wanted to hear was one.

Kaili closed her eyes, brought up her personal construct, and screamed into the unending darkness for her sister.

Nothing echoed back. Anela Zabora had not spoken since Perion City.

In the construct, Kaili collapsed on the floor, sobbing.

"I'll wait," she said, speaking into her hands.

"Are you okay?"

Kaili opened her eyes and saw the woman with the knee-high boots standing in front of her.

"It's a man, isn't it?" she asked, scrunching her nose and raising an eyebrow.

"No," said Kaili. "A woman."

"Oh, oh." Knee-highs wandered away to the sinks and pretended to wash her hands.

Kaili stood and began to undress. She kicked off her shoes and placed them in a cubby inside the locker. Taking off her socks allowed her to feel the soft, micro-fiber mat on the floor running the length of the lockers. There were two plastic hangers on a small steel rod inside, and she used them to hang up her sweater and blouse. She folded her pants and began removing the rest of her jewelry.

"Is that why you're here?" asked the woman from the sinks. "Did she break your heart?"

Could a memory break a heart?

"It's not like that," said Kaili. She pulled a white robe out and hung it on the locker door. With a quick snap of her fingers, she undid her bra and slipped the robe on.

"I'm pretty sure my husband is cheating on me." The woman dabbed a washcloth on the makeup beneath her eyes. "Which is fine with me; *I'm* certainly not going to fuck him. I'll spend his money, yes, but a woman's got to have standards."

Kaili nodded as she folded her underwear and laid them on the pile of clothes in the locker. She shut the door, set a random combination on the keypad, and locked it.

"Maybe he could pay for mine too," said Kaili.

The woman was still chuckling politely as Kaili exited the locker room.

She walked down the hall in the plastic sandals and sat down on a long, white divan in the relaxation room. A small laugh escaped her lips. She had to tell herself it was okay to find humor in the strange things said by Bonnie Diaz. Knee-highs would have laughed too, had she known Bonnie Diaz was the primary shareholder at Diaz Investments and that her recent stock maneuverings in regards to Perion Synthetics had netted almost four million dollars. To have come out of Perion City with nothing and everything warranted both regret and happiness. If Anela were still around, she would have probably told Kaili to focus on the bright side.

And yet, it wasn't the same as hearing her sister's voice in her head.

"Ms. Diaz?"

Kaili looked up and saw a girl in purple scrubs standing in the doorway.

"I'm Ginger," she said. "I'll be assisting Dr. Jenkins today. If you will follow me, I'll show you to your room." She waited for Kaili to join her in the hallway and then led her around a curve to the left. "We're going to be in the fifth room on the right."

Room five was rectangular, barely eight feet across but double that in length. The pod sat on a thick, metal pike in the center of the room with its doors open; the inside glowed yellow from the lights beneath the stasis gel.

"And you've got no biochip, is that correct? No Guardian Angel no one told you about?" asked Ginger.

"No," said Bonnie Diaz.

"I'd rather die," said Kaili Zabora, to herself.

Ginger closed the door and rolled a cart closer to the pod. She pulled a tray of electrodes from a metal box. "If you'll take off your robe, I can get these placed and have you draped before I bring Dr. Jenkins in."

Warm air rose from vents on the floor, providing a blanket of heat so Kaili could feel comfortable standing naked while Ginger applied electrodes to various points on her body.

"Have you ever done this before?" asked Ginger.

"Not like this," said Kaili.

"It's the way of the future. We're building another location downtown and next year we'll have an office in Westport. Couple decades from now, we'll all be living like this."

The construct bloomed; within it, warehouses grew in a massive grid, each one containing racks upon racks of stasis pods, their occupants' bodies suspended while their minds wandered the endless sea of empty registers in VNet.

"We'll see how my body takes six months," said Kaili. "Then we'll talk about spending the rest of our lives jacked in."

Ginger smiled as she gave Kaili a once-over. "You're going to be fine. When you come out and get a look at what we've done, you'll fall in love with yourself." She stepped aside and gestured to the pod. "If you'd like to lie down on your back, I'll get you covered up."

Kaili sat down on the lip of the pod and put one foot at a time into the stasis gel.

"If it's too hot, let me know," said Ginger.

Maybe those lights at the bottom were actually heat lamps.

Kaili let the warm gel envelope her body. It rose in swells on the sides of her legs and ribcage. It trickled into places that made her smirk.

Ginger laid a white towel over Kaili's body, covering everything from her ankles to her neck.

The gel nipped at Kaili's earlobes, and she shuddered.

"There's nothing to worry about," said Ginger. "Stasis is perfectly safe."

Kaili laughed. She could give a shit about going under for a while.

"It's not that," said Bonnie Diaz. "I just haven't been to VNet in forever."

Ginger put her hands on her hips. "How long has it been for you?"

Since before Perion, thought Kaili.

"A decade or more, give or take."

"Well, then you're in for a surprise, aren't you?"

The door opened after a curt knock. An older man with features like Chuck's walked in carrying a palette. He glanced at Ginger and then smiled at Kaili.

"Ms. Diaz, how are you? Comfortable?"

Kaili nodded as the gel clung to her hair.

"Good, well, your vitals look fine. Nothing showed up on the tox screen. Let's get you jacked in so we can get started on your treatments."

"Sounds good," she replied, not really listening. The warm cocoon pulled her towards sleep.

"Ginnie, let's get the sedative going." Then to Kaili, "We're going to take your brain offline for a while until we've got you stabilized. Then you'll wake up, so to speak, and be logged into VNet for the duration. You'll be on a temporary Soleil Rouge permit, so you'll be getting a specialized Personal Assistant to explain the accommodations to you. They will be able to answer any questions you have, including the progress we're making out here. Do you have any questions for me?"

Just do it, she thought. She could see herself standing on the edge of the infinite rabbit hole, just waiting for someone to push her in.

"No," she replied.

"Great, then I will see you on the other side, Ms. Diaz."

A plastic mask came into view; Ginger placed it over Kaili's nose and mouth. "Breathe deeply and slowly," she said. "Start counting back from one hundred."

"One hundred," said Kaili. "Ninety-nine."

"Sleep tight," said Ginger. "Dream of beautiful men in warm climates."

Her face lost all definition and turned to smoke. Kaili grasped at it with her mind as she fell into the void.

For a time, she walked the beaches of San Diego with Rick as the sun forever set on the watery horizon.

And then, lucidity pulled her into a construct.

She found herself sitting on bent knees in the center of an ill-defined space. Ribbons of light shot out from beneath her at ninety-degree angles. They repeated, shifting a few degrees, until they had constructed a blue-white floor of viscous light. Kaili felt the pressure increase on her knees.

Behind her, footsteps sounded, perhaps made by Le Soleil Rouge's custom Personal Assistant.

It took an eternity to turn her head.

Standing there in her blood-red dress was Anela.

Kaili fought to find her voice. "Are you... are you real?"

Anela simply smiled as she offered her hand, electric current pouring from her fingers.

CODA TWO

Robert Gantz
January 2016

The taxi crept along the streets of Umbra, dodging bleary-eyed youths who couldn't be bothered with crosswalks. David Yates observed the distracted population from the back seat, tired from his trip, but unable to tear his attention away from the sensory overload pouring in through the half-open window. Umbra blocks were tightly packed; the neon of one storefront bled into the next, creating a never-ending pastiche of dancing lasers, scrolling code, and inviting women. Together, it was a light show that refused to be ignored. When Yates looked down, he saw it reflected in the puddles on the evercrete sidewalks. Looking up revealed lustrous animations racing along the Umbra Canopy.

A young girl in a tattered, brown jacket stumbled into the street, causing the taxi to brake abruptly.

Yates held tight to the metal cylinder in his lap.

"Open your eyes, sugar tits," said the driver, barely audible over the thumping of distant bass reverberating through the car.

He didn't know how wrong he was.

If anything, these lost and wandering sheep needed to close their eyes against the unreality surrounding them. Umbra was an optical delight like no other, but it held no real information, no truth. The people walking its streets were neon blind, unable to see anything but the pretty veneers and flashing lights. They needed a thick tarp cast over the world, and not just for the sake of their sight, but for all of their senses.

More than anything, they needed to silence the many voices in their heads, the entertainers and celebrities and advertisers who drowned out their own common sense.

The taxi bit the curb at 301 Nand Street and came to a stop, its gears grinding as the driver forced it into park.

"Saint Barbara's in less than twenty minutes. What'd I tell you?"

"Thank you," said Yates, thumbing away twenty-five bucks on the meter.

Warm and misty air had settled in Umbra. Yates felt it reach over his blazer and into the collar of his button-up. Sheep crisscrossed in front of him, the pierced nipples of men and women poking through tank-tops and cut-off shirts. They barely glanced at the tall man with the square haircut as he maneuvered through them to the front doors of Saint Barbara's.

An access panel lit up at his approach, casting a blue light over the *no trespassing* sign hung above it. Yates tapped out the code on the worn buttons and got a harsh beep in return. The blue LEDs flashed red. He tried again with similar results.

"That's Umbra for you. Everything's amazing but nothing works."

Yates turned to the voice and saw a middle-aged man step out of the crowd. He was dressed in black except for lines of neon green streaking across his button-up at random intervals. His slim face held augmented eyes of a similar emerald color.

"Mind if I try?" he asked.

Yates took a step back and watched as the man typed the same code and then banged on the door just above the keypad. The panel responded with a whir and switched from blue to green. The man nudged the door open with his knuckles.

"Thank you," said Yates, extending his hand. "Mister…"

"Gattis, Frank Gattis. And it was nothing." He turned to peer inside. "I remember when Saint Barb's closed in what… '08? Would you mind if I came in and took a quick look around?"

"All are welcome, my son," said Yates.

Gattis was able to find the light panel to the right of the doors; the can lights in the ceiling were still in good shape and ramped up to a warm glow.

The church wasn't even half the size of the WG in Perion City, but Yates hadn't purchased the building for its main chapel. He looked around for the doors to the right and left of the cramped rostrum. They led to a space in the back originally used as dorms. There were ten, eight by eight rooms, each just big enough to hold the deprivation tanks he had ordered. With those tanks, he would transport the distracted throngs to what he saw as a silent nirvana, a state of being free of the feed.

"Well, they certainly let this place go to hell," said Gattis. "Pardon the pun."

Yates traced a finger over the back of a pew; it came away coated in thick black dust.

"What you see is not always the truth," he said. "Underneath, she is still a church. She will shine again."

"No offense, but the average Umbrat doesn't care much for churches. That's why Saint Barbara's went under in the first place. I hope you've got some serious bankroll because donations will be hard to come by."

Yates found a shelf along the left wall near a bank of melted candles. He placed the cylinder upon the warped wood and stepped back.

"I do," he said, "thanks to a generous donation from a friend. It will be enough to sustain the church for several years. By the time the money runs out, I will have shown this city the value of my way and they will support me."

"Your way?" asked Gattis. "Which way is that?"

Yates smiled and walked to the center aisle where Gattis stood. He put his hands behind his back.

"Do you yearn for a new way, my son?"

"That depends on what the new way entails. Are you reviving a church or starting a cult?"

"What's the difference?" asked Yates. "I just want to quiet the agitated mind and help people hear the music and smell the flowers and see the things no one else sees."

Gattis crossed his arms.

"You can see what no one else sees? Are they supposed to take you as the new messiah?"

"I'm not some supernatural son of a sky-god," Yates replied. "I simply know *how* to see. For instance, those irises of yours are brown beneath your latticework; you changed your color to encourage people to look you in the eye. Your shirt is damp around the shoulders, which means you were waiting in the rain for quite a while before my taxi dropped me off. You underestimated the travel time between here and Umbra Terminus."

Gattis tried to smile. "Anything else?"

"Yes, there is one more thing. That red glow beneath your cuff means your sliver is recording everything we say, making you an aggregator and a purveyor of distraction. Do I have that right?"

"Spot on," said Gattis, chuckling. He flashed a laminate that had been tucked into his belt. "Frank Gattis, with Banks Media out of Los Angeles. Pleasure to finally meet you, Dr. Yates."

"I haven't been out of Perion City a full day and already the vultures are circling." Yates shook his head. "I have nothing to say to the media. I would like you to leave, Mr. Gattis."

"*After* you've answered my questions. I'm investigating the disappearance of one of our aggregators. He went off the grid about the same time all hell was breaking loose in Perion City and hasn't been heard from since. As a former employee and resident, I figured you might know something."

Yates sighed. "What is his name?"

"Cameron Gray. He arrived in Perion City on November 9th of last year."

"I heard his name," said Yates, "but I never met him. I do know we would have been better off if he had never come to Perion City. If it weren't for your kind, no kind of hell would have broken loose at all."

"So you admit, there *was* some hell?"

"Leave now, or I'll call the police." Yates pulled out his phone.

"Ask for Commissioner Webb," said Gattis. He cleared a spot on a nearby pew and sat down. "I'm sure he'll send a dozen men right over."

Yates thought about the shotgun he had used to put Truman down. It wouldn't arrive until the next day along with the rest of Yates' possessions. He found a spot on the wall and arched his back against it, trying to relieve some of the pain.

"What do you want?"

"I want to know where Cam is. We're all very concerned."

"Like I said, I never met him. I knew someone who did though. He said your man was detained by Perion personnel."

"They *invited* him," said Gattis. "Why would they detain him?"

"There was an incident, a fire at a warehouse. I assume he was involved."

Yates glanced at the shelf.

"And who is that?" asked Gattis, pointing to the cylinder.

"I've had a long trip. If I tell you about him, will you leave me alone?"

Gattis nodded. "Give me something I can feed, and I'll get out of your hair for a while."

"That is Robert Gantz," said Yates, taking a deep breath. "He was a dear friend and a decent man. He died defending his ideals and those he loved. I knew no other man in Perion City who held closer to the righteous path."

Yates closed his eyes and began recounting the life of Robert Gantz as he knew it to be: a dedicated public servant; a man open to the words of a higher power; full of love; bound by a sense of duty; a servant of justice. He left out small details such as Robert's love of the drink, his casual swearing, and other vices only mentioned in the confines of the confessional.

Over the next half-hour, Yates took Gattis through the years, from their first meeting after a Sunday service to their final night together in Perion City, where a war-torn Robert had walked through his doors frightened by the possibility of losing yet another person for whom he cared deeply. There had been a finality to the way Robert spoke, an understanding about what the night held for him. Despite knowing the danger, he had plunged in headfirst, his thoughts only of Joseph Perion.

"They cremated his body," said Yates, "and there was a funeral. Robert had no next of kin; all of his accounts were payable on death to me for some reason. I stayed only as long as necessary to transition someone else into my role and then

Robert and I moved on. Now I'm here telling you this story instead of getting some much-needed rest."

"It pains you to speak about him," said Gattis.

"Only to you." Yates stepped away from the wall. "Perion City was doing fine until aggregators started raining from the sky like a plague. Your relentless pursuit of a story led to nothing but trouble. What you do, the business you're in, is a blight on humanity. The last thing this new generation needs is someone like you whispering in their ear twenty-four hours a day." His voice echoed off the high ceilings of the church. "We have become too addicted to information. The saturation has blinded us all. Someone has to step in and remind the people there is only one true reality and it isn't virtual and it isn't augmented. It's time we step back from the precipice."

"And if they don't want to?"

"Then I will drag them."

Gattis nodded and stood up. He pulled back the sleeve of his shirt to reveal his sliver. A quick tap dimmed the red LED.

"It's a nice story, Doc, but it'll never feed. We do half a dozen segments on information dependency every week and no one gives a shit. Local and national governments have been hands-off for years. No one cares except for the few crackpots who think they can save the world from itself. You've lived in Perion's utopia for too long, my friend. Any chance we might have had for our own perfect world died with the free Net at the end of the last century. We are living in a hell-bound world and the only thing you can do is try to make the ride more comfortable."

"There is salvation for those willing to listen."

"Whatever you say," he replied, walking to the exit. "Thanks for your time, Dr. Yates. I'll be back in a few days once this Gantz story makes the rounds. If you remember anything or hear anything about Cameron Gray, I'd appreciate a message."

Gattis pulled a twenty from his wallet and dropped it along with a business card in the donation box next to the door. "See you around," he said.

The room filled momentarily with techno music as the door opened and closed. When it was quiet again, Yates returned to the shelf to examine the urn.

Robert's name was etched vertically along the cylinder, punctuated by a PCPD badge. Yates stared at the intricate designs and wondered if Robert's God had welcome him into His arms or turned him away at the last moment. Were there any sky-gods hiding in the clouds who would accept a drunken cop into their afterlife?

"I didn't tell him everything," said Yates to the urn. He thought back to the funeral, to the stark white room where Robert's ashes sat atop a marble pedestal.

The faces of those few who stood around it flashed by one by one until settling on Joseph Perion.

"He was there." Yates cleared his throat. "There were few words, but I saw it in his eyes. He loved you. Maybe not as you loved him but loved you nonetheless."

Yates picked up a pack of matches from the shelf. They were old and brittle, but he managed to get one lit. He selected a large candle and set it next to the urn.

He said a silent prayer to any sky-gods who might be listening.

The flame danced in the valley of Robert's name, turning silver to gold.

CODA THREE

Joseph Perion
February 2016

"And in that way, we will honor my father and make his dreams a reality."

Joe put the phone down on the thick arm of his chair. Sitting across from him, Nico Shaw hit the pause button on the stopwatch.

"I'm not sure about the last line," said Joe, rubbing his face. He'd rehearsed the speech several times a day for the last two weeks and every time he got to the end, he felt the importance of his message taper off with a whimper. "I want to close with something stronger—a resolution or a promise like Dad used to do."

Nico nodded and took out his palette. He scrolled to the end of the speech. "If you're going to ad-lib, I'd at least jot down some notes so you don't get lost. The last thing you want is to look uncomfortable out there."

Joe thought about the many things he wished he could say, but most of them were directed at specific people, not the world at large. He wanted to reassure Dad about the fate of the company. He wanted to tell Gantz what Cyn had done to the synthetic babies. Nico needed to know how proud Joe was that he had remained clean for the last few months.

Then there were the department heads, the VPs, and the individual contributors who had defected, who needed to know how much their absence pained the company. What could Joe say to bring them back? How could he convince them everything was going to be alright?

So maybe the speech wasn't about justifying himself to the world. This was an opportunity to speak directly to those who had jumped ship and those who were still inching towards the railing.

"We're moving forward," said Joe. "The company is pushing through. Things are back on course."

Nico tapped out the fragments on his palette and then looked at his sliver.

"Why don't we take a little break, boss? We'll be starting soon."

Joe nodded and looked to the windows. Outside, the crowd had been growing steadily since dawn, packing the parking lot of Perion Terminus a half mile back to I-10. Aggregators from every feed in the country stood shoulder to shoulder in the crisp February morning waiting to hear what the son of Perion had to say. Joe understood their curiosity; the last news to come out of the PC had been the announcement of Dad's death back in December. The short statement had caused a panic on the feeds and in the market. Though Joe had wanted to reassure the world, Nico had suggested silence. The tactic paid off in the end; the frenzy subsided, the stock price recovered, and the world went back to caring about celebrities and consumer electronics before the year was out.

One side of the terminus faced the back of a temporary stage, the first structure ever built by synthetic hands outside of Perion City. Joe thought it was an ill-conceived experiment put forth by a self-destructive Chuck Huber, but when the synnies made it past the PNR without any issue, he abandoned any thoughts that his lead engineer might just want to watch the synthetics burn.

Synthetics beyond the walls of the city…

James Perion's dream had intruded into reality.

Joe turned at the sound of a door opening and watched as his new police chief walked in rubbing his hands.

"How is it out there?" asked Nico.

"Cold, but secure, Mr. Shaw," said Chief Parker. "Got all the aggregators and reporters and looky-loos penned up six feet from the stage. My men are in the moat every three feet. Got some sharpies up top brandishing to discourage any quick movements."

"That's a little much, don't you think?" asked Joe.

"Unlike your father," said Nico, "you don't have a son to pass the company onto. We'll stop over-planning when you produce an heir."

He joined Joe at the window.

"Dad didn't have me until he was fifty."

"That doesn't mean you have to follow his example," said Nico. "Those people out there are waiting to hear *you* speak, Joe—not your father. They want to know what you think and how you view the world and what you're going to do to leave it a better place. Stick to the speech, speak plainly to them, and keep your ad-libbing to a minimum. We're going to clean up the company's image and get back some of the prestige we lost with the Gil and Roberta incidents and all of that starts today, right now."

Joe looked his assistant in the eyes. And to think it only took his father dying for Nico to shape up.

Chief Parker put his finger to his ear. "They're ready for you, Mr. Perion."

Joe waited for Nico to straighten his tie and then headed for the door.

The cold air bit at Joe's cheeks, but the mid-morning sun melted away the chill as he snaked through the security detail to the short staircase behind the stage. He lingered on the first step to look back. Nico gave him a thumbs-up sign. With a deep breath, he walked out onto the stage.

A smattering of applause greeted Joe, but it was drowned out by a swell of voices. Hundreds of them spoke at once, asking questions Joe couldn't decipher. He put his hands out, asking for quiet as he approached the podium. There, Nico had left him a palette with his speech already loaded. When he cleared his throat, the desert finally became silent again.

"Good morning," he said, his voice echoing from the many speakers set up around the terminus. "Thank you all for coming today. I'm happy to have you here as we begin a new chapter at Perion Synthetics. For years, we have promised a synthetic utopia, a world where humans are spared from the dangerous and the mundane. While our greatest minds worked towards that goal, you gave us your time, your patience, and your encouragement. I want to assure you we will repay that kindness."

"When?" yelled a voice from the crowd. A murmur of agreement followed.

Joe looked down at the palette. The highlight around the next word in his speech blinked off and on.

"When we're ready," he replied. "When the synthetics are ready."

"When will that be?" called another voice.

"I don't have—"

From the right, someone asked, "What about Vinestead?"

"What about them?" asked Joe.

"Will you beat them to market?"

Joe laughed as he swiped a finger across his palette. "Fisher Price is going to beat them to market," he said, stepping out from behind the podium. He approached the edge of the stage.

"Is that really all you people care about? Perion Synthetics versus Vinestead International? Do you think I wake up every morning worrying about other companies dumping inferior products on the market? We are in the business of synthetics here. Intelligent. Automated. Safe."

Joe smacked his hand with each word.

"Safe?" asked a voice. "Since when have the Perions ever been concerned with safety?"

A hush fell over the crowd as Arthur Sedivy and his bodyguards pushed through the barricades to the left of the stage. One of his men put a nearby box in front of the stage so Arthur could climb up.

Joe looked around for Parker, but the chief had disappeared.

What would James Kirkland Perion do if Arthur Sedivy crashed his press conference?

"Arthur," said Joe, presenting his biggest smile. "What a pleasant surprise. I wasn't expecting to see you here. Surely VFeed could have spared an aggregator?"

Joe cringed at his father's voice coming from his mouth.

"No," said Sedivy, joining Joe at the front of the stage. "I had to come myself." He turned to the crowd. "I had to hear the lies for myself! I knew you would stand up here and tell these fine people your synthetics are safe, when in fact, we know them to be anything but."

The screen behind the stage stuttered on a frame from the Perion reel and then went to black. When the image returned, it took Joe a moment to recognize an aerial shot of Perion City. The image zoomed in.

"November 14, 2015," said Sedivy. "An aggregator named Gilbert Reyes livecasts as he struggles with a Perion synthetic. We lock into his signal just before it goes dead."

A few gasps went up from the crowd.

"We believe this is Gilbert Reyes trying to escape the synthetic. He is then surrounded by Perion agents. And…"

The image was blurry, but there was just enough detail to see Gil shake and go limp. The crowd around him dispersed, leaving his body lying there on the grass in the courtyard.

Sedivy leveled an accusing finger.

"This boy will have you believe Perion synthetics are perfectly safe, that by giving them free will, by giving them the *choice* to disobey the three laws, they will somehow be superior to all other synthetics on the planet. Unlike these mad scientists, we built Vinestead Synthetics with the three laws as a foundation. We are firmly committed to the idea that the protection of humanity comes first and foremost. It should *not* be optional and certainly should not be an add-on feature."

Joe put his hands up.

"And here it comes," said Sedivy. "Like father like son, trying to explain away the loss of a human life. What lie do you have for a murdered United States citizen? Or should we wait for you to hire a new head of public relations? Who will do the lying now that your father is gone?"

It was true; Joe had spent the last few months trying to step into his father's shoes, into the stuffy world of meetings and negotiations and glad-handing. Joe couldn't shake the feeling he was simply pantomiming, going through the motions as a second-rate James Perion, his performance feeble compared to the machine who still roamed the basement of the Spire. At what point would he stop being the son of James Perion and just be Joseph Michael Perion, CEO of Perion Synthetics?

Sedivy took a step closer, his voice shifting to a whisper. "I outlasted your father, Mr. Perion, and you're not half the man he was. I will see your company burned to the ground."

What would James Kirkland Perion do if Arthur Sedivy threatened him in front of the world?

"There will come a time when you have to make a choice," said the memory of James Perion.

Beside him, Victoria Perion smiled at Joe. "All must walk their own path to the dust."

The question popped into his head before he could stop it.

What would Joseph Michael Perion do if Arthur Sedivy threatened him in front of the world?

Off to the left, Joe saw Nico climb onto the stage in slow motion. He ran towards Joe, his arms outstretched. To the right, the crowd undulated like the sea, spraying him with vitriolic questions directed at both Perion Synthetics and Vinestead International. The chaos swirled, the memories of James and Victoria Perion faded into the noise.

"Go hide in your spire, Mr. Perion. While it's still standing."

All must walk their own path to the dust.

And James Perion has taken his last steps.

Joe felt his lead knuckle catch the right side of Arthur Sedivy's nose. Blood erupted in a thick spray; it ran freely over the Vinestead CEO's mouth and splattered onto both men's shirts. Joe kept expecting Sedivy to put a hand out as he fell, but the man simply keeled over in one smooth arc. His head smacked the stage, silencing the crowd.

Nico got his hands on Joe's chest and pushed him backwards. His lips moved, but the words were muted.

"Joe. Joe!"

The red hue of the world fizzled out and Joe caught eyes with Nico.

"How was that for an ad-lib?" he asked.

CODA FOUR

Gilbert Reyes
February 2016

Gil spent Valentine's Day and most of the night staring at Roberta's faintly beating heart through the open wound in her chest. He had spent two months at the workbench trying to repair the damage, rarely leaving the back room at the safe house in El Cajon to do anything but check the security monitors or answer a call from Kaili. When those calls stopped coming, Gil planted himself next to the synthetic approximation of Jacqueline Dulac and used his newfound focus and limitless energy to repair the connections that so many bullets had torn apart.

He worked on her through the evening, soldering broken pathways to link her heart back to the idle power sources throughout her chassis.

Her lips had just begun to move beneath the veil Gil had draped over her face when the lights in the safe house went out.

Gil listened as the generators wound down, as the whirring of the fans in the equipment around him began to diminish.

The room fell silent.

He stood next to the workbench with his hand on Roberta's, closed his eyes.

The TSR Ayudante code had died along with Gilbert Alejandro Reyes some three months ago, but the memories of Patrick "Meltdown" Kumanov had crystalized during the transition to a synthetic existence. Thinking back to the Margate days was easier than ever now. No longer were those nights spent beneath the synth haze a foggy playback in Gil's rush-addled mind. Those memories had transcended the biological and found a permanent home in the non-degrading ones and zeros of his Katsumi-brand synapses. He would never forget Meltdown's face now, would never forget how the rusher's eyes had dimmed when he spoke of the world above the world, the nirvanic plane reserved for the enlightened.

"Why do you think we created religion in the first place? It's our nature to reject the idea of a single reality, of an immutable world. We long to be above it, to separate ourselves from this prison. That is why the synth flows, my friend. The code shows us the borders of this world and takes us beyond them. Reality cannot be escaped, but the borders can be transcended."

Meltdown's ramblings became more coherent each time Gil accessed them, translating themselves from Margate mush to something approaching insightful. For the first time in his life, Gil understood what the rusher had been trying to tell him all those years ago. And yet, something was lost in the translation, some bit of humanity or perspective that had made the insight feel more real. Storing the accumulated wisdom of Patrick Kumanov as binary data had normalized the content, made it more instruction manual than aphorism.

Gil closed the Margate file and returned his attention to the safe house. He reached out with his enhanced senses, took inventory of each room, the configuration of the furniture, the locations of stashed weapons, the various exits, the explosives meant to bring the house to the ground—the data streamed faster than he could consciously handle, but his processor ate it up, giving him complete awareness of the building.

Footsteps in the mud. Rubber soles on the evercrete.

The vibrations moved through the safe house, as loud as gunshots in Gil's ears. He imagined the back porch and the reinforced, sliding door. The intruders were vague blobs in his mind, but where they interacted with the house, Gil saw feet and gloved hands. One of them placed something on the wall along the top of the back door. Fingers jabbed like jackhammers until an electronic beep pierced the relative silence.

Gil had Roberta slung over his shoulder and was halfway down the escape tunnel when the first explosion hit. It was followed by smaller reports—the caustic pop of a flash-bang, the soft hissing of tear gas. It would have been disorienting had there been any humans in the living room.

"You think they want me or you?" asked Gil.

Roberta said nothing. A line of oil descended her arm; drops fell from her outstretched fingers.

Gil didn't even look back. The hatch over the tunnel was well-disguised, and he had sealed it from the inside with a steel slab half a dozen men couldn't lift. Even if the surprise guests managed to get through the barricade, they would be buried alive when they triggered the explosives Gil had placed at the midpoint of the tunnel.

"That's why you ring the doorbell first," said Gil.

The tunnel opened into the storeroom of an abandoned bakery two streets over from the safe house. Gil broke the padlock on the other side of the hatch with a single punch. The opening was too small to carry Roberta on his shoulder, so he held her by the hand and dragged her up the ladder.

Once out of the hatch and crouching on the floor, Gil reached out beyond the walls of the storeroom and heard people on the sidewalk talking and laughing, filling the night with noise pollution. Putting Roberta on his shoulder, he moved to the door and gave the knob half a turn.

The veneered door splintered in front of him as automatic fire tore jagged lines across its face. Gil ducked, putting a dent in the wood floor as his knee came down hard.

"Fuck," he said.

They knew about the safe house. They knew about the tunnel.

He squeezed Roberta's legs in his right arm and thought of Jackie. How much did they know about his girls?

Gil loaded the Margate file and searched for some words of advice from Meltdown. Maybe somewhere in that synth-saturated mind of his was some Zen bullshit that might get Gil from the storeroom to the Ford Focus parked out back in one piece.

"We're confined by the idea of a path," said Meltdown, his cadence shaky from the Smashed Peas. "Oh, the path is blocked, the path is open, the path must be taken. We forget to ask the question *what path?* What is this unstoppable river of causality you speak of?" He sat up and leaned over the low coffee table. "Fuck the path, my friend. You are above it. You are beyond it."

Gil took inventory.

Kneeling had been automatic, a way to keep the bullets from poking holes in his body the way Gantz had poked holes in Roberta. Judging by the spray along the wall, there were at most two or three shooters. Though they were putting out a lot of bullets, they didn't seem to be aiming.

It would all depend on how fast Gil could move from the storeroom, across the prep area, to the back door. He ran the calculations in his head, but the numbers appeared jumbled. They fell apart and reformed as words.

Fuck the path.

Gil tightened his grip on Roberta and tensed the pistons in his legs.

Somewhere above the whizzing of bullets, he heard a magazine drop to the floor.

The door was little more than splinters; it gave way easily as Gil pushed through it. He glanced at the front of the store as he pumped his legs, saw four figures, two on each side of the entrance. Barrel flashes lit three of their faces while the fourth struggled to get a new mag inserted. Gil scooped up an empty crate and whipped it towards the front of the store. It caught one of the shooters in the shoulder, altering their aim.

Gil slammed into the wall opposite the storeroom and then made a break for the back door. Bullets pinged off the sheetrock and scraped at the synthetic flesh of his arms. A few lodged themselves in his back and he wondered how many were hitting Roberta. He hadn't had time to secure the inner shield over her heart before carrying her into the tunnel. If a bullet made it through…

A sharp wind cut across Gil's face as he stumbled into the parking lot behind the bakery. He grabbed the hidden key from the front wheel well of the Ford Focus and managed to get the door unlocked and Roberta in the back seat before the gunmen caught up. He climbed behind the wheel and threw the car into reverse. Bullets tapped out a proximity warning on the hood as he pulled away from the building.

When the rear bumper tapped a chain-link fence, he shifted into drive and peeled out.

Late night revelers had filled the Las Palmas parking lot with their bouncing cars; they honked at the POS Ford tearing through their ranks. Gil turned out of the shopping center onto Chase Avenue and smirked at the street sign as it passed by.

He only made it a couple of miles from the bakery before three pairs of headlights began swerving in the rearview mirror. Gil cut across unfamiliar side streets in an attempt to lose them, always pushing towards the highway he knew to be somewhere westward. He ran a red light at El Cajon Boulevard and careened through the parking lot of a twenty-four-hour pharmacy. The car rattled as the tires crossed two sets of railroad tracks. Finally, the highway appeared. He drove alongside the roadside barrier until he could get on.

When the headlights appeared again, Gil made a U-turn at an emergency crossover. As he passed his pursuers, bullets shattered the rear window. Gil looked back to see Roberta covered in shards of glass.

Fucking Perion. Did you send these men, Joe?

Gil pushed the beater up to ninety miles per hour. He had no idea where he was going, so he tried to make his getaway as random as possible. Every time an exit for another highway or bypass came up, he took it, guiding the car ever southward. Numbers of highways he had never driven flew past: the 8, the 125, the 54. Every time he took an exit, the rearview mirror cleared, only to be filled again a minute or two later.

The police took an interest as Gil turned onto the 805. Their flashing lights replaced the light blue HIDs. As they got closer, Gil counted two motorcycles and one SUV.

Gil thought about how he might explain his synthetic body to law enforcement. He couldn't even talk to Benny Coker about it, couldn't tell his former boss he was still alive and immortal and indentured to Calle Cinco's Kaili Zabora. Would the cops believe his story? Or would they consider him a wayward product built by the man who donated hundreds of thousands of dollars to the state police every year?

In the distance, the garish lights of the United States gave way to the forced darkness of the MX. Traffic on the highway thinned as cars turned away from the border. Gil pressed the accelerator to the floor and pushed the engine to its limit. In the mirror, the cops kept pace.

Gil glanced over his shoulder at Roberta sprawled out in the back seat.

"Sorry, baby. This is the only way."

Spotlights previously trained at the glide path to the border sprung up and blinded Gil. Apertures in his eyes closed and opened; filters slipped into place to deal with the glare. Sirens ramped up as shadows moved beyond the lights.

Doubt flickered across a logic gate.

It was one thing to run from the boys in blue, but to run into the waiting arms of MX *soldados?*

Gil ducked behind the steering wheel as large-caliber gunfire tore through the hood. The windshield cracked in jagged cuts until it was opaque. At the last second, Gil leaned his head out of the window to make sure the car was pointed between the booths.

A bullet caught him in the cheek, forcing his head backwards into the door frame. He felt the steering wheel slip from his hands as the car drifted to the right. The front passenger tire caught a barrier just beyond the booth, pulling the car into a retaining wall before bouncing it in the other direction.

Gil tried to avoid an evercrete barrier, but the Ford struck it hard on the left side, launching him into the air over the line of cars waiting to enter the United States.

Reality shifted as the car rotated. Gil saw the frightened faces of drivers as he sailed over them, close enough to reach out and drag his fingers over the tops of their cars.

He could almost touch…

Auxiliary lights on a pickup truck smashed into Gil's shoulder; his outstretched arm wedged between them even as the Ford continued its arc. There was a sharp tug at his waistline, and then Gil was falling into the pickup's bed, landing amongst various gardening supplies. A loud crash followed, punctuated by a shrill scream.

Roberta. His heart skipped a beat.

Jackie. It froze completely.

Gil tried to stand, but looking down, he found he no longer possessed legs or even most of his torso. The damage feedback hit him all at once, drowning out the commotion around him. He wasn't even aware of the MoA infantry surrounding the truck, nor did he notice the mustachioed *soldado* climbing into the bed.

The cries of severed wires, of tendrils with no sensors, were deafening.

Above them, very distant and echoing, was a voice.

It took Gil a moment to realize it was coming from the *soldado.*

"¿Qué chingado eres?"

The barrel of his machine gun pressed into Gil's chest.

"¿Qué eres?!"

The *soldado* reached down and grabbed Gil's torn collar.

Spitting synthetic blood, Gil managed to croak, "What?"

The man's face came closer.

In a thick MX accent, he asked, "WHAT... ARE... YOU?"

CODA FIVE

Cynthia Mesquina
March 2016

The dealer's name was Huy.

He had a funny face and a funnier way of talking, but when the lights were down and the synth was flowing through Cyn's veins, he was so much more than an ill-fitting Italian suit hanging on a coat rack. There was tenderness in his augmented arms; they hummed with the same power as Cyn's, born from the same factory on the mainland.

Cyn had come to the other side of the world to escape the scene for a while, but landing in the port city of Da Nang had shown her there was no getting away from the tech. She had met Huy her second week in-country, and it had been his idea to come to the floating sanctuary of Hon Toan, some fifteen miles off the southernmost tip of Vietnam. The remoteness of the islet, the clear air lacking the stench of technology, had allowed Cyn to breathe for the first time in months.

The hour was somewhere in that indeterminate period between night and morning. Moonlight shone in through the slats in the window facing the beach. Cyn was wide awake, staring at the ancient fan in the ceiling as it spun its blades of petrified palms in lazy circles. Beside her, Huy lay on his stomach, the thin sheets pushed down to his lower back, revealing the cubist tattoos running up both sides of his spine. His rear ribs poked through the skin, highlighting thin lines of black fractures which broke off in random, almost fractal-like patterns. Cyn reached out and dragged a fingernail over one of the light blue cubes, as if it were some stray acrylic to be scraped off.

"Sleep, girl," said Huy. He lifted his head from the pillow and turned it to face Cyn. The veins on his face glowed a light blue.

"Can't." Cyn pulled the sheet to her chest.

"Bad dreams?"

"No," she lied.

"Sweet dreams?" Huy opened his eyes.

"What?" asked Cyn.

"Sweet dreams," said Huy, reaching across Cyn's stomach. He pushed his body against hers. "About candy."

Not candy. *Candice.*

Cyn took a breath. It caught in her nose; she put a hand up to cover the noise.

Huy propped himself up on his elbows, his hair a tousled mess and his eyes glimmering. The augments in his irises gave off a blue aura. He had perfect night vision, so if there were any tears collecting in Cyn's eyes, he would surely see them.

"Tell Huy," he said.

Easier said than done.

She had never spoken to anyone about her experiences in Perion City. Her feed in the Lincoln Continental archive stood on its own. Even Lincoln, with his constant questions and unwavering curiosity, had simply let her go, had driven her to the airport under the cover of night and put her on his private jet. She changed planes in Vancouver, travelling first class on a commercial flight for the trans-Pacific part of her trip. The last few legs through Tokyo and Shanghai were less glamorous, but Cyn took comfort in the knowledge she was putting more miles between herself and the PC.

"You have secrets. Tell Huy."

The waves crashed on the beach, ceaseless and powerful.

Cyn closed her eyes. The files were opening against her will, the memories pouring out, rushing up the beach of her conscious mind to obliterate whatever temporary structures she had constructed there, whatever life she thought she had built as refuge from a pain that lingered on. Forgetting those events had been the only way to stem the tide, to keep away from the current running within the ocean, a thread of tiny fists, sparkling eyes, and a smile so perfect it could have been engineered in a lab.

Huy exhaled; his breath crossed her cheek.

"They thought I left," she said, grabbing Huy's hand and holding it to her chest. "They told me to go, but I went down instead, down to where I first met Candice's brothers and sisters. No one was guarding them. The racks stretched on and on. Too long. Too many of them. That's when I knew. Candice wasn't a prototype. They were making thousands."

Huy slipped his hand from hers and stroked her hair. He wiped away a tear from her cheek.

"I burned them. I burned them all. I stood there and made sure nothing was left. No one tried to stop me. No one was waiting when I tried to leave. They had to have known, but they let me do it. They let me kill them all."

"You see them?" asked Huy.

"I *hear* them," said Cyn. "Crying. So loud. All those screaming voices."

"Huy help you forget."

"There's not enough synth in the world."

Huy traced a line down Cyn's cheek to her neck, to her chest. He drew the sheet back and ran his palm over her breast.

"More to Huy than synth."

"Yeah?" asked Cyn. "You got something that will burn out every memory I have of that place? Because that's what I want. To forget."

"Not with Ayudante," he replied, touching her forehead lightly. "Not with equipment here. We go to mainland."

Back to the flashy lights and electronic pulse, back to the data seeping from every exposed jackport like running faucets emptying into the open sewers the people called streets. Just thinking about the muck collecting on her boots, the brown, pungent liquid worming its way through the leather, into her socks, around her toes, made a shiver go up Cyn's spine. Somewhere deep down she knew she would one day have to plunge headfirst back into the pool, but couldn't that day be put off for another sunset, for another synth-filled week of ignorant bliss, where memories stayed hidden in the shadows and the only feelings to contend with were the ones rising from the valley of her legs?

"Are you sure you could do it?"

"Nothing for sure," said Huy. He slipped off the bed and walked to the door, shadows dancing on his enhanced muscles. "Huy get you water."

His footsteps grew distant in the short hallway.

The horizon outside was still dark; the first inklings of sunrise were still a few hours off. The wood floors groaned beneath Cyn's feet as she swung her legs over the side of the bed and stood up. Each footstep echoed in the small cabana, as did the squeak of the patio doors when she opened them. Cyn put her arms on the railing and looked out over a dark blue ocean streaked with shimmering white. The sea breeze wrapped around her body, calling forth the goose bumps even as her augments began to warm. Something was in the air, something familiar.

Cyn scanned the horizon: the black fins racing through the water, grains of sand sparkling amongst the shells on the beach, and the trees reaching for the ocean but not daring to get too close. Finally, looking off to the right to the lone pier where the weekly supply ship docked, she saw a shadow exiting a small boat. The hulking silhouette stood on the pier talking to someone before finally turning its eyes up the coastline to Cyn's cabana. The way it lumbered up the beach, the way the pimp cane swung forward as if to ward off any attackers, told Cyn it could only be one person.

She grabbed a robe from the chair by the bed and stepped barefoot onto the cool sand. The slope of the beach carried her down to the water where she waited patiently.

Lincoln Tate put his hand to his head to secure his hat as the breeze picked up.

"What are you doing here?" asked Cyn.

His eyes fell to Cyn's feet and came back up slowly.

"Nice to see you too," he replied.

"Cut the shit," said Cyn. "I asked you for some space. You agreed. So again, why are you here?"

Tate looked around at the sparse islet.

"Primitive," he said. "No transmission lines, nothing to tie you to the mainland. Of course, there are always the satellites, but I'm guessing no one here has a receiver. You're completely cut off, aren't you?"

"It's better this way," said Cyn. "Far less noise. No feed in my ear all day."

Tate leaned his head back and scratched his chin. "Must be nice to just opt out of the world. Let someone else deal with it, right?"

"You came all this way to lay some guilt trip on me?"

Tate stuck his cane in the sand and removed his hat. From inside, he pulled out a code card and offered it to Cyn.

"Things have been happening," he said.

"I don't give a shit what Perion is—"

"Not Perion," said Tate. "It's quieted down on that front. People are losing interest in your replays. This time next year, they will have forgotten all about it."

"But I won't," said Cyn, crossing her arms.

Tate waved the card around as if it were a piece of candy.

Cyn grabbed it and shoved it under her armpit.

"I'm done feeding," she said, looking out over the water again. "The scene is dead."

"This has nothing to do with the feeds, nothing at all."

"Then what?" asked Cyn. She pulled the card out, examined the hexagonal scales on both sides, and put it back.

"VNet," said Tate, following Cyn's gaze to the horizon. "Something is happening in VNet."

"May it burn in hell." She spit into the sand.

"One of my contacts got wind of a bounty, something I think you'd be suited for. The payout would be enough to secure an unprovisioned Ayudante chip."

Cyn looked at Tate. There was a smile on his face, but he was serious.

"Yes, you know what that means," he continued. "Memory suppression, complete synaptic control. All the advantages of ReTread without sacrificing every bit of your soul."

Candice's face rose out of the surrounding darkness, erupted into flames, and receded.

Cyn shook her head. "All this way just to offer me a job."

"Wasn't the only reason," said Tate, reaching out to touch her face.

"Don't. Just don't." She retreated a few steps. "You really believe you can get me a clean Ayudante? Top of the line? Next gen?"

"Yes. It will be waiting for you when you get back, so long as you retrieve the target."

"And where exactly is the target?"

"South America, we think. For obvious reasons."

Tate didn't have to explain. If the target had fled to South America, they had done so to get away from Vinestead.

"Level of difficulty?"

"It would test you."

Cyn nodded, thought it over. The idea of putting her augments to use again made her arms tingle.

"Believe me," said Tate, "I see the appeal of staying on the bench. What you've got going here… the lack of tech, the slow pace, the boy toys."

Cyn looked over her shoulder. Huy was standing on the porch of the cabana, a glass in one hand and a 9mm in the other.

"I can see the code crawling beneath your skin, Cynthia; you and I both know this isn't enough for you. Sooner or later, you'll want back in. You'll want to walk through hellfire and come out unscathed. You'll want to *feel* something more than this empty place. Do this so you can move on. We'll swap in a new chip and scrape every last bit of VTech out of you."

Tate touched her on the arm.

"Do this so *we* can move on."

Cyn thought of the first day she had walked into Tate's office in Umbra to demand a job. And now, here they were on the other side of the world with the tables turned.

"I'll need to think about it," she said.

"I know," said Tate. "I'll be on the boat. We leave in half an hour." He uprooted his cane and slipped his hat onto his head. "Don't be late."

Cyn examined the code card as Tate turned for the pier. She glanced at Huy standing on the porch; he opened his arms in response.

"Linc…"

Tate paused, his expensive shoes sinking into the damp sand.

"What's the target's name?"

"I don't know," he replied, resuming his walk. "He just goes by G."

CODA SIX

Cameron Gray
March 2016

"I'm asking you to reconsider. I can make you a very rich man, Cam."

It was mid-morning in downtown Sacramento. Spring had recently returned to the city in the form of newly populated flower beds set in front of every other street-level business between Meridian Plaza and Capital Park Terminus. Each came with a small placard indicating they were part of a city beautification project, a way to counteract the dominance of asphalt and evercrete.

The citizens of Sacramento played along for the most part, standing outside their shops with watering cans, nodding to customers, fully aware direct sunlight would only come around noon when it was high enough to pierce the spiky growth of skyscrapers and towers. A few hours of sunlight a day were just enough to keep things growing, to keep small, red and yellow flowers blooming, breaking up the endless background loop of glass and gleaming metal.

"More money than you know what to do with."

Cam switched his phone from one ear to the other and used the sleeve of his suit to wipe his forehead. The humidity was trying to suffocate him. Unlike other cities that built their grids in straight lines, Sacramento's downtown streets meandered, cutting off the breezes that should have brought relief to the pedestrian traffic.

His suit felt warm, whether from the humidity or his nerves, he wasn't sure. Being on the phone with Donato Banks made his heart race; he hadn't taken a call from his former boss in months. Cam had answered the phone on the off chance he wanted to apologize.

Instead, Donato Banks was trying to negotiate.

A woman stood at the crosswalk with her toy poodle, dressed in jeans that ended at her shins and a pink tank top. She eyed Cam's corporate uniform and smirked.

"I don't want your damn money," said Cam, winking at the woman.

"Then what do you want?" asked Banks.

The light changed and Cam followed the woman across the street.

Banks had asked a good question, but did he know how long Cam had already spent thinking of the answer? The last four months in hiding had produced numerous questions and plans and ideas about what to do next, where the money would come from, and how much he wanted to see Banks suffer for what he had done. Visions of assault and murder plagued Cam's nightmares, but in the morning when he sat on the edge of his bed in some random hotel, he knew violence wasn't the answer. Banks would never apologize. He would take the phrase *it's just business* to the grave. It wasn't until winter broke in California that Cam realized how he could hit Banks where it would hurt him the most.

"I want you out," said Cam. "Resign your position."

There was laughter on the other end of the phone.

Cam stopped at another crosswalk and observed Meridian Plaza on the other side of the street. Trees lined the outer perimeter; lawyers and financial analysts in smart suits and tight skirts walked between them, briefcases in one hand and steaming lattes in the other. Their destination was the Citigroup building in the center of the plaza, a thin, tan rectangle rising seventy stories, reminding Cam of a giant tongue depressor stuck into the earth.

After crossing the street and entering the plaza, Cam paused at one of the benches set inside the tree line.

"Men like me don't resign," said Banks. "Men like me run the world, whether people like you want to admit it or not."

Cam idly counted the windows on the east side of the Citigroup building. Behind that tinted glass were the men Banks was referring to. They were the ones who manipulated the economy for their own massive profits, contributing nothing but reaping everything. The urge to walk into the building and start asking tough questions rose and fell.

"You think you're untouchable," said Cam. "But you're not."

"Neither are you," said Banks. "You think because I come to you with an offer that you're somehow better than me? I'm doing this as a courtesy because I like you, Cam. I'm giving you a chance to come down off your high horse and make a deal that will benefit both of us. Do this, and you will never have to work again. Just give me my story, and the world is yours."

Cam touched the code card in his breast pocket.

"It's my story," he replied.

"Bullshit!"

Cam leaned away from the distortion.

"I financed the entire operation," continued Banks. "They were my contacts that got you into the city, my connections that allowed you audience with Perion executives. Without me, you never would have made it past the front gate. You stood on my shoulders to get this story. I want my cut of the action and some goddamn appreciation!"

Cam looked at his sliver. He had ten minutes until his meeting across the street.

"Oh, I appreciate it, Mr. Banks. I appreciate you deciding my life was worth less than your story. You turned me into a fucking guinea pig."

"You took the assignment willingly," replied Banks.

"You tried to have me killed!"

"And what makes you think I'm done trying?" screamed Banks.

Cam looked up and took inventory of the crowd. Most people were power walking their way across the plaza, their minds lost to thoughts of how best to screw over the housing market or how to keep some corporate philanderer with deep pockets and a penchant for Ukrainian prostitutes out of prison. Cam could find nothing threatening in the stream of people; he chided himself for being so jumpy. It wasn't as if Banks' reach extended this far north...

"You should have taken the money," said Banks.

The phone beeped twice as a dozen men suddenly broke rank to face Cam. They paused for a moment; one of them had his head cocked to the side, as if listening to instructions.

From his whisperer, thought Cam.

Shoving his phone into his pocket, Cam bolted for the street. Meridian Plaza stretched out in front of him, its occasional flagstones marking his lead-footed escape from his pursuers. His new shoes weren't built for running; they slid as he weaved in and out of the crowd. Banks' men pushed men and women aside, creating a rolling tide of screams and obscenities. Their lack of discretion told Cam they were being paid well, and he wondered if their instructions were to take him dead or alive.

The first shot rang out as Cam hit the curb. There was no crosswalk in the middle of the block, and the six lanes of traffic were moving just fast enough to be dangerous. He had intended to wait for an opening, but the shrill ping of a bullet ricocheting off a nearby lamppost spurred him into an impromptu game of Frogger. Cam ventured a glance backwards, saw the lawyers and bankers hitting the deck in their fancy clothes, and then stepped into the street.

A delivery truck nearly ended the game straight off, but Cam was able to pivot out of the way at the last second. A taxi screeched to a halt only a few feet away; the sound of its horn washed over Cam as he stutter-stepped to the side. He waited for another cab to pass by before darting for the solid yellow line in the middle of the street. Only three lanes of traffic separated him from safety, yet he found his legs would not move.

Unlike the Citigroup tower in Meridian Plaza, the Vinestead West building came right up to the edge of the block, leaving barely enough room for five people to walk shoulder to shoulder down the sidewalk. Entrances to the building were in the middle of the block and consisted of two sets of double doors flanking a revolving door large enough to wheel a gurney through.

Looking over his shoulder, Cam saw two men step into the road. They didn't have their weapons out, just open hands waiting to grab hold of their target.

No, thought Cam. Banks wasn't going to win this one. Now more than ever, his former boss needed to be put in his place.

Cam jumped back into traffic as the men neared. Horns sounded from all directions, drowning out the shouts from the frightened crowd. He made it past the two inside lanes without incident, but a bike messenger clipped him only a few feet from the curb. Cam fell, absorbing the impact in the palms of his outstretched hands. His chest hit next, but he was able to roll away from the street and regain his feet. He struggled for air as he pushed his way through the revolving door. One of the panes shattered in front of him.

Stumbling into the lobby, Cam immediately put his hands in the air.

There were seven automatic rifles pointed in his direction, each of them peeking out from behind one of the support columns that surrounded the atrium. Standing directly in front of Cam was a tall Indian woman with an oval face and deep red lips. She wore thin, black glasses that disappeared into a tight bun of black hair.

"You should get down," she said, almost casually.

Cam hit the floor. He listened to the bullets whine above his head for several seconds before tapering off. Twisting on the floor, he looked back at what remained of the revolving door, now nothing more than a frame set atop a carpet of broken glass. Outside, cars stood in the street with their doors opened. Half a dozen gray suits lay prone on the sidewalk, while across the street, the rest were scattering. Cam took inventory of his body. Though his suit was dirty and torn along one cuff, his body had come through undamaged. He rolled onto his back and let out a deep breath.

"You must be Cameron Gray," said the woman.

Cam groaned his way to a sitting position. He took a few deep breaths before standing up.

"That's me," he replied, brushing the dust from his suit. "And you are?" he asked, extending his hand.

The woman put her hands behind her back. "I am Anjali Harishandra, and I am very busy, Mr. Gray. I understand you have something for me."

"You have no idea," said Cam, reaching into his pocket.

"I could venture a guess," said Anjali, looking past him to the swath of destruction stretching across the street.

"Here," said Cam, offering her the code card, "load this."

"I don't know what kind of woman you think I am, Mr. Gray, but I can assure you I didn't get to where I am today by loading random cards from strange men who show up with armed assailants in tow."

Cam sighed. "Just load it, lady. You're going to want this content. VFeed is a joke, but *this* will change all that."

Anjali stepped forward and gestured to one of the pillars. A member of her security detail stepped forward.

"If there is anything on this card that doesn't sit right with me, this man is going to put two bullets in you. The first one you will feel. The second one you will not."

Cam watched the man lift his rifle, holding it slightly lower than level.

"Understood," said Cam, handing the card over. "It's pure feed. Just the highlights."

Anjali took the card and held it to her jackport. She inhaled sharply through her nose as she tilted her head back.

The rifle rose.

"Easy," said Cam, putting a hand out towards the muzzle.

Anjali opened her eyes and smiled.

"Right?" asked Cam.

"Indeed," she replied, waving the rifle away. "I suppose we should head upstairs and discuss payment options. We're prepared to go as high as seven figures."

Cam shook his head. "I don't want your money."

Anjali put her hands behind her back again and asked, "Then exactly what do you want, Mr. Gray?"

Cam looked around the atrium. A nearby monitor showed the Vinestead feed in all of its insignificance. Benny Coker had subsidiaries with more subbers than VFeed. Though Vinestead's joke of a media feed was small, it did have potential, not to mention unmatched capital backing. Money, resources, connections; they were all at the disposal of VFeed aggregators. And yet, the subbers steered clear.

The Perion story would make VFeed number one overnight.

He pointed a trembling finger to the vidscreen.

"I want your whole goddamn feed."

THANK YOU

Perion Synthetics is the third book of **The Vinestead Anthology**.

If you enjoyed this book, please consider leaving a review.

Each standalone novel in the Vinestead Anthology tells a small part of a larger epic: the rise and fall of Vinestead International, the exploits of a rogue artificial intelligence named Lassiter, and a seemingly endless stream of idealistic hackers—each convinced they're the hero of the story.

Enjoy them in any order.

Xronixle (2007)

Veneer (2011)

Guardian Angels (2012)

Perion Synthetics (2014)

Por Vida (2017)

Brigham Plaza (2019)

Hybrid Mechanics (2020)

Vise Manor (2022)

House of Nepenthe (2025)

To learn more about the Vinestead Anthology and explore additional titles, please visit:

danielverastiqui.com

9 781967 847044